Emily Wilde's
Encyclopaedia of Faeries

Emily Wilde's Encyclopaedia of Faeries

Heather Fawcett

DEL REY New York

Published in the United States by Del Rey, an imprint of Random House, a division of Penguin Random House LLC, New York.

DEL REY and the CIRCLE colophon are registered trademarks of Penguin Random House LLC.

LIBRARY OF CONGRESS CATALOGING-IN-PUBLICATION DATA
Names: Fawcett, Heather (Heather M.), author.
Title: Emily Wilde's encyclopaedia of faeries / Heather Fawcett.
Description: New York: Del Rey, [2023]
Identifiers: LCCN 2022000431 (print) |
LCCN 2022000432 (ebook) |
ISBN 9780593500132 (hardcover) |
ISBN 9780593500149 (ebook) |
ISBN 9780593597620 (international edition)
Subjects: LCGFT: Magic realist fiction. |
Romance fiction. | Novels.
Classification: LCC PR9199.4.F39 E45 2023 (print) |
LCC PR9199.4.F39 (ebook) |
DDC 813/.6—dc23/eng/20220218
LC record available at
https://lccn.loc.gov/2022000431
LC ebook record available at
https://lccn.loc.gov/2022000432

Printed in the United States of America

randomhousebooks.com

20 19 18 17 16 15 14 13 12

Book design by Virginia Norey

Emily Wilde's
Encyclopaedia of Faeries

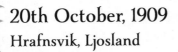

20th October, 1909
Hrafnsvik, Ljosland

Shadow is not at all happy with me. He lies by the fire while the chill wind rattles the door, tail inert, staring out from beneath that shaggy forelock of his with the sort of accusatory resignation peculiar to dogs, as if to say: *Of all the stupid adventures you've dragged me on, this will surely be the death of us.* I fear I have to agree, though this makes me no less eager to begin my research.

Herein I intend to provide an honest account of my day-to-day activities in the field as I document an enigmatic species of faerie called "Hidden Ones." This journal serves two purposes: to aid my recollection when it comes time to formally compile my field notes, and to provide a record for those scholars who come after me should I be captured by the Folk. *Verba volant, scripta manent.* As with previous journals, I will presume a basic understanding of dryadology in the reader, though I will gloss certain references that may be unfamiliar to those new to the field.

I have not had reason to visit Ljosland before, and would be lying if I said my first sighting this morning didn't temper my enthusiasm. The journey takes five days from London, and the only vessel to get you there is a weekly freighter carrying a great variety of goods and a much smaller variety of passengers. We ventured steadily north, dodging icebergs, whilst I paced the deck to keep my seasickness at bay. I was among the first to sight the snowbound mountains rising out of the sea, the little red-roofed village of Hrafnsvik huddled below them like Red Riding Hood as the wolf loomed behind her.

We inched carefully up to the dock, striking it hard once, for the grey waves were fierce. The gangway was lowered by means of a winch operated by an old man with a cigarette clamped nonchalantly between his teeth—how he kept it lit in that wind was a feat so impressive that hours later I found myself thinking back to the glowing ember darting through the sea spray.

I came to the realization that I was the only one disembarking. The captain set my trunk down upon the frosty dock with a *thunk*, giving me his usual bemused smile, as if I were a joke he only half understood. My fellow passengers, it seemed, few that there were, were headed for the only city in Ljosland—Loabær, the ship's next port of call. I would not be visiting Loabær, for one does not find the Folk in cities, but in the remote, forgotten corners of the world.

I could see the cottage I had rented from the harbour, which astonished me. The farmer who owned the land, one Krystjan Egilson, had described it to me in our correspondence—a little stone thing with a roof of vivid green turf just outside the village, perched upon the slope of the mountain near the edge of the forest of Karrðarskogur. It was such stark country—every detail, from the jumble of brightly painted cottages to the vivid greenery of the coast to the glaciers lurking on the peaks, was so sharp and solitary, like embroidered threads, that I suspect I could have counted the ravens in their mountain burrows.

The sailors gave Shadow a wide berth as we made our way up the dock. The old boarhound is blind in one eye and lacks the energy for any exercise beyond an ambling walk, let alone tearing out the throats of ill-mannered sailors, but his appearance belies him; he is an enormous creature, black as pitch with bearish paws and very white teeth. Perhaps I should have left him in the care of my brother back in London, but I could not bear to, particularly as he is given to fits of despondency when I am away.

I managed to drag my trunk up the dock and through the village—few were about, being most likely in their fields or fishing boats, but those few stared at me as only rural villagers at the edge of the known world can stare at a stranger. None of my admirers offered help. Shadow, padding along at my side, glanced at them with mild interest, and only then did they look away.

I have seen communities far more rustic than Hrafnsvik, for my career has taken me across Europe and Russia, to villages large and small and wilderness fair and foul. I am used to humble accommodations and humble folk—I once slept in a farmer's cheese shed in Andalusia—but I have never been this far north. The wind had tasted snow, and recently; it pulled at my scarf and cloak. It took some time to haul my trunk up the road, but I am nothing if not persevering.

The landscape surrounding the village was given over to fields. These were not the tidy hillsides I was used to, but riddled with lumps, volcanic rock in haphazard garments of moss. And if that wasn't enough to disorient the eye, the sea kept sending waves of mist over the coastland.

I reached the edge of the village and found the little footpath up to the cottage—the terrain was so steep that the path was a series of switchbacks. The cottage itself rested precariously upon a little alcove in the mountainside. It was only about ten minutes beyond the village, but that was ten minutes of sweaty inclines, and I was panting by the time I reached the door. It was not only unlocked, but contained no lock at all, and when I pushed it open, I found a sheep.

It stared at me a moment, chewing at something, then sauntered off to rejoin its fellows as I politely held the door. Shadow gave a huff but was otherwise unmoved—he's seen plenty of sheep in our rambles in the countryside around Cambridge, and looks upon them with the gentlemanly disinterest of an aging dog.

Somehow the place felt even colder than the outdoors. It was as simple as I had imagined, with walls of hearteningly solid stone and the smell of something I guessed to be puffin dung, though it could also have been the sheep. A table and chairs, dusty, a little kitchen at the back with a number of pots dangling from the wall, very dusty. By the hearth with its woodstove was an ancient armchair that smelled of must.

I was shivering, in spite of the uphill trunk-dragging, and I realized I had neither wood nor matches to warm that dingy place, and perhaps more alarmingly, that I might not know how to light a fire if I did—I had never done so before. Unfortunately, I happened to glance out the window at that moment and found that it had begun to snow.

It was then, as I stared at the empty hearth, hungry and cold, that I began to wonder if I would die here.

Lest you think me a newcomer to foreign fieldwork, let me assure you this is not the case. I spent a period of months in a part of Provence so rural that the villagers had never seen a camera, studying a river-dwelling species of Folk, *les lutins des rivières*. And before that there was a lengthy sojourn in the forests of the Apennines with some deer-faced *fate* and half a year in the Croatian wilderness as an assistant to a professor who spent his career analysing the music of mountain Folk. But in each case, I had known what I was getting into, and had a student or two to take care of logistics.

And there had been no snow.

Ljosland is the most isolated of the Scandinavian countries, an island situated in the wild seas off the Norwegian mainland, its northern coastline brushing the Arctic Circle. I had accounted for the awkwardness of reaching such a place—the long and uncomfortable voyage north—yet I was realizing that I had given little consideration to the difficulties I might face in leaving it if something went wrong, particularly once the sea ice closed in.

A knock upon the door launched me to my feet. But the visitor was already entering without bothering about my permission, stamping his boots with the air of a man entering his own abode after a long day.

"Professor Wilde," he said, holding out a hand. It was a large hand, for he was a large man, both in height and around the shoulders and midsection. His hair was a shaggy black, his face square, with a broken nose that came together in a way that was surprisingly becoming, though in an entirely uninviting way. "Brought your dog, I see. Fine beast."

"Mr. Egilson?" I said politely, shaking the hand.

"Well, who else would I be?" my host replied. I wasn't sure if this was meant to be unfriendly or if the baseline of his demeanour was mild hostility. I should mention here that I am terrible at reading people, a failing that has landed me in my fair share of inconveniences. Bambleby would have known exactly what to make of this bear of a man, would probably already have him laughing at some charmingly self-effacing joke.

Bloody Bambleby, I thought. I haven't much of a sense of humour myself, something I dearly wish I could call upon in such situations.

"Quite a journey you've had," Egilson said, staring at me disconcertingly. "All the way from London. Get seasick?"

"Cambridge, actually. The ship was quite—"

"Villagers stared as you came up the road, I bet? 'Who's that little mouse of a thing, coming up the road?' they were thinking. 'She can't be that fancy scholar we've been hearing about, come all the way from London. Looks like she'd never survive the journey.'"

"I wouldn't know what they were thinking about me," I said, wondering how on earth to turn the conversation to more pressing matters.

"Well, they told me," he said.

"I see."

"Ran into old Sam and his wife, Hilde, on the way up. We're all very curious about your research. Tell me, how is it that you plan on catching the Folk? Butterfly net?"

Even I could tell this was meant to be mocking, so I replied coolly, "Rest assured that I have no intention of *catching* one of your faerie folk. My goal is simply to study them. This is the first investigation of its kind in Ljosland. I'm afraid that, until recently, the rest of the world saw your Hidden Ones as little more than myth, unlike the various species of Folk inhabiting the British Isles and the continent, ninety percent of which have been substantively documented."

"Probably best it stays that way, for all concerned."

Not an encouraging statement, that. "I understand that you have several species of faerie in Ljosland, many of which can be found in this part of the Suðerfjoll Mountains. I have stories of Folk ranging from brownie type to courtly fae to investigate."

"I don't know what any of that means," he said in a flat voice. "But you'd be best confining your investigations to the wee ones. No good will come of your provoking the others, for yourself or for us."

I was immediately intrigued by this, though I'd of course heard hints of the fearsome nature of the courtly fae of Ljosland—that is, those faeries who assume near-human form. But my questions were forestalled by the wind, which blew open the door and spat a great breath of snowflakes into the cottage. Egilson shouldered it closed again.

"It's snowing," I said, an uncharacteristic inanity. I'm sorry to say that the sight of snow drifting into the fireplace had me edging once again towards morbid despair.

"It does that on occasion," replied Egilson with a touch of black humour that I found preferable to false friendliness, which is not the same as saying I appreciated it. "Not to worry, though. Winter isn't here yet, it's just clearing its throat. These clouds will open up momentarily."

"And when will winter arrive?" I enquired grimly.

"You'll know it when it does," he said, a sideways sort of answer that I would soon grow accustomed to, for Krystjan is a sideways sort of man. "You're young to be a professor."

"In a sense," I said, hoping to discourage this line of questioning with vagueness. I am not really young for a professor now, at thirty, or at least not young enough to astonish anyone; though eight years ago I had indeed been the youngest professor Cambridge ever hired.

He gave an amused grunt. "I've got to be getting on with the farm. Can I help you with anything?"

He said it perfunctorily, and looked to be on the verge of slipping away sideways through the door even as I replied quickly, "Tea would be lovely. And firewood—where would that be kept?"

"In the wood box," he said, puzzled. "Next to the fireplace."

I turned, and saw the aforementioned box immediately— I had taken it for some sort of rudimentary armoire.

"There's more in the woodshed out back," he said.

"The woodshed," I breathed with relief. My fantasies of freezing to death had been premature.

He must have noticed the way I said it, which unfortunately

had the distinct cadence of a word never spoken before, for he remarked, "You're more the indoors type, are you? I'm afraid such folk are rather thin on the ground around here. I'll have Finn bring the tea. That's my son. And before you ask, the matches are in the matchbox."

"Naturally," I said, as if I had noticed the matchbox already. Damn my pride, but I couldn't bring myself to enquire as to its whereabouts after the wood box humbling. "Thank you, Mr. Egilson."

He gave me a slow-blinking look, then drew a little box from his pocket and set it upon the table. He was gone in a swirl of icy air.

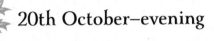

20th October—evening

After Krystjan left, I barred the door with the plank that must have been set against the wall for that purpose, and which, like the damned wood box, I had failed to note before. Then I spent an entirely unproductive twenty minutes scrabbling about with the wood and the matches, until there came another knock.

I opened the door, praying that this visitor's relative politeness boded well for my survival.

"Professor Wilde," said the young man on the threshold in that faintly awed tone I have encountered before in rural villages, and I nearly melted with relief. Finn Krystjanson was a near-mirror image of his father, though narrower of midsection and with a pleasant set to his mouth.

He shook my hand eagerly and tiptoed into the cottage, starting a little at the sight of Shadow. "What a handsome beast," Finn said. His English was more heavily accented than that of his father, though still perfectly fluent. "He'll give the wolves something to think about."

"Mm," I said. Shadow takes little interest in wolves, seeming to place them in the same category as cats. I can't imagine what he'd do if a wolf ever challenged him, other than yawn and give it a swat with one of his dinnerplate paws.

Finn eyed the cold fireplace and debitage of snapped matches without surprise, and I suspected that his father had already warned him of my capabilities. *Indoors type* still smarted.

In a few short moments, he had a hearty fire crackling and a pot of water set upon the stove to boil. He chattered as he worked, directing me to the stream behind the cottage, which I understood to be my only source of water, the cottage not being plumbed; the outdoor privy; and a shop in town where I could purchase supplies. My host would provide my breakfast, and dinner could be had at the local tavern. I was on my own for the midday meal only, which suited me well, as I am accustomed to spending my days in the field when conducting research and would pack my own light repast.

"Father says you're writing a book," he said, heaping logs by the fire. "About our Hidden."

"Not just the Hidden," I said. "The book is about all known species of Folk. We have learned much about their kind since the dawning of this era of science, but no one has yet ventured to assemble this information into a comprehensive encyclopaedia."[*]

He gave me a look that was both dubious and impressed. "My, but that sounds like a lot of work."

"Yes." Nine years of it, to be specific. I have been working on my encyclopaedia since earning my doctorate. "I hope to complete my fieldwork here by spring—the chapter on your Hidden Ones is the very last piece. My publisher is eagerly awaiting the manuscript."

The mention of a publisher seemed to impress him all over

---

[*] There are, of course, detailed compendia pertaining to specific regions, e.g., Vladimir Foley's *Guide to Russian Folklore*. And Windermere Scott has her *I'll Take the Iron Road: A Rail Journey Through the Otherlands*, but this is a narrative account of her travels and highly selective in nature (Scott also undermines her credibility by including ludicrous accounts of ghosts).

again, though the furrow in his brow remained. "Well. We have plenty of stories. I don't know, though, that they'll be any use to you."

"Stories are of great use," I said. "Indeed, they are the foundation of dryadology. We would be lost without them, as astronomers cut off from the sky."

"They're not all true, though," he said with a frown. "Can't be. All storytellers embellish. You should listen to my grandmother when she gets going—she'll have us hanging on every word, yes, but a visitor from the next village will say they don't know the tale, though it's the same one their own *amma* tells at her hearth."

"Such variation is common. Nevertheless, when it comes to the Folk, there is something true in every story, even the false ones."

I could have gone on about faerie stories—I've written several articles on the subject—but I didn't know how to talk to him about my scholarship, if what I said would be nonsense to his ears. The truth is that, for the Folk, stories are everything. Stories are part of them and their world in a fundamental way that mortals have difficulty grasping; a story may be a singular event from the past, but—crucially—it is also a pattern that shapes their behaviour and predicts future events. The Folk have no system of laws, and while I am not saying stories are as law to them, they are the closest thing their world has to some form of order.*

I finished simply, "My research generally consists of an amal-

---

* Esther May Halliwell's *Essays on Meta-Folklore* includes an overview of how our thinking has evolved on this subject, from the scepticism of the Enlightenment, in which faerie stories were viewed as secondary to empirical evidence in understanding the Folk—if not completely irrelevant—to the modern view of such tales as elemental to Faerie itself.

gam of oral accounts and hands-on investigation. Tracking, observations in the field, that sort of thing."

If anything, the furrow had deepened. "And you—you've done this before? You've met them, I mean. The Folk."

"Many times. I would say that your Hidden Ones would be unable to surprise me, but that is a talent universally held by the Folk, is it not? The ability to surprise?"

He smiled. I believe he thought me half akin to the Folk at that point, a strange magician of a woman conjured into his midst in a village little touched by the outside world. "That I couldn't say," he replied. "As I've only known our Folk. That's enough for one man, I've always thought. More than enough."

His tone had darkened a little, but in a grim rather than an ominous way, the sort of voice one uses when speaking of those hardships that are a fact of life. He set a loaf of dark bread upon the table, which he informed me quite casually had been baked in the ground via geothermal heat, along with enough cheese and salted fish for two. He was quite cheery about it, and seemed intent on joining me for the humble feast.

"Thank you," I said, and we gazed at each other awkwardly. I suspected that I was supposed to say something else—perhaps enquire about his life or duties, or joke about my helplessness—but I've always been useless at that sort of amiable chatter, and my life as a scholar affords me few opportunities for practice.

"Is your mother about?" I said finally. "I would thank her for the bread."

I may be a poor judge of human feeling, but I have had plenty of experience with putting my feet wrong to know that it was the worst possible thing to say. His handsome face closed, and he replied, "I made it. My mother passed a year and more ago."

"My apologies," I said, putting on a show of surprise in an attempt to cover the fact that Egilson had included this information in one of our early letters. *What a thing to forget about, you idiot.* "Well, you've quite a talent for it," I added. "I expect your father is proud of your skill."

Unfortunately, this inept rejoinder was met with a wince, and I guessed that his father was *not* in fact proud of his son's skill in the kitchen, perhaps even viewing it as a degradation of his manhood. Fortunately, Finn seemed kindhearted at the core, and he said with some formality, "I hope you enjoy it. If you need anything else, you can send word to the big house. Will half seven suit for breakfast?"

"Yes," I said, regretting the change from his former easy conversation. "Thank you."

"Oh, and this arrived for you two days ago," he said, withdrawing an envelope from his pocket. "We get mail deliveries every week."

From the way he said it, he saw this as a source of local pride, so I forced a smile as I thanked him. He smiled back and departed, murmuring something about the chickens.

I glanced at the letter, and found myself confronted with a florid script that read *The Office of Dr. Wendell Bambleby, Cambridge* in the upper left corner, and in the middle, *Dr. Emily Wilde, Abode of Krystjan Egilson, Farmer, Village of Hrafnsvik, Ljosland.*

"Bloody Bambleby," I said.

I set the letter aside, too hungry to be vexed just then. Before I tucked into my own refreshments, I took the time to prepare Shadow's, as was our custom. I collected a mutton steak from the outdoor cellar—to which I had been directed by Finn—and set it on a plate beside a bowl of water. My dear beast devoured his meal without complaint, while I sat by the crackling fire with my tea, which was strong and smoky, but good.

I felt some regret at having poorly repaid Finn's kindness, but I didn't mourn the absence of his company—I had not been expecting it.

I gazed out the window. The forest was visible, starting a little higher up the slope and giving off the inauspicious impression of a dark wave about to come cresting down on me. Ljosland has little in the way of trees, as its mortal inhabitants denuded much of the sub-Arctic landscape. However, a few forests remain—those claimed, or believed to be claimed, by their Hidden Ones. These are largely comprised of the humble downy birch, along with a few rowans and shrub willows. Nothing grows to a great height in such a cold place, and what trees I could see were stunted, tucking themselves ominously into the shadow of the mountainside. Their appearance was mesmerizing. The Folk are as embedded in their environments[*] as the deepest of taproots, and I was all the more eager to meet the creatures who called such an inhospitable place home.

Bambleby's letter sat upon the table, somehow conspiring to give off a kind of negligent ease, and so finally, once I had finished the bread (good, tasting of smoke) as well as the cheese (also good, also tasting of smoke), I took it up and slid my nail through the seam.

My dear Emily, it began. I hope you're settled comfortably in your snowbound fastness, and that you are merry as you pore over your books and collect a variety of inkstains upon your person, or as close to merry as you can come, my friend. Though you've been gone only a few days, I confess that I miss the sound of your typewriter clack-clacking away across the hall while you hunch there with the drapes drawn like a troll mulling some dire vengeance under a bridge. So woebegone

---

[*] Here of course I refer to Wilson Blythe's Wilderfolk Theory, widely accepted by dryadologists and often referred to as the Blythian school of thought. Numerous guides have been written on the subject, but essentially Blythe views the Folk as elements of the natural world that have gained consciousness through unknown processes. According to Blythian thought, then, they are tied to their home environments in ways we humans can barely hope to grasp.

have I been without your company that I drew you a small portrait—enclosed.

I glared at the sketch. It showed what I considered a highly unfaithful rendering of me in my Cambridge office, my dark hair pinned atop my head but terribly dishevelled (that part, I admit, is true—I have a bad habit of playing with my hair whilst I work), and a fiendish expression on my face as I scowled at my typewriter. Bambleby had even had the gall to make me pretty, enlarging my deep-set eyes and giving my round face a look of focused intelligence that sharpened its unexceptional profile. No doubt he lacked the ability to imagine a woman he would find unattractive, even if he had seen said woman before.

I was certainly not amused by the caricature. No, I was not.

Bambleby then went on at length about the most recent meeting of the dryadology department faculty, to which I would not have been invited, being only an adjunct professor and not a tenured one, including many entertaining observations about how prettily the light caught at Professor Thornthwaite's new hairpiece and asking whether I would agree with his theory that Professor Eddington's relative silence at such convocations suggested a mastery of the open-eyed nap. I did find myself smirking a little as he rambled on—it is hard not to be entertained by Bambleby. It is one of the things I resent most about him. That and the fact that he considers himself my dearest friend, which is only true in the sense that he is my sole friend.

Part of my reason in writing, my dear, is to remind you I am worried for your safety. I speak not of whatever unusual species of ice-encrusted faerie you may encounter, as I know you can handle yourself in that regard, but of the harshness of the climate. Though I must confess a secondary motive in writing—a fascination with the legends you've uncovered about these Hidden Ones. I urge you to write to me with your findings—although, if certain plans I've set in motion come to fruition, this may prove redundant.

I sat frozen in my chair. Good God! Surely he was not thinking of joining me here? Yet what else could he have meant by such a remark?

My fear ebbed somewhat, though, as I sat back and imagined Bambleby actually venturing to such a place as this. Oh, Bambleby has done extensive work in the field, to be sure, most recently organizing an expedition to investigate reports of a miniature species of Folk in the Caucasus, but Bambleby's method of fieldwork is one of delegation more than anything else; he settles himself at the nearest thing that passes for a hotel and from there provides directives to the small army of graduate students constantly trailing in his wake. He is much praised at Cambridge for deigning to provide co-author credit to his students in his many publications, but I know what those students put up with, and the truth is that it would be monstrous if he did not.

I was unable to convince even one of my students to accompany me to Hrafnsvik, and I very much doubt that Bambleby, despite his charms, would have much better luck. And so, he will not come.

The remainder of the letter consisted of assurances of his intention to provide the foreword to my book. I felt a little ill at this—a combination of relief and resentment—for though I do not want his assistance, particularly after he scooped me on the gean-cannah changeling discovery, I cannot deny its value. Wendell Bambleby is one of the foremost dryadologists at Cambridge, which is to say that he is one of the foremost dryadologists in the world. The one paper we co-authored, a straightforward but comprehensive meta-analysis of the diet of Baltic river fae, earned me invitations to two national conferences and remains my most cited work.

I tossed the letter into the fire, determined to think no more of Bambleby until the arrival of his next letter, which would no doubt be swift if I did not reply with a haste sufficient to his self-regard.

I turned to Shadow, curled at my feet. The beast had been watching me with solemn dark eyes, concerned for my well-being in the wake of my panic. I discovered another chilblain upon his paw and fetched the salve I had purchased specially for him. I also took the time to comb through his long fur until his eyes drooped with pleasure.

I removed my manuscript from my suitcase, carefully unfolding the protective wrapping, then laid it upon the table. I flicked through the pages, savouring the crisp sound of the heavily inked paper, ensuring they were still in order.

It is a heavy thing, presently totalling some five hundred pages, not inclusive of the appendices, which will likely be extensive. Yet within these pages, like specimens threaded with pins and trapped behind glass in a museum display, is every species of faerie yet encountered by Man, from the mist-dwelling bogban of the Orkneys to the ghoulish thief known as *l'hibou noir* by those inhabiting the Mediterranean country of Miarelle. They have been alphabetized, cross-referenced, and paired with figures where available as well as a phonetic guide to pronunciation.

I let my hand rest briefly on the stack of pages. I then set atop the manuscript a paperweight, one of my faerie stones*

---

* Faerie stones can be found in a variety of regions, being particularly common in Cornwall and the Isle of Man. They are unimpressive in appearance and hard to recognize with the untrained eye; their most distinguishing feature is their perfect roundness. They seem primarily to be used to store enchantments for

—devoid of magic now, of course. Beside it, at a right angle, I placed my favourite pen—it bears the Cambridge crest; a gift from the university when I was hired—ruler, and inkwell. I surveyed the tableau with satisfaction.

Now, with the world swathed in the total darkness of provincial villages, and my eyelids growing heavy, I am off to bed.

---

later use or perhaps for the purposes of gift-giving. Danielle de Grey's 1850 *Guide to Elfstones of Western Europe* is the definitive resource on the subject. (I am aware that many dryadologists today ignore de Grey's research on account of her many scandals, but whatever else she was, I find her a meticulous scholar.) A faerie stone with a crack down it has been spent and is thus harmless. An intact stone should be left untouched and reported to ICAD, the International Council of Arcanologists and Dryadologists.

21st October

Normally, I sleep poorly in foreign accommodations, but I surprised myself by resting soundly until Finn's promised knock came at half seven.

I rose from the straw-stuffed bed that took up nearly the entirety of the little bedroom, shivering in the cold. The only fire was in the main room, and it was down to the embers. I threw a robe over my nightdress and padded to the door with Shadow at my heels.

Finn greeted me with the same formality into which he had retreated yesterday, setting upon the table a tray of bread—still warm despite the chilly walk from the farmhouse—as well as a bowl of some form of quivering yogurt and a disturbingly large hard-boiled egg.

"Goose," he said when I enquired. "Did you not bank the fire last night?"

I confessed that I had little idea what this signified, and he kindly demonstrated a particular method of stacking the wood and raking the coals within the fireplace that would ensure a long, continuous release of heat as well as easier re-ignition come morning. I thanked him with perhaps an overabundance of enthusiasm, and he smiled with his former warmth.

He enquired after my plans for the day, and I stated my intention to become acquainted with the surrounding terrain.

"Your father informed me in his letters that within the Karrðarskogur can be found a variety of brownies, as well as trooping faeries," I said. "I understand from my research into the scant accounts of your Folk that the courtly fae are more apt to travel with the snows, from which I gather that sightings of their ilk will be unlikely for some days yet."

Finn looked astonished. "Did my father use those words?"

"No. *Brownies* and *trooping fae* are the two largest subcategories of common fae invented by scholars—your people, I believe, refer to the common fae as 'little ones' or 'wee Folk' when you make the distinction at all. They are, as you know, usually quite small, child-sized or less. Brownies are solitary and are generally those faeries who involve themselves in mortal affairs—thefts, minor curses, blessings. Trooping fae travel in groups and keep mostly to their own."

Finn gave a slow nod. "And I suppose, then, that you have a separate word for the tall ones?"

"Yes, we place all humanlike faeries into the category of courtly fae—you understand, then, that there are two main groupings of Folk, courtly and common. As far as the courtly fae are concerned, there are too many subcategories to list, and I've little idea whether any of them will apply to those you call the 'tall ones.' "

"We rarely call them anything," Finn said. "It's bad luck."

"A not uncommon belief. The Maltese are much the same. Though their courtly fae are more troublesome than average, having an unfortunate habit of creeping into houses at night to feast upon slumberers' vital organs."

He showed little surprise at this gruesome detail, which puzzled and intrigued me. The Maltese Folk are singularly vicious—on that front, they have no known equals among the fae. What manner of Folk inhabited this forbidding country?

"I'd have thought you'd want to settle in first," he said, casting a dubious look around the cottage. "Finish your unpacking, buy some provisions. Say hello to the neighbours. You'll be here a while."

The last item in this list nearly made me shudder. "Not long at all, from a scholarly perspective," I said. "My return passage is booked on a freighter departing April the first. I shall be very busy. Some dryadologists spend years in the field." I added, with the aim of inserting into Finn's mind a sense of the polite distance I customarily keep between myself and the locals: "And as for the neighbours, doubtless I shall meet them at the tavern tonight."

Finn's face broke into a grin. "That you shall. With the harvest done, some folk rarely leave the place. I'll let Aud know you'll be there—and Ulfar. That's her husband, he runs things. He's a nice enough sort, though a bit of a cold fish. You won't get many words from him."

This recommended Ulfar to me far more than Aud, though I did not say so. "And I gather from your father that Aud is the . . . goði, is she?" I tripped a little over the unfamiliar word, which I understood indicated a sort of village headwoman.

Finn nodded. "These days, it's a ceremonial thing, but we like to keep the old traditions going. Aud will certainly be able to supply you with stories of the Hidden. And I know she'll take a fancy to any stories you have of London. We likes tales of the outside world around here."

"Yes, well, we shall see what the evening brings. My visit may be short, depending on my fatigue after today's endeavours."

He did not appear put off. "If you're wearied, Ulfar's beer will put you right. Some folk say it's an acquired taste, but it'll warm your belly and grease your tongue better than anything the world over."

I forced a thin smile. I expected him to depart, but he only stood there, gazing at me. I recognized his expression, for I've seen it before: that of a man trying unsuccessfully to slot me into one of the categories of womanhood with which he is familiar.

"Where are you from, Professor?" he said with a hint of his former friendliness. I think he is the type who can never keep someone at a distance for long.

"I live at Cambridge."

"Yes. But where are your folk?"

I suppressed a sigh. "I grew up in London. My brother lives there still."

"Oh." His expression cleared. "You're an orphan?"

"No." This was not the first time someone has assumed that about me. I suppose people are often looking for a way to explain me, and a childhood of neglect or deprivation is as good as any. In truth, my parents are perfectly ordinary and perfectly alive, though we are not close. They have never known what to make of me. When I read every book in my grandfather's library—I must have been eight or so—and came to them with certain thorny passages memorized, I had expected my mother and father to offer clarity—instead, they had stared at me as if I had suddenly become very far away. I never knew my grandfather—he had no interest in children, nor anything else besides his society of amateur folklorists—but after he died, and we inherited his house and possessions, his books became my best friends. There was something about the stories bound between those covers, and the myriad species of Folk weaving in and out of them, each one a mystery begging to be solved. I suppose most children fall in love with faeries at some point, but my fascination was never about magic or the granting of wishes. The Folk were of another world, with its own rules and customs—and to a child who always felt ill-suited to her own world, the lure was irresistible.

"I have been at Cambridge since I was fifteen," I said. "That is when I began my studies. It is home to me, more than any other."

"I see," he said, though I could tell that he didn't at all.

After Finn departed, I unpacked the rest of my things, which, as I had expected, took but a moment—I brought only four dresses and some books. The familiar smell of Cambridge's Library of Dryadology wafted out with them, and I felt a shiver of yearning for that musty, ancient place, a haven of quiet and solitude in which I have whiled away many hours.

I glanced around the little cottage, which still smelled of sheep and was a home to many a cobweb-laying spider, but I've little patience for housework and soon gave up the idea. A house is merely a roof over one's head, and this one would serve me adequately as it was.

Shadow and I finished our breakfast (I gave him most of the goose egg), and I filled my canteen with stream water and tucked it into my backpack along with the rest of the bread, my box camera, a measuring tape, and my notebook. Thus prepared for a day in the field, I turned my attention to banking the fire per Finn's instructions.

I raked the poker through the embers, then stopped. I pushed aside the husk of a log, reached within, and drew out Bambleby's letter. I blew at the ash and skimmed the elegant cursive. It was entirely unscathed.

I added wood to the fire, stoking the flames, and tossed the letter back in. It did not catch. The fire coughed smoke, as if the letter were an unpleasant obstacle lodged in its throat.

"Damn you," I muttered, narrowing my eyes at the heavy stationery staring insouciantly back at me from the flames. "Am I supposed to keep the bloody thing under my pillow?"

I should, I suppose, mention here that I am perhaps ninety-five percent certain that Wendell Bambleby is not human.

This is not the product of mere professional disdain; Bambleby's impossible letter is not my first piece of evidence regarding his true nature. My suspicions were aroused at our initial meeting some years ago, when I noticed the sundry ways in which he avoided the metal objects in the room, including by feigning righthandedness so as to avoid contact with wedding rings (the Folk are, to a one, left-handed). Yet he could not avoid metal entirely, the event including a dinner, which invariably involved cutlery, sauce boats, and the like, and he mastered the discomfort well enough, which indicated that either my suspicions were unfounded or that he is of royal ancestry—they are the only Folk able to bear the touch of such human workings.

Lest I appear credulous, I can attest that this was not enough to convince me. Upon subsequent encounters, I noted sundry suspect qualities, among them his manner of speaking. Bambleby is supposedly born in County Leane and raised in Dublin, and while I am no scholar of the Irish accents, I am expert in the tongue of the Folk, which is but one with many dialects, yet possessing a certain resonance and timbre that is universal, and which I hear whispers of in Bambleby's voice in occasional, unguarded moments. We have spent a significant amount of time in each other's company.

If he is Folk, he likely lives among us in exile, a not uncommon fate to befall the aristocracy of the Irish fae—their kind rarely goes without a murderous uncle or power-mad regent for long. There are plenty of tales of exiled Folk; their powers are sometimes said to be restricted by an enchantment cast by the exiling monarch, which would explain Bambleby's need to resign himself to an existence among us lowly mortals. His choice of profession may be part of some fae design I cannot guess at, or it may be a natural expression of Bambleby's nature, that he should set his sights upon acquiring external affirmations of self-expertise.

It remains possible that I am wrong. A scholar must always be ready to admit this. None of my colleagues seem to share my suspicions, which gives me pause, not even the venerable Treharne, who has been doing fieldwork for so long he likes to joke that the common fae no longer hide themselves away when he comes, seeing little difference between him and some old, lumpen piece of furniture. And for all the stories of exiled Folk, it's not as if any have been discovered in our midst. Which lends itself to one of two conclusions: either such Folk are exceptionally skilled at camouflage or the stories are false.

I removed the letter, still wholly unburnt, and tore it to shreds, which I folded into the ashes. Then I put Bambleby from my mind, twisted my hair into a knot atop my head (from which it would begin its escape almost immediately), and threw on my coat.

The loveliness of the view outside stopped me in my tracks. The mountain fell away before me, a carpet of green made greener by the luminous dawn staining the clouds with pinks and golds. The mountains themselves were lightly ensnowed, though there was no threat of a sequel in that cerulean canopy. Within the hinterlands of the prospect heaved the great beast of the sea with its patchy pelt of ice floes.

I set off with a light step, much heartened. I have always loved fieldwork, and I felt that familiar rush of excitement as I contemplated the field in question: before me lay uncharted scientific territory, and I the only explorer for miles. It is in moments like this that I fall in love with my profession all over again.

Shadow ambled along at my side on our way up the mountainside, sniffing at mushrooms or the melting frost. Sheep eyed me with their characteristic look of incurious anxiety.

They danced a little at the sight of Shadow, but as he only lumbered contentedly by, his snout more engaged by the earth than the familiar woolly boulders that dotted the fields of his stomping grounds in the Cambridgeshire countryside, they soon ignored him.

The forest slowly folded me into itself. The trees were not all stunted, and in places they formed a dense, dark canopy over the narrow path.

I spent most of the morning surveying the perimeter, wading in and out of the trees. I noted mushroom rings and unusual moss patterns, the folds in the land where flowers grew thick and the places where they slid from one colour to another, and those trees which seemed darker and cruder than the others, as if they had drunk of a substance other than water. An odd mist billowed from a little hollow cupped within the rugged ground; this I discovered to be a hot spring. Above it, upon a rocky ledge, were several wooden figurines, some half overgrown with moss. There was also a small pile of what I recognized as rock caramels, the salty-sweet Ljosland candies that several of the sailors had favoured.

After taking some photographs, I dipped a hand in the spring and found it pleasantly hot. The temptation arose in my mind, for I had not bathed properly since leaving Cambridge, and I felt the salt of the journey upon me still like a second skin. Yet it was dismissed quickly; I was not about to go frolicking about an unfamiliar country in a state of undress.

A small sound came then from the wood behind me, a sort of pitter-patter not unlike the continual drip of wet from the forest boughs. I was instantly alert, though I gave no sign. Shadow raised his head from the spring to sniff the air, but he knew what was expected of him. He sat himself down and watched me.

Some people think that the Folk announce themselves with

bells or song, but the fact is that you will never hear them unless they wish to be heard. Should you be approached by an animal, you will likely notice the rustle of leaves, the snapping of twigs. Should you be approached by a faerie, you may hear nothing at all, or only the subtlest of variations in the natural soundscape. It takes years for a scholar to master the necessary powers of observation.

Affecting a weary traveller's appreciation of the view, which did not require much effort, the weather continuing fair, I ran my gaze along the forest's edge. I was not surprised to find no evidence of any observer, apart from the chitter of a squirrel and the runic scatter of bird prints.

To continue the pretense, I slid my feet from my boots and dipped them into the spring. I took a few moments to review my mental catalogue of alpine brownies, particularly those who dwell near springs, with an eye to behavioural patterns.

I reached into my backpack, where I keep a variety of trinkets I've gathered over the years. But what to choose in this case? Some gifts are favoured by the Folk of different regions, while others give offense. I know of a French dryadologist who was driven mad by his research subjects after presenting them with a loaf of bread that, unbeknownst to him, had begun to mould. Their malice when insulted is nearly as universal as their caprice.

I selected a little porcelain box which held an assortment of Turkish delights. Tastes vary greatly among the Folk, but I know of only one recorded instance of an offering of sweets going awry. I set the box upon the ledge; for good measure, I placed atop it one of my few jewels, a diamond from a necklace I inherited upon my grandmother's death. Such gifts I reserve only for very special cases—some of the common fae covet jewels; others don't know what to do with them.

I began to murmur a song.

They are the night and the day,
They are the wind and the leaf,
They lay the snow upon the rooftop and the
   frost upon the landing.
They gather up their footprints and carry them
   on their backs.
What gift is greater than their friendship?
What blade cuts deeper than their enmity?

My translation is clumsy; I've no ear for poetry. I sang it in the tongue in which it was composed, that of the Folk, which prosaic scholars simply call Faie. It is a rolling, roundabout speech that takes twice as long to say half as much in English, with many contrary rules, but there is no lovelier language spoken by mortals anywhere in the world. By some curious quirk—one which has caused much consternation among those adherents to the Hundred Islands Theory*—the Folk speak the same language in every country and region where they are known, and though the accents and idioms differ, their dialects are never so variable as to hinder understanding.

I ran through the song twice, which I had learned from a hobgoblin in Somerset, then let my voice fade into the wind. I had performed the necessary introductions, so I put my shoes on and departed.

---

* The theory that each faerie realm exists on an entirely separate physical plane. Folk might travel from one realm to another on rare occasions, but otherwise scholars argue that the realms have historically had little to do with one another. I myself see this as narrow-minded nonsense, yet the theory remains popular among the older generation of dryadologists, those who tend to sit as department heads and write the most heavily referenced textbooks, and thus it will likely be with us for some time.

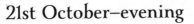

21st October—evening

Shadow and I left the Karrðarskogur behind and headed into the fells. A rough road wound its way up into the mountains north of the village, which I followed until it petered out—likely it was only a track used by sheep farmers. I carried on, though the ground was boggy in places from the melting snow. Eventually my determination was rewarded as I crested the summit of one of the lower mountains.

Beyond, my view was largely obstructed by another, much higher range of mountains, a great convocation of them jutting messily from the green earth brandishing their glacial raiments. Ljosland is a labyrinth of mountains, you'll understand, as well as fjords and glaciers and every other sharp-edged formation most hostile to Man. Between the peaks, the landscape was crushed down into what I supposed were valleys, chasmed and boulder-strewn.

I paused at the summit—partly to bask in a sense of accomplishment—to write in my journal. The Folk do not confine themselves to forests alone, and I know from my correspondence with Krystjan that many Ljoslanders believe the volcanic boulders that jut out of their landscape serve as doors to their realm. I recorded the largest of these as well as those that piqued my interest for sundry reasons, whether by dint of their elaborate peaks or the telltale presence of running water or fungi.

The day was done. I was muddy, chilled, and thoroughly happy. I had established what I considered a useful boundary within which to conduct my research and made contact with one or more of the common fae. It was, of course, possible that the brownies of Ljosland subsisted entirely off sea salt and leaves; found the sight of jewels as offensive as iron; hated music with every fibre of their beings. But I theorized that this was unlikely, and that furthermore they would share commonalities with the Folk of other northerly latitudes—the mountain *alver* of Norway, for instance. Bambleby was sceptical on this point. Well, we will see which of us is right.

I would gladly have sent my excuses to Finn and the headwoman, but my rambles had left me very hungry. And so, my happiness dimming somewhat, I directed my steps towards the village.

The tavern was well-situated in the heart of the village, though this characterization was debatable given the jumbled nature of Hrafnsvik, its dishevelled scatter of homes and shops. A group of men clustered outside, smoking. Two of these were Krystjan and Finn.

"*Voilà!*" Krystjan said, which drew a laugh from his compatriots. "Good evening, Professor Wilde. On the hunt today, were you? Where is your butterfly net?"

More laughter. Finn shot his father a dark look. He gave me a smile and guided me through the doors.

The entire village of Hrafnsvik appeared to have crammed itself into the tavern. Children tore through the establishment, half-hearted reprimands following in their wake, while the aged clustered about the enormous fire. It was cosy in the manner of all such country establishments from England to Russia, a wash of shadows and firelight, crowded with bodies and cooking smells, its ceiling held up by what looked like driftwood logs. Above the bar, where one might find a pair of antlers on the continent, there hung instead the tremendous mandible of a whale.

Finn went around the room, introducing me, which was easily accomplished as most faces had turned from their conversations to stare at me the moment I entered. I was unexpectedly grateful for Finn's presence—I despise the awkwardness of approaching strangers, even without language barriers. I had, of course, been teaching myself as much Ljoslander as possible over the past year or so, but one can only progress so far without the tutelage of a native speaker.

"This is Lilja Johannasdottir," Finn said. "Our woodcutter. She has an *alfurrokk* behind her house—a door to the faerie world. Several of the little ones have been seen passing in and out."

The maiden smiled at me. She was broad-shouldered and beautiful, with round red cheeks and a cascade of flaxen hair. "Pleased to meet you, Professor."

We shook hands. Hers was large and covered with innumerable calluses. I asked after the location of her abode so that I might investigate the feature. She looked startled.

"Aud won't object, I don't think," Finn said quickly.

I was puzzled. "Surely there's no reason why she would?"

"It's fine, Finn," Lilja said. "I'd be pleased to welcome you to my home, Professor."

I encountered similar reticence from several other villagers, though in each case, Finn, smiling and polite, smoothed the waters. I wondered if the locals had not fully understood the purpose of my visit, though it was clear that Krystjan had not hidden the details of our correspondence.

Eventually we came to the table of the goði, Aud Hallasdottir, who looked up from her conversation with two rough-

looking women to smile at me. I found myself abruptly caught
in a tight embrace. Aud stepped back, her hands still on my
shoulders, and informed me that I would dine at her home at
my earliest convenience. I acquiesced, telling her that Finn had
notified me of her expertise where the Hidden Ones were concerned, and expressing my gratitude for any information she
could share.

Finn's smile took on a fixed quality, and Aud blinked. She
was a short, broad woman with two deep lines between her eyes,
the only visible sign of her age. I had only a moment to wonder
where I had gone wrong before she nodded and said, "Of course,
Professor Wilde. Please, sit down, and allow my husband to
serve you. He makes an excellent mulled wine—you must take a
bottle home with you. I've been in that cottage of Krystjan's,
and find it very drafty."

I told her politely that she was very kind, but that I insisted
upon paying for my refreshments. As a rule, I avoid accepting
favours from the locals while conducting fieldwork, as I dislike
the potential for partiality it produces. Every village has its
share of scandals where the Folk are concerned, mysterious
pregnancies and the like, and my job as a scholar is not to cen-
sor but to decide upon the inclusion of such accounts in my
research—with names redacted, of course—based on scientific
merit.

Aud nodded and excused herself to discuss something with
her husband, Ulfar. I had not been introduced to him yet,
though I was constantly aware of him looming at the back of
the tavern. He was not a tall man, but something about the
heavy brows and sharpness of his countenance, which created
little peaks and valleys of shadow, gave him the quality of a
brooding mountain. I at first thought him to be glaring at me
as he moved about the room, serving up platters of fish and

bread or a nearly solid dark stew, until I noticed that he looked that way at everyone.

Finn seemed oddly flustered after my conversation with the headwoman, and I began to worry that I had given some offence. However, Aud reappeared with a smile and a table prepared for me—close to the fire, a position from which she had needed to evict a trio of sailors, who complied without noticeable objection. One woman remained at the table, and I sensed that no command, from a headwoman or otherwise, could move her from her preferred spot. As I seated myself opposite, she smiled at me.

I smiled back. She was a woman of advanced years—so advanced, in fact, that I felt momentarily as if I had never truly known old age. Her eyes were mere slits within that wrinkled countenance, her hands a riverbed of spots. But the eyes were a vivid green, the hands moving rapidly through the wool hooked around her fingers, which she seemed to be knitting without the aid of needles.

"Thora Gudridsdottir," Finn said, before retreating towards the bar. Shadow tucked himself under the table and contentedly worked at a mutton chop.

"They're laughing at you," the old woman said. "They'd never do it to your face. Well, Krystjan, maybe. They call you a—you don't have a word for it in English. It means something like *library mouse*."

My face heated, though I kept my voice even. "There are worse epithets, I suppose."

"They also say you are a silly foreign girl who lost her head over some faerie back home and now trots round the world on her parents' penny looking for a way back to his world. They can't fathom another reason why you'd be doing this. Makes no more sense to them than a sheep taking it into its head to look for wolves. If you make it through the week, you shall astonish them. Bets have been placed."

This speech concluded, she went back to her knitting.

I had not the least idea how to respond. My stew steamed before me, my spoon held foolishly in my hand. I set it down. "Do you agree?"

Thora Gudridsdottir's bright gaze was wholly focused on her knitting. I almost disbelieved that she had spoken at all, so intent was she on her work, her person butterfly-fragile but eminently well cared for, the picture of a beloved grandmother in her dotage. She didn't look up as she let out a rude sound of disbelief. "Do I agree? Why would I be telling you any of this, if that were so?"

I appreciate blunt people. It takes the guesswork out of conversations, and as someone who is terrible at guesswork and always putting her feet wrong, this is invaluable. I could only say with perfect honesty, "I don't know what to make of you."

She nodded approvingly. "You're clever. And how do I know?" She leaned forward, and I found I had to do so too, all my supposed cleverness bewitched by this strange old woman. "Because you've seen them, and lived."

I gazed at her, stunned. "How do you know that?"

She made that rude noise again. "I've a grandniece at university in London. When Krystjan told us you were coming, I wrote to her and she sent me some of your papers."

I nodded. "Well, my successes with other Folk may have little bearing on my fortunes here."

She gave me a pitying look, as if wondering why I'd bothered to say something so obvious. I felt the need to keep talking, for some reason, to justify myself or perhaps my presence. "And, of course, most of my interactions have been confined to the common fae. I've studied the enchantments left behind by the courtly fae—the tall ones—as well as numerous firsthand accounts, but I've never met one." Besides Bambleby, perhaps. "May I ask if you've encountered the Hidden Ones yourself?"

She picked up her knitting. "My money is on a month. Krystjan gave me poor odds. Please don't disappoint me—I need a new roof."

"Here we are," Finn said, setting a bottle of mulled wine on the table. "I hope this will do, *Amma*."

"Idiot," Thora said. "Ulfar's stuff tastes like piss. How many times have I told you?"

Finn only sighed and turned to me. "Aud would have me ask if everything is to your liking."

"Thank you, yes," I said, though I had not yet tasted the stew. "Thora is your grandmother?"

"She's grandmother to half the village, give or take."

Thora made that rude sound again.

The door swung open, admitting a swirl of cold, and a disheveled figure stood framed against the darkness. It appeared roughly woman-shaped, but it was difficult to tell given the many layers of coats and shawls. The figure did not proceed further, but simply stood upon the threshold with the night billowing at her back.

"Auður," called Aud, then she went to the stranger's side, murmuring something. The firelight fell upon her face, revealing a young woman in her middle twenties, her mouth slack, her eyes darting ceaselessly without appearing to see. She gripped Aud's arm tightly, and when Aud directed her to a chair, she sat in a boneless slump.

Curious, I drifted to the woman's side. "Is she well?"

Aud stiffened. "As well as can be expected."

Ulfar set a bowl of stew before the girl. Auður did not look at it, or him.

"Eat," Aud said in Ljoslander. Auður picked up her spoon and mechanically filled her mouth, chewed, and swallowed.

"Drink," Aud said. Auður drank.

I watched them with growing confusion. There was something both uncanny and abhorrent about the way in which Auður responded to Aud's instructions, like a puppet on strings. Aud saw me watching, and her face darkened.

"I would ask that you refrain from including my niece in your book," she said.

I understood, and gave a slight nod. "Of course."

I know of several species of Folk who are in the habit of abducting mortals for the thrill of breaking them. In truth, it is something most of the courtly fae are given to on occasion. I once met a Manx man whose daughter had taken her own life after a year and a day spent in some horrific faerie kingdom so lovely that its beauty became as addictive as opiates. Others have endured torments and returned so changed their families barely recognize them. But in Auður's manner and expression, its scrubbed-clean quality, I found something I'd never encountered before. And for all my expertise, it sent a shiver of foreboding through me, a sense that perhaps, for the first time in my career, I was out of my depth.

"Does she live alone?" I enquired.

"She lives with her parents, as she always has."

I nodded. "May I call upon her?"

"You are a guest here, and are welcome anywhere," her aunt said, lightly and automatically, but there was a brittleness in her smile that even I could recognize, and so I retreated to the fireside. Auður continued to eat and drink only when instructed to, and when the meal was complete, she sat with her head slumped and her hair in her face until her aunt took her home.

"Is she always like that?" I said.

Thora gave me a brief, sharp look, then nodded. "That child would carve out her own heart if someone ordered her to."

There was a cold sweat upon my brow. "What did they do to her?"

"What did they do?" Thora repeated. "Did you not see? She's hollow. There's less substance there than the shadow of a ghost. But at least she returned."

The words had an emphasis that made me swallow. "And how many others did not?"

Thora did not look at me. "Your dinner is growing cold," she said, and there was something beneath the pleasantness in her voice that I did not dare challenge.

When Shadow and I returned to the cottage, we found the embers still hot in the woodstove, a fact that filled me with an ill-fated pride. I decided I would read for a time at the fireside, if only to put Auður from my mind, for she had unsettled me more than I cared to admit. Reaching into the wood box brought me swiftly down to earth, though, for I found only two logs remaining.

I chewed my lip, shivering lightly. I recalled Krystjan's reference to the woodshed, and wished, abruptly, that I had taken Finn's advice and "settled in" instead of spending the day charging hither and thither about the countryside. There are times when my scholarly enthusiasm gets the better of me, but I have never had cause to regret this so deeply before.

Well, there was nothing for it. I lit the lantern and thrust myself back out into the snow. Fortunately, the woodshed was easily located, tucked beneath the eaves. My heart sank, however, when I looked within. The wood had not been cut into logs, but piled up in huge chunks that would never fit into my humble stove.

I was shivering in earnest now. Shadow, perfectly comfortable in his bearish coat, grew anxious at my distress. Correctly intuiting the woodshed as its source, he proceeded to attack the door.

"Stop that, my love," I admonished. I hefted what appeared to be a whole segment of trunk and grimly set to work. I took up the axe set atop the woodpile and placed the trunk upon a stump. Then I swung.

The first time, I missed. The second too. The third, I buried the axe in the wood, where it stuck fast and would not be dislodged.

I wrenched on it. I stuck a foot against the stump and wrenched again. And though I am not usually the sort for cursing, I've no doubt I withered a few weeds with the stream of filth that fell from my lips.

Eventually, weary and cold and aching in my shoulder from the reverberation of the axe, I gave up. The axe I left in the shed stuck deep into the wood, projecting what I imagined was a kind of sadistic triumph. I went into the cold cottage, added the remaining logs to the fire, and draped all the blankets I could find over the bed. I did not wish to finish the day's entry, but habit lent me the necessary fortitude. Now to sleep.

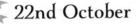

22nd October

I **awoke warm** enough this morning, but only because I was thoroughly swaddled in my blankets, Shadow snoring against me. But the moment I poked my foot free, I yanked it back. The cold had claws.

I could not ignore the knocking, though, which commenced predictably at half seven. I forced myself from bed but wrapped the blankets around me, dignity be damned, and admitted Finn to the cottage.

He cast a glance at the stove, winced, but made no comment. He set my breakfast upon the table.

"What is this?" I said in disbelief.

The loaf of bread was a blackened husk. There was no goose egg, nor egg of any sort, and no butter, but there was a little bowl of something gelatinous and greyish-green.

"*Đangssaus*," Finn said. "My father thought you might enjoy it. It's a kind of—" He searched for words. "Relish? Made from seaweed. It's for toast."

"This certainly qualifies."

His face fell. "I'm sorry, Professor. My father arranged the breakfast this morning. And somehow, without my noticing, the bread was knocked into the fire."

I sat down heavily. "Well, at least the tea is hot."

He smiled. "I made sure of it."

I set my head in my hand, which was pounding from the wine. "Might I enquire what I did to displease your father so?"

"It's not so much my father who is displeased. It's Aud." He added quickly, "My father is old-fashioned. He does not respond well to an insult to his *goði*."

"What? I said nothing to offend her." I reviewed the events of the previous evening. "Clearly there has been a misunderstanding."

Finn looked into the wood box. "Let me assist you with this, at least."

"That's quite all right." A hard, cold anger was forming in my stomach. "I was just about to get to it myself."

He raised his eyebrows and made no comment. Seconds after his departure, I heard the sound of an axe splitting wood in the yard.

I admit that I am disheartened by this news. My research requires the villagers' assistance—I rely as much on local lore as the evidence gathered with my own eyes and instruments in forming an accurate picture of the Folk. That I have already managed to offend the headwoman of Hrafnsvik does not bode well.

I think I can guess the source of Aud's anger—clearly, she is protective of her niece, and worried that I would publicize her affliction and make a spectacle out of her. I am determined to meet with her at the tavern today to plead my case.

Or perhaps tomorrow.

23rd October

I can hardly hold pen to paper, my hand shakes so. The cottage is cold as a grave, naturally, but that is not the reason.

I have met one.

I did not expect success upon setting out today—I had little yesterday, and returned home after a long exploratory ramble too wearied to do anything other than eat a bit of cheese and tumble into bed. In the morning, I obtained from Finn a detailed map of the Karrðarskogur and nearby mountains and divided it into grid sections of one square mile, extending ten miles in each direction (twenty miles being the upper limit of what I estimated I could walk in a day). Before commencing my systematic search, though, I wished to further familiarize myself with the terrain and develop an intuition for the place. Thus intentioned, I set off towards the sulphuric spring I had explored previously.

I located it without much trouble, puffing away in its forest bower, a useful landmark. I was delighted to see that my offerings were gone. As I turned to casually scan the forest, I caught a wink of light. There, in a knob of volcanic rock jutting from the ground, was the diamond, pressed into the stone like a tiny doorknob.

I settled myself by the spring, removing my boots once again. I anticipated a long wait before my friend noticed my presence.

I had spent barely a moment there, however, when I felt the smallest of tugs on my coat.

A faerie crouched beside me. It was very small, its frame skeletal with a face full of teeth and two sharp black stones for eyes tucked beneath a ravenskin that it seemed to wear as a sort of cloak, but the skin had been poorly cleaned and the eyes were absent. It had all the substance of cobwebs and was both there and not there; viewed from certain angles, it was merely the shadow of a stone, and from others, a live raven. It was digging around in my pockets with fingernails the length again of its spindly arms and sharp enough to slit my throat without my noticing the injury immediately.

I was not surprised by the creature's appearance, despite its unsightliness, but I had not been expecting it. I did not shriek or start away, of course, but I stiffened ever so slightly.

Immediately, the faerie was gone. I followed its progress by the birds, which fell silent in the tree to my left.

"It's all right," I said coaxingly in Faie, for it was clear that the faerie was young. Only the juveniles startle easily, in my experience, while adults have more confidence, particularly the ones who look like that. "I've come to bargain."

"For what?" came a small voice out of the forest, nearer than I had guessed.

"For whatever you like," I responded, "if it's in my power to give it."

It was a neat answer that has gotten me out of many close calls, for whatever you promise a faerie you must provide, or you will lose everything.

"I like skins," the faerie said. "Will you give me a bearskin?"

"And how do you know what bears are?" For there are none in Ljosland.

"How do you think?" it replied. "From stories. I like those too."

I thought it over. "I will give you a beaver skin." Oh, I was going to miss that hat. "We will see about the bear. Now will you hear what I want in return?"

"I already know that." The faerie was sitting on the edge of the spring—I would not have known if it hadn't spoken, for it was like a fold in the ground. "You're a noser. Poke, poke, poking your nose in. You want to know about me, but I shan't tell you anything."

"Why not?"

He—it was a he, I think—seemed not to expect the question. "I don't like talking about myself."

I tried not to let my delight show. The faeries of Ljosland should have known nothing about scholars—*nosers* are what the common fae call us on the continent. Not unless the faerie realms overlap, as I have argued on numerous occasions. The Folk can slip through locked doors and disappear into trees. Why would an ocean or mountain range keep them separate from one another?

"Then we seem to be at an impasse," I said, affecting puzzlement. "Why ask for anything if you already knew what I wanted, and that you would not grant it?"

The faerie looked down at his hands, blushing and mumbling to himself. I reached into my backpack and drew out the remnants of Finn's burnt loaf. Sighing heavily, I broke it in half and began to chew.

"That looks foul," the faerie said. He was beside me now, his long, long needle-fingers curved over the edge of a rock.

I spat out a piece of the crust. "My host is a poor cook."

"I'm a very good cook," the faerie said as soon as the sentence left my lips. I smothered a smile. Many of the common fae need little convincing to aid mortals and in fact enjoy the arrangement.

"Are you indeed?"

He nodded, suddenly solemn. "I shan't tell you my secrets. But I will bring you bread if I may have the skin."

I pretended to think it over. "Very well."

I rummaged in my backpack and pulled out another tin of Turkish delights. I popped one into my mouth, then held out a handful to the faerie. His black eyes bulged.

"An offering only," I said. "Not part of our bargain."

He swelled with pride. Ljoslanders regularly leave offerings for the common fae, but I wondered if this little faerie had ever had something left for him in particular. He speared the candy upon his fingertips and was gone, not in any direction I could perceive; he seemed to step into the landscape as if it were a door. I gathered myself and continued on my walk, already composing a description of the faerie for my encyclopaedia, as delighted with my progress as the faerie had been with his sweets.

28th October

The weather has taken a turn. Some days have proven too foul for me to set foot out of doors, a combination of hail and sleet. I have been able to explore another section of forest, where I found a smaller hot spring and—high above the village—the edge of a glacier. I spied several cavernous fissures amongst the ice where the villagers had left food offerings long ago. I wondered what faerie, or faeries, had abandoned the place.

I was not worried about missing my new friend, for the Folk are not bound by time in the way that we mortals are. He would have my bread for me whether I visited next week or next month. I sent off a letter to my brother with sufficient funds to purchase a bearskin. He will grumble and write to me with complaints that he is very busy with his shop and his wife, not to mention their four children, and that he hasn't time to assist with my faerie escapades, but he will send it all the same.

My breakfasts continued to be burnt. One morning, my butter had tiny fish bones in it. Yet I could get no explanation from Aud as to how I had offended her. When I attempted to apologize for questioning her about Auður, she gave me a perplexed smile and assured me that no apology was necessary. I was beginning to conclude that the whole thing was some wild imagining of Krystjan's, until I visited Hrafnsvik's only shop. That is when the fear that I would freeze to death was replaced by the fear that I would starve.

I took the long way, navigating the steep switchbacks below the cottage and strolling past the Egilson farm. Krystjan and Finn have a handsome home, rustic but large, with more windows than is common in the village. It is set back from the road at the end of a meandering lane lined with many outbuildings— livestock, hay, farming implements. Sheep grazed against the tall blue mountains.

The weather had ceased its blustering storms and settled into a rainy pattern, dark clouds clustering over the mountains. I wondered if I would ever get used to them rising from the earth like a terrible wave, spitting fantastical waterfalls.

The shop, a rickety structure painted a vibrant red, was closed for no apparent reason, so I waited outside as the drizzle turned into a cold, hard rain.

Across the road was another farmstead, much smaller than Krystjan's. A mangy goat browsed in the grass amongst a flock of chickens. At the end of the farmer's lane was a house that had once been blue; the paint had largely peeled off, and the roof was sagging. There was something about the house that made me wish to look away. If not for the animals, I would have thought the place abandoned.

A thin hand pushed back a faded curtain in the upstairs storey. Something about the hand was terribly wrong, though I could not place it. It may have been the way it moved, a sort of spiderish twitch. For a moment, a face peeped out at me. It was so white that I thought it must have been painted, topped with a dark thatch of hair. Child-sized it was, and while I could not make out any features, I sensed it was smiling. It pressed a hand to the glass as if in greeting, and I started. The hand was covered in blood.

The figure was gone as abruptly as it had appeared, leaving the bloody handprint behind. Habit made me disregard my thundering heart and look away, and I counted to ten. When I looked back, there was no sign at all of blood.

"Hm," I grunted aloud. I would have to make inquiries regarding the owners of the farmstead. I wondered if they were aware they had a faerie living within their walls. My inquiries would have to be discreet, as I did not like the looks of the creature.[*]

I was interrupted by the appearance of Groa, the shopkeeper. Plump and smiling, she issued a great quantity of apologies as she admitted me into the shop. Her English was not fluent, but with my smattering of Ljoslander we managed to cobble together an understanding.

The shop was cheery and warm, cluttered with an impressive assemblage of goods, from food to farming and fishing implements. I nearly tripped over a sewing machine on my way to the counter. I requested flour, milk, butter, smoked fish, and tea, and Groa also encouraged me to take a few mutton sausages and a box of fresh carrots, leeks, and cabbage.

Humming to herself, she wrapped my requests in paper. I felt warmed just being in her presence, and though I have not much talent for small talk, I found myself compelled to ask her a few questions about herself. She was older than I had first guessed, and had run the shop alone for twenty years since the death of her husband. She informed me that the blue house belonged to a young couple named Aslaug and Mord, who lived with their

---

[*]   The scholarly community has long since moved past such dated distinctions as seilie or unseilie, light or dark, in reference to the Folk, recognizing the general tendency towards malevolence that exists even within seemingly beneficent fae (see de Grey and Eichorn's *Tutelary Spirits*). But there are certainly those whose chosen sport is to frighten and spread misery wherever they go.

son, Ari. Her cheer dimmed a little when I broached this topic, and I did not press her.

"How much?" I enquired, and she cheerily named an exorbitant sum ten times what such supplies would cost in Cambridge.

I had to ask her to repeat herself. She did so, just as cheerily, seeming not to notice my consternation. She bustled about the shop, chattering absently about the buns she left outside for the wee ones—I should have pressed her on this score, but I was too flustered.

I emptied my pockets—quite literally. At this rate, I would run through the entirety of my funds in less than a month.

"Wait!" Groa said. She placed one of her small glazed cakes, wrapped in cloth, atop the bundle in my arms, and tapped her lips. "Aud says you do not wish to be treated as a guest, but to pay foreigners' rates for everything. But I cannot resist. My mother's *svortkag* is for everyone, and it is priceless. Please accept."

I nodded, a grimness settling inside me. Shadow and I made our way back to the cottage, where I deposited our supplies. Then, the dog having settled himself in for an afternoon nap on my bed, I made my way to the spring alone.

As before, I seated myself by the water and removed my boots. I admit that I am increasingly tempted to do more than this. I continue to have difficulty with the firewood, managing to cut only a few pieces if I am lucky and relying on Finn for the rest. But Finn is not always available, and so I am hesitant to use the fire for anything other than maintaining a bare minimum of warmth in order to ration my fuel. Thus, I have heated water for bathing only once, and that a small quantity. I still feel as if I am thinly layered in salt from the voyage north, like a bookshelf that has been left undusted.

My friend was prompt in arriving. I had the beaverskin ready, and he marvelled over it for a very long time. Beneath his grue-some ravenskin he looked much like a branch, covered in au-tumnal moss. He discarded the raven and, after pulling and prodding at the beaverskin, folded it over his shoulders.

Noticing me watching him admire himself, he blushed. He pushed the grass aside and wrapped his sharp fingers around a fine loaf of bread. It smelled of sulphur, but was perfectly golden and soft.

"Thank you," I said quietly. I had certainly not intended to rely on the Folk for sustenance—my bargain with the little fa-erie was to have been for the purposes of trust-building only.

Well. There was nothing for it. I tucked the loaf away, feeling low. I couldn't help but worry that I was harming my scientific objectivity through this arrangement, and that put the cap on a day of frustrations. Or so I imagined then.

"When you run out, I will bring you more," the faerie said, turning from the spring, in which he had been admiring him-self.

"In exchange for?"

"Nearly nothing," he said. "Only clear a path from my tree to the spring when the snows come."

"And which is your tree?" I enquired, though I had already guessed. The faerie pointed to a lovely white aspen, clad in moss like himself, the only one I had noticed in that part of the forest. Thinking back to the loaf Finn had served me with breakfast, all yeast and salt, I had no choice but to agree.

I hurried back to the cottage, intending to spend the rest of the day adding to my notes. That morning, Finn had pointed out several faerie rocks scattered about the farmstead, and I had a mind to map and investigate each one.

The rain started up again as I walked. My boots sank into mud up to the ankles, and I was quickly soaked through and shivering. I nearly ran back to the cottage, an ill-advised decision, for the slope was treacherous even in fair weather. I slipped and ended up on my back in the mud.

Once I finally slogged my way up the cottage steps like some ungainly monster of the mountains, I almost failed to notice that the door was ajar. I thought first of Finn, and then I thought, strangely, of the pale face and the bloody hand. Breath coming fast, I pushed on the door.

A sheep stared back at me.

No—two sheep. One stood upon the carpet, enjoying the heat of the coals, while another roamed to and fro, chewing at something green.

Green. My cabbages!

The table where I had left my groceries was askew, the pitcher of milk shattered on the floor and Groa's *svortkag* smashed into bits that seemed to be scattered everywhere there wasn't milk. The sheep had also overturned a pile of my books, and half-chewed pages decorated the flagstones with hoofprints on them—not *my* book, thank God; I had put that carefully back into my trunk. Shadow sat in the bedroom doorway, politely puzzled as he watched the baggy field-dwellers bulldoze their way through his home. Good dog that he was, he'd given no thought to obstructing the sheep's rampage, having been admonished many times against menacing them.

I erupted into shouts, a mixture of commands in English and Ljoslander alongside various garbled ejaculations of no meaning at all. I lunged at the nearest sheep, intending to pry the remnants of the cabbage—worth more than the sheep itself—from its maw, but the creatures only took fright and stampeded round and round the cottage. No sooner had I managed to force one towards the door than its companion got it into its head to run in the opposite direction. More books were trampled, the frying pan and various pots tumbled off their hooks with a clang, the wood box tipped onto its side, and the armchair fell atop one of the sheep, setting off a storm of hor-rified bleats quickly echoed by its accomplice. Shadow, noting my distress, leapt into the fray, but as he could do nothing to the sheep, he merely ran aimlessly amok, howling, which had a predictable effect upon the interlopers. Amidst the chaos, I did not hear the knocking at the door, which grew louder by the second, nor the creak when it opened.

"God's grace, Em," came a lilting voice from the threshold. "I've never heard such— Ah! Away with you, woollen rat!"

This last was directed at the sheep, which, having had quite enough of the screaming madwoman in the cottage, now sought the relative peace of their rain-soaked abode. Together they hurtled at the tall, black-clad figure obstructing their egress, sending him sailing back down the stairs.

Shadow followed them out the door, still barking (for he had established that he was allowed to bark at the sheep, at least), and plowed into the figure who had been collecting himself from his tumble onto the grass, knocking him over once more.

The figure lifted his head, revealing himself as none other than Wendell Bambleby.

"Any more?" he called from his sprawl at the foot of the stairs.

"What?" I shouted. I believe I had gone slightly deaf.

"Any more of your demented beasts lurking within? Should I simply lie here until they take their leave?"

"They're not mine," I felt it necessary to say. "Well, one of them is."

Bambleby was not alone. In his wake trailed two young per-sons whom I recognized as his students, though I could not recall either of their names—Bambleby is regularly trailing stu-dents, you see. The young woman—red-haired and wide-eyed in a way that gave her a perpetually bewildered look—reached down and helped him to his feet.

As he brushed himself off, I began to comprehend that Wendell Bambleby was standing outside my cottage. You would think this would have happened before, but there hadn't been space for it amidst the pandemonium.

"Dear Emily," Bambleby said as he tugged a leaf from his hair. The hair was golden and entirely perfect, like the rest of him. "Always one for the unexpected."

He gave the girl who had helped him a smile so thoughtlessly beautiful that she seemed momentarily incapable of movement, before turning his amused black eyes upon me again. His slender frame was clad in its customary blacks, all immaculately tailored from the line of his cloak—which had an upturned collar—to the folds of his scarf. You would not think a scarf could be tailored, until you met Bambleby. His age was difficult to place, though I knew it to be twenty-nine, for he had told me.

"I, unexpected?" I managed finally. "What the bloody hell are you doing here, Wendell?"

"What am I doing here?" he repeated with a breath of laughter. "Well, I thought to myself, why take a first-class carriage to the south of France for sabbatical when only five days of seasickness can grant you the luxury of a fishing village in an icebound wasteland? What do you think I'm doing here, Em?"

He motioned to the students and then swept up the stairs and past me into the cottage. The students bent to collect a large quantity of luggage—several bags each, and a trunk. They too tromped into the cottage.

"Oh, God," I said to no one in particular. And I had thought I had been at my wit's end with the sheep.

"This place looks as if it's being tenanted by raccoons," Bambleby noted, looking about him. His graceful Irish brogue formed a bizarre contrast with the recent din, which still rang in my ears. "And why isn't the fire lit? Enjoy the cold, do we, Em?"

Now, I have never once suggested he call me *Em*, and am in fact accustomed to greeting the sobriquet with a stony glare. "The fire isn't lit because I am nearly out of firewood," I said. I settled myself in the chair in an attempt to collect my scattered wits. "Perhaps you'd care to rectify that?"

He frowned at the fireplace. He was such a picture in his splendid blacks (collar upturned), framed against the dusty dishabille of the cottage, that I had to laugh; it was as probable a sight as a prince in a cowshed. I know Bambleby has been in the field, and I suspect he was somewhere else entirely before that, but I only know him set against his oak-panelled Cambridge office, the warm cathedral of the library, the manicured leafiness of the university grounds with their stone fountains and statuary.

"Henry will take care of all that—won't you, dear?" Bambleby said. The faintest alarm had come upon his face at my suggestion—either he hadn't any idea of how a fire came to be or he was in terror of dirtying his sleeves.

The hapless Henry, who had the sharp-edged proportions of a man not a day over twenty, nodded eagerly and set to prodding the sullen wet logs with one of the candlesticks. Now, I was no enemy of poor Henry's and should not have been amused by his ineptitude, but I will admit that I watched this performance for several minutes without comment. Wendell drifted off down the hall with his unnamed and equally hapless admirer, clearly viewing his duty as complete.

"There are only two additional bedrooms," he informed Henry upon his return. "I shall give you two the larger of them. See to all that later," he instructed Lady Hapless, who had begun to lift the trunk again. "We must first make this place liveable. Emily, I must warn you away from your own bedroom temporarily. If you hadn't already noticed, the sheep have been in there too, and they've given it rather a smell. Em?"

He seemed to look at me properly. "What have you done to yourself? Is this some sort of camouflage, to fool the Folk into thinking you're one of the flock? Oh, don't look at me like that, you're the one who turned our cottage into a byre."

"*Our* cottage!"

He ignored me. *Tsk*ing over the empty cauldron, he said, "Henry, let's collect water. I noticed a stream out back. Lizzie, perhaps we could gather up the rubbish?"

In the space of a few minutes, Henry had water bubbling over the fire (started with pages of my ruined books), and I had a cup of tea in my hand. The two of them were sweeping and scrubbing up the mess while Wendell leaned back in the other armchair he had dragged over to the fire, offering occasional directives phrased as suggestions. I had changed clothes and done what I could to wash off in the stream out back, which wasn't much, if I'm being honest. I could still feel the mud clumping in my hair.

"This is quite good," Bambleby said, helping himself to another piece of toast. It was the faerie's bread, warmed over the fire. He looked perfectly comfortable slouched in his chair in that gracefully boneless way of his, clad in a fresh cardigan. "You say the creature is a brownie?"

"Yes—tree. Though he also seems to act as a guardian of the spring, which is unusual." I do not like to admit it, but I was in better spirits, and this was not only due to the tea. Unwelcome as his presence was, Bambleby was a piece of Cambridge, and I felt more myself with him there.

Bambleby stretched, interlacing his hands behind his head. "Dunne noted a similar phenomenon among the Finnish *keiju*. What did she call it? Elemental decoupling?"

I snorted. "Dunne invents theories to hide her shoddy methodology. You cannot generalize about such things with her sample sizes."

Bambleby murmured assent. I realized that he was smiling at me sleepily. Lizzie would have been beside herself with blushes at that smile, but I was too used to him. I simply gazed levelly back, waiting for him to explain this latest outrageousness.

"I missed you, Em," he said. "It was strange not having you across the hall, scowling at me."

"I wonder at your ability to detect my scowls through the wall. Are your senses heightened in other ways?"

I was needling him. I do this sometimes. I believe Bambleby knows my suspicions about him.

"You alone have the talent of scowling loudly. I've often wondered how you manage it." He turned to Henry. "Summon our host, would you? I've a mind to have a hot meal before I retire. And do ask after the possibility of dessert. Nothing elaborate— an apple tart or bread pudding will suit. God in Heaven, but I am tired of fish stew and sailor's bread."

I could not imagine such a message eliciting a favourable response from Krystjan Egilson, so naturally I said nothing. Bambleby leaned forward and took my hand. "I suppose you've guessed why I'm here. Let me assure you, it's not what you think."

"Oh?" I knew exactly why he was here. To take credit for my research.

"I have the utmost respect for your abilities, Emily. Please do not interpret my presence to mean that I think you'll make a mess of this opportunity. Nothing could be further from the truth."

I withdrew my hand, shrivelling into a ball of anger. "Oh, wonderful."

"I'm here to assist," he assured me, perfectly oblivious.

"And I'm sure that this desire to be helpful has nothing to do with a fear that someone other than yourself might get the credit for conducting the first comprehensive investigation of a yet unproven species of Folk?"

He gave me a wide-eyed look of surprise. "That wouldn't be very sporting. I like to think that I've always been a good friend to you. Why else would I have volunteered to write the foreword to your encyclopaedia?"

I was going to club him over the head with my encyclopaedia when it came out. Was it really necessary for him to always be reminding me that I needed him? "As a matter of fact, my findings are quite advanced," I said. "So you may discover that whatever research you undertake here only serves to back up my conclusions."

"Indeed?" To my chagrin, he looked excited rather than resentful, and I realized that he truly did see us as colleagues rather than competitors. The problem with Bambleby, I've always found, is that he manages to inspire a strong inclination towards dislike without the satisfaction of empirical evidence to buttress the sentiment. "Will you show me the data you've collected thus far?" His eagerness was interrupted by a yawn. "Tomorrow, perhaps?"

I tapped the rim of my mug, watching him. "What form do you anticipate this assistance taking, precisely?"

He gave me a different sort of smile, and I felt a chill creep down my back. There is something that Bambleby does which would be noticeable only to those who spend a great deal of time around the Folk. It is the way in which his emotions seem to slide through him like water, one giving way to another as abruptly as waves on the shore. This changeability would seem disconcerting or false on a human face, but it is just the way the Folk are made.

He leaned forward. "Are you familiar with the International Conference of Dryadology and Experimental Folklore?"

His voice had a teasing edge, for of course I was familiar. ICODEF is the most prestigious conference in our field, held annually in Paris, to which I had not once been invited. Bambleby went every year, damn him.

"I'm a featured speaker this year," he said. "There is a particular sponsor attending whom I wish to impress. Very deep pockets. It could mean funding for not one but several research expeditions I have been putting off for lack of resources. Few things would be more impressive than a paper presenting even preliminary findings of a heretofore unknown Folk. As you say, these Hidden Ones are regarded with scepticism by even the most open-minded of scholars. But, as I've always argued, the fact that the Folk are absent in other regions of Arctic and sub-Arctic Europe cannot be taken as evidence of their absence in every winter country."

I narrowed my eyes. "I've not been invited to ICODEF this year. Will you credit me in a footnote?"

"We will present our findings together. I will impress my sponsor. You will make a name for yourself and set the scientific community clamouring for your book, which I understand is out next year."

He sank back into his slouch, looking merry, utterly convinced that I would be delighted. I kept my expression bland, to deny him that pleasure at least, but of course there was no option besides agreement.

Bambleby was being modest—no doubt an oversight of fatigue. He was not merely a featured speaker at ICODEF this year; he was likely the only one people would be talking about, though I doubted the reasons were entirely to his liking.

"I planned to see through the winter here," I said. "To attend ICODEF would mean departing Hrafnsvik—"

"February the first," he said. "At the very latest. The plenary is on the tenth. And, well, we need a day or two to settle in, don't we? I have already promised half a dozen of our continental colleagues that I would dine with them on the Champs-Élysées—you will come along, of course—among them Leroux and Zielinski. She's been awarded some sort of medal by the Polish queen and has been rather big-headed about it—snubbed three-quarters of her old circle, though I've managed to stay in her good graces . . . They say even the king of Paris may make an appearance this year; if so, I'm sure I can convince Leroux to make the introductions . . ."

My heart gave a nervous flutter. That would shorten the duration of my field study drastically. I would have only three months—three months!—to accomplish what took most scholars a year or more. Could I do it?

Instead of answering, I sipped my tea and said, "I'm a little surprised you were invited back this year. But I suppose the furor over the Schwarzwald expedition has died down somewhat."

He slouched deeper and became preoccupied with his sleeve. "A misunderstanding, that. I've no doubt future studies will validate my findings."

"Of course." I'd no doubt they would do the opposite. I suspected that Bambleby's paper concerning the snow-weavings of the trooping faeries of the Schwarzwald was not the first of his to contain exaggerated or patchy evidence, but it was probably the first he had entirely falsified.

Probably. Wendell Bambleby's research is all flash and dazzle, and he has an uncanny knack for uncovering outlandish new faerie rituals and enchantments that turn much of the related scholarship on its head—a knack I have often found less uncanny than suspicious.

Shadow placed his head on Bambleby's knee, and he reached

his long fingers down to stroke the dog's head. In the early days of our friendship, Bambleby had been unsure of Shadow, often appearing to have little idea of what to make of him, so much so that at times I wondered if he had ever seen a dog before. But Shadow had no such hesitancy. From their first meeting, he regarded Bambleby with a thoughtless and entirely undeserved ardour that would have filled me with jealousy had I not already been so secure in Shadow's affections. As time went on, Bambleby grew accustomed to offering hesitant pats in return, and now—to my chagrin—they are old friends.

"This book of yours is important to you, isn't it?" he said. He reached into his briefcase and pulled out a stack of neatly typed pages. I recognized the excerpt I had sent him last month, comprising the first fifty pages or so.

"You've read it?" I demanded.

"Of course." He riffled the pages—they were much marked-up with his elegant scrawl. "It's quite remarkable. I'd like to see the rest once you've had it typed out."

I was startled by the flush that crept up my neck at his words. I've never attached particular consequence to Bambleby's opinion of my work, but I suppose it wasn't just about his opinion. The encyclopaedia has been mine alone for the better part of a decade. It is one thing to think highly of one's own research, quite another to hear that opinion corroborated.

"Remarkable?" I repeated.

"Well—it's never been done before, has it? An encyclopaedia of faeries? This will form a cornerstone of all scholarship on the subject for years to come. Probably it will lead to the formation of new methodologies that will enhance our core understanding of the Folk."

He said it without any hint of flattery. I could only reply honestly, a little overwhelmed, "Yes, that was the intention."

He smiled. "I thought so. You don't need the chapter on the Hidden Ones, you know."

"It will be less impressive without it."

"And who is it you are wishing to impress? Ah." He leaned back in his chair. "The faculty position. That's it, isn't it?"

"And if it is?" I couldn't interpret the look on his face. "You don't think I have a chance?"

"Well, you're a little young—"

"And you're not?" Cambridge had given him tenure two years ago, the bastard.

"I'm an exception." He said it absently, looking down at the pages, and a smile came over his face. "When is old Sutherland retiring?"

"This fall." I was leaning forward, twisting my fingers together. "I plan to put my name forward when I return. It would give me money. Resources. I wouldn't have to scrape together the funding for a one-month expedition; I could run multiple field studies at once if I chose. Think of the discoveries I could make, the mysteries I could solve. And—" And I would never have to leave Cambridge, I almost said.

"Yes." He flicked another page. "And you shall shut yourself away forever in those old stones with your books and your mysteries like a dragon with her hoard, having as little association with the living as possible and emerging only to breathe fire at your students."

He has an irritating way of understanding me, at least in part, which is more than anyone else does—no doubt some faerie gift of his. "You intend to stay here, do you?" I said, to change the subject.

"Where else? This is not the sort of place for a hotel, is it? I received your host's assent to my enquiry the day after I wrote to you, and departed Cambridge immediately thereafter. I assumed he would have told you."

I winced. "Egilson and I have not been on the best of terms."

"What?" He gave an exaggerated affectation of surprise. "Dear Emily. Don't tell me you've had trouble making friends."

My scowl was interrupted by the creak of the door. As before, Krystjan strode into the cottage without knocking. I could tell by his expression that Bambleby's message had been as well received as I had guessed. Lizzie trailed behind him, looking uselessly apologetic.

"Mr. Egilson!" Bambleby was on his feet immediately, his smile broadening. "I see that you don't stand for formalities, my good man. How refreshing. I must convey how much I appreciate your hospitality at such short notice. I had heard tales of the warmth and generosity of your compatriots, but you have gone above and beyond."

He said all of this in accented but fluent Ljoslander. It stopped Egilson in his tracks, but only for a moment. "Professor," Egilson said warily, accepting the proffered hand. I could see his frostiness melt a little upon exposure to the onslaught of Bambleby's charm, but he was a hardy man, and his smile was tight. "There's been a misunderstanding. You're welcome here, but unfortunately, we aren't in a position to provide meals—beyond the essentials at breakfast, of course. I run a large farm—you understand."

He had responded in English, which Bambleby acknowledged with a grateful smile that somehow managed to convey an admiration for Egilson's fluency. I detected a distinct hint of amusement in his gaze that, fortunately, seemed to evade Krystjan's notice. "I understand entirely. I hope you don't think I expected you to prepare our repast. I was, of course, offering to cook for your family."

Egilson blinked, his reserve dissolving into amazement. "You were."

"Oh, God," I muttered. "Please say yes."

Bambleby clapped Egilson on the shoulder. "Of course. It's customary in Ireland for the guests to prepare at least one meal for their hosts. As a token of appreciation. What is your preference? We have some supplies here." He stormed about the cottage, collecting the smashed remnants of the cabbage and carrots along with the smoked fish I had purchased, managing to convey a cheerful but manic energy. I could see from Egilson's face that he was envisioning Bambleby unleashed upon his kitchen.

"I— While I appreciate—" Krystjan began.

"Say nothing about it. I've a recipe for spice cake that'll set your mouth on fire. That's how we like it in Ireland. And as for the mains . . ."

"Truly, Professor, it's all right." Krystjan was smiling— a grudging but very real smile, not his customary smirk—as Bambleby stomped about, radiating good cheer. "You've only just arrived. I couldn't trouble you to cook for my son and me. Not that I don't appreciate the offer."

Bambleby stilled, blinking. Cabbage leaves swirled in his wake as in a contrary wind. "Really? Well, if you—"

"Finn's putting together a stew. We'll send some down to the cottage. If that's all right."

"Of course, my friend," Bambleby said. Then, to my astonishment, he added, "And I've no preference between the bread pudding and the apple tart." He snapped his fingers. "How rude of me! Emily, dear, which would you rather?"

I found myself suppressing a laugh. "Apple tart would be lovely."

"There we are." Bambleby smiled at Krystjan, who blinked as if trying to clear his vision. "And we'll talk tomorrow, won't we? It's my custom to interview the townsfolk—those of stature, you understand—at the outset of these investigations. It's good to get a lay of the land. I've no doubt you're inclined to be helpful?"

As he spoke, he moved closer to Egilson, taking the man's hand again.

"Of course," Egilson murmured, helplessly staring. Bambleby's eyes are not actually black, but the green of a forest at dusk, something you notice only when you are very close. I have seen people become lost in that gaze, foolishly wandering about and entangling themselves in thorns and God knows what else— Krystjan was certainly not the first. He should have looked away, counting to ten or focusing on his breathing or other mundane distraction, but of course he has no experience in evading the tricks of the Folk.

I cleared my throat. Krystjan blinked at me as if only just realizing I was there. "Thank you, Krystjan," I said. And I suppose some of Bambleby's mischief must have infected me against my will, for I added, "And we'll take a half dozen goose eggs with breakfast tomorrow."

Krystjan nodded like a man struck over the head and exited the cottage, politely pulling the door shut behind him.

"Spice cake?" I said.

Bambleby tumbled back into his chair. "How hard could it be?"

"Have you ever made spice cake?"

"I've certainly eaten it."

"Have you ever made *anything*?"

"That's neither here nor there."

I snorted. My stomach gave such a growl that Bambleby wrinkled his nose. It had been days since I'd had a proper meal, I realized.

"Could we build the fire up?" Bambleby said, indicating by means of the plural first person Henry and Lizzie.

Henry strode gallantly over to the wood box, where he frowned. "It's empty."

Wendell looked alarmed. I said, "You'll find more out back. There's a woodshed. My axe is in the garden." Still buried in a stump from my last attempt, but I saw no need to clarify.

"Ah," Bambleby said, "the woodshed," in precisely the same tone I had used upon my arrival. And thus we commenced our partnership.

29th October

Egilson was prompt in preparing our supper, which was accompanied by a dozen buns and, perhaps as a form of apology for the lack of apple tart, a basket of greyish-blue fruits aptly named iceberries. Finn delivered the lot, along with his apologies—there were no apples to be had in Hrafns-vik, and he had no experience with bread pudding, but he hoped we would enjoy his *briðsupa*, which he and Krystjan guessed to be the closest Ljoslander approximation. It was made with rye bread and plenty of cinnamon, cream, and raisins, and smelled divine. Bambleby exclaimed over everything, and he and Finn were soon chatting up a storm, for Finn, it seemed, had nursed a secret desire to visit Ireland since boyhood. Such quarry posed a negligible challenge to Bambleby's quiver of charms, and indeed, Finn ended up drawing up a chair and joining us. The cottage echoed with the sounds of their merriment, with the occasional comment thrown in by Lizzie or Henry. As for myself, I was happy to eat a hot meal without the burden of conversation, as Bambleby well knew, and he did me the kindness of ignoring me. And I don't know how he managed it, but somehow the evening ended with Bambleby retiring early whilst Lizzie, Henry, and Finn heated water and cleaned the dishes. With only the slightest twinge of guilt,

I too retreated to my room, my absence unremarked upon and, I suspect, barely noticed.

When I admitted Finn this morning with our breakfast, he looked predictably disappointed not to be greeted by Bambleby.

"He's still asleep," I said, my stomach rumbling at the sight of breakfast, which consisted of two perfect loaves, the requested half dozen eggs, an array of marmalades without any seaweed in sight, smoked fish, and lamb sausages. "Do you have any coffee?"

Finn's face fell. "He takes coffee?"

"Yes, and the stronger the better."

"Ulfar might have some," Finn said thoughtfully. "It isn't common around here."

"I'm sorry," I said. "He's very particular about breakfast." I felt a little guilty, but I was the one who would have to listen to Wendell's complaints, not Finn.

Naturally, Finn found this charming rather than aggravating, and smiled. "It's not a bad thing to be particular about."

Lizzie and Henry rose soon after and ate their fill, then drifted about at loose ends, looking for something to do. I was already fed up with having so many people underfoot, so I sent them both out to chop more wood. I regretted not having something more educational for them to do, but if they were put out by such a menial assignment, they gave no indication, which told me everything I needed to know about what they were used to from Bambleby.

He showed himself some time later, long after I'd begun seriously considering setting off without him, our agreement and ICODEF be damned. Had I asked him to come here? No. Did I need his assistance? Of course not.

"Morning," he yawned upon emerging from his bedroom, looking resplendent in a black dressing gown that somehow managed to connote the robes a king might wear to a masquerade, though the effect was somewhat spoiled by his golden hair, which went in all directions.

"Finally," I said, but before I could go on, he held up a hand.

"Not before breakfast, Em," he said. "Please."

"I was merely going to point out the coffee," I said. Bambleby was allergic to serious conversation—or indeed, any work at all—that took place before breakfast. We ate it together at Cambridge whenever we were both on campus, and had done ever since he found out that I didn't ordinarily bother with it. He'd reacted with a horror befitting a confession of murder and immediately swept me from my office to his favourite café on the university grounds, which was nearly hidden by a conclave of oak trees and overlooked the River Cam. A full hour later, after what he referred to as a "lean" breakfast of eggs, fried tomatoes, several rashers of bacon, toast laden with butter and blueberry jam, and a baked oatmeal with pears, together with copious amounts of black coffee, which he drank sweet enough to set your teeth on edge, he had declared himself satisfied. I had thought that perhaps he had some philosophy about it the way people have about tea, how it can make every problem less grim or the day seem brighter or some such, but he just blinked at me when I asked him about it and replied, "Oh, Em. What *isn't* so important about breakfast?" Well, it's true that I don't have headaches in the morning anymore, since falling into the breakfast habit, and I suppose my stamina is improved, but really, to carry on so about a meal.

"You say this is coffee?" he said, flipping open the tin pot, which Finn had left on a rack over the fire, along with the kettle and toast, to keep warm.

"Yes. Ulfar had some beans, apparently. Though I understand from Finn that they are of uncertain provenance."

"This will be a long winter," he said, and helped himself to the tea. I ate too, slathering marmalade on toast and having a go at one of the goose eggs, for despite my hunger I'd eaten little earlier, being preoccupied with thoughts of the day—it's not uncommon for me to forget to eat when I am buried in some academic mystery. Bambleby tried everything, including the smoked fish that I did not consider a breakfast food, declaring it of a high standard.

"I think I'll wander up to the hot spring Finn was describing," he said with a satisfied stretch after he had finished his third cup of tea. "Wash off some of the ferry."

"I thought we could go over the plan for the day," I said evenly. "I've been waiting for over an hour."

"Have you? Well, you're welcome to join me."

"I'm fine, thank you."

He reached over and plucked a grass blade from my hair—which, as usual, was already half out of its bun. "Of course you are."

"We haven't even established our research design. We have *three months,* Wendell. How are we supposed to work together? That is our agreement, is it not?"

"I don't recall any formal agreement. I recall a great deal of scowling and a few attempts at impugning my character, but that could characterize many of our conversations."

I folded my arms.

"My research tends to have a certain flexibility," he said, swallowing a bite of toast. "I don't like being too rigid in my approach to fieldwork."

I had guessed he would say that. "In this case, my preference is for naturalistic observation as a primary method of data collection. I've already made a rough map of the study area—roughly ten square miles of wilderness—noting suspected faerie features. I intend to return to as many as possible to attempt to observe the common fae in their native environment. It's unlikely we shall have a chance to do the same for the courtly fae, given their skill at evading human detection; thus we shall have to base our analysis of their ways and habits on ethnographic interviews with the villagers. There is a woman in Hrafnsvik who has been mistreated by the courtly fae—Auður Hildsdottir. If I have the time, I plan to visit her today, along with another household that I believe is home to a brownie. This alone would be a significant discovery, as the literature suggests that the Hidden Ones dwell within the natural landscape only."[*] I paused. "I wish to accomplish two objectives—firstly, to identify the species of Folk that dwell here, and second, to describe their interactions with the mortal inhabitants."

Bambleby knelt to scratch Shadow's ears. "Why not give your map to Lizzie and Henry? Let them go tramping through the wastes, they're quite good at it. As for this Auður, I understand from your field notes that she is a mute. What do you expect to get out of her?"

I blinked. "You read my notes?"

"Last night. How would you characterize the brownie you saw in the house?"

"I suspect it to be a wight of some sort," I replied.[†]

"How dull," he said. "I hate wights—such tedious creatures. Perhaps we should divide our efforts. You go poking about the haunted house whilst I introduce myself to our headwoman. If we're to be interviewing the locals, etiquette would suggest we start with the one in charge."

---

[*]   Bran Eichorn, whose mother was a Ljoslander, wrote one of the few papers on the subject of the Ljosland Folk, though his research is based entirely on oral accounts—it is unclear if he visited Ljosland himself. I will not name the paper here as it is a poor example of scholarship, being mostly a screed disguised as a rebuttal against Danielle de Grey's "The Importance of Hearth Faeries in the Northern Latitudes" (*Modern Dryadology*, Spring 1848). Eichorn spent much of his early career obsessed with de Grey.

[†]   Over the last two or three decades, the word "wight" has evolved in academic discourse to refer to all those household brownies whose behaviour towards their host has become centred around malevolence.

"Let's leave the tavern for this evening, shall we?" I said, knowing that if he went there now, he would not come out again till midnight, and not because Bambleby is much of a drinker, but because he would encounter so many targets for his conversation.

He smiled. "As you wish. I approve of your plan, Em. This field study was your initiative, after all."

"I take that to mean that my name will go first in the paper we present at the conference?"

"Of course," he said calmly, as if there had never been any doubt in his mind. Perhaps there hadn't. His expression was perfectly open in that disconcerting way he has of moving from mischief to guilelessness in the space of a heartbeat. Bambleby never attempts to charm me in the way he did Krystjan. It would not work if he did, and I suspect that he knows this.

He swallowed the last of his tea, gave Shadow another pat, and wandered out the door.

"Where are you going?" I demanded.

"I told you. I won't be long. Take the time to scribble in that journal of yours."

"And you're just going to go wandering about the country-side like that?" I said, waving a hand at his robe.

The amusement returned. "You needn't worry about me, Em."

"Worry!" I scoffed, but the hem of his robe had already vanished through the door.

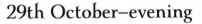

29th October—evening

He was lying, of course. After I finished the morning's journal entry, he still hadn't returned, so I decided to set out on my own as originally intended. Henry and Lizzie I sent off with my map to investigate a series of volcanic features, as Wendell had suggested. They seemed to understand my directives, though I couldn't help missing my own students. I trusted them, for they were chosen on the basis of their qualifications and diligence, not their ability to put up with nonsense.

The sky was that peculiarly rich shade of blue it assumes in the autumn, and the sea was studded with little fishing boats. Groa waved cheerily at me as I passed the shop—as well she should, given that I'd likely doubled her month's earnings. Suffice it to say that I did not stop by for a chat.

Nobody answered when I knocked upon the door of the blue house. The two goats kept an eye on me, bleating their disapproval from behind the fence.

"Hello?" I called in Ljoslander, knocking again.

I thought I glimpsed one of the curtains twitch. Seconds later, the house filled with screams.

My hands flew to my ears. This was ineffectual in deadening the screams, which went on and on. It was impossible to place whether the voice was male or female—what was certain was the desperation and torment. The screams had the cadence of a winter gale, and I could feel the cold radiating from the cracks round the door.

Wonderful, I thought. The wight was toying with me.

I lowered my hands. As the screams rolled over me, I politely knocked again.

Gradually, as I showed no evidence of being terrorized, the screaming subsided. I had no interest in whatever gruesome trick the wight would devise next, so I motioned to Shadow—who had not heard anything amiss—and we wandered around the side of the house.

There I saw in the distance two figures: a man milking a goat and, much farther away, where the land sloped towards the beach, a woman walking alone. She was framed against the sharp blue waves and looked very lonesome. The goat gave a worried bleat, and the man turned and saw me. He finished his task and approached.

"You're the professor, I suppose." He was a small, dark man with a weathered face overwhelmed by a thick beard. "Aud told you about our son."

Instantly, I understood. The creature I had seen in the window had not been a wight at all. It had been a changeling. I have never known a changeling in manner so like a wight, neither in the course of my own research nor in the literature. Changelings are monstrous offspring produced by the courtly fae, weak and sickly creatures who bring misfortune upon a household for as long as they remain there, but they are not vicious or malevolent. My interest in this place grew by the moment, and I was pleased that I had brought my notebook.

I held out a hand. "My name is Emily Wilde. When was your son taken?"

He paused, then took my hand. "Mord Samson. My wife is

Aslaug—she's on one of her walks. I thought Aud would have told you?"

"Aud told me nothing. It was simple inference."

"I see." He gazed at me for a moment. "She doesn't like you."

Something about this man, the grim lines of his face, perhaps, which had the opacity of a windowpane, prompted me to agree, "She doesn't like me."

He smiled at that, barely. I had the impression that even such a smile was a rare occurrence. "It was five winters ago. Ari was a baby. Barely a year old."

Now I was very interested indeed. Already, the behaviour of the Ljosland Folk was diverging from what I knew. "A year is quite unusual. The Folk abduct newborns—I've never heard of one taking interest in older children. Apart from the boggarts of Scotland, of course, but they do not leave a boggart-child in place of the one stolen away."

I realized that I sounded excited, and that Mord was watching me with raised eyebrows. "I'm sorry," I said, and it sounded perfunctory to my own ears, yet for some reason, Mord smiled again.

"It doesn't matter a whit to me," he said. "That is, whether you're sorry or not, whether you will put us in your prayers. We had plenty of prayers and sorries when Ari was stolen away, and we've had plenty since. Can you help us?"

"That's—" I stopped. But something about him made me unafraid to be honest. "That's not why I'm here. I've come to catalogue your Folk for the purpose of science."

He merely nodded. "And yet you are here, and it's clear you are more canny as to the ways of the Folk than any priest, and that gives me hope. I would invite you in, but I'm afraid that the hospitality you will find under my roof will not be to your liking. And I would not wish to frighten your handsome companion."

He gave Shadow a pat on the head, and the dog sniffed him approvingly. "That's fine, Mr. Samson," I said. "He's used to the Folk. As am I."

Mord looked dubious, but he did not stop me as I let myself into his house.

Nothing was amiss. A humble reception room and hearth gave way to an even sparser kitchen with iron pans hung upon the wall. The screams did not recommence, nor did I observe any bloody handprints. Shadow, however, sniffed the air and emitted a grunt.

"Yes," I said. "Stay close to me, dear." To Mord, I said, "Will your wife be gone long?"

"A while. Walking eases her mind. She does it every day, until the snows come." He looked out the window, and written plainly on his face was the weary certainty that the snows would not be long in arriving. "I suspect Aslaug will like you. She and Aud have never gotten on."

I was startled into a smile. Mord motioned with his hand. "Ari's in the attic."

"I see," I said, wincing a little as I remembered Bambleby's comment about haunted houses. "Are you cold, Mr. Samson?"

He glanced down at himself. He had removed his coat, revealing another beneath it. "Aslaug and I are always cold. It never leaves us, not even in midsummer."

I had my notebook out, and was scribbling my initial observations. Part of me was aware of how hard-hearted I must have seemed, but I was too caught up in my scientific interest to worry over it, and in any case, Mord did not appear offended by me.

I took a step towards the stairs. Immediately, they transformed. Each stair became a gaping mouth, glittering with teeth and furred with a wolf's dense pelt. A bitter wind funnelled into the room, smelling of snow and pines. The wolves snarled and snapped at the hem of my coat.

I turned to Mord. He had started back in horror, but there was a dullness to it, and he did not cower long.

"You see such visions often?" I said.

He blinked. Annoyance came into his eyes, and he frowned at me as if expecting pity. His face softened when he encountered only dispassionate interest. "I know they aren't real," he said.

"I see." I thought about living in such a place, beset by such violent illusions. I thought about days following days, and years following years.

"Mr. Samson," I said, "would you bring me an iron nail and a little salt?"

He blinked but went to fetch what I had requested. When he returned, I asked him if the small coat I had spied hanging on a hook on the door was his son's. He nodded.

"Thank you," I said, and I placed the coat in my backpack. "I'll return it, I promise."

I mounted the stairs. Mord drew in a sharp breath. He did not follow me, which was just as well. I would have stopped him.

Shadow padded alongside me as wolves champed at my ankles. I could see the stairs through the illusion, and Shadow could not see the illusion at all—at least, I think he cannot see fae illusions. I suppose it is possible that he sees them but is indifferent.

In the attic I found a little bed and a cosy rug of undyed wool. Upon the bed sat a boy, pale as moonlight on new snow. I stopped short, for the creature was nothing like the changelings I have encountered before—ugly, spindly things to a one, with the brains of animals. The boy's long hair was bluish and translucent, and upon his skin was a glimmer like frost. He was beautiful, with an uncanny grace, his eyes sharp with intelligence.

A distant part of me was struck by how much he reminded me of Bambleby. Though they looked nothing alike, there was a kinship that I could not put my finger on, which was perhaps more absence than feature, a lack of something coarse and mundane that characterizes all mortals.

My stomach twisted at the realization that this creature was the first of the courtly fae I had ever questioned. I was uncertain if the feeling was excitement or terror.

"You tricked me," the changeling said crossly.

"You have it backwards," I said, adjusting the sleeves of my coat. I had turned it inside out before entering the house, enabling me to see through any illusion the faerie chose to show me. "I merely sidestepped your own attempt at trickery. Would your true mother be pleased to know how you welcome a guest?"

"Go away." He was angry, and not just at my evasion of his enchantment. He had not liked me mentioning his faerie dam.

"I am going to ask you a few questions," I said. "I would recommend ready answers. I am aware of the cruelty you are inflicting upon your foster parents, and it has not inclined me to be generous with you."

Another blast of winter wind greeted this statement. The beams rattled in the ceiling.

"Are you happy to be the cause of suffering?"

"I don't care," the child snapped. For he was a child, for all his power, and he glared at me with a child's stubbornness. "I don't want to be here. I want my forest. I want my family."

"And what has become of your family, that they should send you to live among mortals?" I was particularly interested in the answer to this question, for most of what we know of changelings is guesswork. It is the habit of courtly fae to leave changelings in the hands of mortal parents for a period of months or years, and then swap them again without ceremony (if the changeling has not died in the interim, which is not uncommon), but no one knows precisely why they engage in this behaviour. The leading theory suggests a motive of idle amusement.

The changeling's lovely face twisted. He leaned forward. "If you do not go away, I will fill Mord's thoughts with such horrors that he will wish he was dead. I will give Aslaug dreams of burning and rending and the screams of everyone she cares for echoing in the night."

A shudder ran through me, but I maintained my bland demeanour. Wordlessly, I withdrew the handful of salt and began scattering it about the room.

"What's that?" he said, interest replacing fury in the space of a breath. He pinched some between his fingers, smelled it. "Salt? Why are you doing that?"

I stopped, silently cursing. Salt binds faeries, but perhaps in Ljosland it works only on the common fae, or not at all. I withdrew the iron nail.

"You can't kill me," he said.

"No," I agreed. To kill a changeling is to kill the child it has replaced. They are always bound together by a powerful enchantment that neither time nor distance can dispel. "I can hurt you, though."

I gave Shadow a signal, and he snapped at the child's foot, distracting him. I thrust the nail into the changeling's chest.

Almost into his chest. The faerie moved, and the nail ended up in his side. The screams that followed were worse than those before, like winter given voice. The faerie seemed to dissolve, becoming a creature of shadow and frost, with eyes that shone like the blue heart of a flame. It is thought that all courtly fae are like this underneath; their humanlike forms are only a guise they assume. While killing them is a tricky business, a wound wrought with metal may force them into their weaker, insubstantial selves.

I knew all this, but only as theory. Seeing the faerie's true face, for all my determination, froze me entirely. It was a moment before I regained my senses.

As the faerie continued to wail, I withdrew his coat from my pack. "I shall give you this if you answer me." I was pleased that, while my hand shook, my voice did not.

"Give!" the changeling shrieked. He was cowering in the corner. He could still have hurt me, I think, but was too upset to think of it. Of course, if he had, I could have withheld the coat.

The Folk are bound by many ancient laws, some of which give mortals a great deal of power over their well-being. Mortal gifts strengthen faeries, be they food or jewels, but clothes have a particular power, in that they help the Folk bind themselves to the mortal world, and, in the case of the courtly fae, their mortal guises.

"I have your attention then," I said, as the changeling's shrieks diminished to sobs. "Let us start with your parents."

In the end, the faerie told me little. He would only moan about his forest and his beloved willow tree, and the many paths the Folk built underground and through the deep snows, lit somehow with moonlight. This was all interesting enough, but quickly grew tiresome; by the end of an hour I knew the number of the willow's branches and how many stars the faerie could see from his window, but little else. It was a myopic view of the courtly fae, filtered through the eyes of a self-absorbed child, and thus not particularly helpful.

Either the changeling did not know or he could not remember why he had been brought to Hrafnsvik, though he did believe that he would be taken away again, and swore a great many dire revenges upon me when this occurred. Once I had tired of his moaning, I handed him his coat. He drew this around his body and huddled in the corner, shuddering, as slowly he gained weight and substance again.

I did not leave Mord and Aslaug wholly unprotected, of course. I told them about the inside-out trick I had used with my clothing—this would not prevent the visions, of course, but it would lessen their hold over them. Aslaug, returned from her walk, welcomed me with a warmth I did not expect, but she was an unsettling sight—far too thin, her eyes shadowed, and her hair lank. She hummed almost constantly, and at times seemed to become lost in herself, oblivious to conversation until Mord went to her side and squeezed her shoulder. While I am first and foremost a scientist and value my objectivity, I would have helped them if I could. But I saw no way of doing so.

I returned to the cottage to compile my notes. It was empty, though I could see two tiny specks upon a distant mountainside that I recognized by the colour of their cloaks as Lizzie and Henry. I caught the flicker of a spyglass and guessed they were observing the rock formations below. As for Bambleby, I had no idea. Perhaps he had drowned in the spring.

I decided to venture thither myself. I wished to pay my respects to my new friend; one can never predict the effects of being kind to the common fae, and I still hoped to earn his confidences.

The spring was deserted, but I was content to remove my boots and wait. I splashed my face with water, and then, after a quick glance over my shoulder, plunged my head under.

I scrubbed my hair for the first time since arriving in Hrafnsvik, dislodging dirt and leaves that I hadn't even realized were there. When I finished, I squeezed it out and tied it back up, feeling infinitely better. It was as if I had washed off some of the darkness from the farmhouse.

The afternoon held the sort of borrowed, ephemeral warmth that interrupts the advance of winter sometimes, and I found myself wondering what summer was like in this place. With the sun filtering through the trees, I was feeling quite content. I ate my lunch while I waited, after first restocking the faerie's candy. He had not liked the caramels one bit, complaining that they stuck in his teeth. The chocolates, though, he had instantly taken to. I would have to write to my brother for more; no doubt sweets at Groa's shop would cost me their weight in gold.

The brownie—whom I have taken to calling Poe in my head, in honour of the tattered ravenskin he once wore—took longer to show himself than usual. When he appeared, it was on the opposite bank of the spring, and his form so blended with the forest floor that I could see him only when he moved.

"Good day," I said politely. "Is something the matter?"

"Your friend was here," he said hesitantly.

"Bambleby? Was he rude to you?" Damn him to Hell if he was. I had not spent days building trust with this creature only to have him ruin it.

Poe shook his head. "He brought me peppermints. I like peppermints."

"What, then?"

Poe kept shooting me anxious looks. His needle-fingers went *tappity-tap* like rain upon the damp grass. Finally he burst out, "I don't wish to see him again!"

"Then you shan't," I said. "I shall instruct him to stay away." Oh, would I.

The faerie's eyes grew huge. "You can command a prince?" He rushed on before I could speak. "I don't wish to make him angry. He was kind, but I fear him. My mother always said to keep out of their way. The high ones, the queens and kings and great lords. They will trample you under their boots like mushrooms, little one, she always told me. Keep your head down. Keep to your tree. When he asks me questions, I have to answer them. I don't like his questions."

I had gone very still. The brownie had used a word in the faerie tongue that has several definitions—it can mean *lord* or *sir*, or another simple mark of respect. But I knew, said in that manner, with a slight lilt down the middle like a fold, it meant only one thing.

"You say he is a prince," I repeated, clearly enunciating. "You're certain of this?"

The faerie nodded. He came very close, close enough for me to smell the sap on his skin, which mingled strangely with the familiar smell of my old beaver hat—this he had torn apart and woven into a lumpy coat. Quietly, he said, "He wanted to know about the doors."

Little shivers were scudding down my back. "The faerie doors? That lead into your world?"*

He nodded. I sat back, my mind wheeling. I have long suspected that Bambleby is part of the faerie aristocracy. That he is—or was—in line for one of their thrones is something I had not guessed, though that was not what alarmed me.

What does he want with faerie doors? Are his questions mere academic curiosity?

"Did he ask you anything else?"

Poe shook his head, and my suspicion grew. "What did you tell him?"

---

* All dryadologists accept the existence of those doors that lead to individual faerie homes and villages, such as those inhabited by the common fae. Theories about a second class of door are more controversial, but I myself believe highly credible, given the stories we have of the courtly fae. These are thought to be doors that lead deep into Faerie, into a world wholly separate from our own.

The faerie was almost sitting in my lap now, his long fingers curled possessively about my cloak. "That there are no doors here, in this forest. I've never seen one. Maybe the doors move with the snows, with the high ones. Maybe they carry them hither and thither as the wind blows down from the north." He frowned. "They will be here soon."

My hands tightened on the grass. "How did my friend react to this information?"

"I don't know. He left after. I am glad he's gone."

As the brownie seemed distressed, I reminded him of the chocolates I had given him. In truth, my kindness was partly out of concern for my cloak—now striped with holes from Poe's touch—as well as the leg underneath it. He hastened to check on his little hoard and then disappeared into the forest, returning with a loaf of bread still warm to the touch. He seemed calmed by the ritual, and by my appreciation of him. I promised to return on the morrow—alone.

I spent the next hour wandering the forest. I told myself that I was conducting a survey of the possible faerie paths I had noted during a previous wandering; but in truth, I needed the walk. What on earth was I to make of this revelation regarding Bambleby? Not all Folk have grand designs in their interactions with mortals, and I had come to think of him as an aristocratic dilettante. Yet did he have other reasons for cultivating a career chasing stories of his kindred?

More important, did it matter? I had my book to worry about, a book that could make my career, and why should I care about Bambleby's intentions, provided he did not get in my way?

I was distantly aware that most people would have a different reaction to the discovery of a faerie prince in their midst, but I paid this little heed.

Shadow was before me, his head down as he sniffed at a jumble of mushrooms. Upon consulting my map, I noted these seemed to have moved from their previous location some yards away. Now, it is possible they were formed during the most recent deluge, but I thought not. They had a shape about them that my trained eye recognized, something twisted from its natural pattern and purpose. Perhaps it was a gathering place.

I grew calmer as I sank into my work, and the next few miles passed pleasantly enough. If anyone were to claim greater happiness in their careers than I do in poking about sunlit wildwoods for faerie footprints, I should not believe it.

Shadow suddenly surged ahead, his tail flashing among the thinning undergrowth. I followed him to a clearing, where I found, slumped against a tree in the sunshine with his long legs stretched out before him and his hat drawn over his face, none other than Bambleby. He seemed to have found the greenest part of the forest, which had little greenery left—a small grove of conifers.

He did not awaken from his nap when Shadow flopped down beside him, but he did when I kicked the tree, which showered him with a rain of needles.

"Is that all you ever do?" I demanded.

"Dear Emily," he said, stretching like a cat and rubbing Shadow's ears. "How was your day?"

"Delightful." As he showed no evidence of bestirring himself, I grudgingly seated myself on the grass. "Our friend in the village was no wight, but a changeling of the courtly fae. I had to interrogate the creature with iron. Unassisted."

"I'm sure you held your own, as you always do." The hat slid back down his forehead. I took it from him, and he blinked in the sudden sunlight.

"Oh dear. What have I done to earn that basilisk stare?"

"We have agreed to work together. Yet now I hear that you have seen fit to trample on my research. The brownie by the spring, whose trust I have spent days in cultivating, would barely speak to me after your visit."

"What?" He looked genuinely baffled. "I brought the little one peppermints and asked a few questions. Nothing more."

"He seemed frightened of you." I added quickly, "Though he would not say why. In any case, you cannot go there again."

"Your wish is my command, Em." He regarded me with amusement. "Is that all that has upset you? Surely there are other brownies in this wood for you to pester if that one has soured on you."

I thought quickly, hiding it behind a frown. It had become clear to me, in a way that it never had before, that it would be wise for me to be frightened of Bambleby. And if I could not muster fear—a dubious proposition, to be sure—I should at least attempt wariness, if for no reason other than that he is Folk. My suspicion is suspicion no more, but fact.

"You have done nothing since your arrival but laze about," I told him. "As well as jeopardize the only meaningful connection I have established with the Hidden Ones. You don't realize how hard I have been working, Wendell, or how important this is to me."

"I do, though," he said, and I was alarmed by how earnest he became. "And I'm sorry, Em, if I've given you reason to think otherwise. I assure you that I have been working quite hard today." He looked down at his sprawled self. "More or less. I walked a great deal of the Karrðarskogur. I even discovered a small lake high upon the mountain with evidence of kelpie habitation. Well, whatever they call such creatures in this blasted cold country."

"Kelpie?" My mouth fell open. "What lake? I saw no lakes."

He looked far too pleased with himself. "That's because you missed it, my dear. It was about half a mile beyond the extent of your map."

"Show me."

He groaned. "But I just *came* from there. You are far too vigorous for a scholar. Another day, please. Why don't you tell me about your interview with our new changeling friend?"

He was changing the subject, but I admit I had little energy for climbing up into the peaks after the day I'd had, and so gave him a summary of my interrogation at the farmhouse.

"He is terrorizing them, Wendell," I concluded.

"So it seems," he said, though he did not appear particularly interested. "And he would tell you nothing of his parents?"

I shook my head. "The motives of the courtly fae in stealing children have never left the realm of academic speculation. If only we could ask one of them."

"Wouldn't that be nice," he said blandly.

I gritted my teeth. "Otherwise, I don't know how we'll ever figure out their purpose in this instance."

"Purpose? Or purposes? The Folk are diverse in many ways; no doubt this is one of them."

I could detect no hidden meaning in his words, and so decided to take them at face value. Perhaps he truly had no idea why the Folk of Ljosland stole children. Indeed, he was so detached about the whole thing that I felt a sliver of doubt enter me. Yet what reason would Poe have had to lie about Bambleby's identity?

"I would like to at least try to help."

"Help whom?"

I wanted to shake him. "Mord and Aslaug!"

"Ah. How do you propose to do that? Their son will die if the changeling is killed. If we somehow chase it from its abode, it will die, and thus the outcome is the same." He leaned back against the tree, his eyes drifting shut again. "Besides, it would hardly be professional. We're here to observe, not interfere."

I watched him carefully. "Perhaps you could visit them."

His eyes opened to slits. "And what will that accomplish?"

His voice was as bored as ever, but there was an undercurrent of something that made me feel as if I was edging onto dangerous ground. Only I didn't care. I knew that if I left Mord and Aslaug with the changeling without making every effort to free them from its poisons, I would regret it until the end of my days.

"I don't know," I said, meeting his gaze levelly. It was true enough. I don't know what powers he has or what he is capable of. "Perhaps you can get more information out of the creature than I could. The Folk of Ljosland clearly find you disagreeable company, for reasons unimaginable to myself."

He laughed. His eyes become very green when he laughs; you wonder if the colour will spill from them like sap. "I hardly recognize you, Em. I never would have thought that you of all people would come to care for any of these villagers. Are they not mere variables in your research?"

"It's not that I *care* for them," I said heatedly, before realizing that my offence rather made his point for him. I could tell by his smile that he knew it too.

"I'll pay your afflicted horticulturalists a visit tomorrow," he said. "Will that suit?"

"Thank you." I stood, feeling off-balance and wishing to escape the conversation. "Perhaps we can return to the cottage. I would like to review your notes, and hear what your students have discovered."

"Very well." He looked at me woefully, as if expecting me to help him up. I folded my arms. With a dramatic groan, he pulled himself to his feet with his customary grace, and we departed the Karðarskogur.

30th October

Bambleby insisted on a visit to the tavern last night, naturally, a divertissement eminently acceptable to our two assistants, who were wearied from their work in the field. Lizzie and Henry, both attractive if bland ambassadors of the scientific community, were warmly welcomed by rustics and gentry alike, and bonded quickly with the village youth over their enthusiasm to sample the local wallop. Bambleby, of course, was in his element. With a speed that I suspected to be record-setting even in his books, he soon had half the tavern roaring with laughter over one of his many stories of foreign misadventure, delivered in charmingly accented Ljoslander, whilst the other half gossiped about him at a distance, including several ladies whom I overheard scheming over private invitations of a decidedly unacademic nature. The result was easily the most enjoyable evening I have spent in Hrafnsvik, as the villagers largely forgot about my existence amidst the gale-force winds of Bambleby's personality. I was delighted to sit in the corner with my food and a book and speak to no one.

Bambleby seemed particularly drawn to the beautiful wood-cutter, Lilja, and spent a good portion of the evening—when he was not occupying his proverbial hour upon the stage—wooing her by the fireside. I am afraid that one source of my enjoyment was in the continued politeness with which she received his attentions, which never warmed beyond tepid. It seemed Bambleby had never encountered such a result before, given the puzzlement in his gaze, which kept straying in Lilja's direction from across the room. This too was met with an amiable wall of obliviousness.

The only person to converse with me was old Thora Gudridsdottir, who heaved herself into the other chair at the corner table. "Not much for entertainment, eh?" she said.

I gestured to the academic tome in my hands. "This is much more entertaining than stories I've been subjected to more than once."

"What a cold fish you are." Unlike Finn, Thora did not appear to mean it as an insult. "Not one to be charmed by a pretty face, eh? What on earth are you reading?"

I explained that it was a treatise on the Russian forest faerie, the *leshy*, whom some scholars theorize to be cousins of the Hidden Ones of Ljosland (those inclined to entertain the idea of the Hidden Ones). Thora seemed intrigued and asked many questions.

"May I borrow it?" she said.

"Of course," I said with some surprise, and handed her the book. "Perhaps, after you've read it, you could offer your opinion on the merits of Wilkie's theory."

She snorted, thumbing through the pages. "I don't need to read this to know that it's nonsense. There's none like our snow-dwellers, neither in this world nor the next."

I blinked. "Have you encountered other Folk?"

"I've encountered *them*. That's enough."

"Have you?" I was so filled with questions that I could not work out which to utter first. She seemed to recognize this and gave another snort.

"I will not speak of them here," she said. "Nor should I speak of them anywhere, this close to winter, but if you visit my house upon a midday when the sun shines and the wind is fair, I will answer your questions. Those I have answers for."

To this I eagerly agreed. She went back to the book, occasionally blowing air through her nose in sharp bursts, though her gaze often strayed to Bambleby. I enquired whether she wished to move closer to hear his stories.

"Oh, I prefer to enjoy the view," she said with a cackle that I couldn't help but smile at. She motioned to Shadow, curled up at my feet beneath the table, his large black eyes tracking the currents of the gathering, but always returning to me, regular as clockwork. "That's quite a singular dog. Had him long?"

"Some years now," I said. Thora asked a number of questions about Shadow, and I told her the tale I'd invented of our meeting, which I try not to vary. It's easier, I've found, to have only one story to remember.

I must have enjoyed myself at the tavern, for I slept a full half hour later than habit the following morning. When I rose, I found the cottage empty and Shadow dozing contentedly by the fireside, having already been fed his breakfast. Bambleby's cloak was gone, as were those of his students, and the remains of their breakfast were scattered upon the table.

I was astonished. Had my lecture actually penetrated Bambleby's head? Or was he off interrogating the common fae about faerie doors again? Either way, I was happy to have a few moments of peace, and settled myself at the table with my notes and a cup of tea.

Bambleby's door swung open, and I nearly jumped out of my skin. A freckled, redheaded young woman poked her head out.

"Oh!" she tittered, adjusting the sheet wrapped round her. "I thought I was alone."

"As did I."

She seemed to take no notice of my tone, but slunk smiling

into the main room, mischief on her face that she seemed to imagine I would take part in. "Did he leave?"

"Miraculously, yes."

The girl—one of Thora's many granddaughters, I believe—settled herself, sheet and all, opposite me at the table and indolently helped herself to the remains of the breakfast. She proceeded to question me about Bambleby's past, particularly in reference to his dalliances, a subject upon which I could have spoken volumes had I elected to take leave of my senses. I replied with answers so staccato that she soon began to smirk at me, imagining me jilted or jealous, or both. Thankfully, Shadow frightened her when he padded up to the table, hoping for scraps, and she exited the cottage shortly thereafter.

The morning was grey and windy with intervals of sleet, as miserable a face as a sky can put on, so I ventured only as far as the spring for my now habitual visit with Poe. I spent the remainder of the morning with my notes and Bambleby's, which were exactly as cursory as I had expected them to be. Patches of blue sky appeared around noon, and so I donned my hat and coat and packed my camera, intending to venture up to the mountains to hunt for Bambleby's supposed kelpie, which Thora had informed me was known as the *nykur* in Ljosland.

I was just stepping through the door, however, as Bambleby came striding up the path, collar notably askew, looking put out. He started a little at the sight of me, then looked guiltily away.

"What has happened?" I said, already dreading the response. "And where on earth have you been?"

"It seems I must resign the field," he said. "I displease you when I sleep late. I displease you when I rise early. I displease you when I do exactly what you tell me to do, when you tell me to do it. I cannot win with you, Em."

"Yes, that's enough of that." I narrowed my eyes. "You visited the changeling."

"Indeed. Though I'm afraid I could get little information from him, and that is because he has none to give. He does not know when his parents will return, nor why they abandoned him here."

I scanned the path as he strode past me into the cottage. "Where are our assistants?"

"I thought it best to leave them at the tavern with their pockets full of coin."

I did not like his tone one bit. "And what was the cause of this munificence on your part?"

He took his time in answering, using Shadow as an excuse as he greeted the dog with a lavish display of affection. "I brought them along to the farmstead."

"Oh, God." I stared at him. "Why would you do such a thing? That is not a creature to be dealt with by amateurs!"

"I am responsible for their education. An opportunity to study a changeling in person is invaluable to any budding scholar. Besides, you made it sound as if the creature was nearly *harmless*, Em."

"I never said the word! If you think—"

"Well, you implied it. And you mastered that thing with a bit of iron! You are every inch as fearsome as I always supposed you to be."

"The iron was of less importance than a knowledge of the ways of the Folk, gleaned through extensive reading and experience in the field. Such an understanding takes years."

He gave me a look that I found difficult to interpret. "Had I known what that changeling was, the power it possesses, I would not have let you go there alone. I am a better friend to you than that."

"I didn't need your help," I snapped. "I handled the situation adequately."

He pressed his hands to his face. "Yesterday you were angry at my lack of assistance. Today you bite my head off for helping. You are the most contrary person I have ever known."

That took the wind out of me. Being labelled contrary by Wendell Bambleby would stop any sensible person in her tracks. "I suppose I could have been more forthcoming," I said grudgingly. I sat down at the table. "Well. What are we to do?"

"I don't know." He sat opposite me, drawing one knee up and resting his arm on it. With his other hand, he spun one of the empty teacups. "I don't know what visions the creature showed them. I only know they were ghastly, given their reactions. Yet they both seemed calmer with some food and wine in them. I shall give them tomorrow off."

I felt a niggle of guilt. "I suppose I should have mentioned," I said, "that I did not leave the creature in the best of moods yesterday."

He tilted his head at me in a look of wordless exasperation.

"Well, what visions did it show *you*?" I said, to redirect his attention.

"Oh, it doesn't matter. Cold and ice and bloody wolves howling away." The teacup rattled against the table as it spun. "Suffice it to say that I've met with worse Folk than that brat. Mord and Aslaug seemed disappointed that you did not accompany me. Did you realize you were capable of inspiring affection in others?"

"Only narcissists and layabouts, I thought."

He leaned back, a smile playing on his mouth. "You know, Em, you could make life so much easier for yourself if you tried to be liked once in a while."

"I do try," I said, overloud. His words stung more than he could have guessed. I tried and tried—or at least, I used to, and nothing had ever come of it.

"Well, either way, you've outdone yourself this time. How you've convinced almost an entire village to hate you in the space of a week is beyond me. It will not make our research here easier, given the necessity of *talking* to said villagers."

I gave a wordless sound of frustration, running a hand through my hair and dislodging yet more of it from its tie. He was right, and I hated it. "I did nothing to set them against me. Only somehow I offended Aud, and it seems the others are offended on her behalf."

"Tell me," he said, using his knee to push the chair onto its back legs.

Scowling, I gave him an account of my ill-fated visit to the tavern. By the time I was through, he was wincing and shaking his head.

"Oh, Em," he said. "*Em.* Did you do no research at all before coming here?"

Now *that* galled me. "No research! What do you—"

"I don't mean the Hidden Ones. I've no doubt you scoured all of Cambridge for every passing reference to them—I can picture you terrorizing the poor librarians now. I was referring to the mortal inhabitants of this delightful winter wasteland."

He flicked open his satchel and pulled a book out, which he tossed to me. "What is this?" It appeared to be written in Ljoslander.

"A novel," he said. He pulled out another book, which I barely caught. "On the smutty side, I'm afraid—not to your tastes at all. That one's an account of a very dull trade war. Here." He pulled out a third book, also in Ljoslander. "A biography of their last queen. That one's not bad—she shot one of her suitors in the foot. By accident, of course."

I folded my arms. "Thank you, but you needn't go on. I understand."

"Do you? Can you even read Ljoslander?"

"Well enough to get by," I lied, for I had no intention of listening to him brag. Bambleby is irritatingly adept at languages. Small wonder—the Folk can speak any mortal language they encounter. As they flit through the physical barriers erected by mortals, so too do they evade those of our cultures.

"Hospitality is important to these people," he said. "You'd know that if you'd bothered to learn anything about them at all. You offended Aud by insisting on paying for your supper."

My mouth fell open. "That's it? That's why she hates me?"

He sighed. "Perhaps if you were not so covered in prickles, she would have forgiven you by now. But if there's anyone who could encourage others to go looking for excuses to take offence, it is you. And then you compounded the mistake by barging into her village with your questions, and without seeking her permission first."

"I cannot believe that the villagers require her permission to speak to me."

"Of course they don't. You should have sought it regardless."

I put my head in my hands. Bambleby was right, damn him. "Well, what are we going to do?"

"You are going to have to allow her to be kind to you," he said. "To welcome you as a guest. And to do it in such a way that she will not simply assume I told you what to do."

"I have absolutely no idea how to achieve that."

"I know." He thunked his chair down and gave me a considering look. "I didn't say I wouldn't help you, only that we must not let on to Aud. We need to work through this before we go much further in our research. The villagers were evasive with me last night whenever the subject turned to the Hidden Ones. My friendship with you means that I will not get much from them, either."

I groaned. "Can't you charm them into giving you what you want, as you usually do?"

"Probably. But that will take time. Do we have it to waste? As you are so fond of reminding me, we have only a few weeks."

I stared at my hands. Thora would speak with me, but I could not base my research on the testimony of a single person.

I have always hated this sort of thing. I would sooner interview a dozen bloody changelings than navigate my way through this thicket of social conventions. I thought to myself that perhaps I should simply avoid conversation altogether going forward, seeing as I always make a mess of it.

"My dear Emily. I've never seen you look so dejected." He was regarding me with affection—and something else, but it was gone before I could name it. "Why don't we go for a stroll? You can entertain me with a list of your demands. Then I can find a nice place for a nap whilst you hunt for some common fae to harass."

"I wish to see the lake," I said, already on my feet. I wanted more than anything to put the conversation from my mind. "You say you found a footpath?"

He groaned a little at that, but I was already out the door, and so he donned his coat and followed.

31st October

I arose to darkness and silence. Bambleby's enthusiasm for early rising, it seems, was short-lived—well, fine; I shall have plenty of quiet to write in my journal. I have just opened the shutters; a landscape of white and shadow gazes back at me as I pen these words.

Bambleby and I made it to the lake yesterday after a steep climb. It was one of those scenes that froze me in place, a little cup of velvety blue between towers of rock. At our backs was the furious arctic sea, thick with ice, too much of it visible from that height. *Too much* rather summed up the place, I thought as I hurried after Bambleby, who apart from giving the volcanic stones scattered here and there a few desultory kicks seemed barely conscious of the feral nature of the surroundings. The wind yanked on my bun and sent the loose strands lashing against my face.

Though we found only tenuous evidence of the *nykur*—misshapen prints in the frozen muck by the water's edge, which I photographed—I returned with my spirits improved. As Finn had informed us that the weather was changing, evidenced by the looming cloud upon the horizon, I determined to make the most of the sun and set off on another survey of the eastern peaks, whilst Bambleby, despite lacking any visible signs of fatigue, pleaded exhaustion and retired to the cottage.

Solivagant, I misjudged the distance and returned in the dark, the stars a thick glittering above me like a spill of treasure. I could not help pausing to stargaze, a pastime I indulge in but rarely in Cambridge, the nights there being blurred by gaslight and hemmed in by trees and towers. By the time I clambered up the little mountain path to the cottage, our students had returned from their sojourn at the pub rather the worse for wear and had gone to bed early to sleep things off.

I hardly recognized the cottage whereupon I stepped in from the windy night. The fire merrily crackled, and the whole space was illuminated by strategically placed oil lamps that had not been present before. Woollen rugs scattered the floor, and the windows were hung with curtains. And there were *things* atop the mantel: pretty things that seemed to have no purpose at all. I recognized one from Bambleby's office, a little jewelled mirror that flashed merrily in the firelight, but others seemed to be artefacts of Hrafnsvik, including a Madonna carved from whalebone and a little seascape painted on a scrap of driftwood.

Bambleby himself was seated at the fire, mending a curtain. He explained to me that he had borrowed most of the furnishings from Krystjan, including the curtain that he was presently repairing and which he intended to be strung up in the kitchen.

I hardly heard any of it through my amazement. "You are darning curtains? You?"

"My family has a talent for needlework," he said merely, his fingers moving with an improbable deftness.

I informed him that the cottage had been perfectly satisfactory as it was, to which he replied that the place had been so dank and cheerless as to be suitable only to bats and unsociable gargoyles brooding over their books, and he would sooner put his eyes out than endure weeks of such wretched environs. I contemplated unleashing Shadow and his muddy paws upon

Bambleby's efforts, but the truth was that even I could see that our humble abode was much improved, with a sense not only of warmth but of safety, an enveloping cosiness whose source I could not wholly put a finger on. I settled for brooding over my books for the remainder of the evening, ignoring him completely, which he hates above all else.

🌿 **I'm afraid that,** since writing the last, things have turned upside down.

Finn was late with breakfast, which did not at first alarm me, given the conditions. I pulled a chair up to the window and watched the snow fall as I brewed tea. I had not forgotten my promise to Poe, and did not look forward to plunging into those drifts, though I estimated the snowfall at less than a foot.

As I sat, a sort of inexplicable dread grew within me, a sense that I was the only person for miles about. I stood abruptly and threw open Bambleby's door, banging it into the wall.

From the bed came a sort of confused mumbling, and there was a flash of golden hair. Yet my relief was fleeting, and I was already stamping down the hall when Bambleby croaked, "Em? What the bloody hell?"

The students' room was empty. I had known it would be, somehow. Not only that, but their trunks were gone, their cloaks. I stormed back to Bambleby's room, banging the door again, and flung back the curtains.

"Good God," he muttered from his pillows. "If this is your manner of setting an alarm, I am asking Krystjan to install a lock."

"They're gone."

"What?"

Moments later, there came a knock at the door. Bambleby

answered it, having roused himself at last. I knew it wouldn't be them, and it wasn't; Finn's worried face gazed back at us.

"Thank God," he said. "There are rumours going around town that you set off this morning in Bjorn Gudmunson's boat, bound for Loabær. It's rough weather for sailing."

I exchanged a look with Bambleby. "The rumours are half true. Our students, it seems, have absconded. But what on earth are their plans in Loabær?"

Finn shifted his weight, looking guilty. "From Loabær, there are merchant ships to London that depart every other day. Perhaps they've a mind to board one."

Bambleby gave him a level look. "Perhaps?"

"I may have—heard them discussing it with Bjorn yesterday in the tavern," Finn said, adding quickly, "I had no idea they intended to leave today."

"Thank you, Finn," I said grimly. We took our breakfast from him—bread and cheese only this morning; he hadn't had time for anything else, what with the burden the storm had added to his chores. Several sheep were missing, it seemed, and the weight of the snow had caused the roof of an outbuilding to collapse.

Bambleby paced back and forth. While I had calmed somewhat, he seemed to grow more and more agitated. "This is a fine thing. We are nearly out of wood."

Trust him to be concerned with his own comfort, when his students could that very moment be drowned in an icy sea. I said as much, and he waved his hand. "I met Bjorn. He's a man who knows his business. He wouldn't have taken on a suicide mission."

I watched him for a moment—I don't believe I've ever seen him so unravelled. "Have you ever travelled abroad without servants? I'm sorry, students."

He narrowed his eyes at me. "There has never been a need."

"I see." If I hadn't been worried about our research, I might have been enjoying myself. "What are we going to do? We have limited time, and now we are without our assistants to help with the data gathering."

"I'm sure we'll muddle through," he said distractedly. I could tell he wasn't worried one whit about data gathering—well, why would he be, if he was used to fabricating said data? No, he was wondering who would prepare his tea and wash his laundry.

"We will have to roll up our sleeves from now on," I said, placing heavy emphasis on the first word.

Bambleby collapsed into one of the armchairs, looking faint.

There was no water left for the washing up after breakfast, so I donned my boots and tramped outside to the stream. The snow had ceased, and the sky was a soft eggshell colour, the mountains dreaming under their woollen blankets. There was a loveliness in the forest's absence of colour, its haunted dark framed by grey-white boughs, as if the snowfall had winnowed it down to the essence of what a forest is.

My sense of peace was short-lived. The stream was covered in ice too thick to pierce. I slipped trying, covering myself in snow. In a burst of inspiration, I filled the pot with snow, then set it over the fire. Bambleby was outside by the woodshed, looking like he was trying to solve a mathematical equation. For some reason, he had pushed away the snow with his boot so that he could stand upon the frosty grass. I actually felt a little sorry for him, shivering despite the weight of his cloak, for he reminded me of some temperate tree or bush, transplanted and forced to grow in some northerner's garden against its will. I hefted the axe and placed a log upon the stump.

"Perhaps we should send for Finn," Bambleby said.

"I'm perfectly capable," I replied, though the axe was of an unnerving Ljoslander design and nearly came up to my shoulder.

I swung. The dull blade glanced off the log, which went careening into a tree, dislodging a small avalanche of snow. My axe buried itself in the stump; unbalanced, I fell over.

He looked appalled. "Good God, what a violent process."

I dragged myself to my feet, cheeks flaming as I brushed the snow from my backside. "It's not supposed to go like that."

"I won't be helping." He backed up a step, raising his elegant hands. "I'll cut off my foot. Or you will."

"Oh, come on." I wasn't looking forward to trying a second time, and in my anger, I couldn't help baiting him. Baiting a faerie prince! An unfortunate habit I have fallen into, that. "Do you not heat your houses with wood," I said, all innocence, "in the place you come from?"

He gave me a withering look. "I'm quite happy to say that, in Dublin, we have servants to deal with these things."

"Well, this is not Dublin, and I'm not getting anywhere. You have to help."

"I do not. Give it one of your scowls; it will split itself in two."

"God!" I went to impale the axe in the ground in frustration. Unfortunately, Bambleby, contrary creature that he is, had just stepped forward to remove it from my possession. I redirected my swing just in time to avoid relieving him of his arm, but not fast enough to save his sleeve.

"Dammit!" He pressed his hand to his arm, and at first I thought it melodrama, but then the snow beneath him began to turn pink.

"I knew it," he snapped as blood leaked through his fingers. "I knew you would be the death of me. I wish you had chosen my foot. This is my favourite cloak."

"Hang your cloak!" I shoved him towards the cottage. "Get inside! You're bleeding!"

"I will not bleed any less indoors, you utter madwoman."

But he allowed me to shove him inside, leaving behind him a

trail of blood like tiny red footprints. To my horror, the pot of snow I had set over the fire had unbalanced itself during the melting, falling onto its side and extinguishing all but a few embers. Shadow, having been roused from his nap by the fireside, sat sneezing in the smoke.

When we peeled away Bambleby's cloak, we found that the iron of the axe had bit deep, down to the bone. A scrap of flesh hung loose like a ghastly piece of cloth. As there was no water to wash the wound, I settled for a temporary dressing using scraps of my scarf. By the time I finished, Bambleby's arm was blood-soaked, and his face was white.

"Just stay there," I said.

"Oh, must I? Let's head up to the fells again."

"Quiet." I was a storm of anxiety—the missing students, the rapidly cooling cottage, the water pot, the blood everywhere. It took me twice as long as it normally did to light the fire again, and I was forced to use the last of our logs. Then there was the business of heating more snow in the pot, which I was now in terror of overturning. I was equally concerned by the dearth of quips from Wendell's direction. I went to examine the wound again and was alarmed to find a puddle of blood on the floor.

"Why are you still bleeding?" I demanded, absurdly offended.

He let out a breath of laughter. He was resting his head upon his uninjured arm. "Em. You nearly severed my hand."

I shook him. "Tell me what to do!"

"I have no idea." His voice was faint. "I have never been injured before. I don't much care for it."

I let out a string of curses. My mind ran through everything I knew about the Irish Folk, flipping through stories like the pages of a book. There was the tale of a faerie lord injured in battle who had been tended by a mortal girl, after which he turned her hair to gold and she lived as a queen, buying herself a new house with every new inch of hair she grew. Another story of a faerie maiden turned into a tree which a woodcutter half cut down, only to realize his mistake when the tree began to sob. There were plenty of stories of Folk nursed back to health by mortals, but none ever explained *how*; they were told because people loved hearing that the Folk ever needed mortal aid and about the lavish rewards they granted after.

"I need stitches, I think," he said.

"Can you do it yourself?"

"No." He sounded so certain that I did not think to question him. I tightened the scarf and helped him to his bed, then I ran.

I went first to Krystjan's door, but no one answered my frantic banging, and I was left to assume they were off in some fold hunting their errant sheep. I then ran to the village, and must have looked an utter fright when I clattered through the door of the tavern, for Aud, standing by the counter with her frowning husband, exclaimed, "My God, Emily! Who did this to you?"

She grabbed me by the shoulders. I was so astounded that I could only stare at her, which seemed to alarm her even more. Realizing that she was referring to the blood on my hands, I pulled myself together and explained the situation.

Aud listened with a stillness that reminded me of the mountains. In Ljoslander, she said, "Ulfar, Thora, Lilja, come with me."

"*Já*," Thora said, taking up her cane and drawing herself to her feet. "Eventually."

I don't remember much of the walk back to the cottage. I recall Aud holding my arm and murmuring, "He'll be all right, don't worry. He will." Then we were at Wendell's bedside, and the sheets were soaked in blood. His skin was the colour of old ashes, and his eyes were closed, his golden hair flame-bright against the pallor.

Ulfar tossed herbs into the water, and Aud washed Wendell's

arm. She sewed up the wound with the same steadiness and was done before Thora stomped up to the door. The old woman laid her hand on Wendell's forehead and clucked her tongue.

"What?" I demanded, overloud. There was a ringing in my ears.

"Nothing," Thora said. "You must have nicked a vein. He's lost plenty of blood, but that's no death sentence. He should recover once he gets some food in him." She gave me a wink. "He's prettier when he's asleep, eh? You don't notice that big mouth of his."

She shuffled into the kitchen and began banging pots and pans. Someone must have summoned Groa, for she appeared shortly after with a basket of meats, vegetables, and cheeses, greeting me with her customary cheerful indifference. The kitchen din intensified, but still Bambleby did not stir.

My mind had begun to work again by this point, and I remembered the tale of a prince of the Irish Folk, held captive at the bottom of a lake by a water sprite, and the faerie princess who had liberated him with—with—

With a token of the world above. I dashed out the door, even as I mentally cross-referenced the tale with others concerned with faerie potions. Yes—it could work. Nobody even noticed my going, apart from Lilja, who was in the yard making short work of the woodpile. She slung the axe over her broad shoulder and called something after me, but I was already halfway up the mountainside.

The forest was silent as I ducked beneath the boughs, holding its breath in that curious way the wilds do after a snowfall. I floundered about for a time, for the drifts were deep in places, filling my boots with snow.

There it was. A red willow, scrawny and malcontent, the only tree that I was certain grew also in Ireland. I wrenched free a handful of browned leaves and ran back to the cottage. Bambleby was alone in his room, still asleep, still pale, while the women filled the kitchen with noise.

I stared from Bambleby to the leaves in my hand, suddenly unsure. Perhaps there was no need for my desperate remedy? But there was something in Wendell's face that made the terror churn within me again. When looked at from certain angles, he seemed to lose substance, as the changeling had done. My tangled thoughts drifted into place, and I recalled that the faerie princess had brewed a tea—yes, a tea. For the prince's weakness had come not from drowning, but being severed from his own green world. I filled a cup with hot water from the pot and took it back to Bambleby's bedside, where I crumbled the leaves into it and held it to his lips.

There was a noise in the doorway. I turned and found that Aud was watching what I was doing with a queer expression on her face.

"Why—" she began, and as her gaze strayed to Bambleby, fading in and out against the pillow, as if his edges had been subtly blurred, I stepped between them to block her view.

I don't know why I did this; surely his secret is nothing to me. But I wasn't quick enough, in any case, and Aud went very still, like a deer noticing the snap of a twig. We stood frozen like that for a moment, and then her face grew hard. I felt certain she would flee, or perhaps knock the cup from my hand, but it was only her inborn decisiveness reasserting itself.

"Here," she said, stepping forward. "Not like that."

She tilted Wendell's head back, spilling his hair across the pillows. Her hand shook ever so slightly, then stilled. A mouthful of the tea passed his lips, and he swallowed.

I was staring at her. "It's not—I mean—"

"*You're* clearly mortal." She didn't look up from her task. "And he hasn't harmed you. That's something, I suppose."

"He wouldn't," I said, then stopped. Then, "He doesn't know. That I know, I mean."

She pursed her lips and said nothing for a moment. "Well, isn't that perfect?"

I blinked, astonished to see a smile playing on her lips.

"They're so full of themselves, the lot of them," she said. "They love their games and their tricks. This may be the funniest thing I've heard all year. I hardly know the man, but I've no doubt it serves him right."

A burble of laughter escaped me. Wendell muttered something. Aud handed the cup back to me and returned to the kitchen without another word, leaving me staring after her.

I got another mouthful of the tea into him before his eyes drifted open and he shoved my arm away. He grimaced and pressed his sleeve to his mouth. "Good God, what is that? Couldn't axe me to death so you've turned to poison, is that it?"

To my horror, I burst into tears.

Bambleby stared at me, and I have never seen him more astonished. "Em! I was only—"

I fled the room, too embarrassed to stay a second longer. I leaned against the fireplace and tried to control myself, while Shadow pawed at my leg, distressed.

"What on earth is the matter, child?" Thora called at me from the kitchen.

"Nothing, nothing," I choked out, then went outside. I lost my inclination to cry in the bitter cold, and so gave Lilja a hand hauling the chopped wood. In the space of minutes, she'd filled our wood box twice over. Bambleby was up and looking himself again by my third trip, in the kitchen laughing with Aud and Thora about something.

"Where is Ulfar?" I said, though I didn't care.

"Out back, patching up a hole in the wall," Aud said. "I must speak to Krystjan—he should not be accommodating guests in a hovel. It's a wonder you haven't frozen before now."

"No lodging is a hovel after you've been put up in a Swiss crypt advertised as a slice of Alpine serenity," said Bambleby, all charm as he elicited another round of laughs while neatly side-stepping Aud's insult of our host. We sat down and had a meal of lamb stew, mussels, and a delicate pancake made from ground moss, and if Aud's gaze kept drifting to Bambleby more often than necessary, he seemed to think nothing strange about it, surprising me not one whit.

"Now, there'll be no talk of payment," Aud said to me after, a flintiness coming into her voice. I stammered out my assurances on that point, and something in my voice—or perhaps my bedraggled state—seemed to soften her, and she gave my hand a squeeze.

"Be careful," she said, and there were several layers of meaning in it, none of which I was in a state to parse.

Then they were all gone, leaving behind the echoes of their voices and merriment.

Bambleby turned to me, puzzlement all over his face, but before he could say a word I announced my intention to visit Poe at the spring—for I had not yet fulfilled my vow to clear the snow from his home, and in truth it was much on my mind—and hurried outside with Shadow at my heels.

I find myself cringing as I read this over; ordinarily, I try to keep these journals professional, yet on this expedition I find myself continually struggling to meet this standard. I blame Bambleby, of course. I suppose one must expect some blurring of boundaries when one works with the Folk.

12th November

There are now two Hrafnsviks in my mind: the one that existed before Wendell's injury, and the one in which we found ourselves afterwards.

We have entertained a steady trickle of visitors over the past few days, so many that I have had little time for either journaling or venturing up to Poe's spring for a visit. They come with offers of food and assistance, but also with stories of the Hidden Ones.

"I suppose it is because Aud pities us now," I said. "They all do. We have proven ourselves inept at the basics of existence in this place."

"Oh, Em," Wendell said. "It has nothing to do with pity. Aud has forgiven you because you let her help you."

"She helped *you*," I pointed out, but he shook his head as if I were being obtuse.

"Why did you offend her initially?"

"Because I did not ask her permission to interview the villagers."

Again he shook his head. "That was part of it, perhaps, but also you refused to allow her to treat you as a guest. If you do not admit kindness from others, you cannot be surprised when they fail to offer any."

"I don't see what that has to do with your arm," I muttered, more to end the conversation than anything. To my surprise, he did not persist in arguing the point, merely gave a breath of laughter and went to fix tea.

Within the span of a single day, I learned more of the ways of the Ljosland Folk than I gleaned during the entirety of my research heretofore. In the space of two weeks, I may have gathered enough material for not only a chapter, but an entire book.

To summarize broadly: the interactions of mortal Ljoslanders with the common fae follow established patterns seen on the continent. Offerings are left for them, most often in the form of food; those with wealth and status are expected to leave trinkets, with mirrors and singing boxes being especially favoured. Mortals will sometimes enter into bargains with the common fae—like my bargain with Poe—but this is seen as dangerous given their unpredictability, and a road taken only by the desperate or foolhardy. None of the common fae of Ljosland dwell within households; that is the key difference.

As for the courtly fae, they are wholly unique.

They are, above all else, elusive. Few mortals have laid eyes on them—of the villagers of Hrafnsvik, Thora alone makes that claim, and she only spied them once from a distance a very long time ago, whilst playing with her schoolfellows in the woods. Their courts move with the snows, and they dwell for much of the year in the mountainous north and interior of the country, where winter never rests. They love music and hold elaborate balls in the wilderness, particularly upon frozen lakes, and if you hear their song drifting on the icy wind, you must stop your ears or burst into song yourself, or be drowned by it and swept insensible into their realm. For they are also hungry.

They have a particular fondness for youth in love. Those who are drawn into their dances are invariably found wandering alone the next day, alive but hollow. It was not always so; it is said that the courtly fae of Ljosland were once a peaceable people, if somewhat standoffish with mortals. No one is certain when the change occurred, but this behaviour has persisted for many generations.

Auður is the only living victim of the courtly fae in Hrafnsvik. But another boy was taken last winter, two girls the winter before that, and three years ago, a child of fifteen. Victims of these Folk are continually drawn to the winter wilderness after their abduction, and will wander into the night in their shifts or shirtsleeves when their guardians are distracted, to be found frozen a little distance from town. The "tall ones," it seems, have no interest in taking them back.

It seems clear these creatures are increasingly drawn to Hrafnsvik, though it is unclear why. Until recently, the village had not lost anyone to their bizarre vampirism in more than twenty winters. Their stories reflect this; it is said in many villages in the south and west of Ljosland that the "tall ones" take from every generation one youth (naturally this youth is said to be of surpassing beauty and/or talent, particularly musical talent, a feature that will not surprise scholars even superficially versed in folklore). Yet here in Hrafnsvik, five have been taken in the last four years.

I mentioned stories, and I will turn to those now. Most, unsurprisingly, concern encounters with the common fae. I have thus far recorded a round dozen, some fragmentary (perhaps part of a larger saga?) and others filling multiple pages. I will summarize here those that I find most intriguing—later I will choose one of them for my encyclopaedia.

The Woodcutter and His Cat

(NB: I have been informed that this is the oldest folktale of Hrafnsvik origin, though one villager argues that it drifted here from Bjarðorp, a village ten miles to the east. The story follows a familiar pattern in folklore: faeries often aid mortals in roundabout ways, and their generosity is instantly turned to vengefulness if their gifts are unappreciated.)

A woodcutter dwelt at the edge of the forest in a tiny hut that was all he could afford, and he could barely hold body and soul together. In his youth, after a night of drinking, he became lost and wandered into the mountains. He lost his right hand to frostbite and was terribly disfigured.

The woodcutter struggled in his work, naturally, and was sometimes forced to borrow money from his brother, who never missed a chance to rail against his foolishness, though the brother was a rich man whose larder was always full.

Near the woodcutter's house, along a path that was sometimes there and sometimes not, was a faerie tree. Its leaves were red and gold no matter the season, and abundant even in winter, and it was huge and hoary, with knots like windows for the Folk to peep through. Though lovely, it was an off-putting thing, for the sun never touched it, and its boughs were cold and clammy, the ground sodden with dew.

The village priest often visited the woodcutter to complain about the tree. This was in the days when the Church tried to stand against the Folk and sent dozens of poor priests on doomed missions to kill or convert them. But the woodcutter was too fearful of the Folk to cut it down, and the priest went away disappointed.

One winter's eve, after a particularly frustrating argument with the priest, the woodcutter decided that he might as well see if the faeries would help him—if not, he would consider cutting down their tree, just to silence the tedious priest.

The woodcutter travelled along the path that was sometimes there and sometimes not. The faerie tree was all aglow in the darkness, its golden light spilling over the snow like coins, and the woodcutter heard the distant sound of bells and the clink of cutlery. He knelt and asked for the faeries to give him a new hand. He waited for a long time, but there was no reply; the music played on, and the Folk attended to their dinner. The woodcutter went away disappointed.

In the morning, he woke to find a white cat seated at the foot of his bed. The cat was beautiful, with strange blue eyes, but it would not let the woodcutter touch it. The woodcutter knew that it was a present from the Folk, and while he was disappointed they had not given him the hand he had asked for, he knew that it was dangerous to scorn a faerie present.

As the days wore on, though, the woodcutter grew less patient with the cat. It followed him everywhere, even into the woods, watching him all the while with its unnatural eyes, and it ate all the woodcutter's food. One night, it gobbled down the lovely ham his brother had given him, leaving only the bone. The woodcutter grew so frustrated that he threw rocks at the cat and chased it into the forest. The next morning, he woke to find it perched at the end of his bed, watching him. The woodcutter's brother laughed at his predicament, and the priest lectured him even more for keeping such an unnatural beast around, and altogether the cat brought the woodcutter nothing but woe.

The woodcutter's mother died after a long illness and left him a little money. Shortly after, the woodcutter's childhood sweetheart, whom he loved despite her vanity and selfish ways, decided she was no longer disgusted by his scars or one-handedness and agreed to marry him. She and the cat did not get along. It was always hissing and scratching her, and if she left any knitting around, it undid every stitch. Eventually, the cat drove the woman mad, and she ran back to her own village, where she hid at her parents' home and refused to speak to her husband.

The woodcutter was so enraged that he picked up his rifle and chased the cat into the forest, where he shot it. The next morning, though, he awoke to find the cat at the foot of his bed, watching him.

The woodcutter realized that something drastic had to be done. He took his axe and went into the woods, pretending to go about his usual business. The cat followed him, as it always did, purring. Once the woodcutter had reached a quiet spot, he split the cat in two with his axe.

The next morning, there was no cat watching him from the foot of the bed. Feeling pleased with himself, the woodcutter took up his axe and travelled along the path that was sometimes there and sometimes not. He planned to destroy the faerie tree, just as the Folk had destroyed his happiness. But no sooner had his first stroke resounded through the woods than he heard music in the distance. It was not the song of the simple Folk who dwelt in the tree, but the music of the tall ones, and they were calling him. Terrified, the woodcutter tried to stop his ears, and then he grabbed hold of the tree like a drowning man, even as his feet started to move towards the song.

At that moment, the white cat stepped out of the shadow of the tree. The cat told him that it had protected him all along. When the woodcutter's brother, tired of charity, had poisoned his food, the cat had eaten it. When the woodcutter's wife had taken the woodcutter's money in secret and gambled it away, the cat had chased her out of the house. And every time the woodcutter had gone into the woods, the cat had protected him from the tall ones, muffling their song with its purring. But now the cat was dead, and it could no longer protect him.

The woodcutter was never heard from again. Though the faerie tree still stands, the path that is sometimes there and sometimes not has closed to mortals, and it may never be found again.

The Tree's Bones

A successful whaler lived alone at the edge of a bay. Much of his success came from his *fjolskylda,** who had sworn to protect him from the tall ones and other wicked faeries in exchange for habitation of his house during the new moon. The whaler found this an advantageous bargain, for he needed to travel to town once a month anyway to sell his catch.

The whaler's path into town ran through a forest inhabited by a great many Folk, who never gave him a lick of trouble. One day, though, as he neared the halfway point of his journey, he came upon a strange white wolf, larger than any he had ever seen, standing in his path. The wolf gave a howl, and more wolves appeared, each one larger than the last. Terrified, the whaler mounted his horse and fled back home. He was so afraid that he forgot all about his bargain with his *fjolskylda* and ran inside just as they were sitting down to dinner at his table. Instantly, the faeries vanished. From the shadows, a voice scolded him: "Never again will we dine here, and never again will you have our protection. You need not have run from the wolves, and thus you have betrayed us twice over—in distrusting our promise to you, and interrupting a fine banquet."

The whaler cursed his mistake. He delayed his next visit into town, and delayed it again, until he had to choose between tak-

---

* A charming Ljosland term that can be loosely translated as "family," used to describe a bond formed between mortals and brownies. Brownies in Ljosland, as in other countries, sometimes attach themselves to one household, and exclusively provide magical services to its inhabitants. Often they dwell in a rock feature somewhere on the property. The bond seems to be generational, though further research is needed to determine whether this is a variable thing, as it often is on the continent (cf. Northern Italy, where the brownies choose a favoured mortal with whom to bond, but often abandon any offspring upon his/her death).

ing the forest path and starvation. So, he set off along the path, full of weariness and worry, and sure enough, as he neared the halfway point, he met the white wolves again. This time, they chased him into the forest along a faerie path until they came to a huge tree. Its bark was as white as the wolves, and it was fat with blossoms and green leaves, though it was then nearing the start of winter.

The whaler gave a cry. Hanging from the branches was a gruesome assembly of corpses—the skeletons of other travellers, as well as animals and birds. The wolves threw off their wolf skins, revealing themselves as Folk, and commanded the whaler to bring them the bones of his next catch.

The whaler went away weeping. He knew that the faeries must have some terrible reason for what they were doing, but without his *fjolskylda*, he was powerless to deny them.

The next month, he brought them the bones of three whales. The faeries strung them up in the tree beside the other bones. The whaler noticed that the faeries hung the bones on one side of the tree only. When the whale bones had been hung, the tree gave a tremendous groan and leaned a little to the north. The faeries ordered the whaler to bring them the bones of his next catch.

The next month, the whaler brought the faeries the bones of four whales. These they hung from the tree, and when they did, the tree gave another groan, and leaned farther to the north. The whaler grew afraid. He realized that this tree must be the gaol of the faerie king, who had gone mad many years ago and been locked away by his subjects. The faeries ordered the whaler to bring them the bones of his next catch.

The whaler begged his *fjolskylda* for help, but none would heed him—none except the most elderly among them, a faerie woman whose head came up only to the whaler's belt, who had grizzled hair so long it trailed behind her and gathered all manner of leaves and mud. The faerie promised to help him only if he agreed to marry her. The whaler shuddered in disgust, but he gave his word nevertheless, for he feared the mad faerie king above all else, and knew there would be great woe throughout Ljosland if he were allowed to escape.

The faerie took the whaler to her family graveyard, where they dug up the bones of the dead. Then they snuck through the forest to the white tree and buried the bones under the boughs. The next month, the whaler brought the faeries the bones of seven whales. As before, they hung them from the white tree, but this time, the tree gave no groan, nor did it move. Furious, the faeries ordered the whaler to bring them the bones of his next catch, as well as the bones of the whaler's horse.

The next month, the whaler brought them the bones of ten whales, as well as the bones of one of the faerie horses buried in the graveyard. The faeries hung them from the tree, but again, the tree neither moved nor spoke. The faeries turned on the whaler, convinced that trickery was afoot, but before they could reach him, the bones of the dead horse gave a whinny. The skeletal hands of the dead faeries rose up out of the dirt and strangled the servants of the wicked king. They had been holding on to the roots of the white tree, preventing it from falling over and releasing the king from his prison. The whaler, much relieved, hung the dead bodies of the king's servants from the south side of the tree.

The whaler married his faerie bride, and though she remained as shrivelled and unlovely as ever, the whaler never broke his vow to his wife, and she rewarded him with three strong children who drew whales out of the deeps with their beautiful singing. And the whaler died an old, rich man, quite content.

The Ivory Tree

(NB: I include this particular story in part because it falls outside the usual patterns. I hypothesize that it has either been purposely truncated or is so new that it has not yet been worn and smoothed into a more pleasing shape.)

There was once a young girl of such surpassing beauty that all her neighbours whispered she had faerie ancestry. Her golden hair turned white when the winter sun touched it, and she sang so sweetly that even the wind upon the mountaintops quieted its howls to listen. Her mother had been just as lovely, and when she died in childbirth, the midwife swore that half her body had simply melted away, leaving only the skeleton behind. And so she must have been half fae through her father, for his identity was unknown.

The girl wished to marry a carpenter, a handsome young man much respected in the village, but he was afraid of her. The young man was also afraid of offending her, given her faerie ancestry, and so he gave her an excuse, saying that his wife must have a sizeable dowry. He knew that the girl, an orphan dependent on her uncle's charity, was penniless.

The girl was a friend to all the simple Folk, and often ran with them in the woods, particularly after fresh snow had fallen, for her feet left no prints in fresh snow, only that which had breathed the air of the mortal world. One day, she came across a faerie she had never seen before. He had no body, only two black eyes and a swirl of frost where his cloak should have been. The other Folk warned her not to speak to him, but the girl did not heed them. The bodiless faerie led her deep into the woods, where they came upon a beautiful white tree with bark smooth as bone. The faerie told her that such a dowry would greatly please her beloved, who could surely hew wondrous treasures from bole and bough alike.

The girl hesitated, for she knew it was a great crime to cut down a faerie tree—which surely the white tree was—but she was too in love to resist. She took up an axe and began to chop. But before her third stroke fell, a great wind went up, and the tree's leaves dropped upon her. The moment they touched her, she went mad. She returned home, donned her uncle's sealskin cloak, and packed a bag as if for a journey into the mountains. The carpenter, a vain young man who enjoyed revelling in the affection of one so beautiful as she, though he had no intention of marrying her, came to pay a visit and caught her in the act of fleeing. He tried to stop her, but she killed him with a touch that froze his heart.

When the townsfolk found the carpenter's body, they pursued the girl with dogs and horses and sleighs. They found her eventually, still marching doggedly into the wilderness, her eyes alight with madness, and shot her dead.

Now, I have paired these last two stories because it is a common belief in Hrafnsvik that the white tree that drove the girl mad is the same tree from the tale of the whaler, which held a faerie king. What's more, some of the older villagers are convinced the tree can be found in the Karrðarskogur. Thora swears she stumbled across it once, in her youthful trapping days, and has offered to provide directions.

When I informed Bambleby of my intention to search for the tree, as I desperately wish to photograph it for my encyclopaedia, he was full of arguments. Naturally, he assumed I would drag him along, which was indeed my intention, as nothing could amuse me more than watching Bambleby slog through miles of snow with nary a nap in sight, though I had little interest in arguing with him about it. I left him to his blustering in the cottage, where he was supposed to be drafting our abstract but kept wandering off to make tea or stand by the window and expostulate about the cold. I grow increasingly convinced that he obtained his doctorate by means of faerie enchantment, so difficult is it to imagine him applying himself to anything resembling work.

14th November

Today I went to Groa's shop to gather supplies for our journey to the tree. By Thora's estimation, the hike will take about three hours each way. The village is carpeted in snow, partially melted by a storm that came in from the sea; I have been assured by Krystjan that the recent fall is but another clearing of the throat by Old Man Winter; when he truly settles himself over Hrafnsvik, I will know it.

Upon exiting the shop with my parcels, I could not help my gaze from straying to the farmhouse across the road. The curtains were drawn as usual, the sheep huddled in a corner of the field. Altogether the place had such an unwholesome air about it that it was hard to look away, dark smoke drifting sluggishly from the chimney like the ooze of an infected wound.

Mord was coming round the front of the house, and he gave me a wave before disappearing inside. I stared in astonishment at the side of his head, which was mottled with bruising, and returned to the shop to question Groa.

For once, the merriness dimmed in her pale eyes. "He was out rescuing his wife the other night," she told me. "She nearly took a tumble into the sea. He pulled her back just in time."

"I see," I replied, and we left unsaid the oddness of a man

sustaining such bruises in that scenario. Back at the cottage, I reported the news to Bambleby.

"Well, what did you expect?" He had absconded from his notes entirely and was seated by the fire rubbing Shadow's ears. "The creature is clearly bent on driving both of them insane. I don't know who the miserable wretch imagines will care for its needs after its guardians have thrown themselves into the sea. They should kill it now and be done with it."

"And kill their son in the process?"

"Their son may at this moment be suffering any number of torments. He may never be returned to them. We don't know."

He went back to Shadow's ears while I fumed. I have not been able to convince him to care about Mord and Aslaug's plight.

"It could be worse," he said. "Mord and Aslaug are unlikely to fall prey to these snow ghouls when the weather turns. It seems that fate only threatens the lovesick and naïve, and I've no doubt they've been disabused of naïveté where love is concerned."

He saw my face and gave one of his theatrical groans. "Tell them to be kind to it."

This was the last thing I had expected him to say. "What?"

"They keep the changeling shut away in an attic. Spoiling the brats rotten is the only way to appease them." He drummed his fingers on his knee. "Like you do with Poe. Really, Em, I thought you would have worked this out."

I watched him. "And that's what the parents of stolen children do in Ireland, is it?"

"The clever ones." He rubbed his nose. "Just don't ask me to pay my respects again, please. I can't abide children, mortal or Folk."

15th November

We have found it. We have found the tree. When we set out on our expedition, I was expecting either a scientific triumph or utter catastrophe.

Well, I should have expected both.

The morning was dark, the wind clawed with frost crystals. I was unsurprised to find Bambleby still asleep at the appointed hour. He was near impossible to wake, and I began to fear I would have to drag him from the bed. I could not determine if he was wearing anything, that was the problem.

"I see now why you faked the Schwarzwald study," I said. "And here I thought it was ruthlessness!"

"Laziness, Em," he intoned from his pile of blankets. "Do you know how dense that bloody forest is? And you're well aware what sort of ground trooping faeries can cover in a single afternoon. Horrid, self-involved Folk."

"You would know," I said blandly. He roused himself eventually amidst a volcanic cloud of grumbles and remonstrances, and we set out.

In the end, it was easy.

In my earlier rambles, I had stumbled across the river that the tree grew beside, and as Thora had said it could be found downstream, past an elbow-bend, downstream we went, albeit slowly. The snow was too shallow to warrant snowshoes, but the partial melt had created unpleasant little ice streams atop which the snow sat like a bridge made of feathers. Our feet remained dry, courtesy of the furred Ljoslander boots we had purchased prior to departure, but the going was awkward over such cumbersome terrain.

It was Bambleby who saw the tree first.

He came to a sharp halt, his brow furrowing. I caught a gleam of white through the trees ahead, different in quality to the surrounding snow. Shadow began to whine.

"Is that it?" I marched onward, cursing as my boot broke through another rind of ice. I pushed a branch aside and drew in a sharp breath.

There was no doubt that the tree before us was *the* tree; it could have stepped from the tales into the forest. It was centred in an oddly round clearing, as if the other trees had all felt inclined to back away, and was towering but skeletal, its trunk only a little wider than I was and its many, many branches arching and tangling overhead, like a small person propping up a tremendous, many-layered umbrella.

But the strangest thing about the tree was its foliage. There were leaves of summer-green mixed in with the fire and gold of autumn; tidy buds just opening their pink mouths, and, here and there, red fruits dangling in clusters, heavy with ripeness. These fruits could not be easily identified; they were roughly the size of apples, but furred like peaches.

I felt a happy little glow start in my chest, for the tree—though utterly terrifying, when viewed from an objective standpoint—was so evidently, obviously Folk, while at the same time it was like nothing I had seen before. Oh, I wished to learn everything about it.

"What in God's name are you doing?" I called to Bambleby, who had not moved from the riverbank. "Come and tell me if you think there really *is* a king trapped in here."

I could see him only in parts, through the forest: a smear of gold; a hand on one of the trees; the edge of his black cloak. "Emily," he said, "come away from there."

A dreaminess fell over me, and I almost took a step. But then my hand clenched reflexively on the copper coin I carried in my pocket—it's something I've practiced many times whenever a faerie has tried to bewitch me.

He had never done that to me before. It *was* him doing it, not the tree—I could hear it in his voice. I was suddenly filled with a fury of such force my vision swam, and which drove away the last vestiges of his enchantment.

"I will not," I replied, a dagger in each word.

He seemed to start back. "Please, Em," he said in his ordinary voice. "Please come here."

"Why?"

He seemed to think. "Don't you trust me?"

That threw me. But only for a moment. "Of course not."

He fell to irritated muttering, chafing his arms and pacing back and forth. I turned back to the tree, keeping a hold on my coin. Despite my anger at Wendell, his reaction made me cautious. I paced slowly around the circumference, taking photos. I did not touch the tree, and I kept an eye out for errant leaves that might fall upon me, bewitching me in some ghastly way. When the branches moved against each other, an odd, high sound was produced, like someone whistling out of tune.

"Well, that's a perfectly ordinary sound for a tree to make," Bambleby called. "Nothing at all to worry about."

"Have you ever considered," I said, removing my measuring tape from my bag, "that I might be more capable than you think? I have written dozens of papers, read hundreds of analyses. I've also had numerous firsthand dealings with the Folk, from hobs to bogles to an extremely self-entitled aristocrat."

"I don't doubt that most of your success to date is the result of cleverness. But have you ever considered how much you owe to luck?"

My hand clenched. I finished the measurements without replying—base and canopy. Then I withdrew my field book and began taking notes. I scraped at the snow and found, trapped beneath it, a thin carpet of leaves. As I worked, Bambleby's grumbling and stomping reached a volume one normally associates with teams of horses.

"If you would only tell me what you're so worried about," I said calmly. If I am being honest, I was rather enjoying myself.

"I can't," he said through his teeth.

"Can't or won't?"

"I literally and physically cannot tell you."

"Stop being dramatic."

"I am *not*," he said, with the most dramatic groan I have heard him utter. Shadow seemed to take inspiration from his histrionics and whined louder.

I turned back to the tree. I could almost *hear* him stewing. Well, let him. I fetched a pair of metal tweezers from my pack and carefully plucked a leaf from the frost. It was lovely, segmented like a maple and white as the trunk and boughs, though it also had a coating of short white hairs, like some sort of beast. I placed the leaf within a small metal box I habitually use to collect such samples, many of which have found their place in the Museum of Dryadology and Ethnofolklore at Cambridge. Unfortunately, the wind chose that moment to stir the leaves I had uncovered. I leapt aside as quickly as I was able, but one of them brushed my bare fingertips. I felt a shock of cold, as if I had plunged my hand into ice melt.

"Dammit," I muttered. I pressed the coin to my hand immediately, and the pain lessened.

"What?" Bambleby said. His hearing is inconveniently sharp.

"Nothing. I thought you'd gone, but then I saw that you hadn't."

"That's it," he said. "Shadow, go and collect your suicidal mistress."

I laughed. "Shadow only responds to me. You think—"

Shadow burst from the trees and leapt upon me. I fell into a snowbank, and before I even knew what was happening, he had grabbed my cloak in his teeth and was dragging me.

"Shadow!"

The dog seemed not to hear my shrieks. I slid over snow and roots, and my backside barked painfully against a rock. The land sloped a little towards the river, and with one final tug, Shadow slid me the rest of the way like an ungainly sledge to land in a heap at Bambleby's feet.

I gathered myself, panting. "Shadow!" I snapped, full of fury and betrayal, and he hung his head low, that terrible doggish guilt in every line of his body. But he did not move from his position between me and the tree.

"Good boy." Bambleby seized my hand and dragged me along the riverbank. Oh, I was going to kill him. I wrenched him so hard that he stumbled but did not fall, catching himself with that infuriating grace that he often tries to conceal. I yanked him again so that we were facing each other and grabbed his other arm, the better to shove him into the river. His green eyes widened with outrage when he realized what I was intending, his golden hair falling into them—horrendously unfair that he should look beautiful even when he's angry, instead of going blotchy and beady-eyed like a normal person. If I hadn't been decided on sending him into the river before, I was now.

That was when the land broke open, showering us in snow

and dirt. Roots wormed their way out from the soil, white and smooth as bone. They twined themselves around Bambleby and yanked him onto his back, then dragged him towards the white tree in an uncanny mirror of what I had undergone.

"Wendell!" I lunged forward, trying to wrench the roots away from him. They showed no interest whatsoever in me, nor Shadow, who pounced and worried at them until they fell away. But more rose to take their place.

"Why does it want you?" I cried.

"Why do you think, you cold-blooded lunatic of a woman?" he yelled, clawing at the ground. This was followed by a series of curses in what I assumed to be Irish.

I stabbed at the roots with my pocketknife. At the same moment, though, my mind was racing through stories, texts, journals. "Can you not—can you not say it?"

He gave me one of his impossibly green glares. We were nearing the base of the tree, where a hollow like a mouth had yawned open, black and writhing with roots like white worms. "No!"

"Oh," I breathed. My pocketknife was having little effect, but I kept up the stabbing nevertheless—I believe I stabbed him once, accidentally, for I had gone back into my mind. "You can't reveal to me that you're Folk—it must have been part of the enchantment that exiled you from your world. Isn't that it? I've heard of that—yes, that account of the Gallic changeling. And isn't it a peripheral motif within the Ulster Cycle?* Bryston's theory was that—"

---

* There are, in fact, several stories from France and the British Isles which describe this sort of enchantment. In two of the Irish tales, which may have the same root story, a mortal maiden figures out that her suitor is an exile of the courtly fae after he inadvertently touches her crucifix and burns himself (the Folk in Irish stories are often burning themselves on crucifixes, for some reason). She announces it aloud, which breaks the enchantment and allows him henceforth to reveal his faerie nature to whomever he chooses.

"Oh, God," he moaned. "She wants to discuss theory at a moment like this. I am doomed, aren't I?"

The roots were pulling him deeper. I grabbed at his shoulders and yanked, but I only slipped in the snow and thumped onto my side. Shadow gripped Bambleby's sleeve with his teeth and put his own back into it. Neither of us had the slightest effect.

"Well, what do you want me to do?" I cried. "I know what you are, Wendell—I said it, so you needn't reveal yourself! Can't you use your magic now? Can I help you?"

"Yes, you can stop pontificating at me for half a second so that I can concentrate," he yelled over the lashing roots. "I haven't done this in a very long time. I don't even know if I remember how. And if you would please encourage your fanged familiar to stop mauling my cloak!"

I drew Shadow back. It took all of my strength, for he kept howling and lunging at Bambleby's disappearing body. I don't know what I expected him to do, but something loud and impressive, certainly. What actually happened was both underwhelming and utterly terrifying: he folded himself into the earth and was gone. I have seen brownies and trows do this, of course, but they are brownies and trows, creatures of leaf and moss; they are not Wendell. And then he did worse than that, stepping out of a tree on the other side of the river, creating a horrible confusion within me as my mind tried to convince my eyes that he had come from behind the tree, but of course he had not.

Shadow grabbed at my cloak and started pulling again, but I was already running, and so we ran across the mostly frozen river like a bride from a nightmare, her train supported by a servant. The ice cracked near the far bank but did not break, and Bambleby grabbed me before I fell.

He tried to pull me on, but I dug in my heels and turned to watch the spectacle unfolding on the opposite shore. The white tree itself was still, dreamlike, while beneath it the roots writhed with impotent rage. The river ran too deep; they could not burrow beneath it.

"I want a piece of the bark," I said suddenly.

He gave me such a look of disbelief that I pressed on, "For the paper! We need illustrations, Wendell. Exhibits. How else do you expect people to understand—"

"We can go back there, and you can watch that thing crack my skull open and fill it with monstrosities," he said. "Perhaps I'll sit for an illustration after—what do you think?"

"If I went alone, given that it paid me no mind before—"

He took me by the shoulders and shook me. "What is the matter with you? You are many things, which I will be happy to enumerate later, but obtuse is not one of them."

At that, my old habit, carefully honed, reasserted itself, and I gripped the coin in my pocket. The strange desire that had filled me receded, and I knew that, of course, if I went back, the white tree would seize me, and Wendell would have to come to my aid.

I withdrew my hand from my pocket. But I saw no evidence of the chill that had gripped me when my fingers brushed the leaf. Only—my third finger trembled. I put the hand away again before Bambleby noticed.

"What does the king want with you?" I said, not needing an answer but merely voicing my thoughts as they thumbed through the well-worn stories. "Of course—to possess you. He has no substance left that is not tree."

"No doubt." He was shivering so with the cold that I was a little sorry for him. "I felt him reaching for me the moment I stood above his roots. He is very ancient. His people locked him up in that tree because—well, I don't know. He believes it horribly unjust, naturally. He has been sitting in there fantasizing about revenge and murder and all the rest of it for centuries."

I wondered that he could be so dismissive, when he was exiled royalty himself, but his lack of sympathy seemed quite genuine.

"Fascinating." I watched the roots writhe, already piecing together the entry in my encyclopaedia. Note to self: I must needs enquire after this manner of faerie gaoling; is it a feature in other tales of the Hidden Ones? "No doubt the Folk of Ljosland stay far away from him."

Bambleby was gazing at the tree with an unreadable look. "He is very powerful. He would let me use that power, after whatever bloody rampage he has been plotting."

"You are not thinking of going back?" I said, terror gripping me. "You are bewitched." Oh, God—how would I stop him if he was?

"No," he said, and it seemed to answer more than my question. He turned away, a strange sort of melancholy in his eyes. "No. Let's go home."

Bambleby was nearly silent on the long, tedious journey back, which was most unlike him. I wondered if he was self-conscious after revealing himself to me, but of course that wasn't it. I don't think Bambleby would be self-conscious if he were stripped naked and paraded through the streets of London.

As soon as we got through the door of the cottage, he collapsed into one of the armchairs, nearly insensible. I got his boots off him and discovered that his feet were so white as to be shading into blue. His face, too, was white, and he could not move his fingers. His eyes were very dark, barely any green in them at all now—an interesting phenomenon that I had a mind to examine further, but I managed to quell the scholarly impulse. Only when I had built the fire to roaring and helped him into three blankets did he become himself again, and begin moaning about tea and dinner and chocolate. I would not have obliged his veiled demands, only I was genuinely worried about him, and so I put together an adequate dinner for both of us from the leftover stew Aud had donated in the morning and Poe's latest confection. I even, against my better judgment, gave him the last of the sheep cheese that I had been saving for my own supper—I've grown rather fond of it.

"Your blood is too thin," I said—gloatingly, I'm afraid, for it is not every day that one proves oneself stronger than a faerie prince. "I suppose the Irish Folk are only adapted to dreary rainstorms and the occasional frost. And more rainstorms, of course. Do they have other weather in Ireland?"

He glowered at me from behind his mug—I had made him the chocolate after all. "We cannot all be made of stone and pencil shavings," he replied.

After supper, he fell asleep in the chair, and I helped him to his bed. To my great amusement, one of his conquests showed up shortly thereafter, apparently for a prearranged rendezvous, a pretty, dark-haired thing, yet another of Thora's granddaughters. I was sorely tempted to show her the state of her paramour after a hike of only a few hours, and not a particularly difficult one, for Ljoslanders appear to prize hardiness above all things, amusing myself imagining the dent it would put in Bambleby's appeal.

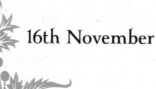

16th November

I expected Wendell to sleep late today, and he did not surprise me; by the time he stirred himself I had already breakfasted and returned from my visit with Poe, whose tree home required shovelling again. It snowed again in the night, a true snow this time. I myself had awoken to the sound of a very strange knock at the door, heavy and rhythmic, and I had a moment of terror, my mind going to tales of ancient winter kings come to demand unfavourable bargains, only to discover that it was Finn, kindly shovelling our steps. The snow was waist-deep in places, with drifts rolling higher like waves, deep enough to drown in and painfully bright beneath the cloudless sky.

After breakfast, Aud arrived on snowshoes with a lump of beeswax and a basket of candles. From the latter rose a powerful smell, a mixture of lemons and rot.

"For the windows," she said. "Light them each night. It will keep the tall ones from your door."

"I see," I said, and proceeded to extract from her the recipe for our paper. The candles were made from fish oil, lemon juice, fermented seaweed, rose petals harvested on the full moon, and the crushed bones of ravens (quantities to be provided in the appendix). It sounded rather fanciful to me—there are human workings, metal for instance, that the Folk near universally disdain, but they rarely take the form of poetic recipes (not that this has prevented many charlatans from making a tidy profit from same). But Aud assured me that the tall ones' music would not pass into the cottage with the candles burning.

I showed the candles to Wendell, when he finally bestirred himself, and he turned his nose up at them. "Snake oil," he said.

I nodded, relieved that he agreed with my assumption. The smell of them unlit made my stomach turn over; the fumes they would release whilst burning didn't bear imagining.

He suggested that I set the candles in the window neverthe-less, to keep us in Aud's good graces. The beeswax, though, struck me as a handy precaution, given the auditory nature of the Hidden Ones' enchantment.

"Will you come with me to interview Auður's family?" I said.

"No," he said. "I will offer myself up to Aud today, I think."

I looked at him askance. Aud was organizing a snow-plowing, a scene in which I could not visualize Bambleby.

He frowned at me over his breakfast. "What? How hard can it be?"

I didn't bother to reply that I doubted it would be very hard, but still more than his soft hands would care for. Indeed, when I next saw him, he was standing in a small knot with Krystjan, Aud, and several other village dignitaries, drinking mulled wine and having a natter while they kept an eye on Finn and the other youth engaged in the grunt work of clearing the road and landings.

My visit to Auður's family was informative but not particu-larly helpful. That is, her parents, Ketil and Hild—both hardy and kind-faced in equal measure, with that greyish touch of sadness—answered my every question, but it was a story with only a beginning and an end. When had their daughter been taken by the Hidden Ones? Two days after Christmas, while fetching mushrooms. How long had she been away? For as long as the moon rose above the mountains at night, which is to say, a little over one week. Where had she been recovered? A hunter found her wandering the mountainside, her basket full of a queer sort of mushroom that melted against his palm.

Through it all, the girl sat in her chair by the fire, empty-faced. Her gaze drifted around the room, occasionally settling on me; I could not help shivering during these moments, for it was like looking through the windows of an abandoned house. I asked questions regarding her condition, of course. In addition to being incapable of speech, she is unable to attend to her own well-being. If ordered to stick her hand into the fire, she would do so; in fact, her left palm bears a scar from the time her mother ordered her to fetch a skillet, forgetting it was still hot from the stove. The only thing she does of her own initiative is wander outside during the longest nights, striding across the snowbound fields without even donning her cloak. She is now tied to her bed every night from the first snowfall to the thaw.

Ketil and Hild were even more interested in asking questions than I, though I could give them little comfort. Not only was I unaware of a remedy that might treat their daughter, I knew of no analogues of her affliction.

Beautiful Lilja arrived in the afternoon to chop our wood, which I'm grateful to say has become a regular favour. I watched through the window as Bambleby flirted, fixing her with many long green gazes whilst his golden hair fluttered in the breeze, even asking her to instruct him in the proper technique, which she did, patient despite his utter lack of improvement. Throughout, she remained cheerfully oblivious, alternately hacking away at the wood and responding perfunctorily to his comments while she wiped sweat from her pretty brow. At one point, I laughed so hard that Bambleby turned and scowled at me through the window. I had heard, through Thora, that Lilja was quite happily committed to a girl from a neighbouring village, but I saw no need to disclose this information to Wendell. It was his own fault, anyhow, for assuming that every woman who walked the earth would be enraptured by his charms.

I spent the day with my books and my notes. Bambleby flitted in and out, contributing absolutely nothing to scholarship, though he did shake out the rugs after exclaiming over their begrimed state and hang some useless woollen tapestry he had purchased from Groa. The effect of his simple ministrations upon the place has been almost alarming; it is virtually cosy. I have never lived somewhere warranting such an adjective, and I am not sure how to feel about it. And anyway, what is the point of decorating a place one is only temporarily inhabiting? When I posed the question to Bambleby, he replied with characteristic solipsism that if I had to ask, I would never understand the answer.

"Come down to the tavern," he said after dark had fallen.

"No, thank you," I said, glancing up from the dryadology journal I was jotting notes from—I was working on the bibliography for my encyclopaedia. "I'd like an early night."

"You don't have to stay long. You'd rather sit here with your nose in a book?"

"Vastly," I said, and he shook his head at me, not in disgust but utter bemusement.

"Very well, you strange creature," he said, and to my astonishment he took off his cloak and settled himself in the other chair.

"You don't have to stay. I'm perfectly content by myself."

"Yes, I've noticed."

I shrugged. I didn't mind him staying; I am in fact used to having him around, not only here but at Cambridge, where he is always poking his nose into my office. He took up that blasted sewing kit of his and attended to his cloak, tucking one leg boyishly beneath him and leaning into the chair.

I am largely incapable of making conversation of a personal nature. I rarely have the inclination, fortunately, but I have had occasion to resent the lack of this particular human skill, as I did then. How many scholars have had the opportunity to question a ruler of the courtly fae? Not one, or none who lived to tell of it.

And yet I could not make myself ask. I suspect that, if I could have convinced myself that my interest was of a purely intellectual nature, I could have managed it. But it was not. This was Bambleby, after all—my only friend. (God.)

"Em," he said without looking up from his work, after I had snuck yet another glance in his direction, "either you are plotting how best to have me murdered and stuffed for one of your exhibits, or you are still concerned that I am bewitched. You are so contrary that I would not be surprised by both concurrently. Perhaps you could set my nerves at ease."

"I am only wondering what in God's name you are doing," I said, taking refuge in the familiar banter.

"What does it look like? You and your hairy accomplice ravaged my cloak." He added a few more stitches and ran his hands over the fabric, folding it this way and that—I could not make out precisely what he was doing. "There."

He tried the cloak on, nodded. If anything, it looked even more magnificent than before, with an elegant billow in the hem, as if the weaver had cut the pattern from his shadow. He saw the expression on my face and raised his eyebrows.

"I can do yours if you like." He grimaced slightly. "And that—that dress."

I looked down at my woollen shift. "There's nothing wrong with my clothing."

"It doesn't fit you."

"Of course it does."

He lifted his eyes to the ceiling and muttered something that I couldn't hear, apart from the distinct words *paper bag*. This offended me not at all, as I afford less than an ounce of importance to my appearance, and still less to his opinion of it.

"You said before that needlework ran in your family," I said after he'd settled himself again.

"Ah," he said, "yes." To my surprise, he did not seem as eager to talk about himself as was generally the case. "Well. I suppose I must gird myself for mockery. I have a very little amount of brownie ancestry, you see. On my mother's side."

I stared. A slow smile crept across my face. "A very little," he repeated severely.

"The *oíche sidhe*," I said, naming the Irish house fairie who, like many of their ilk, operate as a sort of friendly housekeeper, stealing out at night to clean and tidy and make repairs. The well-known tale "The Golden Ravens" is of Irish origin and offers an example of typical *oíche sidhe* disdain for mess and disorder. I include the most famous version of the story in my encyclopaedia—I shall append a copy to this journal.

"Is that usual?" I said. "For a prince to have common fae ancestry?"

He gave me a puzzled look. "How did— Ah, I see. Poe told you. If you are not careful, Em, that creature will come to love you so that he will not let you leave." He went back to his sewing. "No, it is not."

"And is that why you were forced into exile?"

He raised his eyebrows at me, looking amused. "Do you want the whole story?"

"Obviously," I said, unable to keep the eagerness from my voice. "Every sordid detail, in fact."

"Well, I am very sorry to tell you that there is little of that," he said. "Ten years ago, my father's third wife—my mother was his second; the first was barren—decided that she would prefer the sight of her own flesh and blood on the throne. You know how it goes."

I nodded. This sort of ruthlessness is a common occurrence with many of the courtly fae. "Have you siblings?"

"Five, in fact. All older. These she had executed. She sent me alone into exile."

I frowned. "Because you were a youth?"

"No," he said. "It is simply what is done."

I understood. In the tales of the Folk, regardless of origin, no victory or loss is ever certain. There is always a loophole, a door that you may find, if you are clever enough, to lead you out. To twist the story. Wendell's wicked stepmother could not kill him because doing so would close the last door to her own defeat.

"Then you wish to kill your stepmother," I said. "And take your rightful place on the throne. That's why you are looking for a back door into your own world, one she will not be guarding."

He gazed at me in astonishment, then gave a short laugh. "That little rat. I should have guessed he would tell you all."

"Don't be angry with him," I said, alarmed. But Bambleby only shrugged and dismissed Poe with a flick of his fingers.

"Yes, I wish to kill her," he said. "The throne is irrelevant, except as a means to an end."

He rubbed his eyes—they were wet, which alarmed me greatly, as I haven't the slightest idea of what to do when confronted with tears. I nearly threw my handkerchief at him.

"I don't entirely know if you will understand this, Em," he said, wiping his nose. "My cold-blooded friend. But I confess that I miss my home very much. I cannot return while my stepmother lives, obviously. She won't have it, nor will her allies at court. So my only way back is by taking the throne, by making myself so powerful that they cannot be rid of me again."

I leaned back in my chair, mulling it over. My hair was once again coming out of its bun, so I gave up, taking it down and letting it fall over my shoulders. "And you have thus far been unsuccessful."

"I'm well aware you mortals have various theories about how the faerie realms work," he said. "In truth, most Folk don't know much more than you do, because we don't care. Why would we? The laws of nature are too easily altered by those with magic enough to do so. Nothing stays the same. Worlds may drift apart or dissolve or become the same place, like overlapping shadows . . . But we know there are secret ways, forgotten ways, into our worlds. As you say, back doors. I have travelled the mortal realm looking for such a door. No, I haven't found one yet." He rested his head against his fist and gazed into the fire. "You see why it is so important for me to be impressive at ICODEF. I need money to continue my search. That little tempest in Germany has put a damper on investor interest in my expeditions. Our paper can repair my career and fill my pockets enough to search the rest of the continent."

My mind whirred, the pages of my inner library flick-flicking again. I asked him question after question, had him recount every country and village and forest he had visited. I could not help taking notes as we spoke—old habits, etc.—until he exclaimed, "What on earth are you doing?"

"If I am to help you, I require notes," I said.

He blinked at me. "If you are what?"

I gave him an irritated look. "Do you know anyone, mortal or otherwise, with a deeper understanding of the Folk than I?"

He didn't need to think about it. "No."

"There," I said. "I think I can find your door. At the very least, I would like to try. I'm certain I can do a better job than you. Good grief! Ten years." I couldn't suppress a snort. There was something darkly amusing about a faerie lord—one of those same creatures who delight in leading hapless mortals astray in dark wildernesses—being unable to find his way home.

He watched me, his face unreadable again. I no longer think he means to be opaque when he does this; only sometimes what he is feeling is so alien that I cannot intuit it. "Why?"

I paused for the first time to think about the question. "I don't know," I answered honestly. "Intellectual curiosity. I am an explorer, Wendell. I might call myself a scientist, but that is the heart of it. I wish to know the unknowable. To see what no mortal has seen, to—how does Lebel put it? To peel back the carpeting of the world and tumble into the stars."

He smiled. "I suppose I should have guessed as much."

He sounded sad. I suppose he was still imagining his green faerie world. I focused on the scratching of my pen.

"For a time, I thought you must have faerie blood," he said. "You understand us so well. That was only when I first met you. I soon realized you are just as oafish as any other mortal."

I nodded. "My blood is as earthly as anyone's. But you are wrong to say that I understand the Folk."

"Am I?"

"The Folk cannot be understood. They live in accordance to whims and fancies and are little more than a series of contradictions. They have traditions, jealously guarded, but they follow them erratically. We can catalogue them and document their doings, but most scholars agree that true understanding is impossible."

"Mortals are not impossible. Mortals are easy." He rested his head on the chair and regarded me aslant. "And yet you prefer our company to theirs."

"If something is impossible, you cannot be terrible at it." My hand tightened briefly on my pen.

He smiled again. "You are not so terrible, Em. You merely need friends who are dragons like you."

I flipped to a clean page, glad the firelight concealed the warmth in my face. "Which of the Irish kingdoms is yours?"

"Oh—it's the one you scholars call Silva Lupi," he said. "In the southwest."

"Wonderful," I murmured. Faerie realms are named for their dominant feature—statistically, the largest category is *silva*, woodland, followed by *montibus*, mountains—and an adjective chosen by the first documenting scholar. Ireland has seven realms, including the better-known Silva Rosis. But Silva Lupi— the forest of wolves—is a realm of shadow and monsters. It is the only one of the Irish realms to exist solely in story—not for lack of interest, of course; a number of scholars have disappeared into its depths.

"Only you would say that," he said. "Don't worry. I am not as vicious as the rest of them—you may have noticed. I did not see my stepmother's plot coming. I'm afraid I was not much used to doing things for myself back then, and that included thinking. My stepmother encouraged this—she ensured I was never without a host of servants to see to my every desire, nor without a party at which to amuse myself." He slouched down in his seat in a long-limbed sprawl, scowling into the fire.

"Tell me about your world," I said, leaning hungrily forward.

"No."

"Why not?"

"Because you will only write a paper about it, and I don't wish to be an entry in the bibliography. Ask me something else."

I huffed, tapping my pen against the paper. "Very well. If you turn your clothes inside out, do you disappear? I have always wondered."

The dark mood vanished like smoke, and he gave me a youthful grin. "Shall we try it?"

"Oh, yes," I said, an unlikely giggle escaping me. I seized his cloak and reversed it, and he pulled it on.

"Oh," he said, his face blank.

"What is it?" I gripped his arm. "Wendell? What's wrong?"

"I don't—I feel most unwell."

He let me strip the cloak from him, and then he collapsed into the chair. Only after I had made him another mug of chocolate and built the fire up for him again did he start to laugh at me.

"Bastard," I said, which only made him laugh harder. I stomped off to my room, having had quite enough of him for one night.

17th November

I woke some hours before dawn in the quiet of a winter night, snow pattering against the window. Shadow was curled against my back, his favourite position, nose whistling.

I lit the lantern upon my bedside table (both lantern and table had appeared earlier in the week, despite my objections) and held my hand up to the light.

For a moment, I saw something—a shadow upon my third finger. It was visible only from the corner of my eye, and only then when I let my mind wander and did not think of it. My hand was very cold. I had to hover it above the lantern for some minutes before it warmed.

I curled the hand into a fist and pressed it to my chest as an unpleasant shiver ran through me. I lifted the covers, intending to go to Wendell immediately and admit my foolishness. But no sooner had the thought entered my mind than it drifted away again. Even now as I write these words, I must hold tight to my coin to keep them from slipping from my memory. Each time I open my mouth to tell Wendell, a fog arises in my thoughts, and I know that if he were to ask me whether I have been enchanted, I would lie quite convincingly.

"Shit," I said.

I took out my coin and pressed it to my hand. I did not know what manner of enchantment the king in the tree had ensnared me with. What was clear was that I was ensnared. Now, there are faerie enchantments that fade with time and distance if they are not renewed. I could only hope it was of this nature.

If I found my feet taking me back to the tree, I would have to cut off my own hand.

Naturally, I spent the rest of the night in a misery of shame and worry, cursing myself. The worst of it was that Bambleby had warned me away from the tree—if I descended into a murderous rage, or turned into a tree myself, he would be very smug about it.

As soon as the winter dawn ghosted over the snowpack, I dressed and hiked up to the spring in my snowshoes, Shadow at my heels. He does not require snowshoes, nor protection from any weather.

The forest has a different quality now, girded with winter. It no longer dozes among its autumn finery like a king in silken bedclothes, but holds itself in tension, watchful and waiting. In moments like that, I am reminded of Gauthier's writings on woodlands and the nature of their appeal to the Folk. Specifically, the forest as liminal, a "middle-world" as Gauthier puts it, its roots burrowing deep into the earth as their branches yearn for the sky. Her scholarship tends towards the tautological and is not infrequently tedious (qualities she shares with a number of the continental dryadologists) yet there is a sense to her words one only grasps after time spent among the Folk.

I was happy to reach the spring. I'm afraid to say that I have abandoned propriety and taken to bathing in it, a necessity given the awkwardness of heating water in the cottage. After having a scrub, I dried myself quickly with the towel I had brought along and dressed again, balancing myself on one of the heated rocks.

Usually, I waited for Poe to appear before clearing the snow from his tree, as is only polite, but he was unusually tardy. I donned my snowshoes and trudged to his tree, where I stopped. The tree had been scorched. Not from without, but within, as if struck by lightning. Several of the boughs lay broken upon the snow.

I was surprised by the grief that came over me, scattering my thoughts. Yet there was hope. If Poe had run into the woods, he may have become lost. It was a theory supported by anecdotal evidence of the Spanish *anjana*, a tree-dwelling species of the common fae, who rarely stray beyond the land compassed by their roots, and may never find their way home if need drives them from their territory. And so I plunged into the woods, calling for my small, needle-fingered friend. No easy feat, not knowing Poe's true name and being unable to use his language, for fear of what else might hear me. But happily, he showed himself within a few moments of hearing my voice, creeping out from under a root.

"I am lost," he said, wringing his sharp hands. My old hat, now a cloak that he took much pride in brushing and steaming over the spring, was bedraggled and grimed with soot. "They came in the night. I tried to hide from them, for I did not wish to dance. They did not like that, and burned my tree."

Fortunately, I did not have to ask him whom he meant—it was clear from his look that he meant the tall ones.

"There, there," I said. "I will show you the way home."

He hesitated. "For what price?"

I understood his fear; I had to name a price, of course, and he expected it to be great, given his need. This is often how the Folk operate. I had already prepared a reply, however.

"You will answer three questions about the tall ones," I said.

He winced. I knew he hated to tell a "noser" such as myself his secrets, but as this was not concerning him specifically, but his world, it was not a crushing burden. He agreed, and I guided him through the woods. He was perfectly silent at my back, and a very strange Eurydice he made to my Orpheus, or de Grey to my Eichorn.*

He exclaimed over his poor tree, disappearing through a little door I have glimpsed but once, and only then out of the corner of my eye. Soon the snow was darkened with the soot he was scooping from the interior.

"I have broken our bargain," he said glumly, handing me a burnt loaf. "Mother would be very disappointed."

I assured him that our bargain was intact, for the bread was not so burnt that a little scraping would not render it edible. He brightened visibly and settled himself beside me.

"They did not harm my cloak," he said proudly, his long fingers stroking the beaverskin. "It is only a little dirty."

I assured him that the cloak was still most magnificent, and he began the process of steaming it over the spring, hanging it upon a branch that dangled low. Then he turned to his tree, fetching a little shovel from some cranny I couldn't perceive, and began scraping the soot from within. He talked as he worked, an irritated and fearful muttering, and from this I perceived all I needed to know. Promising to return for my three questions, I took my leave of him.

+ + +

* Of course, I refer here to de Grey's disappearance whilst investigating the sinister goat-footed mountain faeries of Austria in 1861, and Eichorn's subsequent vanishing act a year later during one of his many rescue attempts. (Eichorn was convinced de Grey was abducted into Faerie, discounting the commonly accepted narrative of her having taken a fall during a nasty storm.) Decades later, villagers throughout the Berchtesgaden Alps claim to hear Eichorn's voice calling "Dani! Dani!" during winter tempests, though whether this amounts to evidence that one or both remain trapped in some liminal alpine realm is the subject of much conjecture. See *When Folklorists Become Folklore: Ethnographic Accounts of the Eichorn/de Grey Saga* by Ernst Graf.

I ran full tilt down the mountainside, slipping and sliding all the way. By the time I wrenched open the door I was red-faced and panting, my nose running horribly.

I nearly collided with Bambleby, who stood by the table in his dressing gown, looking forlorn. "Finn hasn't been by with breakfast," he told me. Rumpled golden hair completed the picture of indolence as his gaze swept over my pack. "Oh! Our sylvan *pâtissier* has made bread. Have you seen the marmalade?"

"They've taken someone," I said, somehow managing not to beat him over the head with Poe's concoction. "Someone from the village."

"Yes, I rather thought so," he said.

That brought me up short. I did not waste breath asking how he knew, as I would not waste it questioning Poe as to why he wanted a mortal to shovel his lawn, when I have seen him tiptoeing nimbly over the snows. "When?"

"In the night," he said unhelpfully. "And before you ask, no, I don't know who it was. God, but I do hate *singing* Folk. Did you not hear it? Hm, perhaps Aud's fiendish candles work after all. Bloody caterwauling racket. Give me the bells and lutes of my own halls, and hang any pompous minstrels who open their mouths to sully them." He looked at me. "The marmalade, Em."

Something of my feelings must have shown in my face, for he fell back a step, hands raised in a warding motion. Abandoning the bread, I turned and ran back into the winter.

When I crashed through the doors of the tavern, I found nearly half the village gathered there, with Aud fielding questions in Ljoslander. None of them had any interest in foreign bystanders in a moment of crisis, and my arrival was largely ignored. Cursing my lack of fluency, I managed to find Finn in the crowd, and he pulled me aside to translate the situation.

It was Lilja. But of course it was Lilja, the village beauty who could fell trees and cleave firewood as easily as draw breath. They said she had been travelling back to Hrafnsvik with her beloved, a milliner's daughter named Margret who lived in the town of Selabær. They had been taken together, the horse they rode wandering back to its yard before dawn, saddle empty and askew. The other horses had been sent into a frothing panic when it had been stabled among them, a telltale sign of a brush with the tall ones. A search party was being organized, grimly. Lilja's mother, Johanna, who had lost her husband to drowning only a year previous, was being looked after by Thora and her helpers, being near insensible with grief.

Finn then asked me, quietly, if there was anything I could do, given my vast knowledge of the Folk. Unfortunately, Aud chose that moment to conclude her address and join us by the fire, and with the two of them gazing at me with a desperate shadow of hope, I could only promise to think about it.

As I left, Aud entreated me to confer with Bambleby. I could tell from the look she gave me that she was not foolish enough to hope for disinterested aid from one of the Folk, but was willing to offer in exchange whatever was within her power. The loss of two youths, both barely turned twenty, weighed that heavily upon the village.

Indeed, when I returned to the cottage, I found Bambleby dressed and breakfasted (victuals having been delivered by one of Krystjan's farmhands) but far from raring to join the search. I recounted what I had learned at the tavern, and he listened politely (a result, I suspect, of my earlier mood rather than some newfound benevolence on his part).

"Aud is willing to pay for your assistance," I said bluntly.

"Oh?" He looked amused. "Am I to take this as an offer of monetary value, or will she deliver to my door a sheep born of a cow whose wool turns to silver in the moonlight, or some such thing?"

"I think she will give you whatever you want, if it is hers to offer and will not endanger herself or others." I spoke in the careful style in which I am given to negotiate with the Folk, which he seemed to recognize with a kind of weary amusement. He gave a dismissive lift of his eyebrows and turned his gaze back to the fire.

I abandoned caution and spoke to him in my usual manner. "Wendell, be more forthcoming, please. Are you barred somehow from interfering in the sport of your kind?"

"No," he said thoughtfully. "And they are not my kind, Em, particularly; all these silly categorizations devised by mortal minds are about as useful as names given to the wind. If you want the truth, I don't know if it's in my power to rescue our young lovers, and I have no desire to risk my neck trying. Why do you wish to risk yours? You don't care about these people." Surprise dawned in his face. "Or do you? You feel something for Mord and Aslaug, I think. Can it be my cold-blooded friend has come to value the society of these people?"

I opened my mouth to give him the retort he expected, to say that I was motivated by scholarship, pure and simple, that the opportunity to investigate this bizarre ritual was of a magnitude greater than any I had been presented with before, in terms of the ramifications for our understanding of the Folk. It was entirely true, but for some reason, it made me feel unaccountably lonesome.

I looked out over the yard. I could see the axe where Lilja had left it, impaled in the stump—she had taken to coming by nearly every day to restock our supplies. It was such a bleak sight that I quickly looked away.

Yes, I felt something—I am no monster. But would I go after them for their sakes alone, if there were no scientific discoveries to be had?

No. No, I wouldn't.

My life has been one long succession of moments in which I have chosen rationality over empathy, to shut away my feelings and strike off on some intellectual quest, and I have never regretted these choices, but rarely have they stared me in the face as bluntly as they did then.

"Why don't we just pretend?" he said, sparing me from articulating any of this.

I blinked at him. He went on, "We would not have to go anywhere. Let us take a sled a little distance into this godforsaken wilderness, camp out for a night or two, and return with tales of fantastical revelry. Together we could invent a convincing narrative, I've no doubt. The villagers will not sorrow much over our failure—surely they've already guessed that their daughters are lost. We will accept their gratitude for trying, and then we shall go to ICODEF and be showered with praise for being the first scholars to empirically document an encounter with the courtly fae of Ljosland. I shall get my funding. You will make a name for yourself—your cherished tenure will follow soon thereafter. Do you know who was recently appointed to the hiring committee?" He folded his hands and smiled at me.

I held his gaze. I will not lie and say I was not tempted by his suggestion. It would be an easy scheme to carry out, an exceptionally easy one to get away with. I was too practical not to talk through my concerns before ruling the idea out. "You have already earned a reputation for falsifying research," I said. "Would such dramatic claims not fall under suspicion?"

"Ah, that's where you come in, my dear Em. Your reputation is spotless. No one would believe you would participate in a ruse of this magnitude. Of any magnitude. You will launder my reputation most efficiently."

I believed him. But it did not take me more than a moment to make my decision. Perhaps I did not care—could not care—as much as I should for the fate of two youths. But I was also not someone who would put glory before discovery, empty praise before enlightenment. This was about the encyclopaedia, but it was also about something greater than that—the thing that drove me to create the encyclopaedia in the first place.

"We don't know for certain that Lilja and Margret are lost," I said.

He gave a groan and pressed his hands to his face. I waited.

"If you wish it," he said from between his fingers, "I will help you."

I examined him carefully, for I am used to dealing in faerie bargains, and could recognize one in his voice. Yet it was a faerie bargain with only one side, a singular thing indeed. I could not comprehend his motivations.

"I wish it," I said. "Shall I say it three times?"

"I suppose you might as well, you infernal creature."

I did.

"Wonderful," he replied sourly. "Well, don't expect me to help with the packing. I am doing this against my own better judgment. And if the provisions prove inadequate, I am turning the whole mad expedition around."

18th November

The provisions were more than adequate.

The entire village came together in a towering display of generosity and efficiency. By nine o'clock this morning, we had two horses and a sleigh stocked with enough food, firewood, blankets, and assorted comforts to last us days. Somehow, one of the women found time to knit a jacket for Shadow which, combined with the other gifts, left me unaccountably flustered—given my companion's size, it would have taken her hours. Bambleby and I entertained ourselves at the cottage by coaxing a recalcitrant Shadow into his new raiment, which was patterned with flowers and equipped with a jaunty hood. The dog hung his head in abject embarrassment until his tormentors deigned to relieve him of this woollen pillory, and he spent the next hour pointedly ignoring me.

Fortunately, the path taken by Lilja and Margret into the wilderness was clear, for it had not snowed since their abduction, and sailors believed the skies would remain fair for another day or so. As the villagers readied our provisions, Bambleby and I hiked up to the spring one last time.

Poe had made little progress with his tree, though the snow was scattered with soot he had shovelled from the interior.

Bambleby exclaimed in displeasure at the sight of the venerable old tree reduced to a husk.

"Frost-blasted," he muttered. "Disrespectful bloody bogles." Before Poe or I could speak, he touched the tree, and it was healed—ruddy with health and radiant with greenery against the winter pallor. Poe gave a cry and fell upon his sharp knees before Bambleby, trembling, which the latter took no notice of whatsoever. When Poe brought him a magnificent loaf as a thank-you present, Bambleby said rudely, "I am sick to death of bread. Bring me something that will keep me warm in this hellish place."

"Can he do that?" I said after Poe went scrambling back into his tree home, from which arose a queer chorus of clanging and scraping and a sort of bubbling noise. Bambleby only waved his hand and went back to his sulking.

Poe reappeared within the hour with a basket woven from willow boughs, covered with a coarse wool blanket. Bambleby accepted it ungraciously and without even glancing at the contents, even though whatever was beneath the wool steamed intriguingly. I had to take the basket away from him, and found within half a dozen glazed cakes, not unlike those I have seen Ljoslanders consume on special occasions. These would continue steaming until eaten.

Poe answered my questions with something approaching good nature, his black eyes a little damp as his fingers lovingly stroked the roots of his tree. They were simple enough: Where had the tall ones taken the girls? (To the place where the aurora bleeds white.) What do the tall ones fear most? (Fire.)

"Waste of a question," Bambleby said as we departed. "They are of the ice and snow. What else would they be afraid of?"

"Thank you for your advice," I said. "Though I note you waited to volunteer it until after its usefulness had passed. What do you think is the place where the aurora bleeds white?"

"I don't know, but I simply cannot wait to find out. You did not ask your third question."

"How observant you are." In truth, I couldn't have articulated why I withheld the third question, apart from an intuition that it would be important later. It is an intuition I have come to trust, for if you spend enough time studying the Folk, you become aware of how their behaviour follows the ancient warp and weft of stories, and to feel the way that pattern is unfolding before you. The third question is always the most important one.

The laden sleigh drawn by two of the hardy, shaggy Ljoslander horses awaited us in the village. The horses were white, which struck me as an omen of something, though I could not guess if it was good or bad. These were no ordinary horses, but beasts used to picking their way over open countryside laden with drifting snow, and even clambering up mountains.

Aud surprised me before our departure by giving me a hug and kissing me on both cheeks. I flushed and mumbled my way through the experience. She drew Bambleby aside and spoke to him quietly. When he returned to the sleigh, he was frowning.

"What?"

"Aud seems to think I will leave you for dead at the first sign of trouble," he replied. "Either that or devour you myself. She offered me a boon in exchange for your safety."

"I hope you said yes," I said unperturbedly. "You may keep the money. I claim the silver sheep."

He rolled his eyes. Moments later, after another round of tedious goodbyes, we were on our way.

The sleigh glided smoothly over the snow. We followed the road for the first hour. Two of the villagers went before us on horses, men who had been part of the first search party. They showed us the place where Lilja and Margret had left the road, a spot where the Karrðarskogur rolled down from the mountains and cast blue shadows over the wheel ruts and footprints. There the men took their leave, as Bambleby and I would continue on alone, having refused Aud's offer of a guard.

The forest seemed to make a path for us as we followed the clear marks of trampling in the snow, as if the trees had shuffled aside to make way for whoever or whatever had passed there before. Only in places was our way blocked, once by a tall birch that I could have sworn, from a distance, stood to the side of the clearing. The boughs creaked and groaned, and it felt as if the forest was slowly closing the path again, like the healing of a jagged wound.

I got out and walked with Shadow whenever the ground climbed over a hill, to give the horses some relief. I looked back at my footprints in the snow, deriving some primitive form of satisfaction in seeing the mark I'd made on that unfamiliar world. Shadow, loping at my side, left no tracks. He never does.

Bambleby stayed put in the sleigh, wrapped in two blankets and speaking only to complain about the cold. His nose turned a brilliant red from blowing it, the sound of which always seemed to coincide with moments when I was spellbound by the quiet loveliness of the snowy wood. Finally I demanded that he eat one of Poe's cakes, and was relieved by his acquiescence, which spared me the effort of shoving it down his throat.

The cake was warm to the touch, so soft it might have just emerged from the oven, and it transformed Bambleby's mood. He strode alongside the sleigh for the rest of the afternoon without his blankets or scarf, face flushed with warmth, absently brushing his hands through the boughs of this tree or that. Whatever he touched burst into bloom, scattering the snow with leaves like beaten emeralds, red berries, pussy willows and seed cones, a riot of colour and texture crackling through that white world. Soon enough our little wilderness path could have been a grand avenue decked out for a returning general's triumphant procession. Birds hunkered down for the long winter crept out of their burrows, chirruping their alarmed delight as they grew drunk on berries. A narrow fox darted across our path, a starling clutched in its mouth, sparing us a dismissive glance as it slunk back into the velvet shadow.

I tried very hard not to be awed by this flamboyant display of Wendell's. It was the first time I'd seen him be free with his magic, and it left me feeling unsteady and on edge; I realized that I was used to ignoring that part of him, or at least looking past it. As we crested a rise, I turned to see all that colour unfurled across the sleeping landscape, trees jaunty and defiant even as the chill winds snatched at their leaves like nipping wolves.

Towards evening, we came to a mountain pass. The first search party had stopped here—we could tell by the perturbation in the snow, a confusion of hoofprints and boot treads. We carried on a little farther, following the ominous outline of a single set of hooves. The mountains on either side were volcanic-sharp and larger than any earthbound thing should have a right to be, their iced peaks surely closer to the stars than they were to us trudging specks.

"Were they alone at this point?" I wondered aloud.

Bambleby shrugged, perfectly unconcerned. He had donned his scarf and gloves again, but some of the ruddy warmth lingered in his face. "Shall we stop for the night? I'm famished."

I made him continue for another hour, until we came to the heart of the pass. Bambleby sighed heavily, but helped me unload the tent and tuck it into a fold in the mountain's skirts, where we would be protected from the weather. More sighing ensued as we made our fire and our supper, a mix of dried meat, spices, and vegetables that we were to boil with melted snow. He stood staring at the pot as if he had never seen one before until I enquired whether he had ever once in his life cooked his own food—for certainly he would have been waited on even more ostentatiously in his faerie kingdom than he was used to in the mortal realm—and he snapped that he didn't see what difference it made, which was enough of an answer for me. I left him to it, and the burned taste of the stew was worth the enjoyment I derived in watching him flounder about, alternately burning and spattering himself. Afterwards, he retreated in a moody huff to the tent to shroud himself in the blankets Aud had provided, where he withdrew needle and thread and proceeded to mend minute tears in his cloak, muttering to himself and generally making a picture that was like some bizarre inversion of one of the hags of Fate, weaving the future into their tapestries. His seemed like pointless industry to me, with nobody to see us but the foxes and the birds, but the task appeared to lift his spirits, or at least shut him up, so I refrained from commentary.

19th November

I spent today alternating between scholarly excitement at this uncharted scientific territory we were entering and dread that we would be too late—or worse, that we had never had a chance to start with. Lilja and Margret would have travelled more swiftly than us, unladen as they were, but still I worried that perhaps we had stumbled into a faerie trap without realizing it and were now doomed to wander the wilderness, chasing shadows and accomplishing exactly nothing.

"This is no trap," Bambleby said, with such certainty in his green gaze that much of my dread melted away. "Only godforsaken cold, and miles and miles of uninhabitable wastes."

He seemed unable to enjoy the stark beauty of it all, the wild terror of the mountains, the towering glaciers, the little ribbons of time that clung to the rock in the form of frozen cataracts. The aurora danced above us both nights, green and blue and white undulating together, a cold ocean up there in the sky, and even that he barely glanced at. On the second night, he used his magic to summon a thick green hedge of prickly holly and a trio of willow saplings that enfolded our tent in drapery like bed curtains to keep out the chill wind.

"Will you look at that!" I couldn't help but exclaiming as

I sat by the fire, gazing up at the riot of light. I will admit, I wished for him to share the sight with me and was disappointed when he only sighed.

"Give me hills round as apples and forests of such green you could bathe in it," he said. "None of these hyperborean baubles."

"Baubles!" I exclaimed, and would have snapped at him, but his face as he gazed into the fire was open and forlorn, and I realized that he wasn't trying to be irksome—he missed his home. He had been longing for it all along, and this place, so alien and unfriendly, had sharpened the longing into a blade.

As usual, I had no idea what to do with this sort of insight—would questioning him lighten the sadness or make it worse? Should I (oh, God) attempt to hug him? In the end, I merely asked him to draw up additional fencing to keep off the worst of the wind, as I knew he enjoyed using his power thus, and he summoned a hedge so laden with bright berries that it put me in mind of a Christmas tree, as well as an entirely unnecessary carpet of snowdrops at my feet, which I suffered in silence.

I kept my hand carefully hidden in my glove—not that I wished to. I wanted to yank it off and wave in Bambleby's face the band of shadow that swirled there on my third finger, distinct enough now that I knew it for what it was—a ring. It filled me with a terror the likes of which I've never felt before, but I couldn't tell him about it, nor give him any sign that might arouse his suspicion. The enchantment, whatever it was, had me firmly in its grip. Even more worryingly, I sometimes forgot all about it myself. I could only hope that it would not interfere with our expedition.

I watched him out of the corner of my eye as he frowned at the fire, a crease between his beautiful dark eyebrows. Would that he would only grab me and—and—

A flush rose up my neck. What reason would he have to do that?

As usual, Wendell laughed at me when I announced my intention of visiting the restroom, but I didn't care; in the wilderness, one should cling to what dignity one can, I've always thought. Leaving him and Shadow to enjoy the fire, I strode a distance from camp and found a tree large enough to crouch behind (we had left the forest, and all that remained of it were sad, mangy stands of birch here and there). I did my business quickly and hastened back over the snow.

Looking back now, I wonder if I was observant enough. Certainly I was alert—I always am, during fieldwork—but I suspect that the unfamiliarity of the landscape, the high, dark mountains swaddled in snow, lulled me into a belief that no living thing could accost me here, certainly nothing fae, creatures I have spent my career associating with greenery and water and life.

Fortunately, my reflexes are sharp. The instant the light flared through the trees, I halted and gripped my coin. It was a greyish light with no warmth in it, like a star. A wind moved through the trees, and there came a whisper of bells. Had I not been touching metal, I might have been bespelled, and as it was my head still spun a little, but I am used to brushing against faerie enchantments and stood my ground.

They were trooping faeries, and when I did not fall under the spell of their music and move towards them, they grew intrigued and surrounded me. I knew instantly that I was in danger, for they were faeries of the bogle variety, a disputed categorization given to all those common fae with a deathly appearance, low intellect, and malevolent disposition. Bogles are universally and perpetually ravenous, yet they delight in desolate places, leading to theories that they enjoy the sensation of hunger. When they do encounter living beings, they have every manner of unpleasant means to devour them, usually by roasting them part by part in the little cook fires they carry with them everywhere.

They were tall for common fae, though some are of human height, the tops of their heads nearing my shoulders. They were little more than bone with something resembling skin draped overtop, but everything about them was planed and angular like ice chipped into faerie shape. They did not let me see them clearly, melting in and out of the snowdrifts as easily as Poe did with his tree, but what I saw was pale and hoary with frost, with cloaks woven from moonlight, and they had Poe's needle-fingers and matching teeth. Some carried bells, others carried their cook fires in little pots, grey-blue flames fed by the twigs they snapped from the trees as they passed. They circled me a few times, getting my measure as they whispered to one another. Their voices were like the wind stirring the snow, and I could make no sense of them. It is not known if bogles have speech in the human sense; they are very close to animals.

The scholar in me was already formulating questions in Faie; I wished to learn if they could understand me, and not only that, I wanted to draw out the encounter in order to study them. But then one of the bogles was suddenly at my shoulder, its frigid, sharp hand squeezing my neck as it leaned in to take a bite of my ear.

I caught only a whiff of its breath, which smelled of pine smoke and blood, before I jerked aside, spitting out one of the Words of Power.* I have learned two of them, extracted through

---

* First described by Annabelle Levasseur. Exceptionally powerful fae enchantments that, uniquely, can be cast not only by the courtly fae but also the common fae and mortals (though their power is greatly diminished in this latter form). No one knows the origin of the Words of Power. At some point, some powerful faerie enchanter (an awkward term, for the Folk have magic to a one, but I simply refer to a faerie particularly skilled at enchantment), possibly the Ivy Smith who forms a prominent motif in the faerie art of southern England, cre-

bribery from ancient Folk who inhabit forlorn corners of wilderness.

One of the Words is utterly useless. I stumbled across it while pursuing tales of a hag-type faerie in the Shetland Islands—locals were uncertain if it was a banshee or some sort of disgraced runaway courtier of the courtly fae. I never did determine which was true. I came across her at twilight in a huddle of pale rags upon the beach, where she was nearly indistinguishable from a pile of driftwood. She asked me for shelter, which I gave her, of course, leading her back to the inn where I was staying and offering her my bed, whilst I slept on the floor. I even washed her feet when she asked me to—they were very small and curved, like seashells. She was so ensconced in her rags, several layers of gowns that may or may not have been fine once, and a hooded cloak and several shawls, that I never did get a good look at her. When she asked me what favour I would like in return, I said I was currently searching for Words of Power, particularly those that would be useful to me—not really expecting her to know any (few Folk do). To my astonishment, she gave me one without argument—though after she went away and I worked out what it did, I was disappointed. The Word has a single use, and that is retrieving lost buttons. Suffice it to say, I have rarely bothered with it, and I'm at a loss to explain why anybody would go to the trouble of devising such an enchantment. My conclusion: that is faeries for you.

There was little use in summoning buttons in my present predicament, but fortunately, the second Word I'd learnt lends

---

ated the Words, telling them to only a few favoured friends and allies. The oddest thing about the Words (as Levasseur discovered in her interview with a dying member of the courtly fae) is that they can be forgotten by the Folk who learn them, if they are not cast often enough. This is likely why they remain so obscure, even to the Folk—otherwise, why would every power-hungry monarch not know them by now and deploy them against their enemies? (Not that all the Words have an obvious utility.)

the speaker a temporary invisibility—much more practical. Naturally, it had been far easier to track down than the one for buttons—a few judicious bribes led me to the tree of a wizened kobold, who gave me the Word in exchange for a yearling calf.

In any event, when I spoke this Word, the bogles fumbled for me, shrieking in outrage. Unfortunately, the effect of the Word is not long in duration.

Now, I have my pride. I believe I could have dealt with the creatures myself—reasoned with them, offered a fair exchange for my safety, given time. I have done so before. But beliefs and coulds are not much comfort in such situations, and I am not arrogant enough to risk my life for pride with assistance so close at hand. And so I opened my mouth and shouted, *"Wendell!"*

The faeries took no notice of my cry. No doubt they were used to lost travellers screaming for help. One of them grabbed me by my cloak and wrenched me painfully back and forth, like an animal wishing to drag me to the ground. But I did not need to call for Wendell again.

He stepped out from behind a tree—or perhaps *from* the tree; I didn't see. He reached a hand out and snapped the neck of the faerie gripping me, which I had not expected, and I staggered back from both him and the crumpling body. He saw the mark on my neck, and his entire face darkened with something that seemed to go beyond fury and made him look like some feral creature. The faeries scattered like leaves, though they were too intrigued and too stupid to run.

"Are you hurt?"

"No." I don't know how I made myself speak. I have seen Wendell angry before, but this was something that seemed to surge through him like lightning, threatening to burn everything in its path.

He moved his hand, and a hideous tree rose up from the snow, dark and terrifying, all thorns and knife-sharp branches.

The boughs darted out, and he skewered the faeries on them. Once they were all immobilized, held squirming and screaming above the ground, he moved from one to the other, tearing them apart with perfect, calm brutality. Limbs, hearts, other organs I did not recognize scattered the snow. He did not rush, but killed them methodically while the others howled and writhed.

I couldn't move. It wasn't like watching people die, of course—when these snow faeries breathed their last, they melted away like witches in a story—but it was bad enough. Like a cat faced with an overabundance of wounded birds, he didn't bother to finish them all, but left some to flutter and bleed while he dealt with the others. When one broke away, the branch that spitted it snapping under the weight, he actually laughed, a sound with nothing human in it whatsoever, and let the faerie think it had escaped before he calmly magicked himself into its path and tore it in two.

The mad, focused fury left him almost as soon as he'd finished the last faerie to his satisfaction, and then he was shrugging off his cloak and exclaiming over bloodstains that I couldn't see, for to my eyes, they had turned to water. He stomped off to the nearby spring in high dudgeon, leaving me staring at the last few twitching bodies. Then I realized that I could not sit there anymore, nor could I face him when he returned, and so I staggered off into the wilderness.

I paced around for perhaps half an hour, bile in my throat and tears I could not explain stinging my eyes. Slowly—very slowly—the shudders ceased. I grew calm, and was able to see the situation rationally.

My problem was clear—I had not yet learned to see Bambleby as Folk, not truly. Had I done, his display would not have shocked me so. For the sake of my sanity, not to mention both our safety, I had best reconcile my understandings of him, and soon.

When I got back, he was in the tent, mending his cloak yet again. I could not see that there was anything wrong with it and wondered if this obsessive turn his habit had taken was symptomatic of his inability to indulge his nature by making our present existence tidier and more homelike in other respects.

"There you are!" he said, looking up at me in relief when I entered. His voice was ordinary, as if the appalling, violent frenzy of an hour before had been little more than a sneezing fit, something that would have surely terrified me to my bones had I not already been accustomed to his mercurial moods and anticipated it.

That is not to say that it wasn't terrifying at all.

"I was only out walking," I replied, removing my boots and settling myself in my blankets. "You needn't have worried."

He continued to watch me. "Are you certain? When I returned and you were gone, I wondered if I had scared you. I lost my temper, and I'm sorry for it."

I blinked, positively astonished by this display of self-reflection, generally a thing that Bambleby seems to repel. "You have nothing to apologize for. You were protecting me—overzealously, it's true, but I would be foolish to fault you for that." I'm pleased to say that my voice shook only a little, and that a few deep breaths were enough to settle it.

He gave me an odd look; impressed, I think, but at the same time, there was something sorrowful about it. Really, had he *wanted* me to run screaming from him in horror? Good grief.

"Em," he said. "My dear dragon. Here I thought I would have to make amends somehow. I've made a start, I'm afraid."

I followed his gaze to my pillow, upon which rested a thing I did not recognize, woollen and oddly shaped.

I seized it abruptly, indignant. It was my jumper! "How—what have you—"

"I'm sorry," he said, not looking up from the flicker and flash of the needle. "But you cannot expect me to live in close proximity to clothing that barely deserves the word. It is inhumane."

I shook out the jumper, gaping. I could hardly tell it was the same garment. Yes, it was the same colour, but the wool itself seemed altered, becoming softer, finer, without losing any of its warmth. And it was not a baggy square anymore; it would hang only a little loose on me now, while clearly communicating the lines of my figure.

"From now on, you will keep your damned hands off my clothes!" I snapped, then flushed, realizing how that sounded. Bambleby took no notice of any of it.

"Do you know that there are men and women who would hand over their firstborns to have their wardrobes tended by a king of Faerie?" he said, calmly snipping a thread. "Back home, every courtier wanted a few moments of my time."

"King?" I repeated, staring at him. And yet I was not hugely surprised—it would explain his magic. A king or queen of Faerie, the stories say, can tap into the power of their realm. Yet that power, while vast, is not thought to be limitless; there are tales of kings and queens falling for human trickery. And Bambleby's exile is of course additional testimony.

"Oh." He tucked his needle and thread back into his sewing box. "That. Well, it only lasted a day. My coronation was promptly followed by an assassination attempt—and then, you see, my dear stepmother forced me to flee to the mortal world." He lay down and closed his eyes. "It was an eventful day. I did your other cloak, too."

"God." But he was already asleep, so I could not harangue him further, allowing me the relief—I suddenly wondered if that had not been his intention all along—of being too angry with him to be frightened anymore.

–? November

Much as I hate to sully these pages with melodrama, the reality is that these may be the last words I write. I don't know how much time I have, nor how much longer I shall be able to hold this pen, so I will attempt to be concise.

Last night (if last night it was; the movement of time is impossible to gauge in Faerie), I woke to the sound of the accursed tree Bambleby summoned scraping at the fabric of the tent, and the echoes of the bogles in their death throes, as if the tree had gathered up their screams and kept them like souvenirs. Well, try sleeping after that.

I fumbled for my pocket watch, and found it was not yet six. Dawn was a long, long way off.

I looked round for Shadow, and found the turncoat curled up against Bambleby. The dog lifted his head, though, at the sound of my stirring. Wendell was little more than a pile of blankets—he had the lion's share of them, and still awoke complaining of the cold. I could just make out a tuft of gold sticking out from a crack between two quilts.

I went outside, thinking that I might rouse the fire and have an early breakfast. The horses were pressed up against each other, their rumps facing the banked coals.

Above us, the aurora was bleeding.

I stood frozen. The long ribbons of white unfurled all the way to the ground, growing filmier as they went. The green and blue of the aurora was unaffected. It was as if something were drawing the silvery whiteness to earth, like fingers pulling paint down a canvas, to a place just beyond the curve of the mountain—less than a mile away.

For several minutes, I did nothing, merely stood there, carding through possibilities and plans. Once I had chosen a course, I thought on it for several minutes more. Then I ducked back into the tent and dressed, tucking my notebook into my pocket out of habit. I took out the golden chain I kept tucked at the bottom of my book bag, which I had managed to keep hidden from Bambleby this whole time. It has long been a source of amusement to me that he's never had any suspicions about Shadow.

I placed the collar end of the chain around Shadow's neck. He sat up, perfectly silent, understanding my intention in that uncanny way of his.

Wendell did not stir, and given his habits, I doubted he would anytime soon. I draped my own blankets overtop him, to further increase his comfort. In addition to his hair, an elbow, a cheekbone, and a dark-lashed eye were visible.

I brushed my fingers through his hair—partly because I'd always nursed a foolish desire to do so, and partly by way of apology. After all, I might not return from my errand, and if so, he would never forgive me. He might not forgive me if I did, but I could not risk taking him along after that display of his yesterday. Like all the Folk, Wendell is unpredictable, and I had no way of knowing if he would fly into another deranged fury if one of the courtly fae laid a finger on me, and land us in trouble from which we could not extricate ourselves. He had admitted before that he didn't know if he was a match for them. Despite his power, there was only one of him—and that could easily be one too many, given his utter lack of self-control.

No, in this case, I needed levelheadedness, and for that, I could count only on myself.

I donned my snowshoes and set out with Shadow at my side. The leash kept the dog close to me, no farther than the space of three of my strides. I glanced back only once—one of the horses eyed me with a sort of relieved disgust—I was mad, but I hadn't forced him to leave the warmth of the coals, at least. The murderous tree leaned itself over the tent like a doting mother, looking obscenely fat and somehow pleased with itself. The sight was enough to tamp down my doubts.

We walked and walked, my snowshoes softly crunching through the crust of ice laid over the drifts. The mountains slumbered, disturbed only by the fitful touch of the wind, which skimmed small fogs of snow from their slopes. The aurora tumbled to the ground in bursts like silver rain. It was falling into a valley between two great roots of a jagged mountain.

I became aware that we had been walking a long time without our destination growing any closer. We were outside the enchantment, and I needed a way in. I let the leash unfurl so that Shadow strode four paces away from me, then five. Slowly, the light grew near.

We had stepped into their realm.

As soon as I was certain, I drew Shadow to me again. As we moved deeper into the faerie world, Shadow had grown larger. He was now twice the size, his muzzle coming up to my chest. His snout was sharper, wolfish, his paws enormous. But he followed me as calmly as ever, his black eyes trusting.

I climbed carefully up the last slope, bending low. I found a volcanic boulder to crouch behind, and peeped out.

Below us was a frozen lake. It was perfectly round, a great

gleaming eye in which the moon and stars were mirrored. Lanterns glowing the same cold white as the aurora dangled from lampposts made of ice, which framed paths from the lake's edge to a scattering of benches and merchant-stands, draped in bright awnings of opal and blue. Delicious smells floated on the wind—smoked fish; fire-roasted nuts and candies; spiced cakes. A winter fair.*

The Folk gliding upon the ice and strolling easily from stand to stand were not as strange as I had expected. In fact, when I fixed my eyes upon them directly, they looked perfectly mortal, if a little too lovely and graceful. But when viewed slantwise, they were figures of ice and ashes, ashes gone grey and frozen, knife-slender wraiths that at times were not even there, becoming features in the landscape, a phenomenon I had observed with Poe. Their hair was universally silky and white, not like human hair at all, but that of a snow fox or hare, and their eyebrows too, while some had a fine cover of the same hair, or perhaps it was fur, visible on the backs of their hands that disappeared beneath their cuffs.

I heard no music. The Folk upon the ice danced and glided to the same song, that much was clear, but Shadow's presence made me oblivious to it. Naturally, there was a part of me that wished it were otherwise; that I could have been like Odysseus, tied to the mast of his ship. But I had no ship, and no sailors to stop me from drowning myself.

---

* Outside of Russia, almost all known species of courtly fae, and many common fae also, are fond of fairs and markets; indeed, such gatherings appear in stories as the interstitial spaces between their worlds and ours, and thus it is not particularly surprising that they feature in so many encounters with the Folk. The character of such markets, however, varies widely, from sinister to benign. The following features are universal: 1) Dancing, which the mortal visitor may be invited to partake in; 2) A variety of vendors selling food and goods which the visitor is unable to recall afterwards. More often than not, the markets take place at night. Numerous scholars have attempted to document these gatherings; the most widely referenced accounts are by Baltasar Lenz, who successfully visited two fairs in Bavaria before his disappearance in 1899.

I itched for my notebook and camera. I suppose it was cold of me, with Lilja and Margret down there possibly being devoured, but I have vowed to be honest in these pages, even to the last. For some time, I simply watched the Folk and thought nothing about the girls. I thought of Bouchard's discovery of a curious stone slab in Rosetta, and Gadamer peeping through the trees at the goblin city. Was this what they had felt? It was awe, of course, mingled with stunned disbelief. I suppose that when one spends their career working towards a goal, constructing all sorts of fantasies about what that goal will look and feel like, one is left a little senseless when the scaffolding comes crashing down around them.

Eventually, I forced my thoughts back to the missing girls. It did not take long to find two mortals among a sea of Folk alternately beautiful and horrifying—there they were, gliding together on the ice. They could have been two ordinary young people in love, Margret's pretty head resting on Lilja's shoulder. But they moved like dolls on strings, and their smiles were blank and insipid. Occasionally, Lilja would look up, and a frown of confusion would push through the smile. I took heart from this, that there might still be something of them to save.

I didn't try to sneak into the fair—how utterly pointless that would have been. I simply plastered my own blank smile onto my face and wandered over.

Luck was with me, and I managed to find a faerie couple to trail behind at first like a child after its parents, so that the other Folk assumed these two had brought me. They smiled at me, and I smiled back as if I didn't see the hunger in their eyes. In truth, it took my breath away, and I faltered a few times, feeling sick. I began to shake at one point, for there was no difference between this and strolling into a forest filled with tigers.

Shadow, prowling at my side, saved me in more ways than the obvious one. I counted his breaths as they fogged out and the swaying of his tail as he walked. It was an old trick I used to clear my head of enchantment; now I used it to stop myself from running screaming back into the wilderness.

Not one of the faeries glanced at Shadow, not even when he turned his head to nip at their finery out of pure dislike. Once, a man in a sea-grey gown encrusted with jewels with storm clouds in them (they all wore gowns under their cloaks, belted at the waist), jumped when Shadow snapped at his heel, but when he turned to look behind him, his gaze went right through Shadow and into the snow.

Now, there are few dryadologists who could resist the opportunity to sample faerie food, the enchanted sort served at the tables of the courtly fae—I know several who have dedicated their careers to the subject and would hand over their eye teeth for the opportunity. I stopped at a stand offering toasted cheese—a very strange sort of cheese, threaded with glittering mould. It smelled divine, and the faerie merchant rolled it in crushed nuts before handing it over on a stick, but as soon as it touched my palm, it began to melt. The merchant was watching me, so I put it in my mouth, pantomiming my delight. The cheese tasted like snow and melted within seconds. I stopped next at a stand equipped with a smoking hut. The faerie handed me a delicate fillet of fish, almost perfectly clear despite the smoking. I offered it to Shadow, but he only looked at me with incomprehension in his eyes. And, indeed, when I popped it into my mouth, it too melted flavourlessly against my tongue.

I took a wandering course to the lakeshore, conscious of the need to avoid suspicion. I paused at the wine merchant, who had the largest stand. It was brighter than the others, snow piled up behind it in a wall that caught the lantern light and threw it back in a blinding glitter. I had to look down at my feet, blinking back tears, as one of the Folk pressed an ice-glass into my hand. Like the food, the wine smelled lovely, of sugared apples and cloves, but it slid eerily within the ice, more like oil than wine. Shadow kept growling at it, as he had not with the faerie food, and so I tipped it onto the snow.

Beside the wine merchant was a stand offering trinkets, frozen wildflowers that many of the Folk threaded through their hair or wove through unused buttonholes on their cloaks, as well as an array of jewels with pins in them. I could not compare them to any jewels I knew; they were mostly in shades of white and winter grey, hundreds of them, each impossibly different from the next. I selected one that I knew, without understanding how, was the precise colour of the icicles that hung from the stone ledges of the Cambridge libraries in winter. But moments after I pinned it to my breast, all that remained was a patch of damp.

At the lake was a little beach of frozen white sand upon which a number of spectators had gathered. I spied two other mortals in the crowd, a young man and woman draped over the shoulders of two lovely faerie ladies. I did not have to watch them long to know they were far beyond my aid, and turned from their blank stares with a shudder.

Despair overcame me as I gazed into the whirl of dancers. How on earth could I extract Lilja and Margret when I was deaf to the music they danced to? Stepping onto the ice would give me away immediately—I am flat-footed at the best of times, but I doubted even someone trained in the art of dance could fit their limbs into a rhythm they couldn't hear.

As I stood going through my options, there came a rustling at my elbow. A beautiful lady was gazing at me, her rabbitish white hair cascading in a long braid past her waist, her blue-grey eyes perfectly matched to her many-layered gown, which was ornamented with icicles that I thought should have clinked together like bells, but didn't—or I couldn't hear them.

"What a lovely cloak," she said in Ljoslander. I gave her a blank look and said, in English, that I could not understand,

and she smiled and repeated herself in my language. Her gaze as she eyed my cloak was sharp with greed.

I thought at first that I had accidentally donned the cloak Bambleby had been working on—I realized, gazing down at myself, that it flowed fetchingly around my legs as I walked, and kept me warmer than any cloak I've ever owned. But it wasn't; it was the same old cloak I'd worn yesterday, which meant he must have woken last night after I took it off, damn him, and fixed it up, just like one of his ridiculous ancestors creeping about the shoemaker's shop and mending the boots.

"What is a little sparrow of a girl doing with an enchanted cloak?" the faerie lady asked, trailing one long finger down the sleeve. My arm ached with cold for hours after that touch.

I curtsied for her, thinking fast. Why not settle for a version of the truth? "It was a gift, my lady. From the *oíche sidhe*."

I didn't know if she would understand the Irish term, but she seemed to, I suppose in the same way that the Folk can understand and speak English even if they've never heard it before. "Fine workmanship, even for the little ones."

Her attention was drawing a crowd—other faeries stopped to *ooh* and *ahh* over my cloak. They formed a ring around me, which was disconcerting; I could look at only one at a time, which meant that all the others, viewed from the corner of my eye, assumed their spectral halfway forms. Shadow growled deep in his throat. In the faeries' eyes were hunger and avarice, and it occurred to me suddenly that whatever caused them to long for hot-blooded human victims might also lead them to view someone like Bambleby as a particularly rare treat.

Goddamn you, Wendell.

The only good to come of this was that Lilja noticed me too and skated slowly over with her hand linked in Margret's. Margret was a slight, dark-haired girl, barely coming up to Lilja's chin, and pretty in a delicate sort of way. She wore a crown of icicles that hung askew and slowly melted into her eyes so that she was always blinking, a nasty bit of mockery, I thought. Her gaze was blank, but a flash of comprehension dawned in Lilja's eyes, and she stumbled towards me.

I held her gaze and shook my head ever so slightly, then curled my finger once. She seemed to understand, and slowed her stride. She and Margret drifted off the ice, graceful as birds, and wandered to my side, as if they too were merely interested in my cloak. The moment they neared, I made Shadow stand beside them, stretching his leash, so that his magic washed over them both and muffled the music in their ears.

Lilja came back to herself first. It was a strange thing to watch; as if she'd stepped back into her own eyes after cowering in some dark corner. Fortunately, the faeries were not looking at her, but continued pestering me with questions about the cloak, how long I'd had it and did I have any others like it and on and on, which all this time I had been answering in a carefully dull voice.

"Leave our dear guest be," a quiet voice said. A man came forward, his eyes the violet-grey of a winter dawn. He was tall and slender and more beautiful than the others, and he wore a sword of ice at his waist. Though he was more simply attired—no jewels or icicles festooned his clothing—he moved with an arrogant, unhurried grace that I recognized all too well, as if the world was one vast divan for him to laze upon.

My breath caught in my throat. I didn't know what he was, prince or lord or something in between, but it didn't much matter. The crowd fell away, some with bows or murmurs of respect, and we were alone with him.

"Walk with me," he said in a voice that was near enough to music that I surely would have been caught in it without Shadow there. He led us along the lakeshore, summoning little icicle flowers to carpet our feet, as if the symmetry between him and Wendell wasn't already striking enough. Once we'd left the crowd behind, he turned to face me.

Even though I was looking directly at him, at times it felt as if I were staring right through to the stars and mountains at his back. I could read only mischief in his gaze, which frightened me more than the malevolence I saw in many of the others, though I couldn't have said why. Everything about this man made me feel utterly insignificant, like a trinket his gaze had been caught by, which he might at any moment choose, idly, to crush between his fingers.

"You are not enchanted," he said calmly. "I won't bother asking how—why would you tell me? And in truth, I don't care. Humans have their tricks, just as dogs do. All I want is that cloak."

This was a lot to take in all at once, but I paused for only a moment to steady myself before saying, "If so, why bother asking? Why not just take it?"

I had already guessed the answer; I just wanted him to think me ignorant and even more uninteresting than he already did. He answered in just the sort of bored voice I'd hoped for, "It is of little value to me like that. I want it willingly given."

Of course he did; faeries steal when the fancy takes them, but most prefer gifts.* "And in exchange—"

"I will not reveal you," he finished, his tone adding an *obviously* at the end.

I gave him a long look. I will not lie, I was absolutely terrified of him, standing there with dawn-coloured eyes and his ice sword with the starlight reflecting in his face (I mean that literally; his face was at least partly made of ice, and caught reflec-

---

* While it is considered settled fact that the common fae are strengthened by mortal gifts, whether the more powerful courtly fae experience the same benefit is a matter of much conjecture. For my part, I have never seen any reason why this should not be so; that it defies human logic is not a sufficient counterargument where the Folk are concerned.

tions of the stars like a smattering of freckles). I think that, for all my experience with the Folk, I would have cowered before him or perhaps simply given in to my instincts and fled, if he hadn't reminded me so much of Wendell. And somehow, that steadied me enough to say, "You will also place a path before us to lead us from your world."

For the first time, he looked at me as if I had surprised him. I guess he'd never had much reason to bargain with mortals when he could simply sing them senseless and then drain their hearts dry. He smiled slightly and bent to pluck one of the flowers he'd made. He shook it a few times, and the petals unfurled like water melting through his hand. When the water solidified, he was holding a white fur cloak. The fur was coarse—perhaps from a bear?—and as thick as my fist.

He offered it to me, and held out his other hand for my cloak. I was so surprised that I didn't think before I blurted, "That's not what I asked for."

He gave me a look as ancient and unyielding as winter, and suddenly there was nothing about him that was like Wendell. "What use do you have for a path, if you are frozen to death? Your chances of escape are low enough already. Take it and be grateful."

🌿 **We left the** lake as quickly as we could, weaving our way back through the stands. We ducked behind one, and I helped Lilja and Margret turn their cloaks inside out. I didn't bother reversing my faerie-made one.

I taught them the Word next, though it works only temporarily on the common fae, which didn't inspire confidence that it would be effective against these creatures. Lilja looked like herself again, calmer than I in the face of peril, doing what I said without question. Margret was still blank-eyed, though now there was at least a furrow of confusion upon her brow. Her ice crown melted and melted but never got any smaller, and when I tried to take it off her, it nearly froze to my skin.

"Can you help her?" It was the only question Lilja asked me. I saw Auður when I looked at Margret, and knew Lilja did too.

I didn't know what to say, so I simply motioned them on. Murmuring the Word, we slipped past the last stands. While the Word might not have made us invisible to these creatures, it certainly made us less interesting. We kept our pace slow and aimless, as if we were merely off for a stroll. There was no reason for these Folk to think differently—apart from the one with the stars in his face, it was clear that none of them had ever considered the possibility that a mortal could evade their magic. Perhaps none ever had.

At first I was relieved to put the fair behind us. But we hadn't been walking through the wilderness for long before I realized that it wasn't right. The footprints I had left petered out, as if someone had followed behind me with a broom and swept them away, and though we walked for an hour or more, we saw no sign of the little camp Wendell and I had made. The dawn didn't come. The aurora shone above us in all its colours, the stars clustered like swarms of bright bees in an undulating garden.

I walked with my hands shoved in the pockets of my ridiculous faerie cloak. At one point, my fingers brushed something cold and smooth. I drew it out, and found myself holding a compass.

In all honesty, I was too weary to appreciate this impossible magic. "I suppose the cloak gives the wearer what they need," I told Lilja, my voice almost dismissive—well, after all, what we really needed was a door, and you couldn't fit *that* in a pocket. She took the compass and used it to guide us south and east, from whence Bambleby and I had come.

"Is there anything else in there?" she said.

I dug around in the pockets again, but my hands were empty when I withdrew them. She swallowed and turned back to the compass.

I made us keep going, even as hours passed and it became clearer and clearer that we were still tangled up in the faerie world, like a fly struggling in a web. Shadow felt it too. He growled and paced ahead of us and then back again, his nose snuffling at the snow, searching for a way out, like a fold in a stage curtain he might slide beneath.

We had to rest after a while, if only out of sheer exhaustion. I drew Lilja and Margret into my ridiculous cloak, which had an itchy, prickly sort of warmth, as if the garment were irritated by the use I made of it. It made me yearn all the more for my old cloak, even though Bambleby had made it ostentatious. But at least I found a flask of water in the pocket of the faerie cloak, which we shared among the three of us. It seems clear that the cloak was indeed enchanted to supply its owner with whatever he or she requires, though it doles out those gifts in a most miserly way—some food would have been nice, along with the water, or a lantern and some flint. Perhaps it is only miserly when forced to serve mortals.

Margret was stumbling more and more, and we could walk only another hour or two before we had to stop again. And here we are, tucked into a cave in the mountainside. Lilja and Margret are huddled in the cloak, Lilja furiously rubbing at poor Margret's arms, while Shadow continues his search outside for a door to the mortal realm. I have faith in him, my oldest, most loyal friend—if there is a way out, he will find it. I have had to force myself to consider the alternative—that we may need to go crawling back to the Hidden Ones merely to stay alive; how many hours of life that will buy us is not something I wish to contemplate. I will put the pen aside for now and rest briefly.

20th November

Well, what an absolute nightmare of a country this is—even worse than I previously supposed, which is quite the feat; little more than ice and darkness and nasty, hungry things gnashing their teeth. Trust you to have dragged me into it.

I have no doubt, my dear Em, that you will be beside yourself with gratitude when you find that I have filled in the next entry in your journal. When I informed you of my intentions, I believe you glared in your sleep, another superpower of yours. You are snoring now in the sleigh, and Margret and Lilja are similarly wearied, and so with no other options for occupying myself beyond admiring the scenery as the horses bear us back to Hrafnsvik, a dubious prospect at best, I will do you this good turn. You may thank me when you wake.

Naturally, I thought about glancing through what you have written, at least to look for my name, but something stopped me. No doubt it was my chivalrous nature; I certainly can't imagine what else it would be. Ah, you're stirring a little. Strange how you always keep your left hand stuffed into your pocket, even in sleep; I tried to see if you had injured it, and you elbowed me in the face.

Anyway. I suppose I should pick up where you left off, yes? Though let us backtrack a little to set the stage.

It was close to noon when I awoke to find you vanished, and Shadow too. Oh, how I hate this place. Usually upon awakening I experience a few blissful seconds in which I think that I am home again, that at any moment I will hear the rustle of the weeping rowan as it murmurs to itself by my window or the pitter-patter of my cat's feet as she comes to greet me. (Did you know I had a cat back in Faerie? She is not the sort you would like to meet. I would tell you more, but you would only write a bloody paper about her.) But in this foul place, it is so cold that I cannot ever fool myself into thinking I am home, and so I am denied even that brief moment of peace.

You'll no doubt be happy to hear that I didn't rush after you immediately. Of course I guessed that you had concocted some scheme in the night, which you would no doubt carry out with your usual reptilian efficiency, no help needed from the faerie king you have dragged along with you like a half-forgotten doll. I don't mean to say that I was insulted; I was more than happy to have been left behind with the fire and the blankets. But I soon grew bored of waiting, and of worrying that your plans had gone awry, as even the plans of fire-breathing dragons are wont to do sometimes, Em.

And so I took one of the horses and followed your tracks, and very interesting tracks they were, leading me to a frozen lake where there was absolutely nothing to see at all, but of course I knew that I stood outside the door to what I'm sure is a very charming faerie realm, no doubt filled with Folk with icicles for hair or something equally grotesque. I did not bother looking for a way in to exchange pleasantries with the locals, for I could see from your tracks that you had been and gone, sort of, for the tracks led in and out of Faerie, and in and out again, as if you had wandered for some time without being able to extricate yourself from the borderlands of their realm. When I saw that I became very worried indeed, for there was no way of knowing how long you'd been wandering, though only a few hours had passed in the mortal world. I was finally alerted to your presence when that fiendish dog of yours came charging out of nowhere, howling his head off. From the sound he was making, you were dead or dying or frozen into a dessert for some bogle, and so rather than looking for a proper door into their realm, I simply ripped a hole through it, and kept ripping until I found you in that cave.

Yes, yes. It was perhaps not the wisest choice, particularly given what came after. You can delight me with your lectures when we are home again.

I shook you awake, and you said, "Wendell!" in a way that I quite liked, nothing at all like your usual tone. But of course, instead of thanking me for pulling you out of some desperately unpleasant otherworld, you began immediately to harry me with demands, namely that I heal young Margret.

"I can heal her," I told you, "but I can't make her whole again," to which you only gave me a look as if to say, that's good enough, get on with it. Perhaps it was good enough for you, but Lilja was watching me with shadows like bruises under her eyes, and I could tell by her expression that she would give me anything for my assistance, even her own soul, if I meant to be petty and make demands of her, which I did not. As she told me later, she had not slept a wink, but had spent the hours chafing her beloved's arms and blowing warmth into her hands. I spoke to her quietly, and she gave her assent, and then I touched Margret's forehead and melted the crown that the Hidden Ones had placed there. It left behind a rather pretty scar across her forehead and cheekbones, a pattern of jagged snowflakes that gleams like ice when the moonlight shines upon it.

Now, I thought this exceedingly gracious of me, healing the lover of the only woman who has ever spurned me, but I was not foolhardy enough to expect praise from your direction. Lilja, however, pressed my hand hard enough to bruise it as Margret buried her teary face in Lilja's neck, and the charming picture they made was thanks enough for me.

"How?" I enquired, and you must have known from the disbelief in my face that I was helplessly amazed by your feat, marching into some ice faerie realm and making off with two captives, and all that without sustaining a scratch. But you looked away, and seemed to be avoiding looking at Shadow too, so that I immediately began to think about how it had been him who had led me to you, and then about all of his uncanny ways, not least of which is his choice of a creature like you for a master. I patted his head, feeling about for the glamour, as I have never bothered to do before—and why should I; I do not make a habit of looking beneath people's pets to see if there is a monster hiding there—and sure enough, there it was, and when I moved the magic aside, a bloody Black Hound stared back at me, all glowing eyes and glistening fangs.

You looked worried, for some reason, but you calmed down when I started laughing. "Where did you get him?" I said.

"In Scotland," you replied. "He's a Grim. I rescued him from a boggart, who was tormenting him for sport."

Then you told me how you had tricked the boggart into thinking you a long-lost relative of his last master—a feat which had required extensive research into local lore—then bribed him with exotic seashells, for you remembered some obscure story about a boggart whose secret fantasy was to travel the world, boggarts being bound to their crumbling ruins, while I half listened in astonishment. I say half, because I was mostly just watching you, observing the way your mind clicks and whirrs like some fantastical clock. Truly, I have never met anyone with a better understanding of our nature, and that *anyone* includes the Folk. I suppose that's partly why—

Ah, but you really would kill me if I desecrated your scientific vessel with the end of *that* sentence.

Anyway. We strolled out of the cave into the purpling light; it was getting on for evening by that time, and I was thinking longingly of supper. In truth, I was also thinking longingly of my apartments back at Cambridge: the fire crackling in the hearth, my servants hard at work preparing my repast, and one of my mistresses, fetchingly attired, to share it all with— everything as it should be, in other words. You said something in a sharp voice about the blasted aurora, which seemed to be falling to the ground right in front of us, and then I was suddenly on my back with an arrow through my chest.

Now, I have never been shot before, so we will have to add it to the list of pleasures I have experienced since making your acquaintance. You screamed, which I appreciated, and Shadow went berserk, also kind but not much more helpful, but fortunately, Lilja had her wits about her and yanked the arrow out, then threw herself and Margret to the ground.

It was a faerie-made arrow, of course, a shard of pure ice and magic, and with it removed I was able to use my own magic again. Fortunately, the edge of the Hidden Ones' realm was rolling over us again as the wind picked up—I suppose it's intriguing, this travelling faerie realm, as little as it is to my taste— and like all monarchs, I can bend the rules when I am in Faerie, if only a little. Through the agony, I managed to pull at the pocket of time I was in and unravel a few threads. I'm not explaining it well enough for you to understand, I'm sure, but essentially I turned back time, returning to the moment the arrow flew towards me, where I caught it. It's a talent of limited compass, I'm afraid; I can affect time only within a small area— anyone standing much more than an arm's length away is unaffected—and I've only ever managed to undo a handful of seconds. Quite helpful, though, in this instance.

The faerie who had shot the arrow soon made his presence known, striding arrogantly out of the wind to smirk at me. I could tell right away that he hadn't seen my little trick; he'd only seen me catch the arrow. He had eyes like the dawn, and he was wearing some sort of dreadful grey thing that hung from him like a sheet—very much your style—and a cloak made of dead animals of some sort—hideous but perfectly practical attire, I suppose, for an icicle like him.

"You're a long way from home, child," he said to me in Faie, with a condescending tone that I did not appreciate. Unfortunately, he was very old, older even than some of my court's most tedious councillors, so I suppose he had reason to condescend to me. No reason at all to put an arrow in my chest, though.

You were at my elbow then, rapidly recounting the whole story of the cloak and the Hidden Ones' interest in me—unnecessary, really, for I had already gathered that the man had been drawn to the great hole I'd put in his realm, and that he meant to make a meal out of me, hollowing me out like an orange, as he'd done to Auður. My, what an ignominious fate that would have been! I can imagine my stepmother's reaction; I think she would have injured herself laughing. It would not have surprised her.

Anyway, I did not much want to fight him—he looked a mean sort, and I was resentful that after all the effort I'd expended, here was yet another trial to keep me from my supper—so I simply explained to him who I was and gave him a little demonstration of my power to put him off, summoning a very pretty rose garden in the middle of his desolate winter, complete with a handful of bees.

"You were cast out?" he said with distaste, and looked me up and down. "Yes, we have children like you at our court. Indolent peacocks, strutting about with their jewels and their perfumes, teasing one another with vacuous enchantments. Your step-mother did your realm a great favour."

I did not have any time to be angry at that, for before he'd even ended his sentence, he was charging at me with his sword.

I shoved you out of the way first, which cost me; a slash through the arm of my cloak. Then I had to vanish into the landscape, a trick I hate very much here, because even the trees feel like ice when I step into them. He shadowed me everywhere I went, so that I was endlessly spinning and leaping and dodging his sword, and generally making myself ridiculous. I tried to throw my own magic at him, but the sword swallowed it. Of course it was no ordinary enchanted sword—it *was* enchantment, a powerful one at that, probably honed through all the years he'd been alive, just my luck.

"Wendell!" you were yelling, trying for some ungodly reason to get my attention as I dodged and weaved, as if I needed another thing to think about. "Wendell, what do you need?"

I think I replied something ungracious about shutting up; it's all a bit hazy. I managed to get an ordinary blow in when the faerie was looking for me in a hazel tree I'd summoned—I was summoning all sorts of trees and shrubberies, more to distract him than anything else, and the icy mountainside was beginning to look like the domain of some mad hedgewitch. My hand still stings from that blow as I write this; it was like punching solid ice.

You just kept yelling, though. "Think of the stories, Wendell—there's always a loophole, a door! I can find it, if you'd just tell me what you need!"

"A sword!" I shouted back, half hysterical at this point and not thinking for a second that you'd actually pull a sword out of the snow. I was beginning to wonder if I'd have to blast a hole in time itself to get rid of this bloody iceman; and oh, what a mess that would be to clean up. It's not something I've done before, so who knows, I might've blasted myself to pieces in the process, leaving you to put me together again, which I've no doubt you would have managed with perfect detachment.

The next time I took notice of you, you were sobbing all over the snow. Well, I thought, finally she's being sensible. Then I realized that you were sobbing because you'd stabbed yourself in the arm, and not out of concern for my imminent demise. I noticed that your tears were freezing as they hit the icy ground and collecting into the shape of a sword.

Well, that almost killed me. I mean that—I froze for a full second, during which our yeti friend nearly skewered me through. I dodged, barely, my head whirling. One day I would like for you to explain to me how you heard of the story of Deirdre and her faerie husband, a long-ago king, which is one of the oldest tales in my realm. Do mortals tell it as we do? When the king's murderous sons schemed to steal his kingdom by starving it into torpor with endless winter, Deirdre collected the tears of his dying people and froze them into a sword, with which he was finally able to slay his children. It is a tale many of my own people have forgotten—I know it only because that poor, witless king is my ancestor.

I felt the story in my blood and let my magic flow into the sword you were fashioning. Unfortunately, our enemy noticed there was trickery afoot and lunged towards you, so you dropped the sword in the snow. Lilja, though, was once again firing on all cylinders—she snatched up the sword before the faerie could crush it, and threw it to me.

I caught it, of course, and in the same instant I interposed myself between you and him, catching the blade of his sword with my own. From that moment on, things were much more enjoyable. I do like swordplay—I began my lessons when I was virtually still in the cradle, as do all royals in my realm. I didn't kill the man straight away, but made him dance a while first, running through several of my favourite patterns, forcing him back, and then back again. He wasn't bad, though he wasn't much of a challenge, either—few Folk are. It's a pity sword fighting isn't de rigueur in the mortal world anymore. I could end every tedious argument with the department head by challenging him to a contest in the quadrangle.

Anyway. Eventually I grew bored of the whole thing and knocked the sword out of his hand. Then I knocked his head off with one well-aimed stroke, nice and clean and hugely satisfying. In fact, I liked it so much that I wound back time and did it again, just to hear the lovely *thunk* of his head hitting the snow. I had just decided to have a third go at it—for we Folk like things that come in threes, you know—when you roared at me to stop. I turned, and saw that Lilja was being sick in the snow, which distressed me, as I've decided that I quite like her. I'm not sure if it was due to the general mess that accompanies decapitation or the fact that mortals are not used to seeing time moved back and forth like the pages in a book, but I felt sorry anyway. I will have to make amends to her when we return to Hrafnsvik—perhaps she would like a tree that fruits year-round, or a dress that changes colour at her will, which neither stains nor wrinkles? I'll think on it.

I suppose this is as good a place as any to leave things, as I see that you are stirring—I hope you don't mind that I didn't dislodge you when you slumped against me in sleep, your head coming to rest on my shoulder. No, silly me; of course you'll mind, but perhaps I don't care.

22nd November

I thought long and hard about throwing all that into the fire. Well, all right, not *that* long and hard; Wendell's account is helpful, I admit, and in fact put about a dozen research questions into my head—not least of which regards the ability of faerie monarchs to manipulate time—but no doubt he would only smirk if I posed them to him and make some joke about bibliographies. As much as it infuriates me when anyone else so much as touches my journal, let alone has the gall to fill it with their perfect handwriting (for of course his handwriting is beautiful, even when composed in a horse-drawn sleigh), I am not going to let my pet peeves take precedence over scholarship.

I slept most of the way back to Hrafnsvik, which astonished me. During one of my few waking moments, Wendell explained that I had allowed myself to take part in a powerful enchantment—the making of the sword—and as I had no magic myself, the enchantment had instead absorbed much of my mortal strength, and it would take time for that to recover. This fascinating statement immediately filled me with questions: Is that what Deirdre did, sacrificing her own strength for her faerie husband's sake, and is that why she died shortly thereafter? By what alchemy does mortal strength contribute to faerie magic, and is it only the courtly fae who have access to this? But I was asleep again before I could ask him.

Once we returned to the cottage, I tumbled into bed and slept for another night and a morning, and when I awoke, I felt whole again.

"Wendell?" I called. I don't know why I did so—I was on the edge of sleep still, and for some reason the quietness of the cottage alarmed me. But he came into the room, smiling smugly.

"I have been up for hours," he said, which I did not for a second believe. "Shall I send for breakfast?"

"Oh, yes."

He had already eaten, but that did not stop him from helping himself to the food brought by Finn and Krystjan—hearty dark bread, smoked fish, goose eggs, a variety of cheeses, and blueberries that had been canned fresh in syrup, which they had mixed into oatmeal and yogurt and piled with toasted sugar. It was a more elaborate breakfast than any we'd been served before, and even stranger, both Finn and Krystjan delivered it. Bambleby invited them jovially to dine with us, an overture that was immediately accepted. This suited me well, as I was able to eat in peace while Bambleby entertained himself with directing his charms at two willing recipients, both of whom were full of questions regarding our exploits. Lilja and Margret, I learned, had been safely delivered by Wendell to Lilja's family home, and were both in good cheer; Lilja's parents were beside themselves with relief and gratitude, while Lilja's younger siblings were enthralled by the strange but lovely scar upon Margret's forehead. I was more than content that Bambleby had absorbed the initial onslaught of praise, which no doubt factored into his present high spirits. He answered Finn and Krystjan's questions elaborately, and somehow a wolf pack and a fearsome ice storm found their way into our journey to the Hidden Ones' fair, as if the tale was in need of embellishment. The men hung on his every word, which I was used to, but there was something in the way they hesitated in their speech, as if every word directed at Bambleby needed to be carefully selected, and the way Finn cast nervous looks at Krystjan whenever his natural abrasiveness came through—that was entirely new.

"They know about you," I said bluntly after Finn and Krystjan finally departed. "The whole village?"

He helped himself to more yogurt. "Lilja and Margret are clever girls, but even so, you would not need much cleverness to put two and two together after what they saw."

I drummed my fingers on the table. "It's inconvenient. The villagers will see you as some sort of faerie godmother now. You get little work done already without them accosting you night and day for favours."

The smile slipped from his face. "Do you think they will?"

"I have no idea. The Ljoslanders do not have the kindest associations with the courtly fae, so perhaps that will dim their expectations of you. Could you not have taken the girls' memories?"

He gazed at me in disbelief. "You wish that I had addled their minds, after what they went through? Oh, Em."

"Not *entirely* addled," I said defensively. "But you could have taken the memory of what they saw in that valley."

"It doesn't work that way."

"How does it work, then?" I leaned forward eagerly.

"I haven't the faintest idea. I've never bothered mucking about in mortals' minds."

I slumped back with a sigh. "You are no help whatsoever."

"I don't wish to be of *help*." Bambleby lifted his eyes to the ceiling. "I wish to finish off our paper and use it to dazzle the brilliant minds at ICODEF into a magnanimous stupor. Then I wish to take their money and use it to hire an army of students and equipment with which we will find a door back to my kingdom. Speaking of which, I believe we have quite enough material to complete our draft, don't you think?"

My spirits rose at that. "More than enough."

"There is also this," he said, springing from his chair with a grin. When he returned, it was with the white cloak the faerie had given me draped over his arm.

I stared at it. In the light of the cabin, its unnaturalness was heightened—the fur looked less like hair and more like blades of frost. "Did you do something to it?"

"God, no. I'd rather stuff my mattress with snow than tailor any garment of theirs. Not that it couldn't use it." He examined the cloak critically. "I've been keeping it outside, for it melts a little indoors. But if we pack it in ice—"

"We could display it at the conference." My head spun. We had collected an artefact of a species of faerie that had never been studied before. One that said *faerie* in every stitch and crease. It was nothing short of a triumph.

He smiled at me. "Precisely."

He went and put the coat back in the cold, then brought me one of his own notebooks, leather-bound with pages that crinkled smartly and had lavender crumbled into them (of course). To my astonishment, it contained a draft of the abstract and an outline in his irritating handwriting.

"Did you think I would leave you to do all the work?" he said in response to my look.

"Of course I did." I skimmed through the outline and added my own notes here and there. It wasn't bad at all. But then, Bambleby has been published before, dozens of times; I suppose I'd just always assumed that his students did everything for him.

"You haven't included anything about your encounter with the snow prince," I said. "If that's what he was."

"What would I say? That I fought and killed him with a sword forged from tears? I wish to raise eyebrows at ICODEF, but not for that reason."

I didn't reply. In truth, I didn't like thinking back to that scene by the cave. I was used to recording stories of the Folk—I had not expected to become one, had never wished to. I was supposed to remain comfortably outside the stories with my pen and my notebook. I could tell it didn't bother Wendell in the least, and why would it? He *was* a story; he had proven that when he had taken the impossible ice sword and driven back our enemy with the ease of breathing, his blade flashing too quickly for me to follow it. I'd had no idea he was capable of something like that—magic, yes. Displays of physical skill, the sort of skill that requires training and effort? No. Since that night, I feel as if the ground has altered slightly beneath the two of us, as if I cannot see him from precisely the same angle I used to.

"You still haven't explained yourself, by the way," he said, picking at a loose thread on his jumper. "How did you know to pull that sword out of the snow? Sometimes, Em, you are so terrifyingly competent in your dealings with the Folk that I begin to suspect you are a magician."

I snorted. "One doesn't need magic if one knows enough stories." I examined him. "Do you have any doubts about all this? What if the scholarly community learns what you are? Most will fear and distrust you. A select few may try to have you shot and stuffed like one of Davidson's brownies."

He leaned his chair on its back legs. "Nobody at Cambridge will believe it, in the unlikely event that any of them find out what Hrafnsvik thinks of me. Just in case, I'll get out in front of the whole thing when I return, and tell them that our guileless villagefolk were so impressed by our success in the field that they thought us both faeries. That will get a laugh at ICODEF.

Most of our tenured colleagues rarely require much convincing as to the gullibility of the peasantry. You know that, Em—remember the trouble you had giving co-author credit to that Welsh shepherd for your paper on faerie mounds? Your peer reviewers wouldn't let it go to print."

I remembered very well, and thought he was probably right. So what was I worried about? And why was I worried? Surely it was of little importance to me if Bambleby's secret got out. But he was my friend, and I thought he was handling the issue far too lightly.

We were interrupted by a knock at the door. It was one of Aud's sons with a delivery of dried wildflowers, polished shells, and a colourful array of mushrooms that must have taken days of labour to retrieve. Bambleby accepted it perfunctorily and closed the door in the young man's face.

"What on earth am I to do with this?" he muttered, setting the basket down on the table with a clink. "Open an apothecary?"

"They don't know what you want," I said, smothering laughter. "They only know what they give to their own Folk in exchange for their services. You could simply tell them you prefer silver." For this is the customary offering in Ireland, at least for the courtly fae. Almost every species of Folk disdains human metals, yet the Irish fae are unique in their ability to tolerate—and, indeed, to love—silver. It is said that they fill their vast, dark forests with silver mirrors like jewels, which drink in the little sun and starlight that penetrates the boughs and reflect it back at the will of the Folk; it is also said that they use silver to construct fantastical staircases that wind up and up those vast trunks, and bridges that hang between them like delicate necklaces.

"It doesn't matter, for I can't accept any of it," he said moodily. "I made no agreement with these people. I went on that mad goose chase for you."

I frowned a little, remembering our strange, one-sided bargain. "Then I shall buy you a fine set of cutlery upon our return," I said. "As for Aud and the rest, I recommend that you affect a strong predilection for fungi, and declare their debt to you repaid."

"This is all your fault," he said. "If we had only *pretended* to go after those two, like I wanted—"

"Lilja and Margret would be dead or worse," I said. "Is *that* what you wanted?"

He took his time in thinking it over. "No, it isn't. Though I can't imagine the thought troubles *you* much, Em. Lilja came by twice to thank you, and will be back again, count on it. I did not bother to tell her that your motives were not kindhearted at all."

I felt a prickle of disquiet. After all, it was true that I had rescued Lilja and Margret not for their own sakes, but for scholarship. From that perspective, there was nothing to thank me for; indeed, I had as much reason to thank them for getting themselves captured and allowing me the opportunity of witnessing the Hidden Ones' fair.

I went back to drumming my fingertips. Something was nagging at me. I recognized the sensation, though I knew not what it signified, other than that I was missing something important. There was a pattern here in Hrafnsvik; I could feel the edges of it.

I needed time with my notes.

"Oh, God," he said. "I know that look. What dreadful imposition is in store for me now?"

Trust Bambleby to think himself always at the centre of my thoughts. "There is no imposition. I would like you to leave me in peace for a few hours, if that is something within your capabilities."

"I suppose so," he said grudgingly, though I was not flattered by his reluctance to leave my side; Bambleby hates to be without company to talk at. Well, no doubt he would find ready listeners down at the tavern, if he grew bored.

He surprised me, though, when he informed me after breakfast that he intended to go for a stroll.

"I thought you had given up hope of finding your door here," I said. For so I had assumed, given that he had made only the most cursory of efforts.

"Did I say anything about a door?" he said over his shoulder as he pulled his cloak on.

I groaned. "What is the point in being mysterious now? Are there any secrets of yours I don't know?"

"Oh, I'd say there are a few outstanding."

I rolled my eyes and went back to my notes. I couldn't be bothered with him now. "Well, don't go harassing poor Poe again. You're not likely to find such a door in the Karrðarskogur. The courtly fae of Ljosland move their realm about, yes? But only spatially; they dwell forever in winter. The door you seek must be fixed, given that your own realm is fixed—I say *must*, though I am speaking in theoretical terms, of course, as I have never encountered such a phenomenon myself, and can only extrapolate from the literature—so it stands to reason that if it is anywhere, it will be in a place of permanent winter. Namely, a glacier or high peak that never loses its snowpack. I should note here, of course, that I think it highly unlikely that a door such as the one you seek is in this country; there is too little affinity between your realm and that of the Hidden Ones. It is most likely to be found in a similar woodland landscape, green and wet with plenty of oak groves to drink in the small magics of the common fae and create spaces for such portals to manifest—if indeed their existence is the result of mere accident or chance. These sorts of rabbit hole doors—back entrances, if you like—are often said to be accidental, in the stories. Northern Europe is the most likely location; perhaps one of the warmer forests of Russia."

He stood unmoving with his hand on the door, staring at me.

"Yes, I know that's a lot of conjecture," I said, misreading the look on his face. "I've not had time to give it much thought."

He smiled at me, his eyes shining a little too brightly in the way they sometimes did. "We are going to make a very good team, Em."

I snorted to cover the heat rising in my face. "So far, our teamwork seems rather unevenly distributed."

"I may be of use to you yet, my dear dragon." He left me, pulling the door shut softly behind him.

23rd November

After paying a visit to Poe this morning, I returned to find Bambleby vanished yet again. Clearly, he is still looking for his door—why does he bother being so bloody secretive about it? And why not enlist me to help?

Feeling put out, I wandered about the cottage for a while, eyeing the various knickknacks he'd cluttered the space up with and wishing I could be more offended by them. I ran my finger over the mantel—not a speck of dust. I recalled how dingy the place had been when I moved in, yet I'd never observed him dusting.

Perhaps in anticipation of my displeasure, he had left several completed diagrams of basalt rock formations on the table, those which the villagers said were inhabited by the "little ones." This section of the paper I'd assigned to him—at least he had gotten something done. I read over the summary he'd left beneath the diagrams—it was brief, but acceptable.

I sat down to work but found my mind wandering. The weather outside had a quality of softness one finds only in winter; clouds drifted in and away, dreamlike, loosing handfuls of white. The wind was from the north and carried the smell of sulphur from some invisible mountain spring.

I put my pen down and pulled on my cloak and boots. We had a healthy supply of wood, but I wanted some exertion.

The first log split eventually, though I had to take a few swings at it. The second was riddled with knots, and it went flying sideways when my axe struck it. As I went to dig it out of the snow, I heard the soft press of booted footsteps.

"Emily!" Lilja called. Margret trailed behind, both of them smiling at me. "We've just been giving Ulfar a hand unloading supplies at the dock, and came to see if you'd like to join us for some wine. Thora's been complaining about the drinks again, so he thought he'd try ordering a few French bottles."

"Thank you," I said, "but I wouldn't wish to interrupt your chores. Also, I prefer not to imbibe so early in the day."

Lilja's face fell. Only once the words were out of my mouth did I realize how they sounded. "I don't mean to say that it's too early to drink," I clarified. "Only that I do not drink much generally, and thus it is too early for *me*. But those who drink frequently would likely disagree."

They gazed at me, brows furrowed. *Oh, well done*, I thought. How was it that in trying to remove my foot from my mouth, I invariably managed to shove it in even deeper?

I began to sputter something else, but fortunately Lilja spoke first. "You look like you're improving," she said, gesturing at the axe. "Would you like me to give you a lesson?"

I almost wept at her kindness. "Thank you," I murmured.

Looking amused, she took the axe away from me. "I'll show you how I do it, then you can try again."

Margret settled on another stump to watch. Lilja arranged the piece of trunk, rotating it a little in the unthinking way of expertise, changed her stance, then brought the axe down in a swift arc. The wood split, though not quite in half.

"That's how I like to do it," Lilja explained as she picked up the larger half and set it back on the stump. In her callused, capable hands, the axe seemed light and small. "It's easier to split if you strike the edge, not the centre. Now I can do this—"

She swung again, and the piece cleaved in two. "And there you have it. About right for your stove?"

I nodded. I admit I would not have thought I could be impressed by this sort of rustic skill, but Lilja made it look like an art. "You must be much in demand in the village," I said.

"I can split a full cord in an hour," she said, not boasting, but by way of answer. "I've been doing this since I was seven. I wouldn't want any other job."

"And do you also enjoy this form of exercise?" I asked Margret, who had been sitting quietly, swinging her feet with a little smile on her face.

Margret grimaced. "I'd rather be inside at my piano, or reading a book. Chopping wood is Lilja's job. She keeps me warm."

Lilja blushed at her, and then she looked at me with such warmth and gratitude that I found myself asking inanely, "And are there different categories of axe?"

Lilja was very patient with me. She showed me how to grip the axe—I'd been going about it all wrong, apparently, swinging it like a hatchet.

"See these lines?" she said, pointing to the split side of a log, where a network of cracks sliced through the grain. "That's where you aim. I'd go for this one here, myself." She traced it with her finger. "That way you avoid the knot. See?"

"You may be overestimating my skill if you are expecting me to aim at anything smaller than the log itself."

She laughed. "Just do your best."

There was something in the comfortable way she said it that made me feel easier. I split the log in only two strokes. I managed to hit one of the cracks in the next piece, and it divided with a single blow.

Margret clapped. "Well done!" Lilja exclaimed, beaming as if I'd completed a marathon. In truth, I did feel rather proud of myself. It's funny how the practice of such simple, ancient skills can put one at ease.

My progress, though, was rather uneven. My aim began to improve under Lilja's instruction, but I did not have her strength, and I could not be comfortable swinging something so deadly about, particularly after the fiasco with Wendell. After we'd accumulated a little pile between us, she and Margret helped me cart it inside, and I found myself inviting them to stay for tea, though my notes scowled accusingly at me from the table.

"How cosy!" Margret said, and they both looked around the cottage admiringly. For some reason, I did not inform them that the cosiness was all Wendell's making. Not once have I been complimented on my apartments at Cambridge. Well, I spend most of my time in the library or my office, so what does it matter?

Lilja asked if Wendell was in, and both looked relieved when I shook my head.

"Surely you aren't frightened of him?" I enquired.

"Oh, no!" Margret said a little too quickly. "We're very grateful to him for helping us."

"Yes," Lilja said, and I understood then that they *were* afraid of Wendell, very much so, and eager to avoid offending him.

I sensed Margret wanted to pursue the subject of Wendell somehow, but she said nothing more as I made tea. I was relieved they hadn't mentioned the tavern again—I doubt I will ever be easy in such places, particularly when all in attendance insist on approaching you for a warm-hearted sort of chat, full of praise and gratitude that I have no more idea what to do with than one of Thora's skeins of yarn and some knitting needles.

We chatted about my research and my forthcoming ICODEF presentation with Bambleby, and then as I poured the tea, Margret said in a bit of a rush, "Then you and Wendell are not—an item?"

I blinked at her. "I—no. Of course not. We are colleagues. And friends, I suppose," I added grudgingly.

"I didn't think so," Lilja said, giving Margret a *just as I said* sort of look. "What with how he carries on with the village girls."

But Margret's brow was furrowed. "I only thought— The way he looks at you—"

The way he looks at me? I thought about the way Wendell looked at me sometimes, particularly when he thought I wasn't aware of it, and then I felt hot, then cold, then hot again. "I don't know what you mean," I said, turning away to conceal my blush. Good grief, you'd think I was a girl of sixteen.

Lilja kicked Margret. "She probably has someone back home, you goose."

"Do you?" Margret said.

"Oh, no." I busied myself with the toast—one of Poe's palest, softest breads. "I'm always much too busy for that sort of thing."

Margret blinked. "Then—then there's never been *anyone* you fancied?"

"Oh, of course," I said, much relieved that the subject had shifted from Wendell. "There was Leopold—he and I were together a year. We were studying for our doctorates at Cambridge at the same time. He went away to Tübingen afterwards on a fellowship. He asked me to come along, but obviously it was out of the question."

Lilja waited, as if expecting me to go on. "And—that's it?" When I looked at her blankly, she seemed embarrassed and said, "That's it. I see."

Margret was not so tactful. "*One?* That's it? I've been with more men than that, and I don't even like them. And you're—"

She squinted, clearly attempting to assess my age—the furrow in her brow boded an unfavourable conclusion. Lilja elbowed her.

"I suppose I'm just—" I thought it over. "Choosy."

Lilja smiled. "Choosy. I like that."

Margret leaned back with a snort of laughter. "I wish this one had been a little more choosy before I came along."

Lilja kicked her. "Rude."

"You know what else is rude?" Margret leaned towards me. "Burning down a stranger's barn on account of a broken heart."

"Erika didn't burn down your barn!" Lilja said. "It's still standing."

"Thanks to the rainstorm, not her." To me, Margret added, "Lilja has a habit of romancing madwomen."

"I do not!"

"Either that or you turn them mad, then. I suppose I'll be locked up in due course. Perhaps after I set the village alight."

Lilja threw a tea towel at her. It had the cadence of an old argument, and I found myself laughing along with them.

After tea, Margret again invited me down to the tavern, growing quite insistent, in a good-natured way, when I refused. After glancing at me, Lilja put a hand on her arm.

"That's all right," she said. "We should be getting home anyway. My mother likes us to help with the supper." She paused. "Why don't I come round tomorrow for another lesson? I think with a little more instruction, you'll be a natural. If you can fit it in among your research?"

I assured her that I could—I was surprised by how much I'd enjoyed the experience, as well as their company, particularly as it had not involved the company of a dozen others. She gave me another warm smile, and she and Margret departed.

26th November

I spent most of the day poring over my notes and re-reading my journal, unable to focus on either the paper or my encyclopaedia, still beset by the certainty that I was missing something. I turned eventually to my books, in particular those collections of ancient faerie stories in various iterations that dryadologists love more than anything to debate—which version should be given primacy; whether similar tales told in differing regions share a primogenitor. Bambleby had absconded again, and I was left to my fretting until past midday, when there came a knock on the door.

Expecting Lilja and the welcome distraction of another woodcutting lesson, I was surprised to instead find Aud, looking determined. "He did not like our gifts," she said without preamble.

I sighed. I considered telling her that Bambleby required no gifts, but she wouldn't understand that—favours granted by the Folk must always be repaid in a manner that satisfies them, which is not the same as saying that the values must be equal by human standards. I cast my gaze around the room, and it fell upon Wendell's sewing kit.

"Have you any silver needles?" I said. I had observed that Wendell's were made from bone.

Aud nodded slowly, looking puzzled. "Will that suffice?"

"I expect he'd like a mirror or two," I said. "To hang on the wall. But only if they are handsome. And chocolate," I added with some pique, because surely *I* deserved a gift too, for my efforts.

Aud nodded, looking pleased. She went away again, and an hour later, all that I had requested was delivered by one of Bambleby's conquests, the little dark-haired one, who looked both relieved and disappointed to find him absent. I understood how she felt, for I had finally worked out what had been bothering me and was beside myself with excitement to share it with him.

But evening set in, and there was still no sign of him. I decided to go down to the tavern—no doubt I would find him there, happily ensconced in awe and admiration. But when I pushed through the door, only the familiar faces of the villagers gazed back at me. To my horror, they burst into applause and began clapping me on the shoulders. Several of the women hugged me—I didn't note which ones, as my senses were temporarily overwhelmed by this onslaught.

"Leave her be, leave her be," Thora's voice grumbled, and her bony hand wrapped round my wrist and pulled me to her usual cosy and out-of-the-way nook next to the fire.

"Thank you," I murmured, collapsing into the other chair.

She gave a rumble of laughter. "The way you froze! You looked like a startled badger."

I didn't argue with her unflattering choice of metaphor, merely folded myself deeper into the chair. "Have you seen Wendell?"

"Why would I know where that creature's gotten to? He's your faerie. What's the matter?"

I nearly bit my tongue in consternation. My faerie! Good grief. "Nothing is the matter. Only I believe I've worked out the reason why your village has lost so many to the tall ones in recent years. And why it will keep happening, if nothing is done to stop it."

I hadn't meant to tell her, but the words just spilled out of me in my excitement. Thora's face hardened, and she held up a hand. "Wait a moment, girl."

Seconds later, Thora had dragged Aud over to join our tête-à-tête. "What's all this, Emily?" she said, grasping my hand warmly.

"The changeling," I said. "Before his arrival in Hrafnsvik, your village lost few youths to the Hidden Ones. All your stories concur about that—once in a generation, perhaps, often less frequently. Neighbouring villages have not been similarly affected, which means there is something about Hrafnsvik that draws them."

"They wish to take the child back, then?" Aud said, puzzled.

"No. It is a motif that appears often in the literature, which has been called the lantern theory—" I stumbled to a stop. How did I explain this to ordinary people? How did I explain that the stories they tell to children, or for diversion on cold nights spent by the fire, held the deepest of truths—that they were in fact keys to unlocking the secrets of the Folk? "It's as if—the Folk are drawn to places of great magic. Changelings require the greatest magic of all, to take a faerie child and embed him in the mortal realm so securely he cannot be removed. And your changeling is especially powerful. And so the courtly fae are drawn here, even if they themselves have no connection to him, perhaps without even realizing they are being drawn."

Aud's brows were knitted together. "A lantern. Yes. But how do we put the light out?"

"There's only one way." Thora's voice was hard, but she reached out one weathered hand and rested it on Aud's shoulder. "It's what I've been saying for years, Aud. You said no, when it was just Mord and Aslaug that creature was hurting. But it's the whole village now. Which of our children will be taken next, if we do nothing?"

"Ari," Aud said as she let out her breath. "I'm godmother to that child."

"Yes." Thora's voice didn't soften. "And how many other children are you godmother to?"

Aud pressed her hand to her eyes. When she took it away, she looked much older, and I saw the kinship between her and Thora there like a reflection out of time. But Aud didn't acquiesce; instead, she fixed me with a hard look, as if to say, *Well?*

"If we knew his name," I began unsteadily. "The changeling's true name. We could use it to banish him."

Thora leaned back in her chair with a dismissive sound. "We know *that*. You don't think we tried to trick him into telling us, when he first came here? They guard their names closely."

Aud said nothing, merely kept her eyes on me.

"Let me think on it," I said. "Do nothing for now. Please."

"Don't think too long," Thora said, her face dark. "We heard the bells again last night. They've never sounded so regularly before. They will take another child, and soon."

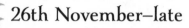

26th November–late

I don't know what to make of this development, which has unnerved me more than any changeling or faerie beast ever could. Perhaps putting my thoughts to pen and paper will help.

After my conversation with Aud and Thora, I went back to the cottage. Wendell had still not returned, and after about an hour, I decided to search for him. We nearly ran into each other on the path leading up the mountain; he came strolling out of the twilight with his hands buried in his pockets and his gaze downcast, frowning and lost in thought. Crystals of snow nestled in his golden hair, which was very distracting. I am used to ignoring his good looks, but that hair of his is a difficult matter. I've observed that most people are taken in by his smile or his eyes, but for me, it's that damned hair—one can't help imagining what it feels like, is the problem.

He lifted his eyes when he heard my footfall, and his face lit. "There you are, Em! Slinking about in the half-light, how very like you."

I didn't bother asking where he'd been. If he wanted to be secretive, let him. Shoving aside my relief at his return, which filled me with an unaccountable feeling of lightness, I said, "I need your help."

"Of course you do. Can we get out of this bloody cold, at least? You won't believe it, but I have a hankering for one of Ulfar's mutton chops—"

I grabbed his hand and dragged him back to the cottage. He seemed a little taken aback, but let himself be dragged, his graceful fingers closing around mine.

"I need his name," I said as soon as we were indoors. "The changeling's true name. How do I make him tell me what it is?"

He gave me a puzzled look. "If you haven't figured that out by now, I doubt you ever will."

I threw up my hands. "Just tell me."

"I don't know how. That's why I said that if *you* haven't figured it out by now, I—"

"Oh, God." I threw myself into one of the chairs. "You couldn't be any less helpful if you tried. I think you are trying."

"Not especially." He sat opposite me. "Why does it matter what the creature's name is?"

I told him what I'd told Aud and Thora. He groaned.

"So now we have to rescue the entire village, do we?" He folded his hands and scowled. "Thank you, but I've had my fill of philanthropy."

"It isn't philanthropy. We still know nothing about this changeling—where it comes from, why it's here. It's a gaping hole in our research. If we can fill it—"

He waved his hand. "We've made enough discoveries already to impress the entirety of academia. 'Further research needed, blah blah blah,' we will write in our conclusion."

"This isn't just about the paper! It's about my book, Wendell. Our knowledge of changelings is inchoate—not just those of Ljosland. There is more to be learned here, and I cannot leave without turning over every stone."

He made no response to that, only gave a tremendous sigh and put his head in his hand.

"In the stories, Folk are tricked into revealing their names," I said. "The one of Linden Fell, for instance—his wife pretended to give birth and then brought him a lamb wrapped in swaddling clothes to look like a child, all so that he would write his name on the baptismal certificate."

Wendell laughed. "I'd sooner freeze to death than write my true name in ink, even if my wife hurled a dozen brats at me. These things are not as easy as they are in stories."

I got up and paced. "We could threaten him."

"Threats must be buttressed with deeds. I'm not interested in tormenting children, no matter how much their parents deserve it."

He frowned at me as he said it, which I ignored, as I was not about to be lectured by Bambleby on matters of morality. I felt little regret over my initial interrogation of the changeling, given the anguish he had inflicted upon his foster parents.

I stopped at the table, playing absently with one of the parcels Aud had delivered. "These are for you, by the way."

He only sighed again. "I told you, I can't accept their gratitude."

"I chose them," I said. "Not Aud. You may think of them as gifts from me."

He looked intrigued and a little alarmed. "From you? Are they covered in thorns?"

He unwrapped the mirrors first, exclaiming over them. They were indeed handsome, as I had requested, with frames made from sun-bleached driftwood carved with intricate patterns of leaves complete with pearl dewdrops. Aud had been clever in her selections, I thought. Wendell spent nearly an hour working out where to hang them, first setting them in one location, then moving them elsewhere. Naturally, they looked beautiful everywhere, and when he was finally finished, the room was even cosier than it had been before.

"Oh, Em," he said, gazing into the mirror he'd hung behind the fireplace, which trapped the flickering light and turned it into something golden and summery—doubtless not an effect mortal hands could have achieved. "You do have a heart after all, somewhere buried deep. Very deep."

"There are also these," I said grudgingly, hoping to head off any mistiness. Unfortunately it was not to be, for Wendell was no sooner gazing at the silver sewing needles than he was brushing away a tear.

"They are like my father's," he said wonderingly. "I remember the flicker of them in the darkness as we all sat together by the *ghealach* fire, with the trees surrounding us. He would bring them everywhere, even the Hunt of the Frostveiling— that is the first hunt of autumn, the largest of the year, when even the queen and her children roam through the wilds with spears and swords, riding our best—oh, I don't know what you would call them in your language. They are a kind of faerie fox, black and golden together, which grow larger than horses. My brothers and sisters and I would crowd round the fire to watch him weave nets from brambles and spidersilk. And all the moorbeasts and hag-headed deer would cower at the sight of those nets, though they barely blinked at the whistle of our arrows." He fell silent, gazing at them with his eyes gone very green.

"Well," I said, predictably at a loss for an answer to this, "I hope they are of use to you. Only keep them away from any garments of mine."

He took my hand, and then, before I knew what he was doing, lifted it to his mouth. I felt the briefest brush of his lips against my skin, and then he had released me and was back to exclaiming over his gifts. I turned and went into the kitchen in an aimless haste, looking for something to do, anything that might distract me from the warmth that had trailed up my arm like an errant summer breeze, and settled for preparing a light repast from the remains of our provisions.

After we ate, I watched him play with the mirrors. When he touched them, strange things appeared—for an instant, I saw a green forest reflected back at me, boughs swaying. I blinked and it was gone, but some of its greenness lingered around the edges of the glass, as if a forest still lurked somewhere beyond the frame.

"Are those the trees you would see in your kingdom?" I asked.

He let out his breath and drew his hand away. "No," he said quietly. "That was merely a shadow of my world."

I gazed at him a moment longer. His mourning was a tangible thing that hung in the air. I have never loved a place like he has, and felt its absence as I would a friend's. But for a moment, I wished I had, and felt this as its own loss.

A strange surety flowed through me like a swallow of cold water. "*Of course.*"

He turned. "What?"

But I was already moving. I fetched the faerie cloak from outside with trembling hands. The fire was high, as Bambleby liked it that way, and the cloak began its steady *drip drip drip* on the floorboards. I dug around in the pockets, fingers brushing against the edges of things that clanked or rustled.

Focus. I drew a breath, plunged my hand inside again, putting every ounce of will and thought into imagining what I needed. And finally, my hand closed on something.

I withdrew it. I was holding a doll. It was carved from whalebone and had hair of willow boughs. Its dress was of dirty, undyed wool the colour of snow, the old snow that is left behind in springtime. And yet the doll was clearly Folk, for it changed— just a little—from one moment to another, and in different lights. When I turned it to the firelight, it seemed to wash the pale dress with gold.

Wendell took it from me and turned it over and over in his hand, frowning.

"It's a token of Ari's home," I said. "The changeling's home, I mean. Something he will recognize."*

Wendell blinked at it a moment longer. "Ah. I see. But I don't think—"

"We shall have to find out," I said in a cool voice, while my heart hammered madly.

🌿 **Aslaug opened the** door for us. Mord was out walking by the sea, she said, something that struck me as strange, for not only was it dark, but Mord does not like to leave his wife alone in the house. She did not admit us, only stood in the doorway, frowning as the winter wind gusted inside and ruffled her thin dress—far too thin for the time of year.

"May we come in, Aslaug?" Wendell said, wrinkling his eyes in a charming smile. He must have put magic into it, for she blinked as if hit with a gust of summer rain, and stepped back.

The house was so cold I could see my breath. Aslaug went back to lighting the fire. The floor before the fireplace was scattered with at least a hundred spent matches and kindling, and the fireplace itself was filled with snow. Despite this, Aslaug had piled firewood in it, as if she could not see the snow or expected it to light regardless.

---

* Such tokens are a motif of changeling folklore. In the stories, they are commonly found in the possession of the changeling; if wrested away, he or she weakens or vanishes entirely, but they can also be used to threaten or cajole the creature into good behaviour. It was commonplace in early- to mid-nineteenth century Britain for museums to maintain collections of supposed "changeling tokens," most of which were of questionable provenance; Danielle de Grey wrote a scathing paper on the subject. Unfortunately, to make her point, she also stole a number of tokens from the University of Edinburgh and replaced each with a cap and bells. The rector was unamused, and the result was a short stay in Edinburgh Prison for de Grey, her second but, sadly, not her last brush with incarceration.

"How long has she been at that?" Wendell wondered. "Aslaug, dear, come away from there. Let's get you warm again."

He bustled around, sweeping the snow into a pot, building the fire, and grimacing at the mess—for the place was a warren of unwashed dishes, ash, and bits of the outdoors scattering the unswept floor. Though he did little that I could see besides shake off a rug and straighten the jumble of plates and cups, the room seemed to brighten. Aslaug remained on her knees by the fire, gazing into the flames and taking no further notice of our presence. At least her shivering had stopped.

Meanwhile, I took up one of the cast iron pots and filled it with embers and kindling—I had been inspired, you see, by the bogles and their cookpots.

Poe had said that the tall ones feared only fire. Well, we would see how deep that fear ran.

I made my way to the staircase, from which a cold wind funnelled, somehow conspiring to bring darkness with it that fought against the new light in the sitting room.

"Will you stop faffing about?" I called over my shoulder, for we weren't here to tidy. Casting a last scowl over his shoulder at the mess, Wendell followed me up the stairs.

The changeling was crouched in a corner this time, and as I entered the room he gave a horrible shriek and sent a pack of snarling white wolves charging at me from a wall of snow, their muzzles crusted with blood. Though I had expected frightful visions, the suddenness of the onslaught made me fall back a step. Bambleby caught me before I tumbled down the stairs.

"There there," he said, stepping in front of me. The wolves vanished instantly. "Tantrums will get you nowhere with this one. She's perfectly heartless and will take no pity on you whatsoever. I speak from experience."

He spoke in Faie, words that vibrated in the air like a song, an effect I could never achieve, no matter how hard I worked on my accent. The changeling stilled, his pale face upturned like a baby bird's, and I could see that he heard an echo of his own kin in Wendell's voice.

"Go away," he said, but there was a miserable hopefulness in it. Wendell turned to me with a look of woe that I ignored.

I drew the doll from my cloak. The air chilled further, and every line in the changeling's body tensed. He whispered something that sounded like "Mersa." Then, "Where did you get that?"

"Do you want it back?" I said. I placed the pot of flickering flames upon the floor. "You may have it, if you give us your name."

The changeling seemed too stunned to speak. He still looked like a faerie, too pale and sharp, but there was more of the child in him now, all wide eyes and confused longing. But I paused only a moment before dropping the doll into the flames.

The changeling screamed. He lunged at me, and would possibly have torn me to shreds had not Wendell been there to hold him back.

"Emily!" Wendell said in a scandalized voice, because of course he could take pleasure in bloody *decapitation*, but something like this would distress him. He need not have feared, though, for I had snatched the doll from the flames before it could suffer serious damage. It was only melted a little.

"I'll ask again," I said over the creature's wails. "What is your name?"

In the end, it was easy. The changeling sobbed and raged at us. He made the room darken and fill with snow that struck us like tiny blades. But then I held up the doll again, the only token of home he'd seen in all the miserable years he'd spent in Hrafnsvik, separated from his own family and world, and placed it in the flames, and he finally shrieked, "*Aðlinduri!*"

I removed the doll instantly and handed it to him. The faerie clutched it to his chest, still sobbing. The tears didn't fall, but froze to his face in braided tracks like an icebound river.

Wendell was shaking his head at me. "You are even colder than I thought, Em," he said, and yet mixed with his complaint was something like fondness. He made no argument as we went to retrieve two of Krystjan's horses and even offered to ride with the changeling. Aslaug had not looked up from the fire as we left the house, other than to shudder as the door opened, and Mord had not returned, and so neither of them had the chance, should they have wanted it, to bid adieu to the creature they had housed and cared for during the darkest years of their lives.

A light snow fell as we rode into the mountains. Aðlinduri sniffled, and did not speak other than when we commanded him by name to direct our horses. But as we travelled farther, he sat up straighter and craned his neck to look in all directions. Misery mixed with a desperate sort of longing in his eyes.

"There you are," Wendell said to him. "You indeed have cause for cheer. You are going home."

The changeling burst into weeping again, and Wendell gave me a baffled look.

We rode for perhaps an hour with the snow tapping at our cheeks before we came to a little gully where the mountainside folded itself around a grove of misshapen willows. Even if the changeling hadn't directed us there, I would have taken it for a faerie door of some sort; though there are many sorts of doors, they all have a similar quality which can best—and quite inadequately—be described as *unusual*. A round ring of mush-rooms is the obvious example, but one must additionally be on the lookout for large, hoary trees that dwarf their neighbours; for twisted trunks and gaping hollows; for wildflowers out of sync with the forest's floral denizens; for patterns of things; for mounds and depressions and inexplicable clearings. Anything that does not fit. The willows before us leaned into one another like fingers interlacing, with a narrow gap at either end. They had a sickly aspect, skeletal and half covered in some sort of lichen.

Wendell dismounted and then lowered the changeling down to the snow. He was still clutching his doll tight to his chest—some of its hair seemed to have refrozen, but not all. Guilt nudged at me, and I could not quash it this time, so I did what I was used to doing with troublesome feelings and shoved it down deep until it was buried by other things.

"Where are we?" I said, for I was struck by an inexplicable certainty that we had come farther than we should have in an hour's time. I had not noticed when the mountains stopped being familiar, when we came into this valley between two long, blue glaciers. Behind us was a seam in the landscape through which the earth breathed out its sulphurous smoke, warm and wet against my cheek. "We are not in the Karrðarskogur?"

"Not for some time," Wendell said absently, as if this fact were of no material importance. And I suppose it wasn't—provided we could get back.

The changeling stood hesitating before the willow grove. For a shadow of a second, I thought I saw a hallway between the boughs, lit with moon-coloured lanterns, beyond which a stair led into the earth and another spiralled up towards a tower made of ice. Then a faerie stepped out of the grove.

She was both like and unlike the Folk I had seen at the winter fair. She was tall and lovely and sharp-edged, and the starlight reflected off her strangely as she moved, like a lake with pebbles dropped into it. But her shoulders were bowed as if beneath a weight, and her grey clothing was tattered and so indistinct she might have been wearing a many-layered sack. Her black hair was tied up and thick with frost.

Her astonished gaze took in the child first, and then swept to Wendell, who was closer than I. "Who are you?" she demanded. "Why have you brought this sorrow upon us?"

"*Mother*," the changeling sobbed, and rushed forward. The faerie woman caught him up in her arms and covered him in kisses. "There, there, my love. There, there."

"My apologies, lady, if I have overstepped." Wendell swept her a bow. "My friend and I thought it best to return your child, who was, I'm sorry to say, quite unhappy where you left him."

"Idiot," she spat. "Who are you, to involve yourself in our doings? Some feckless wanderer from the summerlands, with little more than moss between his ears. You were bored, is that it?"

"You have company in characterizing me so," Wendell said, unperturbed. "And yet why make such a to-do about this? You would have had to fetch him back yourself, eventually."

Her hands tightened on her son's small back. She murmured to him, and he ran between the trees without a backwards glance. A whisper of music filtered through the grove, and I fell into a momentary daze. The faerie woman faced Wendell with cold fury in her eyes, and then—I cannot describe what happened next, other than to say that it was like being struck by something, a wave perhaps. Though not physically—I know, I am making little sense. Already disoriented by the music, I staggered about in a trance of some sort, and came back to myself in Wendell's arms—he had caught me before I could fall, and held me upright.

The faerie woman, meanwhile, had collapsed gracefully to her knees. She placed both hands in the snow and pressed her whole face into it. "Forgive me, your highness," she murmured.

"No, no, no," Wendell said. "None of that. I'm not anybody's highness anymore."

She gazed at him with confusion in her eyes, which slowly cleared. "You are only a child."

"Good grief!" he said. "I will have you all know that, by the measure of the mortal world, I am quite advanced in years."

She glanced at me for the first time, her nose wrinkling. Then, to my horror, she said, "And who is this, a pet of yours?"

Wendell gave a nervous laugh. "I would not recommend pursuing that line of inquiry."

"Well, what do you want?" she said, shifting in the uncanny way of the Folk from humility to rudeness in the space of a breath. "Are you here on business of theirs?"

"I don't know who you mean, but regardless, the answer is no. This business with your son is part and parcel of my plan to return to my kingdom, from which I have been banished."

"A quest?" she said, remarkably unconfused by the illogic of his statement.

"Of a sort." He cast me a brief glower. "A rather winding, meandering one, but one cannot always be fortunate in these cases."

"Who has cursed your trees?" I cut in. It was not what I wanted to ask first, but many of the Folk value indirectness. I was pleased by the coolness in my voice, for I was still wobbly from whatever enchantment the faerie had blasted us with, and also my pride was smarting from the *pet* nonsense.

"It's not only the trees," she said, after eyeing me curiously for a moment. "We are all of us cursed. Root and branch, flake and frost, young and old. All allies of the old king share in his downfall and his misery." She wrapped her arms around herself. "Would that I had been trapped in a tree, like my lord. It is a kinder fate than watching your children wither like ice in the summer sea."

"Then that is why you sent him away," I murmured. My mind flicked through the stories one after another, trying to fit it all into a pattern I recognized. "Then Ari—your son—he is the old king's child?"

Wendell, who had been only half listening, stamping his feet and blowing warmth into his hands, stared at me openmouthed. The woman gave a short laugh.

"Your mortal lover has a mind like crystals," she said. "Sharp and cold. I would like her for my own."

"That's very thoughtful of you," was all he said in reply to this statement, which was appalling on a great many levels.

"Truly," the woman pressed. "Would you trade her? Your power is of the summerlands, but I will gift you with the hand of winter."

"Thank you," Wendell said; he seemed to be struggling to hold back laughter. "But I am satisfied with my hands as they are. And unless you have a key to my forest kingdom across the sea, I will not be trading my mortal lover today."

I was going to kill him.

"Em," he said, "perhaps you could explain this all to me, as you seem to have instantly grasped the situation with your crystalline mind."

"It's not difficult to grasp," I said in as icy a voice as I had in me. "She is loyal to the king in the tree. The Folk who overthrew him have cursed her and her home, and so she sent her child away to keep him safe. But she has told us that she has more than one child, and thus it would follow that she would wish to preserve the most valuable of her brood—and why else would he be of greater value than the others? Perhaps he is also in greater danger too—the changeling bond would keep him safe."

The woman nodded. "He is a bastard. Still, the queen has slain many of her husband's bastards in order to safeguard her claim to the throne."

I frowned. "Then the present monarch is—or was—married to the king in the tree?"

"She was his first wife. He put her aside and married someone else. She sought revenge, and got it, for much of the nobility preferred her to both the second queen and the king. She locked him away forever and had his bride slain."

My head spun, sorting through all this, though I was used to hearing tales of the complicated tangle of murder and intrigue of faerie courts.

Wendell did not appear particularly interested in this information. He had turned up the collar of his cloak and was back to blowing into his hands. "Well, we will take back the mortal child now, if you would be so kind. I am afraid my blood is too thin for lengthy convocations in this weather."

The faerie woman, with characteristic changeability that I suspected I would never grow used to, now seemed to view the unwanted return of her son after a years-long absence as something akin to a minor inconvenience. Her initial fury forgotten, she shrugged and turned towards the grove.

"Wait," I said. The faerie woman paused at the edge of the trees, fixing me with her grey-blue gaze. "Why did the nobility side with the queen?"

She watched me a moment longer, and I could no more read her expression than I could name all the colours in the snow. "The old king was chivalrous," she said at last. "He abided by the ancient laws set down by our ancestors. Namely: we must have fair dealings with the mortals of this land. Kindness is met with kindness, evil with evil. He forbade us from taking them for our entertainment."

My hands clenched. "And the present queen does not."

"The queen?" She smiled. "Oh, the queen and her children have—peculiar appetites. They pluck mortals from their homes like apples ripe from the tree, then drain them dry. It is the sort of sport that suits the fancy of many of the nobility."

🌿 **We made good** time on the return journey, for I had noted and memorized every direction given to us by the changeling, even the smallest commands he gave to the horse, taking her left around a frozen puddle rather than right, for instance. Ari—the true Ari—had been returned to us in an enchanted daze, and soon slipped into sleep swaddled in blankets against Bambleby's chest. He was pale and had clearly been underfed, as is common with human children kept by the Folk, for time is not the same in faerie realms, and also the Folk are thought to be irresponsible child minders. But he appeared well otherwise, clad in a dress and cloak of finely woven lambswool and boots stuffed with straw.

Nobody answered our knock at Mord and Aslaug's door—it was then nearing midnight—but it was unlocked, and so we went inside and laid the child down upon the changeling's bed, which had also been Ari's, long ago.

As we were arranging the blankets, Mord came home. He was shivering and unshaven, and he carried a long knife in his belt, and I wondered how many nights of late he'd been given to wandering the fields and cliffs after dark. He didn't seem to understand what he was seeing, and while he stood blinking at us in the doorframe, Aslaug appeared, still clad in her day clothes. Something in her face shattered, and she threw herself upon the bed, erupting into sobs, which woke Ari, who began to wail in confusion. His crying, though, was a wonderfully mundane sound, unlike anything the changeling had ever uttered. Mord gave a cry and tried to pry them apart, perhaps assuming this was all another horrible faerie trick, but Wendell and I managed to stop him. He sat down heavily on the floor, legs tucked beneath him like a child, and simply stared at his wife and son as Aslaug had stared into the fire. I think he had already decided inside himself that his son was lost, and perhaps his long walks had something to do with the knife he carried with him, ready to be put to a purpose he could never bring himself to actualize.

Wendell gave the room a good sweep with a broom he found

somewhere or perhaps conjured up himself, knocking icicles and frost from the walls, which he later explained to me were the remnants of enchantments woven by the changeling, left behind like cobwebs. I had little idea of what to do, so I simply gave Mord an awkward pat on the shoulder and made to leave. At that, he suddenly rose to his feet and wrapped me in a very strange hug (my back was to him, my arm somehow trapped between us—I have no instinct for this sort of thing) and then, still without speaking a word, he released me and went to his son's bedside.

"Well!" Wendell said after we had returned to the cottage. "What a heartwarming scene! I could get a taste for this philanthropy nonsense."

I snorted. "You will get a taste for it on rare occasions, when it suits your whims, and if you needn't exert yourself too greatly."

He shook his head, smiling. "We are not all alike, Em. You cannot simply compare me against what you know of the Folk."

"I was comparing you against *you*."

He laughed and handed me a glass of wine. I froze, my gaze falling on the mirror behind him.

"You've enchanted it!" I exclaimed, stepping forward. The mirror was filled with trees, a twilight forest that bent in the wind, tossing its branches. Leaves flickered across the glass like bright birds, and lights flashed here and there amongst the shadows. I could have been looking through a windowpane, and for a moment my head swam with the dissonance of it.

"There is nothing green in this place," he said in a complaining tone. "Even the forest is rendered in black-and-white; I feel as if I am in a movie. I must have something to rest my eyes upon."

I gazed at the forest a little longer, the sway and glimmer of it. It was—well, mesmerizing. It had a powerful resemblance to my favourite wood in the south of Cambridgeshire, where Shadow and I were wont to escape on fine summer days. Beyond the familiar curving oak at the edge of the frame should be a little stream. "Is it a faerie forest?"

"Oh—I don't know," he said. "It is leaf and bole and the scent of pine. That's all I care about."

Indeed, I did catch the faintest aroma of needles, now that I was thinking about it. Summer needles on a forest floor, warmly fragrant as they snapped underfoot.

I settled beside the fire, even though I was exhausted; in truth, I felt a little giddy. The snowy ride through that wild country; the conversation with the faerie woman—in and of itself a greater triumph than most dryadologists could hope for in their entire career. The things I had learned in a single night would give me material for a year's worth of papers. I downed the wine and sank back into my chair, my mind already dancing through the additions I would make in my encyclopaedia.

He sat with me, chattering away about our triumphant return to Cambridge and ICODEF, and myriad other things, and not expecting anything substantial in reply, which is one of my favourite qualities about him. It sounds odd to admit that I find the company of such a boisterous person restful, but perhaps it is always restful to be around someone who does not expect anything from you beyond what is in your nature.

After a while, though, I felt an unexpected guilt. "You don't have to stay with me," I said. "You can go down to the tavern and regale the villagers with the tale of our success."

"Why would I do that? I prefer your company, Em."

He said it as if it were obvious. I snorted again, assuming he was teasing me. "Over the company of a tavern filled with a rapt and grateful audience? I'm sure you do."

"Over anyone else's company." Again, he said it with some

amusement, as if wondering what I was doing speculating about something so evident.

"You are drunk," I said.

"Shall I prove it to you?"

"No, you shan't," I said, alarmed, but he was already sweeping to the floor, bending his knee and taking my hand between his.

"What in God's name are you doing?" I said between my teeth. "And why are you doing it now?"

"Shall I make an appointment?" he said, then laughed. "Yes, I believe you *would* like that. Well, name the time when it would be convenient for you to receive a declaration of love."

"Oh, get up," I said, furious now. "What sort of jest is this, Wendell?"

"You don't believe me?" He smiled, all mischief, a look I'd seen from other Folk, enough to know not to trust him one inch. "Ask for my true name, and I'll give it to you."

"Why on earth would you do that?" I demanded, yanking my hand back.

"Oh, Em," he said forlornly. "You are the cleverest dolt I have ever met."

I stared at him, my heart thundering. Of course, I am not a dolt in any sense; I had supposed he felt something for me and had only hoped he would keep it to himself. Forever. Not that a part of me didn't wish for the opposite. But that was when I assumed his feelings in that respect were equivalent to what he felt for any of the nameless women who passed in and out of his bed. And why would I lower myself to that, when he and I already had something that was vastly more valuable?

But he was offering me his *name*?

Once, while following a trail of blue foxberries in the woods east of Novosibirsk, I had tripped over a root and gone tumbling end-over-end down the side of a gully, landing with a great splash in the little stream at the bottom. Luckily, I fell into a pile of sodden leaves trapped in a side channel by the current, and not upon the sharp rocks only inches to my left. But the breath was knocked out of me entirely, and I simply lay there aching from innumerable bruises for several minutes— and yet even then, I hadn't been stunned like this.

He sighed. "Well, I don't expect you to do anything with this information. I have grown rather used to pining, so it won't put me out to keep at it, I suppose."

"I would order you to do all sorts of terrible things," I managed, though my voice sounded very far away.

"You seem to have a talent for that already."

"I would have you accompany me on every field study," I said. "I would have you rising at six and carrying my cameras and equipment everywhere. You would never escape a day of hard work again. And you would certainly have to retract all of the studies you faked."

He glared at me. "Yes, you would do all that, wouldn't you? Well then, instead, why don't you just marry me?"

I said nothing for several minutes. The only sounds were the crackle of the fire and the pit-pat of snow upon the windows. "That's a more sensible suggestion," I said.

He burst out laughing. By the time he finished, he was wiping at his eyes. "Sensible, she says. *Sensible.*"

"Well, it is," I snapped. "I didn't say we *would* marry. But why would I want your name? I don't wish to order you about like a servant. You may keep it, and your mad faerie logic, to yourself."

"Very well," he said. "Is that it, then? Your answer is no?"

"I didn't say that," I snapped, irritated and hopelessly flustered. I thought inanely that this sort of thing would never have happened with Leopold. Leopold had been predictable in every way, and as transparent as spring water. "I'm going to leave," he would announce at a dinner party he wasn't enjoying, and then he would. "I have stopped listening," he would say to a longwinded colleague, and then go back to his book. I was aware that people found him peculiar because of this, but it suited me very well. A kiss would always be preceded by "I'm going to kiss you." I don't know why anyone would mind this— it's very relaxing to know what other people are about to do. I suppose that's why we got on so well. Of course, Wendell has as much in common with Leopold as a rock has with a rooster.

The fire was suddenly far too hot, so hot I'd nearly sweated through my shirt. "Well—I—how on earth am I supposed to answer?"

He threw his hands up in exasperation. "Do you *want* to marry me?"

"That's—that's beside the point." A nonsensical reply, but it came the closest to expressing how I felt. I had never even considered *marrying* Wendell—why on earth would I? Wendell Bambleby! Certainly I'd imagined being with him in other ways, particularly since I'd grown used to having him around— travelling with him across the continent, no doubt arguing half the time; conducting research; scouring woodland and heath for lost doors to the faerie realms. And yes, I liked the prospect of being with him often, or even all the time, and felt a sort of hollowness fill me when I thought about us parting ways. But I couldn't *marry* one of the Folk, particularly not a *faerie king*, even if he was Wendell.

"It's the point in its entirety, you madwoman," he said. "Do you not find me handsome? I can change my appearance to suit whatever direction your tastes run."

"Oh, God." I pressed my face into my hands. "You are not helping."

I said nothing for a while, and he let me think without interruption. Part of the problem, I realized, was that I was not accustomed to thinking about him in such a way. And so I took his hand—tentatively, as one might reach for a ladle they thought might be hot. Then I lowered myself onto the flag-stones by the fire so that we were next to each other, our knees touching.

"What are you doing?" he said, half hopeful and half alarmed. Well, I was glad that I'd unsettled him—served him right, after throwing all *that* at me out of nowhere.

"I am only conducting a test."

He sighed. "Of course. I should have guessed you'd want to be bloodless about this."

"I am not trying to be!"

"You've done nothing but talk at me since I told you I loved you."

"Is that a problem?" For he hadn't said it as if it were. "Were you expecting me to throw myself at you? Would you have then said a dozen pretty things about my eyes or hair?"

"No, it would have been, 'Get off me, you imposter, and tell me what you did with Emily.'"

"All right, be quiet." The bloody fire hissed and crackled away, and a bead of sweat trickled down my neck. Wanting to be through with this quickly, I leaned forward and kissed him.

Almost. I lost my nerve halfway there, somewhere around the moment I noticed he had a freckle next to his eye and won-dered ridiculously if that was something he would remove if I asked it of him, and instead of a proper kiss, I merely brushed my lips against his. It was a shadow of a kiss, cool and insub-stantial, and I almost wish I could be romantic and say it was somehow transformative, but in truth, I barely felt it. But then his eyes came open, and he smiled at me with such innocent happiness that my ridiculous heart gave a leap and would have answered him instantly, if it was the organ in charge of my decision-making.

"Choose whenever you wish," he said. "No doubt you will first need to draw up a list of pros and cons, or perhaps a series of bar plots. If you like, I will help you organize them into categories."

I cleared my throat. "It strikes me that this is all pointless speculation. You cannot marry me. I am not going to be left behind, pining for you, when you return to your kingdom. I have no time for pining."

He gave me an astonished look. "Leave you behind! As if you would consent to that. I would expect to be burnt alive when next I returned to visit. No, Em, you will come with me, and we will rule my kingdom together. You will scheme and strategize until you have all my councillors eating out of your hand as easily as you do Poe, and I will show you everything—*everything*. We will travel to the darkest parts of my realm and back again, and you will find answers to questions you have never even thought to ask, and enough material to fill every journal and library with your discoveries."

And that is where we left things. I don't even know why I am including this, for God knows I do not wish to preserve the details of my romantic life for posterity (and a very short footnote that would be), only I find that writing it all out has made me somewhat calmer. Perhaps I will tear up this entry later.

I know that if I put this notebook aside and attempt to sleep, I will simply run over every argument and counterargument in my head, but what else can I do? Shadow is gazing up at me from his forepaws in a woebegone sort of way, as if I have somehow disappointed him. Traitor.

2nd December (?)

I haven't any idea what the date is, and so I have decided to guess. I believe it may help me stay sane here, if anything can. Everything blends together now, but I vividly remember writing that last entry, how angry I was, as if it were only a day or two gone—perhaps it was.

I must have tossed and turned for an hour at least. How on earth was I supposed to concentrate on research now, with a marriage proposal from one of the Folk dangling over my head? I could almost imagine myself a maiden in one of the stories, but stories didn't leave dirty teacups scattered throughout the cottage, or underline passages in my books—in *ink*—no matter how many times I ordered them not to.

Of course I wanted to marry Wendell. That was the most infuriating thing about the whole business—my feelings conspired against my reason. I will not lie and say my desire was purely romantic, for I couldn't stop myself from imagining the picture we would make back at Cambridge—despite his controversies, Wendell Bambleby was still a celebrated scholar, and yes, we would be a fearsome team indeed. I doubted I would have to worry ever again about securing funding for future fieldwork, nor being overlooked when it came to conference invitations.

It was the thought of invitations—yes, *that* thought—that made me rise from my bed. I yanked open my door, intending to stomp down the hall and—well, throw myself at him. I wanted to see what he would do, but more important, I needed to know if it was something I would enjoy. I was not going to marry someone without making sure of *that*.

But before I could take a step in his direction, a calm settled over me like a dream. Instead of going to Wendell's door, I returned to my own room and dressed in warm clothes. Shadow remained asleep at the foot of my bed, though it was a strange sleep—he twitched and whined, his huge paws batting at invisible foes. I left my room and pulled on my cloak.

As I did, I happened to glance down at my hand. The ring was there, but it was no longer a ring of shadow. It was a ring of ice, polished smooth and patterned with tiny blue crystals.

I knew exactly what was happening, of course. I have had enough faerie magic thrown at me over the years that I believe I have become somewhat inured to it—at the very least, I have trained myself to recognize when enchantment is affecting me; the absence of such recognition is what dooms most mortals. The truth is that it is not impossible to throw off faerie spells if you have a focused mind. But most people don't try, because they fail to recognize that it is enchantment pushing them to dance until their feet bleed, or murder their families, or any other number of horrors inflicted upon hapless mortals by the Folk.

Unfortunately, in this case, the knowledge of my own enchantment was of little use, for it was uncommonly strong magic, and held me like an iron vise.

I did what I could to push against it, to feel about for cracks. I could not stop myself from donning my boots, but I was able to slow the process by fumbling with the laces. Yet eventually, the laces were fastened, and then I was opening the door and stepping into the night.

I managed a single glance over my shoulder, and what did my gaze fall upon but my encyclopaedia, pages stacked tidily beneath my paperweight, little bookmarks sticking out the sides indicating sections requiring revision. That pinnacle of faerie scholarship, which I had only weeks ago likened to a museum exhibit of the Folk, neatly pinned down and labelled by the foremost expert on the subject—that is, me—brimming with meticulously documented accounts of foolish mortals who bumbled into faerie plots and games. The irony was rather too keen to appreciate.

Trying to shout for Wendell was, of course, ineffective. It made sense, the rational, freethinking part of my mind noted, that this would be the case. My feet were being led somewhere—to the king in the tree; the destination burned in my mind like a brand—and naturally the enchantment would not wish me to do anything that placed obstacles in my path.

And yet, it did not want me to be uncomfortable en route—it had compelled me to dress warmly, to don boots to prevent frostbite. And perhaps that aspect of the enchantment could be manipulated to my own purpose.

I focused on my bare hands. They were cold, and would grow colder, the farther I walked. I imagined the tips turning white, the fingers numbing so that I could no longer lift them. I did not try to move my hands—instead, I pushed the desire into the enchantment.

And it worked. As I descended the cottage steps, I reached into my pocket, where yesterday I had tucked my gloves, and pulled them on. I say *I*, but really, it was the enchantment making me do it, just as it had dressed me like a puppet. What I had done was less like reaching out to pull the strings myself and more like reasoning with the puppeteer.

My exultation was dulled by the realization of what I would have to do next. I was able to slow my steps across the lawn in an effort to fortify myself, though I suspect the additional seconds of delay had the opposite effect. I wondered if the enchantment was controlling my stomach too, or if it would be within my abilities to throw up.

And then there before me was the axe, still wedged into the stump. I had left it there myself the previous day—it felt like a very long time ago. I was no longer as pathetic a woodcutter as I had been upon my arrival, thanks to Lilja's patient lessons, though to say that I was *skilled* would be overstating things.

"Shit," I said, or rather mouthed—so the enchantment would allow me to *mouth* curses: what a comfort.

I was able to bend my path to take me to the stump, again by convincing the enchantment that this was the easier course, down the slope rather than up it. It was a gentlemanly sort, this enchantment. But I would not so easily convince it of the merits of my next decision.

I began by imagining wolves. Yes, there were wolves in the forest—how frightening. And here I was, a defenseless woman, wandering into their depths alone and unprotected. Would it not make sense to carry a weapon, as much sense as it made to don my gloves? Yes, of course it would.

Slowly, dreamily, I lifted the axe. The blade—oh, God. The blade was sharp. This was a good thing, from a practical standpoint, but it was not possible for me to see it as such in that moment.

The enchantment was already compelling me to tuck the axe beneath my arm and carry on like a well-behaved little puppet, which it still thought I was. Silly, really, to think of the enchantment as a *person*—but it felt like one.

I placed my hand upon the stump and lifted the axe—oh, only to check that the blade hadn't dulled, of course. Better lift it a little higher to catch the moonlight.

I carried on this way until the last moment, at which point I threw my will against the enchantment with all my might.

For the briefest of seconds, I was free. I thought the enchantment was surprised, but probably that was only my fancy. I knew I would not have more than that single second—certainly it would not allow me a second chance—and drove the axe towards my finger.

I did it the way Lilja had taught me—fixing my eyes on the target, letting the weight of the axe do the work. My other fingers I folded against the side of the stump, to keep them out of the way. I was half convinced I would miss and drive the axe into my hand—it was not at all the same as aiming for a crack in a log, no matter what I tried to tell myself—but I heard Lilja's voice in my head, her offhanded good cheer, as if there was nothing in the world more ordinary than what I was doing, and I didn't hesitate. My aim was true, and suddenly I was gazing at my finger, and it was not at the end of my hand.

It was the most curious sensation. At first, I was conscious only of the enchantment leaving me—it felt like falling, that dream sensation in which there is no ground to hit, only wakefulness. I awoke, and then immediately after that, the pain rolled over me in a red wave.

I staggered about, fading in and out of consciousness. I threw up at one point, I think. But somehow, when I fully returned to my senses, I found that I had wrenched off my glove and pressed my scarf against the hollow where my third finger had been.

I sobbed there in the snow for a moment or two, from relief as much as from the pain. When I'd got that out of my system, I returned to the cottage and bandaged my hand.

Then I set off again for the white tree.

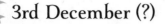

3rd December (?)

I just read over that again. It sounds irrational, if not insane—but I assure you, my mind was quite clear.

Of course I considered waking Wendell. But that would have given me away—the king in the tree would have known I wasn't enchanted if I arrived with Wendell in tow. As a general rule, the Folk do not take kindly to mortals who find ways to break their enchantments—they see it as an affront to their craftsmanship—and so to travel there in an unenchanted state would have been a risky prospect indeed.

I suppose most would ask why I wished to go to the king at all. I cannot answer that adequately, other than by posing more questions. If you give an astronomer a telescope through which he can view an undiscovered galaxy, but allow him only a glimpse of a single star, will he be content? By freeing the king in the tree, I would witness not only the ascension of a faerie king, but the ending of a story I have heard told many times, in many ways. Stories, after all, are so fundamental to their world; one cannot hope to understand the Folk without understanding their stories.

As for a secondary motivation, I admit that it pleased me to think that I could release Aud and Thora and all the others from their fear of the tall ones—for if the king had forbade the taking of mortal youths before, and been overthrown for it, I had no doubt he would do so again once he was freed, if only out of spite. The Folk are, by and large, blinded by pride and incapable of learning from their errors, and even if a mode of thought or behaviour lands them in trouble again and again, each time worse than the one before, they will simply carry on as they always did, which perhaps explains a little of the chaos and absurdity that typifies many faerie stories, and indeed their realms.

I did leave Wendell a note, at least, informing him that I had gone to release the king in the tree, that I had broken the enchantment I had fallen under (I provided no details as to how, in case he flew into one of his homicidal rages and began decapitating the sheep or something), but that I was pretending that I hadn't, and if I was still gone when he awoke, he had better not do anything to give the game away.

First, I went to see Poe. I walked quickly, or as quickly as I could through the knee-deep snow, with a parcel that had recently arrived at the cottage tucked under my arm.

He crept cautiously out of his tree, puzzlement written all over his sharp little face—I had never come to see him at night before. The spring and the grove were a different place now, full of little lights that might have been stars, reflected in the running water or the ice gilding the snow. But I didn't think so, for as I approached the spring, they winked out and then reappeared much deeper in the woods.

"I've come for my third question," I said.

He nodded, though his eyes kept drifting to the package under my arm. To spare him the suspense, I placed it before him. He puzzled a little over the wrapping paper until I told him that it was meant to be torn open—which he did with one sharp and silent finger. He cried out at the sight of the black bearskin which my brother had finally—grudgingly and with many expressions of dismay at whatever faerie nonsense I had mixed myself up in this time, for it's not as if he would believe I would want such an adornment for my personal use—sent from one of the furrier's shops in London.

"This will delight my lady, for it will set off her beauty and dignity to great effect," Poe said. And then he added, in the typical fashion of the Folk, who dole out information like a miser does his coin excepting the occasions when they provide more enlightenment than one would care for, "Though she prefers the skins of mortals."

I chose to withhold my thoughts on the latter half of this characterisation. "Your lady?"

He blushed and lowered his eyes. "His Highness blessed me with a marvellous home. I have had Folk banging upon my door night and day, demanding to marry me. I chose the loveliest, of course."

"Congratulations," I said, genuinely pleased. "May I meet her?"

There came a whisper of movement at the edge of the spring. Poe's sweetheart had been there all along, watching me. There was nothing to distinguish her from Poe, though she was perhaps a little taller, and she wore an odd, pale, filmy garment that I did not care to examine closely. She edged around me to Poe's side, where she ran her fingers over the bearskin. The two held a muttered converse.

"What do you want for such a gift?" Poe said.

"Nothing now," I said. "I will claim my payment at a later date."

Poe's wife regarded me uneasily, no doubt fearing that I would come knocking at their door again with burdensome demands, but Poe murmured something to her, and she seemed to relax.

"I told her that you are my *fjolskylda*," he said. "She understands this. She too had *fjolskylda* in another village, before she came here, and they always made fair exchanges with her and her kin. You will be fair too."

He said all this without any particular warmth, merely as if he were stating something self-evident. I felt tears spring to my eyes nevertheless. I've made bargains with the Folk before, and I can't say why his words affected me so, but they did.

"I will depart these shores before the winter is out," I said. "Wouldn't it be best for you to find a—*fjolskylda* among the Ljoslanders?"

"It doesn't matter where you are," he said simply.

I closed my fist around the bearskin, and then I let the brownie woman take it away. It melted into the forest as easily as a living bear.

"How was the king imprisoned in the tree?" I said.

Poe went still. "It was a long time ago," he said in a hushed voice, "I was only an icicle on a bough* then."

"Ah," I said, disappointed. "So you don't remember."

"Oh yes, I remember—why wouldn't I? And even if I didn't, it's not as if the forest keeps quiet about it, nor the snows. They were quite upset when His Majesty was locked away—of course, snow has a terrible memory, and forgot almost everything by the following year apart from the fact that it was angry, and so it covered everything in a nasty sleet instead of proper flakes. Everything was all turned to mud and grey sludge; it was horrid."

---

* What an intriguing comment this was. Initially I took it as a win for Blythe, to hear one of the common fae link his existence to the natural world (in this case, an icicle). Upon reflection, however, I believe this interpretation to be a tenuous one. The Folk often speak in metaphor. In fact, several years ago I had a conversation with one of the German kobolds in which she referred to herself as a "bud," meaning a child. Yet I know that she did not originate from this form, as I met her parents several days later. And, indeed, Poe has referenced his own mother numerous times during our conversations.

Poe talked quite a lot more to me now than he had when we first met, and as informative as I found his ramblings typically, right now I didn't have time. There would be no way to convince the king I was still enchanted if I tarried too long.

"How was it done?" I pressed. "Some complicated enchantment, I suppose." Because of course, I needed to know how to trap him again if he proved entirely mad and wicked, not merely mad and wicked by the standards of the Folk.

"Not really," Poe said thoughtfully. "The first queen gave him a cloak woven from all the seasons, and then when he fell asleep in it one night by the Lake of Dancing Stars, as he often did, she snipped out the winter and stitched the whole thing back together. Then she wrapped him up tight in the cloak and fastened all the buttons. That trapped him, you see—well, no one could escape a year without winter, not even the king. She planted the king's feet in the woods and turned the silk and wool and gold thread she'd used to weave the cloak into bark and leaf. Since then the tree has grown very tall, and he is still inside it, trapped forevermore."

"Oh," I said faintly. "Is that all."

My hand was throbbing ferociously by the time I reached the tree, every step sending a jolt of fire up my arm. My bandage was bloody, but there wasn't anything I could do about that, other than keep my hand stuffed into my glove and pray that the king didn't notice.

I stood before the tree, which rustled and hummed musically to itself. I wasn't enchanted anymore, but that didn't much matter, for the tree was positively brimming with enchantment—I had noted that before, with Wendell. I think the king was asleep—probably he'd been asleep the whole time, but I've no doubt he was still aware of me, in his dreaming.

I shivered with excitement and terror. I kept my hand firmly wrapped around my coin, but I allowed a little of the enchantment to seep into my mind—merely by relaxing my focus, which wasn't easy, as I was accustomed to fending off faerie enchantments, not inviting them in. Yet it was necessary, for I hadn't the slightest idea how I was supposed to get the king out. The enchanted ring hadn't cared whether or not I brought the axe, so there must be some other way.

The magic murmured at me to move my legs. I did so. It had me stride about the grove, making a pile of snow and then shaping it with my hands. I went down to the stream, broke the ice, then found a curl of bark and filled it with water. This I poured over the snowman—yes, the king had me building a snowman, which perhaps I will laugh over later, but was quite disturbing in the moment, twisting carefree childhood memories up with some huge and terrifying magic—and watched as it froze into silvery ribbons like the indication of hair.

I stood gazing at the ugly snowman I had made, feeling rather foolish and wondering if the king in the tree really meant to step inside the snowman and use it as a vessel. Wendell had said that the king's body had decayed, so he needed to use *something*, but I couldn't really imagine this. Of course, the king was still trapped, so what body he wished to step inside was something of a moot point.

I began to wonder if this was all a mistake. Perhaps the king had only meant to enchant Wendell, but since I'd turned up instead, he'd decided he might as well have some fun with me. Dragging a mortal out of bed to build snowmen in the middle of the night seemed like poor sport to me, but I supposed that being trapped in a tree for centuries didn't afford much opportunity for entertainment. As I was thinking all this, though, a raven fluttered out of the trees and perched on the snowman's shoulder.

Two more followed. They swirled around the snowman, pecking and clawing. When they were done, it looked more like a man—a little more. It was still strange, but no longer hideous. Then, to my horror, the birds fell to the ground dead, blood leaking across the snow from wounds I couldn't see. They stained the snowman's feet like an offering, which I suppose they were.

The tree murmured, and magic prodded me again. But it did not prod me to move, it prodded my *mind*. And that was when I realized—the king didn't know how to free himself. He expected me to come up with a solution.

Well, that set my thoughts whirling. Though in truth, they had already been diving in and out of stories and academic papers, holding them up against what I knew of the Hidden Ones and their disgraced king.

The Word.

The useless, ridiculous, button-gathering Word, which I had long valued as a piece of esoteric trivia, a footnote, perhaps, in a paper I had yet to write. Well, footnotes in dryadology are sometimes like the Folk themselves, leaping out at you from nowhere.

A thrill rushed through me. Looking back, this would have been a very good moment to stop and think through the wisdom of what I was doing, but I was too full of the delight of scholarly discovery (and, I suspect, my own conceit) to stop. I turned to the white tree and spoke the Word.

And what do you know? A button came sailing out from somewhere among the branches. I caught it and examined it against my palm. It was white and desiccated, like old bone, shedding a fine powder against my skin, with an acorn carved into one side. The button began to melt against my palm, and I dropped it into the snow. The tree had given a shudder when the button came free, but now it was still once more.

I spoke the Word again, and out sailed another button. This one had a flower. The next button had a sailboat dreaming among gentle waves.

All told, I spoke the Word nine times, and as the ninth button sailed free, the trunk of the white tree split open like the front of a cloak, the bark billowing—for a moment, it became silk and fine wool churning in the wind that had filled the grove, and then it stilled. The tree gave a sigh and dropped its leaves, buds, and fruits onto the snow with a rustling *thud*.

I stared into the cavernous hollow that had opened in the tree, my heart going like a rabbit's, waiting. When I heard a footfall behind me, I screamed.

"There's no need for that," a voice said. "I don't mind, though. It's been a very long time since anybody was afraid of me."

The Hidden king was kneeling in the snow, *tsk*ing over the dead birds. He seemed at first to resemble the figure of ice and snow I had built with their aid, but with each breath he drew, life came into his body, and he grew more mortal in appearance. It was a little like watching someone rising towards the surface of murky water; one moment his face was little more than indistinct planes of ice, the next he was blinking his pale blue eyes at me and smiling. Of course he was beautiful—is it even necessary to say it? His hair was black with glints of white, his cheekbones sharp above a wide mouth with a natural smile in it. The white in his hair turned out to be small opal beads, and his clothing was a blackened blue with an overlay like ice, beaten thin with a lacy pattern, and he wore a white crown and layers of jeweled necklaces that glittered fetchingly in the dim light. And yet everything he wore was as tasteful as it was beautiful, precisely the amount of adornment one would expect on a king, no more and no less.

"Poor things," he said. "This world is terribly unkind to beasts, is it not? Here we are."

He touched them, and the ravens sprang to life—in a manner of speaking. Their movements were jerky, and they were still covered in blood—one had a broken neck, and its head was bent at a disquieting angle. This one landed on the king's shoulder and pecked his finger when he stroked it, drawing blood. He laughed.

"Hello, my love," he said, striding over to me. "My darling rescuer, who has given me back my body and my throne, and freed me from my eternal captivity."

Before I could recover from my amazement, he kissed me. It was like pressing frozen glass to my lips, like breathing in pure winter. I staggered back a step, coughing, and for a long time after I felt as if I had ice in my lungs.

"I," I began. "I'm not your love. I'm not anyone."

"Oh, don't worry, I know who you are. Years ago, when I was a boy, a seer told me I would one day be locked up by my own people, and only a mousy little scholar could get me out again. I would marry the mouse—which forms a very poetic contrast, don't you think? And together we would rule over my kingdom." He stretched. "Well! I am glad to be out of there. My first order of business, I think, will be a nice bath and a feast of salted plums with caviar. Do you like salted plums, dearest?"

It wasn't easy, in that moment, for me to think like a scholar again. To think at all, really. How was it that I suddenly had faerie kings, plural, demanding to marry me? But I forced myself to be rational and to answer in the way I guessed he would like—yes, I loved salted plums, thank you—and to enquire about the seer.

"I don't know anything more," the king said. "I never got a good look at her—she was all dressed in rags. She was not from here, but was one of the wandering Folk, who go all over."

I thought carefully before saying, "It is kind of you to offer to marry me, Your Highness. But I am not your equal, nor even close."

He gave me an indulgent look, as if I were a child who had correctly counted to ten. "But I must fulfil your every desire, dear one—starting with our marriage. Your modesty does you credit, though—I have a great love for modesty. But what is this?" He touched my wounded hand, swathed in a bandage that was now leaking dark blood upon the snow.

Terror gripped me. There was no way to pretend I was still under his spell now. "I—I wished to release you of my own free will, Your Highness. As a sign of my respect for you."

He looked puzzled at that, but, fortunately, he seemed to take little interest in prodding my motivations. With a shrug, he unwrapped the bandage—I gave a sharp gasp as the pain rolled up my arm—and then, like a magician pulling flowers from a handkerchief, he revealed my hand, fully healed and spotless. The finger was still missing, and its absence was an ache—but it felt like an old one. I wondered if he, too, had some power to manipulate time.

"I—I desire to remain unmarried," I stammered. "As I said, Highness, I freed you out of respect, not because I wished for anything in return. I have a betrothed, you see."

"Oh, well, that's no concern," he said, waving one ringed hand. "I'll see that we adequately replace his dowry. He won't sorrow, then, for it will free him up to marry someone prettier than you."

I could see that the idea that I might prefer not to marry him was completely incomprehensible to him. There was some logic in it, I suppose, given what he had been told by the seer; though I know enough of the self-obsession of the Folk to guess that he would have assumed my devotion either way. So I abandoned that approach.

"As you say, I'm not beautiful." It was a solid objection, for the Folk never marry mortals who aren't beautiful unless they have been forced into it by trickery (and even then, the mortals are often revealed to be beautiful in the end, having been enchanted to look ugly). He could find nothing appealing in my ordinariness, especially now, with my plain shift stained with blood and sweat and my hair in exceptional disarray, even for me, most of it hanging loose down my back.

"That's true enough," he said, looking me up and down with a pained expression. He looked down at himself after, as if he needed to soothe his eyes with his own beauty. "But let's see what we can do."

Before I could say anything, my clothing gave a rustle, and a new gown and cloak spilled from my shoulders like water. It was all in dark blue to match with him, the cloak the darker of the two, patterned with the same iced lace and opals like swirling constellations. My boots grew up past my knees and became a pure white lambskin with jet buckles.

I immediately began to shiver—he hadn't bothered to make anything warm; the cloak was fur, but it was thin and better suited to a spring day than a winter night. He took his time with it, wandering around to see me from the back and place additional pearls in my cloak, or add another pair of earrings— I wore two, one pair a long dangle of emeralds and the other a cluster of pearls shaped like a dove.

He declared himself finished, looking pleased. "There—you are almost pretty now."

"Almost isn't good enough, though, is it?" I said through chattering teeth, my mind racing. "A king as beautiful as yourself should not be marrying the likes of me."

"Oh, no! You see, beauty of mind and spirit is what is most important to me in a wife," he said. "I adore poetry, and the poets say this is the sort of beauty that matters most. Kindness. Generosity. Forgiveness." He winced. "I admit, I struggle with these things myself. Even now, I am filled with a desire to visit many vengeances upon the ones who put me in that tree, including my first wife, whose blood I would very much like to feed to my wolves, cup by cup. But—" He gave me a smile that lit up his entire face. "—I will resist. For I hate cruelty and all other forms of ugliness, and will not abide them in myself."

Behind him, one of the ravens he'd reanimated had begun worrying a rabbit, which shrieked alarmingly—the raven seemed to have little interest in killing it and merely amused itself by tearing at the rabbit's fur. I've never seen a bird behave that way, but the king took no notice.

"What sort of palace would you like, my love?" he said, taking my hand. "We must have somewhere to greet our courtiers. They will know I am free, and will be on their way to pay their respects."

I don't think I could have responded if he had held a sword to my throat. I had imagined many possibilities after freeing him from his prison—this had not been one of them. I felt terror, but mixed into it was something that felt ridiculously like exultation. It wasn't that I wanted to be a queen, or any of the rest of it. But try devoting your life to a field of study so elusive it is almost entirely made up of hearsay and speculation, and then have someone say to you casually, all right, I will now give you a book that will answer every question you ever had, and see if you don't feel the same.

I felt ill. I was beginning to wonder if getting myself into danger had become something of an addiction.

The Hidden king patted my hand indulgently, thinking me either too humble or too stupid to answer. He turned towards the mountains, which peeked their snow-streaked faces through the winter trees, and tilted his head to one side.

A great rumbling started, and then came a series of cracks so loud I nearly threw myself to the ground, fearing lightning. A mist of ice crystals had descended upon the nearest mountain, and within it, a castle had appeared. It looked like a ghost for a moment, a huge, sprawling ghost made of glittering ice, built in levels to fit the slope, and then the mist split open, and it was real.

It took up almost half the mountainside. The king made a dissatisfied noise, squinting at it, and several of the turrets rearranged themselves and a row of outbuildings appeared where there had been none. Another squint, and suddenly there was a road leading up to the castle, broad and paved in huge cobblestones of ice, each with a different flower trapped inside it. I could see the flowers, because he brought the road all the way to our feet, sending trees crashing to the forest floor. The impact shook the ground so that I almost fell over, and I was soon coughing on the swirl of snow the fallen trees had raised. The avenue was lined with lanterns all gleaming with the same moonlight glow as those of the winter fair.

I didn't watch only the castle as it reared up out of nothing— I also watched the king, terrified and fascinated. When he is not speaking or moving, he becomes perfectly still. I mean that— *perfectly*. I speculate that, in those moments, he returns to what he is, a piece of winter given form. It is the same stillness one finds in a frozen lake or trees weighted by heavy snow.

In one last gesture of extravagance, he lifted his hand and, with a sort of brushing motion, moved aside the smattering of clouds in the sky. The aurora shone through, mostly green tonight, or perhaps he summoned it along with everything else, I don't know.

"Yes," he said, examining the monstrous spectacle before us. "Yes, it's a start, I suppose."

His voice seemed far away; my hearing had been deadened by the tumult of

4th December (?)

Somehow, I drifted away from my journal without finishing that last sentence—it's unlike me. I have no recollection of deciding to stop. I am so terrified I might one day forget about my journal altogether that I've decided to carry it with me wherever I go.

Any inclination I felt to revel in the excitement of my situation faded quickly. For I soon realized that the castle summoned by the Hidden king had caused an avalanche that buried several far-flung farmsteads at the edge of one of the neighbouring villages.

"That's unfortunate," he said sympathetically when I told him. "Well, I will give the mortals a great feast to make up for it. It will last for days and days until they are all nearly too fat to move. Will that serve?"

"I should think not," I said, "given that they're probably dead."

"Oh, dear." He seemed very sorry for a moment, but then one of the servants arrived with a trio of white wolves on a leash made of bone and moonlight (a gift sent from the lord of one of the faerie holdings on the northern coast), and he forgot everything else, including me, as they leapt all over him to lick his face.

I tried not to think too hard about how quickly the faerie servants had arrived. I was half afraid that he had conjured them out of the snow, and for some reason, this disturbed me more than anything else. Though there was a lot to be disturbed about, the palace not the least of it.

We hadn't had to walk the long avenue to the palace, which was paved with ice-bound flowers. A carriage had appeared made from black wood covered in slippery frost and drawn by two graceful faerie horses, one white and one black, who seemed to change slightly from one moment to the next—I swear, at one point they even swapped colours. The driver and footman leapt from the carriage and threw themselves at the king's feet in such violent haste one cut himself on the ice.

"Brethilde, Deminsfall," the king said slowly, as if savouring their names. "Where have you been? Not tending to my tree after my queen locked me away, that's certain. Oh, a few servants stayed, but their numbers dwindled, and for a very long time I have been alone."

The servants opened and closed their mouths, trembling, but he only smiled and laid a hand on their heads. "I forgive you," he said warmly, then helped me into the carriage.

"How do your servants know you've been freed?" I said as the horses whisked us along the road.

He gave me a puzzled look. "How do mortals know winter has arrived?" He turned his face towards his castle, and his pale eyes shone. The undead ravens flew ahead, occasionally swooping down to peck at the servants, despite the king's admonishments (though these were few and far between). "My courtiers will soon arrive—I look forward to introducing them to my betrothed." He kissed my hand.

Through my terror, a part of me was fascinated. "Then you don't believe any of your people will remain loyal to the current queen?"

"The pretender? No." He didn't seem annoyed by my question, nor did I notice any bitterness in him to belie his confidence. "The winter knows me, the mountains and glaciers, the aurora and the birds. I can be confined temporarily, but I can't be overthrown, not in the way mortals might think of it."

I noted that he didn't say he couldn't be killed—for certainly the stories suggest faerie monarchs can be gotten rid of that way, not that it isn't a difficult undertaking. I said quickly, "Forgive my ignorance of your ways, Your Highness. I had thought your people might prefer the queen. Only because I was informed that you had forbade them from having a particular kind of sport with mortals, and many Folk resented you for it."

"I'm sure they resented me for a dozen different reasons," he said. "The point of being king is not to be *liked*. It is to demonstrate a nobility of character which your people will take as a template upon which to model their own behaviour."

I digested this. "Then you will once again forbid them from stealing mortals from their homes?"

He gave me his beatific smile. "I will do more than that, my dearest. I will have them release every mortal currently in their possession. Poor things! Mortals are terribly weak, and it is a dishonourable thing for the strong to prey upon the weak, I've always felt." He squeezed my hand. "Does this make you happy?"

I assured him that it did, and he kissed me again and said, "Your nature is a generous one, that you would ask me about this before demanding jewels or other gifts. I will be happy to call you my wife."

Well, that exchange gave me some measure of relief, though I heard Wendell's voice in my head, mocking my philanthropy. And in my present situation, chilled to numbness and facing eternal imprisonment in Faerie, I found my supposed good deed hard to appreciate.

The horses brought us through the tremendous white doors of the palace, into a courtyard lined with galleries of black stone. The palace was a deeply disquieting thing—I found I could see it only out of the corner of my eye; if I looked at it straight on, its lines dissolved into the mountainside's jagged pattern of snow and rock. Fortunately, once we were inside, my vision settled somewhat.

The palace itself was surprisingly simple in its architecture; I had anticipated a warren of grand staircases and corridors that I might locate once and then never again. But it was like a Ljosland winter, stark and minimally adorned, but painfully beautiful. The scale of it, though, was enormous. The courtyard, tiled in ice, could have fit all of Hrafnsvik, and the opposite gallery was so far away that its outline was softened by the ice crystals in the air. A few Folk were there to greet us, and they were like flowers floating upon a vast sea.

It is at this point that my memory begins to warp. I recall the king introducing me, all smiles, while the Folk paid their respects, which they did with a brittle, obsequious politeness. But then, suddenly, I was in the rooms the king has given me, gazing out over the valley, with no memory of how I got there. The view is magnificent but terrifying, as my chamber is housed in the southern gallery, which faces the open expanse of sky and fog between the mountain and the valley floor far below. I can see the snowbound glitter of the forest, and somewhere beyond it, a grey smear that is like wet paint drawn over a canvas, which I guess to be the sea. The mountains stare back at me, grim and uncaring.

17th December (?)

I am never without servants, I don't think. It seems there is always something being pressed into my hands, be it food or drink or warming furs, though I stopped being cold the moment I stepped into the faerie palace, which is how I knew for certain that I was sealed up in the enchantments that bind their world.

Naturally, I have made several attempts at escape. I try to be systematic about it, which is not easy when your mind is being constantly muddled by magic. But I cling to my coin at all times, which helps, as does writing in this journal.

First I tried simply walking through the gates—not because I thought it would be so simple, but out of a desire for thoroughness, to exhaust all possibilities. As soon as I did so, I found myself in my chamber again, and not only that but seated in a hot spring bath that had not been there before, scooped out of the floor in a series of broad steps paved in seashells. Two faerie women were seated beside me, one weaving strands of opalescent seaweed into my hair, which undulated like snakes, the other prattling on about arrogant bards teaching the snow to sing their songs, which it did now at all hours. My muscles were limp, as if I had been there a long time.

I tried asking my servants to take me into the mountains, or the forest—anywhere that wasn't the palace. They never protested, but I have no recollection of them obeying me; it seemed that no sooner had I made the request than I found myself in a bath again, or at breakfast with the king while he merrily recounted his progress in making improvements to the palace.

The king sends a steady stream of craftspeople my way in preparation for our wedding. I was questioned about the menu by two harried Folk who smelled of cake and had icicles spiking their beards—whether I preferred, for instance, star-brewed wine or ale spiced with salt from the sea beneath the sea, and similar nonsensical queries.

I maintained my equanimity as best as I could, knowing that panic was the surest way of losing one's mind in any faerie realm, but I admit that I lost patience a few times.

"I despise wine," I snapped at one of the poor faerie chefs, who leaned back from me as if I'd breathed fire at him. "You will serve beer from barley that grows only during the new moon, which has been brewed together with the bones of singing fish fed a diet solely consisting of honey."

"Yes, Your Highness," the faerie whispered over and over, bowing low, and went away weeping. I refused to speak to the dressmakers who swept into the room after he left and ordered them away before they could even take my measurements.

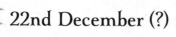

22nd December (?)

It occurred to me today as I stood gazing out my window, which made up the entire southern wall of my chamber, that the forest was nearly buried in snow. In places, the drifts covered all but the tips of the trees.

"Has there been an avalanche?" I demanded of the small army of florists currently filling my chamber, offering me samples of this bloom or that.

The senior florist, a small woman with eyes like black ink and a dress made entirely of ice-glazed petals, frowned down at the trees.

"It is winter, Your Highness," she said.

"Yes," I said through my teeth. "But it seems there is rather *more* winter than there was before."

She exchanged a nervous look with another florist, a narrow man holding an armful of black and grey roses. "The king has returned," he said slowly, as if he didn't understand my question at all and was merely taking a shot in the dark.

A little bead of fear slid down my back at that. When I next saw the king—I believe it was at supper, though it's entirely possible I saw him before then—I raised the question with him.

"Yes, it will be a winter the likes of which has never been seen in Ljosland," he said cheerily, helping himself to more fish. The

Folk pulled their fish from a frozen mountain lake and served them raw on a bed of ice or swimming in a sweet, creamy sauce that tasted faintly of apples. Several varieties were spread before us, the smallest ones—vibrantly striped grey and green—retaining their head and bones, which were meant to be eaten together. We were seated in a cavernous banquet hall with walls of black stone and another floor of ice cobbles, this time with leaves and fir boughs prisoned inside, so that you felt as if you were walking atop a forest canopy. The table was crowded with Folk—what seemed like a mixture of courtly and common, though their faces often blended together in the bone-coloured light. I caught a sneer here, a beseeching look there; the minstrels were playing their flutes, and although the king had ordered them not to enchant me, their songs often made my head swim.

"But what will become of the mortal villages?" I said. "You can't bury them in snow!"

He touched my hand reassuringly, his beautiful face full of adoration. "The mortals here are used to winter, my dear."

"They are not used to fifty feet of it being deposited on their doorsteps," I said, fists clenched on my skirts.

"It will last only as long as my coronation festivities," he promised, and that *really* worried me, for it suggested that he planned to extend the winter until he had finished revelling in his triumph—and anyone who knows a thing about the Folk will easily guess that this would be a substantial period of time.

"You must pull back the snows from the mortal world," I said. "Their animals will die. Their children will starve."

He was only half listening—he motioned to one of the minstrels, and they switched to a song he liked better.

"Children!" he said, smiling. "I'm glad you mentioned them. Children adore winter—do you know they used to leave offerings for us at the centre of frozen lakes at the solstice, to ask us for heaps of snow on Christmas. As if we know anything about Christmas, the silly darlings. I wonder if they still do that?"

The music swelled then, and I forgot what we had been talking about.

23rd December (?)

The worst part of my day is when the king receives visitors. These are supplicants, mostly, faeries both courtly and common who come with gifts and congratulations expressed in varying degrees of desperation. Occasionally, such gifts include the heads of the king's enemies, who conspired to shut him away in the tree or turned a blind eye to the queen's machinations. The heads do not bleed—I am spared that, at least—but they do melt, which might sound easier to bear the sight of, but should you ever witness a corpse whose nose or eyes have simply melted away, you will know what nonsense that is.

Each time, the king exclaims over the cruelty of it. Once he exclaimed for so long that several of the servants began shuffling their feet, their eyes gone glassy with boredom. The lords and ladies bear his displeasure remarkably well, bowing their heads humbly and murmuring apologies, all the while looking pleased with themselves. Invariably, I will find the head turned into some ghastly decoration somewhere, usually placed upon a pedestal and decorated with jewels to make it beautiful, while the lord or lady who so angered the king with their barbarity is suddenly being invited to dine at the king's table and granted tokens of his favour in the form of furs, minstrels, or minor enchantments. When I pointed out that this hardly set a good example, he shook his head and smiled at me.

"The ability to forgive is a great virtue," he said. "Indeed, there are few qualities that are more exquisite or more rare."

He was also given to expatiating on the dire punishments he would dole out to his former wife, the now-deposed queen, who I understood was in hiding somewhere, if his nature was not so magnanimous. As it was, he said, he wished only that she be brought before him so that he could forgive her publicly and gift her with a little land to heal the wound between them. I began to dread the arrival of every messenger, certain that they would bring news that the ex-queen had been disposed of in a dozen stomach-churning ways, perhaps even bringing as proof something worse than her severed head—I did not know what could be worse than that, but I had no doubt the king's courtiers would work it out. I was almost relieved when word finally came that she had been torn apart by the king's wolves, who had mysteriously escaped their kennel one starless night. The king wept for more than an hour, and then at his next banquet, the lady who had gifted him the wolves was seated at his right hand, smirking victoriously at the assembled guests, many of whom fixed her with scowls betraying a grudging admiration.

25th December (?)

As often as I can, I try coming up with reasons why he shouldn't marry me. I tried telling him that I am too dull, as I know no poetry and have a dreadful singing voice; I argued that I know nothing of the politics of his world and would surely make a mess of things.

"Your thoughtfulness knows no bounds, my dearest," he said. "But it's of no matter to me that you are dull or ignorant, as you mortals do not live very long—one hardly has to turn around to find that you have expired. I intend for you to enjoy the brief time you have in this world, and then I will marry a woman of my stature. You needn't worry."

I am growing increasingly desperate. While I don't know how much time has passed in the mortal realm, I know that my wedding date draws ever closer. Not that the Folk give much attention to *dates*—they move with the ebb and flow of the seasons. Once all the details are decided, and everything is ready, we will be married, and everything is almost ready. Folk are gathering from every corner of the king's realm to witness our nuptials, and the palace rings with laughter and music at all hours of the day and night.

But I have one more idea to try. I wish that I could think of something other than flight—a way of limiting this vicious winter into which he has plunged the land—but the truth is, my mind grows more and more muddled as the days pass. I know that I have to find a way to undo what the king has done—what *I* have done—but I also know that if I remain here much longer, I will lose myself entirely.

30th January

That is the date.

I know the date. I feel as if I have touched solid ground for the first time after years at sea.

When the dressmakers announced themselves this morning, after the king and I had breakfasted and he had left me with a chaste kiss, I put my plan into motion.

I had observed that, unlike the servants who trail after me at all times, the craftspeople sent to construct my absurd wedding are not of the palace. They come from far and wide—some are not even from the Ljosland mainland, but remote Arctic islands off the ice-choked northern coast. These Folk are smaller and speak with strange accents. Given that they are not part of the palace and its many enchantments, I thought perhaps there was a way one of them could get me out.

"You are not from the king's court?" I asked.

"Not at all, my lady," the tailor replied. "We are—far too humble for that."

There were two of them, but only one spoke—the man, who now bent to measure my feet. He was small with overlarge black eyes and a sharp face, his hair the colour of dust and his fingers many-jointed and far too long. His companion, an oafish sort of woman whose perpetual mien was an odd mixture of embarrassment and moroseness, handed him a pair of silver shoes. I kicked them aside.

"Her Highness makes it difficult to determine her size," the tailor said in a dry voice.

"Her Highness has a request to make," I replied coldly.

"Indeed? Well, Her Highness need not concern herself with requests, but only demands, which surely she is accustomed to."

As he spoke, he motioned for my servants, who were hovering as usual, to help the mute woman bring in yards upon yards of fabric. He selected a bolt, which—thank God—was neither black nor blue-white, but evergreen with black-and-white brocade.

"I desire a very particular veil," I said, "I wish it to be woven from the white fur of a hare that I have shot with my own hands. You will weave it for me there in the forest, while the blood is still fresh on my hands, for I wish to make of my veil an offering to my dear husband."

Now, I had calculated my request carefully, and knew it to be a sensible one for the Folk, who are given to such gruesome predilections. But the tailor only looked at me in silence, his sharp face unreadable.

"Well?" I demanded. "Is this beyond your capabilities?"

"No, my lady."

"Then take me to the forest. I wish to hunt now." I tried for an approximation of my fiancé's thoughtless imperiousness, though I did not have his good humour to pair it with.

The tailor glanced briefly at my servants, who had removed a yard of fabric for his inspection. He took it and began pinning it to my chemise.

"His Highness cherishes my lady dearly," he said, moving behind me to add more pins. "And what is cherished must be guarded closely, and protected with enchantments like golden chains."

My chest tightened, and I reached out to the bedpost to steady myself. I understood the tailor's careful words, though he would not speak openly, in case it were interpreted as criticism of the king.

The king had used his magic to shut me away in the palace. Each time I had tried to escape, I had found myself thwarted, and if I tried again, the results would be no different.

"If my lady would forgive her humble servant's temerity," the tailor said, "I have another proposition."

"What is that?" I was barely listening. The room seemed to have grown cold and dreamlike, like the years stretching out before me, shut away in that ice palace.

"His Highness has declared tomorrow a day of gift-giving." The tailor's sewing needle flashed in the light as he added a sleeve to the gown, impossibly quickly. "Folk and mortals both have been invited from far and wide to pay their respects to the king and his new bride. I would like to offer you a veil patterned after one that my mother wore on her own wedding night. I believe you will like it better."

"That's very kind of you," I began to say, then stopped. The sewing needle was unusually small and delicate, forged of a very pure silver that darted in and out of the fabric like a fish through a stream.

I gave a sudden, involuntary jerk, and my arm jabbed into the needle. I gave a hiss of pain. When I did, the other faerie tailor, who had been holding her companion's sewing kit and scissors in woebegone silence, let out a growl.

"Shut up, you brainless mongrel," the tailor hissed at her. "It was just a little prick. She's fine."

My faerie servants hadn't noticed this bizarre exchange. They continued to hover, mostly unhelpfully, unrolling more fabric from the bolt so that it dragged on the ground and gathered unsightly wrinkles. I turned to them.

"Leave us," I commanded in my best imitation of queenly arrogance. They exchanged puzzled glances and backed away a few paces.

The tailor looked at the ceiling, and then he turned to the attendants with a smile that somehow managed to be charming, despite his ugliness. "Her Highness is modest," he said. "I must undress her now, and she'd rather we have some privacy."

Oh, God. If I hadn't known it was Bambleby before, I did now. Even through my shock and confusion, I couldn't help glaring at him.

The servants tittered and drifted out, all but the senior of them, who said in a show of loyalty, "I must remain, for the king has decreed that my lady must at all times have someone to fulfil her every desire."

"As thoughtful as that is," the tailor said, "our lady's desires are frequently nonsensical, and right now, she desires you *not* to fulfil them."

He passed his hand over the servant's face, and her expression grew dreamy and unfocused. With a sigh, she tumbled backwards onto the bed.

"Wendell!" I exclaimed, rushing forward. "You can't murder my servants! The king will—"

"Much as I missed being berated by you, Em," he said, "she is only asleep. We needn't worry about your king's wrath."

I found the servant as he had said, drowsing with her eyes half closed. I was so relieved and happy and stunned, a rush of feelings all together, that I could have thrown my arms around him. Indeed, I almost did, but for some perverse reason, I found myself needing to argue with him instead. Truly, I sometimes wonder if some enchantment is at work to render him as disagreeable as possible. "He is not my king," I said.

"No? But you freed him." He shook his head. "How is it that you know how to befriend wild faerie dogs and ferret out Words of Power, yet you missed one of the fundamental rules of dryadology—namely, not cutting wicked kings out of trees."

"I've learned my lesson, thank you," I snapped. "Should you end up trapped in one, I won't let you out."

"You shall have to. I know you too well, Em. You could never survive without having someone around to snarl at."

The other tailor had fallen onto all fours and was snuffling at my feet. I hugged her instead—or *him*, rather, for it was indeed Shadow under the glamour. He licked me, an unappealing experience, and I pushed his head back to ward off further attempts.

I stared at Wendell. He looked nothing like himself—he didn't even *sound* like himself, his voice thickened and rough. Only now that I looked harder, I saw his familiar insouciant lean, the way he gazed at me with a mixture of bemusement and concern. He was several inches shorter than me now, and with his unprepossessing appearance and the palette of greys he wore, he could have faded into the background of any room.

"Oh," I breathed in sudden understanding. "You have turned yourself into one of the *oíche sidhe*."

"Naturally," he said. "My grandmother's blood flows through my veins, and so I may take on their appearance if it suits me— though the process was rather unpleasant." He looked down at his formerly graceful fingers, now spindly with extra joints in them, and grimaced. "And worse than that, I have to *look* at myself every day."

"Could you not have used a glamour?"

"Well, perhaps, but I thought our snow king's enchantments might shred it. This place is stuffed full of them. I risked putting one on Shadow, because if anyone was to reveal him, it would not matter much. He is nobody's enemy."

I gazed at him. "And you are?"

"I have tried multiple times to free you by force, which didn't go very well. I killed several of the king's lords and ladies, though."

My mouth fell open. "He never told me about that."

"Why would he? Anyway, I eventually came up with this idea"—he gestured sourly at his unsightly self—"and after talking things over with Aud, we decided—"

"Aud!" I nearly yelped. "Aud is working to—to *rescue* me?"

"The whole village is working to rescue you, my dear. We've had almost a merry time, plotting it all out."

I tried to picture this, Aud and Thora and Krystjan and the rest in the tavern, bandying about ideas to free me from Faerie, but my imagination failed me utterly—mainly because I could not picture them caring.

"Why?" I said softly.

"Why?" His eyes crinkled with amusement. "You rescued three of their children—and scores more will be spared, no doubt, now that the changeling has been cast out."

"I also freed a faerie king who is perfectly content to doom them to eternal winter."

"Yes, but I managed to convince them that your intentions in that respect were noble."

He said it in an offhand way, not caring if it was true or not. I shivered, though I hadn't felt the cold in days. "They weren't," I said. "Not for the most part. I wanted—" I looked down at myself, at my ridiculous dress. "I wanted to understand the story. I suppose I thought about helping Aud and the others, but I won't lie and say that I didn't think about science first. They should not be risking their lives to help me."

"Emily, Emily," he said. "I'm positively astonished you decided to help these people, whether they came second, third, or fourteenth in your mind. Have you ever done something like that before? Thought of someone other than yourself and your research, I mean."

I glared at him. "You are calling me self-centred? You?"

He shrugged, unruffled by a slight against something he put little stock in, namely, his character. "In any event, these are practical people, and they care more about *what* you did than the *why* of it all. You should have seen Thora's face when I told them you'd been taken. And Lilja and Margret were ready to declare war for you. Not to mention Aud—she loves that boy you rescued like her own child. And as for Ulfar, he swore on his mother's grave they'd get you back—he only let out about a half dozen words in total before retreating into that gloomy mug of his, but still that is more than I've gotten from him in weeks."

I felt an unexpected tightness behind my eyes, picturing the tableau he painted for me. I had been imagining myself all alone in this ice palace, with only my wits between me and eternal enchantment, while they all sat in the tavern as Ulfar's stew bubbled in the back and the wind whistled through the crack in the windowsill that Aud never got round to patching, debating how best to rescue me. As when I had sobbed over Wendell's injury, my reaction alarmed me. I can't recall the last time I cried before coming to Hrafnsvik—likely I had been a small child. I won't be maudlin, yet I couldn't help but feel that something inside me had loosened—something small but troublesome, like a pebble caught in a shoe.

"And—and what did you decide?" I said.

"Aud and the others will pay the king a visit on the morrow, during the gift-giving. Mortals have been invited, so the king will lift the veil on his realm temporarily. They will present him and his bride-to-be with a wedding gift containing a poison that will render him senseless. Things will get rather messy after that, but not to worry—we will use the chaos as cover as we flee."

I sat heavily on the bed, next to my enchanted servant, who dreamed so soundly that she appeared to be drooling. "And this winter will end. Is it bad out there, in Hrafnsvik?"

"Utterly dreadful." He rolled the faerie out of the way and sat beside me. "It snows all day and night, which is very tedious. My own clothes no longer suffice, so I've had to borrow a seal-skin cloak of Ulfar's. I suppose it's warm enough, and I've tailored it adequately, but I cannot get the smell of fish stew out. And then, of course, there are the boots."

I have no doubt he would have gone on at length about the degradations of his wardrobe had I not interrupted, "But this poison will not kill the king?"

"Hmm? No." He gave me a smile ill-suited to a discussion of regicide. "Sneaking poison in amongst the gifts was Aud's idea. We make quite a good team. I tracked down the old queen, who was hiding out in the mountains with her firstborn son. Her allies at court faked her death."

"You tracked her down?" I repeated faintly.

"Yes. Well, I've been looking ever since the king enchanted you during our delightful expedition to his tree-prison."

"You knew!" I exclaimed.

"Of course I knew. Give me a little credit. Anyway, I thought that the queen might know how to break her former husband's hold on you, so I went searching for a door to her court. I found one, a narrow, ancient door high on a forgotten peak, which would not open for me, but coincidentally it was the same door she eventually fled through after you freed the king. I guessed she might make use of it then, and indeed, I found her hiding quite nearby."

"You might have told me you knew I was enchanted," I snapped. "You might have said something that very night, in fact, when we returned from the tree. Or at any other time—we only spent every day together."

"What would have been the point? You would only have denied it—the enchantment would have forced you to. I dropped plenty of hints in that blasted journal of yours."

I thought back to how the enchantment had thwarted me every time I opened my mouth to reveal it, how often I had forgotten that I was enchanted at all. I had to admit he was probably right—well, no, I didn't have to *admit* it.

I tightened my hand into a fist. It was swathed in a white glove, cunningly tailored with elaborate folds and bunches to mask the absence of the third finger. It gave its ghost-ache, which was familiar to me by now.

"And what is to be the queen's role in this?" I said.

"The king will not be worried about her, given that he thinks she was torn apart by wolves, and so she will sneak into the gift-giving ceremony in disguise. Once he has been distracted by the poison, she will kill him, aided and abetted by her allies among the nobility, of whom there are quite a few, though they've been temporarily cowed into subservience to their king."

My mouth was dry. "How?"

He shrugged. "I've left that up to their fertile imaginations."

I lowered my head onto my hands. My mind had stopped whirling since Wendell's arrival—I wondered if he was doing something to counteract the king's enchantments—but I still felt too light, as if I might at any moment fade away. "Well, you will never fool me again."

"What?"

"I will never again believe you to be incapable of hard work."

He shuddered. "Being *capable* is not the same as being inclined, Em."

"Could you free me without killing him?" I said. "Could you imprison him again?"

"No," he said, after a puzzled pause.

"You can turn back time," I said, frustrated.

He shook his head. "Your belief in me is flattering. But at my age, most Folk have only begun to grasp the extent of their powers. This king is older than the mountains. And worse, we are in his realm, not mine. What does it matter? Surely you don't pity him. He will starve everyone in Hrafnsvik, you know, burying them and their fields beneath yards of snow even at the height of summer, if left to his own devices."

I shook my head slowly. "The old queen and her court will go back to abducting mortals. Aud and the others will once again hear their music calling to them on a winter's night."

"I daresay they're used to that."

I quickly abandoned this line of argument—it was silly of me to expect him to care about the wickedness of the Folk when his own people are guilty of worse than the Hidden Ones, if the stories are to be believed. I tugged at a loose strand of hair—the servants had secured it with some contraption of ribbons and pins, but it seemed not even faerie magic could tame it. "Did they *really* plan this—this rescue?"

He smiled. "I knew you wouldn't believe it. Just because *you* have a heart filled with the dust of a thousand library stacks does not mean everybody does. Here."

He handed me a small book with a leather cover, plain in an expensively crafted sort of way. His journal.

"I don't bother writing in it often," he began.

"I could count on one hand how often," I said. "Were I missing half my fingers."

He ignored me. "But I made an effort to document things more consistently after you ran off with the king. You are so obsessed with recording everything about our time here; I thought you would appreciate it. I have marked the entries detailing my conversations with the villagers."

I was tempted to make some remark to answer his library dust comment, but in truth, I was a little humbled by his thoughtfulness.

"Thank you," I said finally. "I will—I will confine my reading to the indicated entries only."

He was only partly listening to me, his attention absorbed by the mirror that hung by my bed, in which he was frowning at his reflection and tugging his cloak this way and that.

"I thought you had only a *little* common fae ancestry," I said, trying to suppress my amusement—though not very hard, I admit.

He scowled. "It *is* a little. I have three other grandparents, all highborn, including a king and queen."

I nodded, pretending to ponder this. Then I said, "There's a bump in your nose now."

He glared at me. "There is *not.*"

"Your mouth is lopsided."

He opened his mouth to argue, but then he just let out a weary groan. "What is the point? I am hideous. I can't wait to change myself back again."

"Don't. I prefer you like this."

He looked surprised, then he began to smile. "Do you?"

"Yes," I said. "You blend into the background. I could almost forget about you entirely. It's refreshing."

Naturally, he found a way to twist this into a compliment. "And am I ordinarily a distraction to you, Em?"

He rose to leave, flicking his fingers at the servant, who grumbled and began to stir. "Your attendants will become suspicious if I tarry much longer," he said. "I will send you a note with your veil to clarify your role in tomorrow's events. Perhaps it will soothe your conscience to know that it is a small one."

As he retreated, he seemed to melt into the grey daylight shadows, and I felt a sudden stab of terror. I didn't want him to leave.

Actually, I wanted him to stay, which was almost but not quite the same thing. I realized with a horrible sort of clarity that I had missed him.

"What is the date?" I said.

He paused, and told me.

"A month," I murmured. "I was off by a month."

He raised his eyebrows. "That's not bad. Most mortals can watch years slip by in Faerie and think them mere days."

"Wendell," I said. "I should—I mean, everything you've done for me, I—"

"Oh dear," he said. "That's how I know you've really and truly been enchanted—you are getting mushy. You will kill me later if I enjoy the moment, so I'll leave you to profess your gratitude to the walls. And anyhow, I must finish your dress."

I did not see him and Shadow leave the room, though I knew they were gone. My servant propped herself up on one elbow, blinking her frosty eyelashes in confusion. Before she had a chance to open her mouth, I berated her for falling asleep and bid her to send in my next visitor.

30th January–later
(presumably)

It was some time before I was able to escape
from visitors and their interminable questions about my
nuptials—which I do not recall answering, though I suppose I
must have done. Then I banished my servants to the doorway
of my bedroom and settled by the window in an overstuffed
white chair that looked like a frozen cake to read Wendell's
journal.

The journal had a silk ribbon attached to the spine, naturally, with which he had marked the page. Though I had promised to confine my reading to the relevant passages, I could not
help flipping back through his earlier writings. I had not un-
derestimated him—there was little there to speak of: a few desultory descriptions of Poe's tree home and various rock
formations the villagers must have pointed out to him and
which he probably only wrote down because said villagers were
standing there watching him expectantly; a few passages he'd
copied from my field notes, perhaps to remind himself to put
them in our paper; a handful of local faerie stories I recalled
him collecting from Thora. He'd only bothered to describe a
few of his days towards the beginning of our stay, and I half
expected to find these full of complaints about my tyrannical
demands or the deprivations of our lodging, but I suppose he

considered written expostulations a pointless effort, for these entries were factual if extremely abbreviated. He had a habit of doodling, marginalia I was inclined to ignore given that a full half of these sketches were of me, including one that made me still. In it, I was bent over my notebook, hair tumbling over my shoulders as it usually does in the evening, my chin on my hand and a small smile on my face. It was very detailed work, each stroke carefully chosen. I could see the places where he'd smudged the ink with a thumb to create shadow—the curve of my neck; the hollow between my collarbones.

I flipped the page—my face was hot, and little shivers ran over me like the strokes of a pen. I focused on the other sketches, some of which were of ghastly trees, huge and grasping yet drawn with a loving hand, and others were of a creature that I eventually understood to be a cat. This was not an easy deduction; he'd only ever drawn it in hints, a few slashes of black ink, as if it was not wholly a material being. Yet there was something about those hints that unsettled me. I could not tell if he was terrible at drawing cats or if he simply had a terrible cat.

I turned at last to the entry he had marked, the day he would have discovered me missing. To my astonishment (self-doubt not being a quality I had ever attributed to Wendell Bambleby), it began with a great many crossings-out, the words illegible now, though I saw the shape of my name beneath the scorings several times.

27/11/09

All right. I shall simply begin. You would want me to be academic about this, wouldn't you? To treat your disappearance like some bloody appendix.

I will skip over my discovery of your letter. Suffice it to say that I will not be letting Krystjan in until I have cleaned up. Things are looking a bit warped, as if in my fury I put a crease in the veil between Faerie and the mortal realm. Poor Shadow! He was so affrighted he fled to the tavern. Never fear, I have given him plenty of pats, as well as an entire bowl of Ulfar's gravy, and I believe he has forgiven me.

(At this point, he seemed to have stabbed the page several times).

Anyway. That was not terribly academic, was it? Only I cannot stop picturing you reading this. I think that I *have* to picture you reading this, otherwise I will go mad. But let me try again.

Once I finished reading your letter—thank you for being so matter-of-fact about this suicidal mission of yours; it's not as if I had just begged you to marry me and might thus be inclined to some emotion about the whole thing—and once I had calmed down afterwards, I naturally set out for the tavern to petition the locals for assistance. Rather, I *tried* to set out; when I opened the cottage door a little avalanche of snow came tumbling in, sending me reeling backwards. Lovely: it had blizzarded in the night, so much that a drift was piled halfway up the door. I collected myself and went hurrying down the stairs too fast, tripped, and plunged face-first onto the snow-shrouded lawn. The wind was vicious—it was cold like I'd never felt before, not even in Ljosland. It took me a quarter of an hour just to wade down the lane, and by the time I reached the tavern, there was such a quantity of snow in my boots and sleeves that I was soaked through and shuddering. Such an enchanting place this is.

Fortunately, Aud and Thora were both in attendance, as well as sundry village youths, having been bestirred from their beds to dig out the village. Aud seemed concerned by my appearance, saying something about my colouring, and it was only then that I noticed I'd forgotten to don my cloak before stepping out into the arctic chill. Aud and Thora kept trying to herd me to the fire, talking endlessly about tea and breakfast, ignoring my protestations, which were rather garbled on account of my lips being turned to ice, until finally I took up the breakfast tray and hurled it against the wall, whereupon it shattered into a plume of leaves and pine cones (I did not mean to do this, only my magic was flaring erratically). I feel rather badly about that now—I believe I scared them, though Aud didn't show it, merely shoved me into a fireside chair with more force than necessary.

"I don't want tea," I informed her when she pressed a mug into my hand.

"Either drink it or have it emptied over your head, you mad faerie," she replied, flinging a blanket in my face.

It was a struggle to hold the mug, and I realized then the state I was in. I am so cut off from my own forests and lakes here in this land of winter, and it weakens me terribly. The tips of my fingers were blue, probably my nose also. Aud must have thought I was dying. Shadow padded up to me and put his head on my knee, all forgiven, as it always is with dogs. If I frightened my cat as I had Shadow, she'd ignore me for days, or possibly put a curse on me, but then cats have self-respect.

Eventually, I was able to speak coherently again. By that time, most of Hrafnsvik had assembled in the tavern, the populace having sensed that something was afoot in that osmotic way of village folk.

"Now," Aud said, "from the beginning."

You could hear the snow blowing against the windows as I told them what you'd done. When I finished, I expected a long pause, the villagers stunned into silence. But Aud said, after only a small hesitation, "We must bring her out, then."

Lilja burst into tears, burying her face in Margret's shoulder. I sank back in my chair, overwhelmed with relief. For I do not know if I could bring you out alone, Em—I have only a shadow of my powers in this world. But with the help of the villagers, I feel a sense of hope.

Finn looked pale but determined, and gave a nod. "I'll gather the brambleberries," he said, and shrugged his way out into the storm as if it was nothing.

"What's that about?" I asked.

"An old tradition," Aud said. "Ancient. In the days when the king in the tree ruled over the Folk of Ljosland, we mortals would summon him by burning dried brambleberries in our hearths."

I found the notion of any monarch of Faerie answering a mortal summons highly amusing, and for such a trifle as perfumed smoke, but Aud was insistent. "He would not always listen," she said. "But sometimes. It's worth a try. If we cannot get his attention that way, we will try sacrificing a lamb."

This seemed more promising. I would never trouble myself over something so silly, but some Folk like to have mortals make a fuss over them, to treat them like some pagan god. "Very well. While you are doing that, I will try to free her by force."

Aud blinked. "How will you find his court?"

"It's easily done." Indeed, I already had a sense of where it was, pressing against the mortal landscape like a seed stuck between two teeth.

They exchanged looks but did not press me for any more tedious elaborations. "We should first try to speak with the king in the—with the king," Aud said. "Perhaps he does not intend to hold her long."

I laughed at that, bitterly. "He intends to make her his wife."

Aud flinched back. "How do you know?"

I felt suddenly weary. "It's only right. She freed him. What other reward would he give her? What else could be sufficient recompense?"

"Madness," Ulfar muttered.

Aud held up her hand, for the villagers had started muttering among themselves. "And you believe you can free her from the king yourself?"

"I can try," I answered.

They looked at me dubiously. I suppose I was not cutting an impressive figure seated there by the fire with my blanket and my tea like an aged grandfather, and my nose constantly in need of blowing. I'd gone through two of Aud's handkerchiefs already.

"We will help however we can," Aud said. I suppose she thought she was sparing my feelings. She needn't have worried. As I said, I am not optimistic about my odds of success. I need these villagers rather desperately.

Aud began assigning tasks, all cool efficiency. Brambleberries were to be gathered and burned in every hearth, and several youths were sent to the next village to consult with their bard, for they have a bard there, and he has collected many stories that may give us some ideas for dealing with this king. I was assigned to show a handful of the men the way to the snow king's court, but not, Aud said, until I had turned a normal colour again—my fingertips still looked a bit blue. She tried to force toast and smoked fish on me, but I couldn't eat a thing.

In part to warm myself, and mostly for a distraction, I paced the length of the tavern a few times, even ducking into the back where Ulfar was preparing an enormous quantity of stew for our strategy session. Oh, God, that kitchen. I've never seen such a mess. I paced back to the fire whilst everyone stared at me and likely worried I'd gone mad, but I couldn't stop picturing that kitchen. It was pleasant to think of something other than you being made to dance until you collapsed or clothed in a gown of icicles, so I began rearranging the pots and generally setting everything in order. By the time Ulfar returned to give the stew a stir, I'd cleaned the majority of the space, though it remained far from satisfactory. Certainly a long way off my father's standards.

"How does one manage to affix toast to the ceiling?" I demanded. This had not been the most offensive example of the kitchen's disorder, but it was the most perplexing.

Ulfar didn't seem to hear me. He stared at his kitchen, those blond eyebrows of his nearly disappearing down the back of his bald scalp. My fingers itched to have a go at his apron, which was filthy and torn, one of the straps fastened to the body with a pin, but I restrained myself. Aud followed a moment later, and she stopped too, staring. You'd think neither of them recognized their own kitchen.

Eventually, Aud seemed to remember herself. "You're looking well enough now," she said a little nervously, as if I'd truly scared her, which was utterly ridiculous. If ever you want to frighten a person, Aud, show them your kitchen.

Anyway. She helped me bundle up in some of Ulfar's things, and I braced myself for another ghastly expedition, this time to show the villagers how to reach the king's court. At least it had stopped snowing.

I was skimming by this point, flipping slowly through the pages. Each day, it seemed, the villagers had tried something else. After their brambleberry fires had come to naught, they had made a sacrifice of a dozen lambs, and then several women had woven a quilt from polar bear hair, which, according to an ancient tale, the king had once accepted as a fair exchange for a stolen village girl. After that had come a series of attempts to sneak into the king's court with Wendell, an elaborate scheme to capture one of the courtly fae in the hopes of some sort of prisoner exchange—this inspired by a similar tale shared by the bard—and then, when that ended in disaster, several parlays with various common fae to elicit information that might be used to set me free. It went on and on.

A drop landed on the back of my hand, and I realized to my dismay that I was *crying*. Never in my adult life had I had someone looking out for me. Everything that I have wanted or needed doing, I have done myself.

And why not? I have never needed rescuing before. I suppose I always assumed that if I ever did, I would have two options: rescue myself or perish.

The whole village, working for weeks. Setting aside their own lives and interests to help me. At first I was horribly embarrassed. But underneath that was something that warmed me to the core, even in a palace of ice.

They are coming to rescue me.

I am not alone.

3rd February

I have spent the last quarter hour simply staring at this page. I must write down what happened that day in the king's palace, but it is all such a tangle of horrors and impossibilities that it feels almost futile to try.

For the scene of a bloody assassination, the king's gift-giving ceremony was a remarkably dull affair. I wonder if this is the context in which all such events unfold, whether all the great murders and intrigues of history were preceded by a series of moments in which dull grey men talked at length about nothing or large groups of people simply waited around, fiddling with their hair or picking lint off their clothes.

I sat fidgeting in my throne beside the king while a long procession of people approached one by one to lay their gifts at our feet, then went to join the crowd of spectators. The throne was made of delicate blades of ice, slotted together to resemble the rib cage of some enormous beast, and piled with furs to keep me comfortable. The king sat in an identical throne, though without the furs, his hands folded politely in his lap. We were in a throne room that wasn't a room, but the vast courtyard in the heart of the palace, where sometimes there were two thrones, a dais, and a long avenue lined with ice statues of glowering Folk, and sometimes there were not.

The weather was a strange and lovely mixture of snow clouds and winter sky; whenever the clouds parted, still spilling their flakes, rainbows alighted upon the mountain peaks. The sunlight turned everything to silver and pearl.

I wore the green dress Wendell had made; he had sent it to me that morning with a note saying that he'd decided it was inappropriate for a wedding, and so why didn't I wear it today? There had been other things in the note, of course, and I had torn it to shreds and tossed it down the mountainside after I'd finished reading. The dress was perfect, every inch of it, covering me in emerald green drapery that flowed like the boughs of a weeping willow, the bodice embellished with crushed pearls that made a whispery sound when I moved. And with it was a matching veil which I wore pushed back from my face. My hair had been swept up by my servants and woven with jewels, but several pieces were already falling into my eyes, proving once again that even magic is not enough to keep me neat. The pearls lining the veil brushed against my forehead, cold and hard.

A faerie woman as tall and slender as evening shadow placed a cage at the king's feet. He motioned to a servant, who opened the cage door, and out sprang a white raven.

"An albino!" the king exclaimed, leaning forward onto his hand, his elbows on his knees. He had a childlike manner about him in such moments that made me wonder at Wendell's description of him—*older than the mountains.* But I never wondered for long. These moments were only flashes, the drops of sunlight winnowed through the deepest and darkest woods. He settled back in his throne, growing far too still again, his magic enveloping us all like wind. He is more magic than person, that is the truth of it. Is this what happens to all the Folk as they age, their power hollowing them out like the fissures in an ancient glacier?

Many of the gifts were for me. There were jewels and gowns

and furs and paintings—done on ice canvases that made everything bleed together far more than watercolours—and a strange, empty box with a base of some sort of pale velvet that the faerie claimed would sprout white roses with diamonds in them if left outside at midday, and blue roses with rubies if left outside at midnight. There were other nonsensical presents along these lines, including a saddle of shapeless grey leather that would allow me to ride the mountain fog, though no explanation was given as to *why* I should wish to do this. The only presents I truly appreciated came in the form of ice cream, which the Hidden Ones are obsessed with and cover with sea salt and nectar from their winter flowers.

The king turned to beam at me lovingly every few moments, and I forced a smile in return while my hands, hidden in my sleeves, clenched into fists. The brief clarity I had felt during Wendell's visit was gone, and my thoughts were foggy. I always felt worse in the king's presence, by which I mean that it was harder to stop my mind from being befuddled and to avoid those disquieting instances where I lost myself for entire chunks of time. It made sense, I suppose; he was the source of the enchantments that held the palace together, that shut his world away from mortal eyes, and that no doubt altered time to suit his fancy. I was like a small planet that, when it drifted too near a massive star, began to tear itself apart.

The more I thought about our plan, the more wrong it seemed, and the more that *wrongness* curdled inside me. It wasn't just that it would mean replacing one vicious faerie king with a more vicious queen; it didn't feel at all like the proper ending to such a story. Mortal maidens forced to marry faerie kings never just lop their heads off and walk away—they are cleverer than that. I thought of the Gottland tale of the hairdresser who wove curses into her braids, so that every time her husband touched her, one of his cherished hunting dogs—who had been menacing the peasants of the countryside—would turn into a fox or some such (the transformations grow progressively more ludicrous as the story unfolds, culminating in a cricket); also of the long-winded epic that is a popular fireside tale in Yorkshire of the shepherdess who enlisted the help of the common fae of the fields to torment her wicked husband by spinning scraps of wool into dolls so uncanny they eventually drove him mad.

The plan Wendell had devised with the others felt like taking the story I'd fallen into and folding it to suit me, putting ugly creases down the middle. And yet, as much as I was convinced that there was another door out of the tale somewhere, I couldn't see it.

My gaze floated over the assembled Folk—they glimmered like a lake full of sunlight, even more shapeshifting as a crowd than they are individually. Where was the queen?

There were a few Folk from elsewhere, from beyond Ljosland, which did not seem to surprise anyone. To my eyes, they seemed even less distinct than the Hidden Ones, barely more than shadows in lovely gowns and fur cloaks, though I don't know if that was my faulty mortal sight or something the king had done to elevate the splendor of his own people.

I itched for my notebook. Whether or not the Folk have regular dealings with Folk of other realms is the sort of question scholars argue over for hours at conferences, and there I was, casually watching the answer stroll up and give me presents.

The next guest drove all such thoughts from my mind. Wendell swept up to the dais, short and drab and indistinct, and gave me and the king a bow. The lords and ladies who had been watching the proceedings turned back to their whispered gossip, dismissing him entirely. I saw the king frown briefly, as if some memory had been triggered. Wendell appeared perfectly at his ease, even a little bored, as he set at my feet a pair of shoes.

I sucked in my breath. The shoes were of white leather and fur, with impractical heels that would add half a foot to my height, but unlike every other adornment I had been presented with, they did not sparkle with frost or ice-encrusted jewels. Somehow, he had woven the fur with the petals of cherry blossoms, as if the pale beast who had owned the pelt had rubbed its back against a tree. When I touched them, a spring breeze fluttered against my fingers, and I smelled rain and green, growing things.

"If you would allow me the honour, Your Highness?" Wendell said. In one quick, graceful motion, he slid the boots from my feet and replaced them with the shoes. They fit perfectly, and oh, they were so warming. I felt astonished that I hadn't realized how cold my feet had been before.

"Thank you," I said, trying to read the meaning of this gift on his unfamiliar face. But he gave me no assistance, only smiled, bowed again to the king, and faded back into obscurity.

The king was watching me with a frown between his lovely blue eyes. "Are you all right, my darling? Your heart is thundering as if it wishes to escape from you."

I swallowed—it would be an understatement to call his knowledge of my heart rate an unpleasant surprise. "The shoes are beautiful."

"Ah," he said, smiling. I didn't think him an idiot, only his expectations of me were so limited that I never found him difficult to lie to. I had the sense that he viewed all mortals as akin to his pet ravens, whose lives revolve around the treats he tosses their way, which made me wonder if he'd ever had a comeuppance before, and I don't mean by a fellow monarch. The literature is, after all, strewn with examples of arrogant faerie lords given their due by artless maidens and practical rustics.

"I should have guessed," he said. "I've been wrong to spoil you with jewels and servants, haven't I? Never fear. After our wedding, I will have my shoemakers fill your rooms to bursting with boots of calfskin and rabbit fur, all covered in diamonds, flowers, and frost; you shall have a different pair for each day of your life."

I didn't care for the way he said this, as if the life of a mortal, measured in ridiculous shoes, was so puny a thing that there was nothing at all extravagant about such a present. He turned his attention to the three guests approaching our thrones.

If my heart had been suspiciously thundering before, now it was a racehorse spooked to a gallop. The mortals stood out against the lovely watercolour gathering of Folk like accidental splotches of ink on a canvas. Aud, Finn, and Aslaug walked steadily, staring in front of them, though as the thrones loomed closer, I could see their resolution falter.

Aud was the bravest. She kept a little ahead of the others, dressed simply but well in her furs with her hair intricately braided. Given her smallness, it was all the more impressive, and I could see the king start to smile. Finn was pale, but I could see that, alongside his fear, there was amusement, as if he could see no other way to react to such an impossible situation.

Aslaug surprised me the most. She had gained weight, and her gaze had lost its cloudiness—she looked like an altogether different person. When she met my gaze, she smiled—a quick, fierce thing that was also a promise.

"Do you know them?" the king enquired, politely nodding at the villagers as they bowed and curtsied.

"Yes," I said, for there was no reason to lie about it. "They are—friends of mine."

"You honour us, Your Highness," Aud said, and swept me another note-perfect curtsey. "And we are honoured to be invited here to pay our humble respects to His Majesty and his bride-to-be, as well as to welcome what I hope will be a new era of friendship between mortals and Folk. It has been too long since we have been honoured with an invitation to your realm."

"I quite agree," the king said. "And you put it prettily too—I know very well there were no invitations made to mortals during the interregnum—only abductions. Rest assured such occurrences will no longer be tolerated."

He gave her one of his kind, beautiful smiles, and I could see that Finn and Aslaug were dazzled; Aud smiled back, though I knew her well enough now to detect a certain opacity about it.

"If I might be so bold as to present His Highness with a token of the mortal realm," Aud said. "It is nothing so fine as the gifts you have so far received."

"Then I'm sure I shall like it all the more," he said with such graceful condescension that several ladies in the audience swooned.

Aud held up the bottle she was carrying. "This is our finest honey wine, which has been maturing for nearly a century of our years. I can attest that there is no choicer vintage in the mortal world."

The king looked positively charmed by such a humble gift. Glasses were brought out by faerie servants, and Aud filled them all, emptying the bottle among the king's nearest courtiers. They drank politely, and showed no ill effects beyond a few grimaces—and why should they? The wine in the bottle was not poisoned.

Aud moved to offer the king a glass, paused, smiled, and handed it to me first. My hand shook as I gripped the stem, splashing wine on my sleeve. The *wrongness* of what we were doing overwhelmed me then, leaving me lightheaded. Those other stories flickered through my mind like dark birds.

I had to be resolute. If I did not go through with our plot, I would be trapped forever, slowly losing more and more of myself, while Hrafnsvik and all the other villages watched their animals die and their shovels break against their frozen farmland.

My fingers white against the glass, I took a sip, and as I did so, I brushed my hair back. A habitual gesture, to keep it out of the drink—my hair, of course, is forever flopping all over the place. But I also brushed the veil Wendell had made for me, loosening a single pearl. The pearl landed in the wine with an insubstantial splash, and dissolved.

I should have felt relief. That was it—my part was done. I had only to pass the poisoned wine to my betrothed. To wait for him to sag forward in convulsions, for the queen and her son and whatever other allies they had among the courtiers to spring forward and finish him. Wendell was already moving—he strolled along the edge of the crowd, moving closer to the thrones as if to improve his view. He would grab me as the king died, and we would flee with Aud and the others in the ensuing chaos.

And yet there I sat, still holding the wine.

Finn and Aslaug began to look worried. Aud alone was at ease, a warm smile still hovering on her lips. But it was not her usual smile, I knew, which was cool and brisk; this smile was a performance.

I leaned forward under the pretense of offering Aud a grateful kiss. She mirrored me, calmly pressing her cheek to mine, though I felt her stiffen slightly with disquiet.

"I can't do it," I murmured. My thoughts blurred together, and I had to dig my nails into my palms to keep myself from slipping through time again. "It's not how it's supposed to end."

I believe I babbled something else, about stories or patterns or I don't know what, for my memory is patchy. I know that Aud kissed me, and I felt her lips trembling. I held her eyes with mine, trying to convey to her that I wished her to tell me what to do, to help me. But she only stared back in baffled silence. And why wouldn't she? She had planned this whole intricate scheme out with Wendell, and now here I was, threatening to bring it crashing down upon us.

Aud quickly mastered herself, hiding her shock under polite surprise. "Her Highness's praise is far too kind."

The entire incident—my hesitation; Aud's embrace—had lasted only seconds. The king was still smiling, perfectly unsuspecting as he murmured to one of his courtiers. He turned to me, holding out his graceful hand—the nails very white and narrower at the tips, as if they would form points if left untrimmed—to accept the wine.

Aud's gaze bored into me. I could see she hadn't understood a word I'd said—unsurprising, given my nonsensical prattling. No doubt she thought I'd gone mad. And perhaps I had, shut away so long in that winter world, encased in enchantments like layers of dreams. Yet in that moment I knew—I *knew*—that if I went through with our plot, it would be to the ruin of us all. I had no evidence to support this, and yet the conviction had its roots in reason, somehow; not in anything specific, but in my accumulated knowledge of the Folk, the resonance of hundreds of stories. This murder was discordant; a snapped string.

I made some motion with the wineglass—I don't know what it was. Probably I would have dropped the glass, shattering it, or perhaps in my agitation I was motivated enough for drama and would have hurled it away. But at that slight motion, Aud sprang forward, knocking the glass from my hand.

The surprise of it launched me to my feet, an inarticulate cry on my lips—it was as if I had awakened from slumber, and a great terror at what I had been about to do rose within me. The king stared at me, then at Aud, then at the wine soaking into the ice. It bubbled and frothed, and then a tendril of smoke went up, as if in the wine there had lurked a flame, now snuffed out.

A murmur of horror went up among the courtiers.

"Forgive me, Your Highness," Aud said with her usual cool calm. "But as Her Highness moved the glass into the light, I noticed that the wine had turned an odd colour—I know our vintage well. I believe the glass itself was lined with poison. No doubt a foul plot hatched by allies of the former queen." She paused as if to process a shock, yet I saw the wheels turning in her mind. "It is fortunate that your betrothed is mortal—no doubt her blood is too warm to have been affected."

Aud gave me a brief, sharp look, and I collapsed back into my throne, still staring at her. She hadn't understood my hesitation—I could see that written plainly on her face. But far from thinking me mad, she had trusted me wholeheartedly, and she had acted, twisting the story into a new shape. An inarticulate sound rose within me, close to a sob.

And yet—it almost didn't work.

The king looked from Aud to the spilled wine, still smoking, then his gaze swept over the assembled courtiers and guests, whose shock quickly turned to terror. As one, they shuffled away from him, bumping into one another. I didn't blame them—the king's expression was contorted, and all the sunlight and playful rainbows had dissolved in a swirl of ice crystals. He looked at me, and I knew my shock showed plainly on my face, while my mouth hung open in an idiotic way—unintentional, but in retrospect, it was the best possible alibi I could have given him. His face softened, and he squeezed my hand.

"There, there, my love," he said. "I'm quite unharmed. You needn't worry."

Then it all began to unravel. There came a series of screams, and a drab, black-haired faerie woman was hauled through the gathering and thrown at the king's feet.

"The traitor queen, Your Highness," one of her captors declared. "She has disguised herself!"

The king made a sharp gesture, and suddenly the huddled faerie was drab no more, but unspeakably beautiful, all sharp lines and frost-glittering skin and white hair that flowed all the way to the ground. At her side she carried a sword, nearly as tall as she and wonderfully incriminating. It struck me that the two faeries who had dragged the queen before the king should not have been able to identify her through her glamour, if the king could not, and I also noted the way their outraged tones contrasted with how they kept swallowing and darting looks at the king. But he did not spare them a glance. His gaze never strayed from the queen.

"I thought I had killed you, my darling," he murmured to the queen in a voice that was almost a caress. I cowered away from him, not caring how I looked.

"You thought, you thought," she spat. Her voice was as lovely as her face, even in her fury. "Your power is matched only by your stupidity, my husband. Twice now I have played you for the fool. I shall rise and play you a third time."

I could not help admiring her self-possession, though her threat struck me as unlikely, particularly as there were suddenly a great many hands upon the queen, striking and shoving her, stripping her of her sword and handing it to the king.

By this time, a number of Folk were running for the doors. Some of the king's guards were mowing them down with their ice swords, though it was impossible to know if their flight was the result of guilt or simple panic. Guests were screaming, and there came the intermittent noise of clashing weaponry. It was chaos—that part of the plan, at least, had come off.

Suddenly, Wendell was at my side with one of the king's guards. "We must get Her Highness to safety," he told the king. He might as well not have spoken, for the king took no heed of him whatsoever, nor of me. He stood before the queen, tapping her sword against the ground, drawing the moment out for the enjoyment of it.

"The show is over, Your Highness," Wendell murmured, dragging me off the throne as he threw a cloak over my shoulders. "Time to put your notebook away."

Aud, Aslaug, and Finn fell into step behind us as we ran. At one point, Wendell drew the king's guard behind a wall, whereupon he brushed the guard's face with his fingers as he'd done to my maid, and the guard collapsed almost comically, as if he were a puppet whose strings had been cut.

I stopped suddenly. We had just run through the first set of doors, beyond which was a hallway that should have led us to the outermost doors of the palace. But instead, we found ourselves in my horribly familiar chambers.

"I'm still caught in the king's enchantments," I told Wendell. "Take the others—you'll be able to escape if I'm not with you."

"Shut up," Aud said, and she gave me a brief, painful hug. She looked at Wendell. "Is there anything you can do?"

"Possibly," he said. "Yes, you're still caught, and this would be a lot easier if he were dead." He glared at me and Aud. "But he's quite distracted right now, which means that his enchantments are wavering. I may be able to find us a way through."

"Here." I hardly recognized Aslaug's voice. She pulled off my cloak, turned it inside out, and put it back on me again. "He's a great lord, I know, but perhaps this will help a little."

Wendell nodded approvingly. He paced back and forth in front of the door, examining it as if it were—well, something other than an empty stretch of air. I watched Aslaug.

"I suppose you're wishing you hadn't come along now," I said.

She snorted. "I've been wishing it ever since I saw that horribly beautiful creature on his throne. How did you keep your hands off him?" She gave me a sly look that I never could have imagined on her face before. "Or did you?"

"Please," Wendell said. "I ask to be excused from any descriptions of marital intimacy. This whole thing is unfair: I asked you to marry me first."

"Oh, that's rich!" I exclaimed, and was about to remind him of his many dalliances, which he'd never hesitated to make *me* aware of, but he seemed to sense the storm coming, and said, "Mustn't tarry. Come, I think I've found a door."

He dragged me from the room, the others following close behind. We came out in a vast cavern full of little hot spring pools where the courtiers liked to bathe. Wendell muttered to himself, and we ran on, until we left the cavern behind and came to a room I'd never seen before, filled with ice statuary.

"I thought you found the door!" I called, panting.

"I have," he said over his shoulder. "But it's a very narrow one, a gap between many layers of enchantment, and it requires some manoeuvring. Come *on!*"

We came next to a side door that led us back to the courtyard, where the ice now ran red with blood, then he made us all leap through a window that brought us to a winter garden, filled with flowers the colour of twilight punctuated with violent hedges, their leaves black and spiky and their berries bright with poison. Another door brought us to the banquet hall, which had a dozen more doors leading off it. Wendell hesitated only briefly, then made a run for the third door to our left. It looked to be a servants' egress, but once we were through, I tripped over a snowdrift and would have tumbled all the way down the mountainside had not Wendell been holding on to me.

"There," he said, smug and satisfied. "Now shall I explain your gift?"

I wanted to tell him to hang his gift, for we were standing on a narrow ledge with only the raging wind and the fall of the mountainside all around us, and I could see no way down, but my teeth were chattering too hard to force any words through them.

He smiled and lifted the hem of my skirt. The shoes he'd given me had transformed—now they were boots going all the way up to my knees, the fur so thick and warm they doubled the diameter of my calves, ending in sturdy wooden snowshoes.

He looked so smug now that I wanted to send him over the side of the mountain, but instead I said, "Thank you," and kissed his lopsided mouth. It had the effect of stunning him into silence, which I enjoyed almost as much.

"This way," he said, looking flustered for the first time since I have known him, and then he led us down into the valley.

4th February

I have read over my last entry, contemplating scratching it out and starting anew, out of some misguided desire to make it all sound more plausible. But Wendell and I will reach London tomorrow, and a day is insufficient time to accomplish that—a year would be insufficient, I suspect.

My memory of the journey back to Hrafnsvik is hazy. The snow, stirred up from the mountainside as we descended to form an icy fog, seemed somehow to mingle with the enchantments that bound me to the king. In one corner of my memory, the journey was one of hours; in another, we were trapped in those mountains for days, wandering haphazardly. I recall Wendell swearing in Irish and Faie as he tried to disentangle me; though we'd made it out of the palace, scraps of enchantment still clung to me like the broken filaments of a spiderweb. I don't remember the others being there at all, and later Aslaug told me that Wendell would appear and disappear, leading them through the mortal realm as he gradually drew me out of the faerie one. I suppose they walked alongside me the whole time, a world away.

My first clear memory is awakening in the cottage—I was lying by the fire in a soft pool of blankets. I was confused by this at first, for my bed would have been more comfortable, until I realized that despite the blazing fire and the layers of furs, I was still shivering lightly. It was a chill that would not leave me for several days, and which I still feel at times when the sea wind picks its slippery way through the cracks in my cabin.

Shadow lay curled at my side and rolled upright with a delighted snort when he sensed I was awake. He shoved his huge muzzle into my face and licked me, while I half patted, half swatted him away. I'm afraid his breath is immune to glamour and smells exactly as you'd expect a Black Hound's breath to smell—rather deathly.

"There you are," Wendell said, his head appearing above my little blanket nest. He looked cheerful and supremely smug. "And how are we feeling?"

"Like I could sleep until spring."

"No time for that, I'm afraid. We leave tomorrow morning—early—for Loabær."

"Tomorrow?"

"You wish to hang about for the aftermath of what happened at the palace yesterday?" Wendell shook his head. "No, much safer to make ourselves scarce. In Loabær, we will seek passage on a merchant ship to London captained by Ulfar's brother—not ordinarily a passenger vessel, I'm afraid, so accommodations will be spartan, but it is our only option, as we have missed the freighter. Ulfar will accompany us to Loabær to arrange things."

"What," I said fuzzily. A hundred thoughts swam through my addled mind, and I grasped at the one that felt most familiar. "What about the paper?"

"I'm just fine," he said, relaxing into the nearest armchair with his hands folded. "A little weary, from dragging you all down from that mountain, but beyond that I am simply glad to be leaving this land of ice. Aud, Aslaug, and Finn are all well."

I glared at him. "I was about to—"

"I'm sure you were." He didn't seem annoyed, though; there was a quality to his smile, as he gazed at me, that I couldn't interpret.

"Aud's gone back to the palace to request a favour from the king," he said. "She should be back by nightfall, all going well."

"A *favour*," I repeated in disbelief. Then I thought about it. "Oh! Of course. She will ask him to put an end to this snow."

He nodded. "He owes her, so I suspect he'll give her whatever she wishes, though one can never be certain. Perhaps he'll shove her onto the throne in your stead."

"That's very nice," I said. "And I'm the hardhearted one?"

He shrugged. "I did advise her against it. Anyway! I'll get you some tea."

I *was* thirsty, I realized, and hungry. He brought me a steaming cup and a plate of Poe's bread, soft and fresh and slathered with marmalade. After I'd devoured the lot, he rose again, and I heard rustling, then he tossed something onto my lap. A stack of pages, neatly clipped together and covered in his elegant handwriting.

"We'll pay someone to type it out when we reach Paris," he said, waving his hand.

"You cannot work a typewriter?" I murmured distantly, staring at the title.

"There are limits, Em."

The title read:

OF FROST AND FIRE: AN EMPIRICAL STUDY OF THE FOLK OF LJOSLAND

Emily Wilde, PhD, MPhil, BSc, DDe, and Wendell Bambleby, PhD, MSc. Hons.

"You finished it," I said once I had regained the use of my voice.

"Read it over," he said, somehow managing to look even more smug.

"I certainly will," I said, so emphatically that he laughed.

"The bibliography is a bit of hodgepodge, but that's your strong suit, isn't it? And the whole middle section on the habits of the common fae is cribbed almost verbatim from your notes. But you might say," he added, examining his hands, "that I did most of the work."

"I would certainly *not* say that."

He ignored me and began a long dissertation on his efforts while I was away as I skimmed the pages, only half listening. He had been honest in confessing his reliance on my notes—the majority of the paper was comprised of them. But he'd spun everything together in an unexpected way, filled with lively speculation and effortlessly clever phrasings that I could not have hoped to achieve. The effect was scholarly yet glamourous, weightier than Bambleby's usual fare yet much more engaging than my own writing.

"I must remain like this for the present, it seems," he said heavily, rubbing his hand over his face. "It's a long and tiring process, changing shape, and I'm not sure I have the patience to start today. But I will be myself again in time for the conference."

"What?" I said, giving him a blank look. Then I blinked, taking in his plain appearance, unchanged from before. "Oh, yes, of course."

He stared at me. "You didn't notice?"

I said that I hadn't, and he stomped off to the kitchen in high dudgeon. In fact I *had* noticed, in a drowsy sort of way, when I'd first awakened, that his hair hadn't returned to its golden waves, and felt a pinch of disappointment. But why would I tell him that?

My encyclopaedia was exactly where I had left it, neatly arranged on the table beneath the faerie stone paperweight, as if it too had spent the last weeks in a separate pocket of time. I rested my hand upon the stack, pressing slightly, relishing the familiar rustle of the paper. Then I noticed something.

I removed the paperweight. There in the margin of page one was Wendell's familiar scrawl. I flipped through the rest of the manuscript, mouth hanging open slightly. He had not added his opinions to every page, but he had clearly read it front to back. He had even taken the liberty of rearranging certain sections and crossing others out.

I opened my mouth to call him back to the room, intending to register my displeasure—for I did not require a co-author for something I had spent much of my adult life compiling. But then I closed it again as I flipped through the notes. Some of his ideas were quite good. Well—I supposed that there was nothing wrong with a little feedback, even if it was of the heavy-handed variety.

A knock came, and I shuffled over to answer it, one of the blankets wrapped around me. Lilja and Margret stood on the threshold, and on the path below were Mord, Aslaug, and Finn. I blinked, startled by so many faces on my doorstep.

Lilja gave me a brief, light hug. "I know you leave in the morning, and haven't the time for farewell parties," she said. "So we thought we'd just come round with some baking and help you pack."

"Marvellous," Wendell said, flopping back into his chair with a cup of tea. "I despise packing. Do come in."

I realized that I should have said this by now, and stepped back to let them all tromp inside, banging the snow off their boots. Mord and Aslaug had brought an almond cake called a *hvitkag*, while Finn had a loaf of the dark Ljoslander bread, baked in the hot earth, as well as some salted chocolates.

Mord looked around the cottage. "Krystjan's fixed the place

up since I last saw it. Calling it a shack would have been generous, then."

He paused before the forest mirror, gazing open-mouthed into the swaying greenery. "This looks like the forest I used to play in as a boy, just outside Loabær. Look! There is the willow with the face in the trunk."

"Where are the tea things, Wendell?" Aslaug asked. "I've brought a bottle of red, too, in case anyone cares for something stronger."

"I'll start with the books," Finn said.

And that was that; suddenly the place was as noisy and bustling as a train station. Finn went back to the main house to fetch spare luggage, returning with Krystjan and several wooden crates. Wendell and I had accumulated a variety of things over the course of our stay, from Aud's gifts to the faerie cloak, which prompted a great deal of curiosity and discussion. Wendell floated about the room, chatting with this person and that, giving off the impression of contributing while doing no actual work at all.

The whole time, I worried that Aslaug or Mord would burst into tears of gratitude or offer some extravagant thank-you gift, and tried to come up with a strategy for how I might respond. Fortunately, they did no such thing, only cheerfully stormed around with the others, folding and packing and calling out questions to me and to Wendell. Eventually I began to worry if perhaps *I* should be the one making some grand gesture of thanks. They had all saved me, after all, as surely as Wendell and I had saved little Ari.

"What's with you?" Lilja hissed at me as we manoeuvred the enchanted mirror into a crate stuffed with wool. "Didn't Wendell heal you?"

"No, I—" I paused. *Had* Wendell healed me? I felt perfectly myself, apart from the chill. "It's not that. I can't think what I should say."

"Why must you say anything?"

"Well—" I hadn't been expecting this. "Because you rescued me. All of you, but especially Finn and Aslaug—"

"What?" Aslaug had come up behind me without my realizing. "Did you call me?"

"Emily feels bad because she wishes to thank us, but doesn't know how," Lilja said, and I went red and began to sputter, to hear it all spelled out so bluntly.

"Oh! Don't be silly," Aslaug said simply, and gave me a hug. "We are as good as family now." Then she went back to bustling about as if nothing had changed. As if it was nothing, what she'd said.

Lilja smiled and squeezed my arm. "Some cake?"

I nodded dumbly. Lilja pushed me into a chair and passed me a plate of cake, and I ate it. It was very good.

The bottle of wine was polished off by Mord, who had spent most of the evening quietly beaming at everyone, particularly when they asked after his son, and telling the same story over and over, about how Ari had taken to putting unexpected objects into his mouth, including the tail of their long-suffering cat. No one seemed to mind.

By the time all the *hvitkag* was gone, I was quite weary, and the clamour of so much company was not helping matters. To my relief, Wendell chose that moment to begin herding everyone out of the cottage, and one by one they went, donning cloaks and boots and wading out cheerfully into the blowy weather, curls of snowflakes spinning through the cottage in their wakes. Wendell glared at the snow and pressed the door closed with a grimace.

"One more," he said grimly, and I didn't have to ask what he meant. Though I was not as relieved to be leaving Ljosland as he was—what I felt was a complicated tangle of things, topmost of which was melancholy. I would miss Lilja and Margret and the others. When had that ever happened before? I was beginning to wonder if the faerie king had changed me somehow.

"Wendell," I said as he neurotically adjusted the doormat, "I believe I know why the king's spell—why it *took* when it did."

He raised his eyebrows. It was interesting—he was not exactly unattractive in this form, when you actually stopped to parse his appearance. It was mostly that he was *muted*, yet this did nothing to affect his natural grace, or indeed his ego.

"Well." I fumbled the words as I thought back to that night. "I was going to— After you asked me about—well—"

"After I asked you to marry me," he said in a tone I thought louder than necessary.

"Yes," I said, trying my hardest to keep my voice ordinary, as if we were talking about our research. I felt ridiculous. Any sane person would have already turned down his proposal. If there is one thing about which the stories, regardless of origin, agree, it is that marrying the Folk is a very bad idea. Romance generally is a bad idea where they are concerned; it hardly ever ends well. And what about my scientific objectivity? It is looking very tattered of late.

"I—that night—I was thinking about it. And I suppose that's my answer. That I would like to—well, continue thinking about it."

He gazed at me with an unreadable expression. Then, to my astonishment, he smiled.

"What?" I said suspiciously.

"I was just thinking that the fact that you have neither roasted me alive for my presumption nor rejected me outright is something to marvel at."

"Well, if you're just going to tease me about it," I muttered, turning away. I was surprised to feel his hand brush against mine—he'd crossed the room without a whisper of sound—his grip feather-light.

I froze, realizing that he was about to kiss me only a second after I knew I was going to kiss *him*. I leaned forward, but he put a hand on the side of my face, very gently, his fingers brushing the edge of my hair. A little shiver went through me. His thumb was by the corner of my mouth, and it made me think of the time when I had touched him there, when I'd thought he was dying from loss of blood. For a heartbeat, all the other moments we'd shared faded away, leaving behind only the small handful of times we'd been close like this, connected somehow like a bright constellation. He brushed his lips against my cheek, and I felt the warmth sink all the way to my bones, chasing out the ice of the snow king's court.

"Good night, Em," he murmured, his breath fluttering against my ear and sending a river of goosebumps down my neck.

And then he went into his room and closed the door.

I stared at it for a moment as if it were going to explain itself to me. I came back to myself with a start and picked up the blankets on the floor, then wandered in a daze to my own bedroom.

Naturally, I found it ridiculously clean.

Wendell and I stood shivering by the dock the next morning, watching the fishing boat captained by one of Thora's innumerable grandsons pull against its tether as the two sailors readied it for our journey to Loabær. Shadow was flopped at my side, yawning big doggish yawns and looking none too pleased to have been roused from his warm bed at such an hour. The world was a blur of shadow and ice, from the heaving sea to the scowling mountains framing the village. Aud had told us that the weather was fair enough to make the journey safely, and that the winds would drop on the other side of the headland, an assessment I could accept intellectually while all my instincts assured me that we would be drowned.

Aud, who had returned as planned the previous evening, called out instructions to the sailors in Ljoslander, looking cheerful. As well she should, for Aud had saved her village—indeed, her entire country. The king, who had only just finished glorying in the vengeance we had left for him like a wedding gift, and was in an exceptionally pleasant mood, had immediately granted her request for an end to the vicious winter and an early spring.

As to my whereabouts, Aud had given the king few clues, apart from offering that she had seen me fleeing the palace in the direction of the valley, in a panic at the thought of pursuit by the queen's minions. Shaking her head, she had remarked that if I had succumbed to the elements or tumbled off a cliff, poor witless waif that I was, it was yet another crime to be lain at the doorstep of the queen's treasonous ambition. The king had seemed barely able to hide his glee at this notion, and had immediately taken up my death as justification for another round of executions, which had no doubt sent even more nobles—those still in possession of their heads—into hiding in the wilderness. As for myself, I was more than happy for my death to be accepted as a boon by my fiancé, particularly as it gave him ample incentive to give up the search for me. Nevertheless, it was well that we were leaving quickly—I wished to prevent any hint of my survival from reaching his court.

Despite the early hour, the entire village came to see us off as we boarded the ship, even little Ari, who buried his head in Mord's shoulder when I said goodbye, as shy as he would be with any stranger.

"Here you are," Aslaug said, handing me a basket of the

sheep cheese I'd come to favour. "It's a silly gift, isn't it? After all you've done."

I mumbled my way through the *goodbyes* and *thank-yous*, but nobody seemed to mind anymore. Lilja and Margret hugged me tight.

"Here," Lilja said, pressing a basket into my hands. I lifted the cloth covering and found five neatly stacked apple tarts. "Finn says you have a liking for them."

"Ah," I began, wincing a little—each tart weighed as much as a brick. "That's very kind, though I'm not sure I'll be able to—"

"Please," Lilja said, a gleam of desperation in her eyes. "That tree, it just—it doesn't stop. I've already got preserves to last a decade. The neighbours are so sick of apples they hide when I knock."

I shook my head. Naturally, Wendell, in typical faerie fashion, had given Lilja a "gift" that created more problems than it solved. I knew that Lilja would be terrified of wasting a single apple for fear of him taking offence. "Throw the surplus to the pigs," I suggested, because wouldn't that just serve him right?

She looked so horrified that I felt guilty. "Or trade them," I said. "Perhaps to a sailor or wandering merchant. You might be surprised by what you get in return." Indeed, I knew half a dozen stories of that ilk—poor, long-suffering mortal gives away a troublesome faerie-made gift in exchange for something mundane, but which reveals unexpected uses. Sometimes *that* is then traded for something even more wondrous, and on and on it goes. I hoped Lilja would end up with a wheel that spun straw to gold.

Aud's embrace was the longest, and when she drew away, her face was wet with tears. Fortunately, Thora stumped up before I had to work out how to respond. (How does one respond to tears?) "Two things," she said, taking me by the shoulders. "One, look out for yourself. Wise men make bargains with the

Folk. Only idiots make friends with them—or whatever he is to you."

Lord help me, I went red in the face at that. "You think I'm an idiot?"

"Even the smartest among us are idiots in one way or another," she said. "Two, I expect you back here in the spring for Lilja and Margret's wedding. My granddaughter does not like to impose on people, but your being there would make her happy, and so I will say it for her."

I smiled. "Of course I'll be there."

"Good girl." She patted me. "Run along, then. I will mail you my—what did you call it? Peer review?"

"Thank you," I said. Thora had promised to read through a draft of the final chapter in my encyclopaedia and provide her thoughts and additions. "And please don't worry about being polite with your criticism."

She blinked at me, and then, as a smile crept over my face, she gave me a surprisingly firm shove. "You've a mouth on you like one of my grandchildren."

My gaze drifted to the village, huddled into the night shore, as my hand went to the little trinket Poe had given me as a farewell gift. He had called it a *key,* though it looked nothing like one, and was in fact a small, impossible coil of bone. In some lights, it seemed to curve counterclockwise; in others clockwise. I had put it on a chain around my neck.

Wendell appeared at my side, having finished giving instructions to the sailors, and twisted his misshapen face into a smile. He'd fixed his uncanny hands and added a few inches to his height, but he was still a long way from his former dazzling self. "Ready?" he said.

The villagers shuffled back a little. They'd all accepted that this strange, grey faerie was the dashing Wendell Bambleby, but that didn't make them any less frightened of him, even though the face he wore now was far less intimidating than his old, painfully handsome one.

As for myself, I barely noticed the difference. I'd never had any use for his beauty, and he was unchanged in every other respect, including his ability to antagonize—he'd tailored all of my dresses whilst I was trapped in Faerie.

We said our last goodbyes, and then we stepped onto the rocking deck. Wendell took his time waving to the villagers and admiring the sight of Hrafnsvik fading into the night. I turned away as soon as I could and did not wave or look back. If I had, I would have seen Aud and Lilja brushing away their tears. I would also have seen the outline of our little cottage, which ordinarily had a curl of smoke drifting from the chimney, but now sat quiet and dark, dreaming. Shadow gave a huff, looking back at me as if certain there had been some mistake. My eyes were wet, and I had to dab at them with my sleeve, turning so that Wendell wouldn't see. *Damn this wind*, I thought.

I hugged Lilja's apple tarts to my chest as I gazed at the grey-white sea, my hand tight around Poe's trinket. The ship sailed on as the sun began to tip its light over the horizon.

13th February

In the end, we missed the plenary.

It didn't much matter, of course. Wendell sat on three panels and charmed his way onto a fourth, and charmed *my* way onto another. I sat through the interminable dinners without overly hating them; I was on familiar ground with scholars, and I even enjoyed some of my conversations, for they were conversations of the mind with nothing to do with small talk or social conventions.

And then it was time for our presentation. I paced about in the little room behind the stage. Through the half-open door I could see the two podiums, as well as the scholars filing into the room in their dowdy suits and dresses. Many of them wore their coats, for if there is one thing that unites scholars, it is complaining about the temperature of conference rooms.

Wendell swept in at last, looking resplendent, all sharp edges and lean grace in his own black suit, as plain as any other scholar's but immaculately tailored. His gaze swept over me in polite appraisal, though I could tell he was suppressing his smile. I glowered back. I was wearing one of the dresses he'd fixed up—out of necessity only, for I hadn't the money to buy new ones in Paris, and we'd had no time to stop in at our apartments at Cambridge.

It had taken him a full two days to return to his former glory, which he had spent mostly in his cabin on the ship, staring into a mirror and muttering to himself as he moved his nose this way and that or stretched his limbs out. It was an appalling process, and I had spent as little time in his company during the homeward voyage as possible.

"The exhibits are prepared," he said, and I nodded. Awaiting us behind the podium were three trunks, one containing the remnants of the faerie cloak, now badly melted but still recognizable; one a necklace the king had given me, a delicate spiderweb of ice chains that, unlike the cloak, didn't melt; the last a jagged spire of volcanic rock from one of Krystjan's fields, in which there was a tiny wooden door that vanished in direct sun. I felt like a magician.

He held out a hand to me. I accepted it, feeling a little shiver as I did, and he smiled. He had seemed especially happy with himself lately; I guessed the source of his pleasure to be his transformation back into his old self.

"We're about to create quite a stir," he said, looking misty at the prospect. "And just think—if you'd finished mulling over my proposal by now and said yes, we could have introduced you as Mrs. Wendell Bambleby. They would never stop talking about us."

I gave him a long, thoughtful look. "What?" he said.

"It's your chin. It's still a little crooked."

His hand went immediately to the feature. "It is not."

I shrugged. "Perhaps it's my imagination."

While he prodded at his jaw, I looked back at the crowd, the assembled scholars arguing quietly with one another or sitting mulishly with their arms crossed, as if already going over their criticisms in their heads. I drew a deep breath, my grip tightening on my notes. Then we stepped onto the stage.

This particular tale is one of the oldest in Ireland, and is told throughout the northwestern counties in varying iterations. Appended here for future reference. —E.W.

The Golden Ravens
or, The Serving Girl and Her Faerie Housekeepers

There once was a kingdom in the bleak and mountainous north of Ireland called Burre, which was ruled by an old queen with twelve sons and daughters, including one who was half Folk. This prince was the youngest of the lot and least likely to inherit the throne; thus, in typical faerie fashion, he went about improving his odds in a roundabout way that nevertheless proved quite effective. He released the queen's three golden ravens into the wild, which had been gifted to her by a powerful witch for luck, and this caused a great sorrow to spread over the land. The queen's other children began squabbling amongst themselves, culminating in treacherous intrigues and assassinations.

After the golden ravens were released, the ordinary peasants of

Burre also met with one misfortune after another. Crops failed, and cursed children were common. One of these was the adopted daughter of a poor serving woman. The daughter was unnaturally clumsy and brought disorder with her wherever she went, which made the serving woman's lot very hard. The mother and daughter were dismissed from position after position, being unable to keep any house clean despite their best efforts.

One bleak winter the mother died, leaving her barely grown daughter to fend for herself. Everyone in town knew the daughter's reputation, and she could not find any work. In desperation, she ventured far into the wild white mountains until she came upon a castle owned by a duchess, the queen's sister. Living in such a remote location, the duchess and her family were always short-staffed, and so the duchess hired the serving girl on the spot.

The duchess set the serving girl a simple task: scrub the floor of the kitchen, particularly minding the corners where spiders had built their nests. But this task was not simple for the cursed serving girl, and no sooner had she scrubbed the floor to a shine than she tripped and upset the spice rack. The spice spilled everywhere, mingling with the damp of the newly washed floor to form a fragrant mud. The serving girl at once set to cleaning it all again, but it was no use: she seemed able only to move the muck from one place to another. She went to bed weeping, certain she would be dismissed again.

But when she came into the kitchen in the morning, she found the duchess in a state of delight. The kitchen gleamed as it had never gleamed before, even the corners, every last spider having been relocated to a luxuriously intricate web high in the rafters. The duchess and her family begged to know how the serving girl had made the floor shine so, like a winter pond in the starlight, and what on earth had she done to the spices, which filled the kitchen with scent as if newly ground?

The serving girl realized that the castle must be home to the *oíche sidhe*, the little faerie housekeepers. They must have plucked up each grain of spice one by one with their clever fingers and dried them with their breath. The girl kept her mouth shut, overwhelmed by her good luck.

As the days passed, the family's respect for the serving girl only grew. Never had they had such shining floors, windows of such purity as if made of air, such fragrant, spotless bedding. They did not know that they only had such things because the *oíche sidhe* had to work twice as hard to clean up the mess made by the serving girl, who could not cross a floor without leaving behind a muddy trail, nor open a window without smearing it with handprints, nor pin the bedding up to dry outside without it being blown across the fields and into some muddy puddle.

But then began a series of strange events. After the serving girl dusted the portraits, somehow managing to summon more dust than had been there before, the portraits the next morning were not only free of dust but everyone in them had their hair combed and their clothes brushed and straightened. After the serving girl washed the duchess's dogs, they were found the next day with their hair in elaborate ringlets. Rearranging furniture would cause rooms and windows to change shape, taking on a rigid and unnatural symmetry. Laundry was the worst of all; after the serving girl had washed it to the best of her lamentable abilities, clothes not only cleaned themselves to spotlessness but grew threads of gold and buttons of ivory, or sometimes became new garments altogether, pyjamas growing into evening gowns and wool socks to silken stockings. If the serving girl cleaned the chicken coop, the chickens would appear the next morning with their beaks polished and their feathers pomaded, looking very self-satisfied. The duchess and her husband began watching the serving girl with concerned looks and encouraging her to take frequent breaks for tea and a lie-down. They did not send her away, though—indeed, they more than doubled her pay to ensure she would never wish to leave.

The serving girl began to fear that she was driving the *oíche sidhe* mad with her impossible messes—she knew the poor creatures did so abhor disorder. Further evidence of this came unexpectedly and unpleasantly in the form of sudden wet smacks to her face when she was working, rather like being struck with a small, invisible mop. The serving girl lived in terror that the *oíche sidhe* would murder her one day.

Eventually, the serving girl snuck out into the woods where an old witch lived and begged for help. In exchange for one of the pomaded chickens, the witch informed her that the serving girl's curse originated in the royal family with the youngest prince, and that only he could undo it.

Fortunately, the serving girl knew the queen and all her children were due to pay a visit to the queen's sister soon. The night before their arrival, the serving girl took her shabbiest dress, freshly stained with kitchen grease, and tore it to shreds, which she scattered over the floor.

When the serving girl awoke in the morning, she found in place of her old dress the loveliest and most eccentric gown imaginable. It was quite clear that the *oíche sidhe* were indeed going mad, for the dress was at odds with itself, one moment deciding to be murky pond green and the next ocean blue or harvest brown. It was festooned with baubles and ribbons like a Christmas tree, including a crystal that showed flashes of strangers' futures and a live hedgehog, which with its tiny claws climbed from pocket to pocket as the mood took it (the dress had an infinite number of pockets).

Dubious, the girl donned the dress and went downstairs. The castle was full of royal attendants and various hangers-on, all bustling about importantly, and in her ridiculous dress, everyone assumed she was a relation of the duchess. She asked one of the ladies' maids where the youngest prince could be found, and she was told: in the garden.

She found the prince wandering the garden with a displeased look on his face, for those whose blood is half Folk and half mortal exist in a state of perpetual displeasure—the typical games of the Folk leave them perplexed, while they find mortal pursuits dull. In truth, the prince was only scheming to obtain the throne for want of anything better to do with himself.

The prince took one look at the serving girl and fell instantly in love with her, just as she'd hoped. Most young men fell instantly in love with her when she was not dressed in rags and covered in stains, as the serving girl was beautiful, with black eyes, pale golden hair, and skin of a darker gold, a strange but irresistible combination. The duchess was furious when the prince expressed his intention to marry her cherished serving girl, but she could not very well gainsay the queen's favourite son.

On her wedding day, the serving girl was elated. Once they were wed, she planned to order the prince to undo her curse—if he did not, as her husband he would have to share it and endure a life of mess and disorder. She was certain that the curse that had plagued every season of her life was soon to be broken.

In a way, the serving girl was right. The *oíche sidhe* fashioned her a magnificent wedding gown—though it was also rather lunatic, having not one but eight hedgehogs roaming the pockets, as well as a bodice that was a portal to Faerie if turned inside out and a train with a ghost hiding in it who disrupted the service with bursts of cackling. At the banquet after their nuptials, the serving girl naturally managed to spill the entire contents of a gravy boat upon herself, and it was the sight of their finest handiwork in ruins that finally broke the *oíche sidhe*.

They swarmed out into plain view as the *oíche sidhe* never do normally, halfling men and women the colour of dust, and began walloping the serving girl with their faerie mops. No one and nothing could stop them, and the wedding guests began to fear that their new princess would be beaten to death. Whenever the prince tried to pull his bride to safety, the hedgehogs would bite him. Golden feathers began to fly through the air, and the wedding guests could not at first make sense of it. The *oíche sidhe* kept whacking and whacking until the serving girl split apart like an overripe plum and became what she had been long ago, though neither she nor the mother who raised her had guessed it—a golden raven, one of the three enchanted birds that the prince had released to bring strife to the kingdom.

The serving girl flitted out the window, free at last, while the *oíche sidhe* dusted their hands and went smilingly back into hiding. They stopped pomading chickens and turning pyjamas into evening wear, which was ultimately a relief to the duchess, who had been down to her last nightgown.

As for the prince, the serving girl's disappearance finally gave him a purpose in life. He retreated to the wilderness to learn magic from witches and any Folk who would teach him. Eventually he succeeded in turning himself into a raven, whereupon he flew off in search of his beloved. In the northeast of Ireland it is said that he is still searching for his golden bride to this day, and that if you listen closely, you can hear her name in the croaking of the ravens.

The story of Emily Wilde
and Wendell Bambleby
will continue in Book 2.

Acknowledgments

A huge thank-you to my brilliant editor, Tricia Narwani, and my wonderful agent, Brianne Johnson, as well as the entire team at Del Rey. Thank you to Nadia Saward and Orbit, Soumeya Bendimerad Roberts and everyone at HG Literary, Anissa at FairyLoot, Jenny Medford, Mandy Johnson, Bree Gary, and Becky Maines.

Thank you to the amazing professionals I have worked with and learned from both past and present, including Alexandra Levick, Jessica Berger, and the team at Writers House, Kristin Rens, and Lauri Hornik. Thank you to my friends and family for their support.

And finally, thank you, reader, for picking this story up. I hope you've enjoyed the journey.

About the Author

Heather Fawcett is the author of middle-grade novels *Ember and the Ice Dragons, The Language of Ghosts,* and *The School Between Winter and Fairyland,* as well as the young adult series Even the Darkest Stars. She has a master's degree in English literature and has worked as an archaeologist, photographer, technical writer, and backstage assistant for a Shakespearean theater festival. She lives on Vancouver Island.

heatherfawcettbooks.com
Facebook.com/HeatherFawcettAuthor
Twitter: @heathermfawcett
Instagram: @heather_fawcett

About the Type

This book was set in Legacy, a typeface family designed by Ronald Arnholm (b. 1939) and issued in digital form by ITC in 1992. Both its serifed and unserifed versions are based on an original type created by the French punchcutter Nicholas Jenson in the late fifteenth century. While Legacy tends to differ from Jenson's original in its proportions, it maintains much of the latter's characteristic modulations in stroke.